ALSO BY JULIAN BARNES

A HISTORY
OF THE WORLD
IN 10½ CHAPTERS

A HISTORY
OF THE WORLD
IN 10½ CHAPTERS

JULIAN BARNES

ALFRED A. KNOPF   *New York*   1989

THIS IS A BORZOI BOOK
PUBLISHED BY ALFRED A. KNOPF, INC.

A portion of this book was originally published in *The New Yorker.*

Library of Congress Cataloging-in-Publication Data

Barnes, Julian.
A history of the world in 10¹/₂ chapters / Julian Barnes. — 1st ed.
p.   cm.
ISBN 0-394-58061-3
I. Title.
PR6052.A6657H5   1989
823'.914—dc20   89-45266   CIP

Manufactured in the United States of America

FIRST AMERICAN EDITION

Facing page 124: Géricault, *The Raft of the Medusa,* 1819.
Louvre Museum, Paris.
© Réunion des Musées Nationaux.

to Pat Kavanagh

CONTENTS

1

THE STOWAWAY

THEY PUT THE BEHEMOTHS in the hold along with the rhinos, the hippos and the elephants. It was a sensible decision to use them as ballast; but you can imagine the stench. And there was no-one to muck out. The men were overburdened with the feeding rota, and their women, who beneath those leaping fire-tongues of scent no doubt reeked as badly as we did, were far too delicate. So if any mucking-out was to happen, we had to do it ourselves. Every few months they would winch back the thick hatch on the aft deck and let the cleaner-birds in. Well, first they had to let the smell out (and there weren't too many volunteers for winch-work); then six or eight of the less fastidious birds would flutter cautiously around the hatch for a minute or so before diving in. I can't remember what they were all called – indeed, one of those pairs no longer exists – but you know the sort I mean. You've seen hippos with their mouths open and bright little birds pecking away between their teeth like distraught dental hygienists? Picture that on a larger, messier scale. I am hardly squeamish, but even I used to shudder at the scene below decks: a row of squinting monsters being manicured in a sewer.

There was strict discipline on the Ark: that's the first point to make. It wasn't like those nursery versions in painted wood which you might have played with as a child – all happy couples peering merrily over the rail from the comfort of their well-scrubbed stalls. Don't imagine some Mediterranean cruise on which we played languorous roulette and everyone dressed for dinner; on the Ark only the penguins wore tailcoats. Remember: this was a long and dangerous voyage – dangerous even though some of the rules had been fixed in advance. Remember too that we had the whole of the animal kingdom on board: would you have put the cheetahs within springing distance of the antelope? A certain level of security was inevitable, and we accepted double-peg locks, stall inspections, a nightly curfew. But regrettably there were also punishments and isolation cells. Someone at the very top became obsessed with information gathering; and certain of the travellers agreed to act as stool pigeons. I'm sorry to report that ratting to the authorities was at times widespread. It wasn't a nature reserve, that Ark of ours; at times it was more like a prison ship.

Now, I realize that accounts differ. Your species has its much repeated version, which still charms even sceptics; while the animals have a compendium of sentimental myths. But they're not going to rock the boat, are they? Not when they've been treated as heroes, not when it's become a matter of pride that each and every one of them can proudly trace its family tree straight back to the Ark. They were chosen, they endured, they survived: it's normal for them to gloss over the awkward episodes, to have convenient lapses of memory. But I am not constrained in that way. I was never chosen. In fact, like several other species, I was specifically not chosen. I was a stowaway; I too survived; I escaped (getting off was no easier than getting on); and I have flourished. I am a little set apart from the rest of animal society, which still has its nostalgic reunions: there is even a Sealegs Club for species which never once felt queasy. When I recall the Voyage, I feel no sense of obligation; gratitude puts no smear of Vaseline on the lens. My account you can trust.

You presumably grasped that the 'Ark' was more than just a single ship? It was the name we gave to the whole flotilla (you could hardly expect to cram the entire animal kingdom into something a mere three hundred cubits long). It rained for forty days and forty nights? Well, naturally it didn't – that would have been no more than a routine English summer. No, it rained for about a year and a half, by my reckoning. And the waters were upon the earth for a hundred and fifty days? Bump that up to about four years. And so on. Your species has always

4

been hopeless about dates. I put it down to your quaint obsession with multiples of seven.

In the beginning, the Ark consisted of eight vessels: Noah's galleon, which towed the stores ship, then four slightly smaller boats, each captained by one of Noah's sons, and behind them, at a safe distance (the family being superstitious about illness), the hospital ship. The eighth vessel provided a brief mystery: a darting little sloop with filigree decorations in sandalwood all along the stern, it steered a course sycophantically close to that of Ham's ark. If you got to leeward you would sometimes be teased with strange perfumes; occasionally, at night, when the tempest slackened, you could hear jaunty music and shrill laughter – surprising noises to us, because we had assumed that all the wives of all the sons of Noah were safely ensconced on their own ships. However, this scented, laughing boat was not robust: it went down in a sudden squall, and Ham was pensive for several weeks thereafter.

The stores ship was the next to be lost, on a starless night when the wind had dropped and the lookouts were drowsy. In the morning all that trailed behind Noah's flagship was a length of fat hawser which had been gnawed through by something with sharp incisors and an ability to cling to wet ropes. There were serious recriminations about that, I can tell you; indeed, this may have been the first occasion on which a species disappeared overboard. Not long afterwards the hospital ship was lost. There were murmurings that the two events were connected, that Ham's wife – who was a little short on serenity – had decided to revenge herself upon the animals. Apparently her lifetime output of embroidered blankets had gone down with the stores ship. But nothing was ever proved.

Still, the worst disaster by far was the loss of Varadi. You're familiar with Ham and Shem and the other one, whose name began with a J; but you don't know about Varadi, do you? He was the youngest and strongest of Noah's sons; which didn't, of course, make him the most popular within the family. He also had a sense of humour – or at least he laughed a lot, which is usually proof enough for your species. Yes, Varadi was always

5

cheerful. He could be seen strutting the quarterdeck with a parrot on each shoulder; he would slap the quadrupeds affectionately on the rump, which they'd acknowledge with an appreciative bellow; and it was said that his ark was run on much less tyrannical lines than the others. But there you are: one morning we awoke to find that Varadi's ship had vanished from the horizon, taking with it one fifth of the animal kingdom. You would, I think, have enjoyed the simurgh, with its silver head and peacock's tail; but the bird that nested in the Tree of Knowledge was no more proof against the waves than the brindled vole. Varadi's elder brothers blamed poor navigation; they said Varadi had spent far too much time fraternizing with the beasts; they even hinted that God might have been punishing him for some obscure offence committed when he was a child of eighty-five. But whatever the truth behind Varadi's disappearance, it was a severe loss to your species. His genes would have helped you a great deal.

As far as we were concerned the whole business of the Voyage began when we were invited to report to a certain place by a certain time. That was the first we heard of the scheme. We didn't know anything of the political background. God's wrath with his own creation was news to us; we just got caught up in it willy-nilly. *We* weren't in any way to blame (you don't really believe that story about the serpent, do you? – it was just Adam's black propaganda), and yet the consequences for us were equally severe: every species wiped out except for a single breeding pair, and that couple consigned to the high seas under the charge of an old rogue with a drink problem who was already into his seventh century of life.

So the word went out; but characteristically they didn't tell us the truth. Did you imagine that in the vicinity of Noah's palace (oh, he wasn't poor, that Noah) there dwelt a convenient example of every species on earth? Come, come. No, they were obliged to advertise, and then select the best pair that presented itself. Since they didn't want to cause a universal panic, they announced a competition for twosomes – a sort of beauty contest cum brains trust cum Darby-and-Joan event – and told contestants to present themselves at Noah's gate by a certain month. You can imagine the problems. For a start, not everyone has a competitive nature, so perhaps only the grabbiest turned up. Animals who weren't smart enough to read between the lines felt they simply didn't need to win a luxury cruise for two, all expenses paid, thank you very much. Nor had Noah and his staff allowed for the fact that some species hibernate at a given time of year; let alone the more obvious fact that certain animals travel more slowly than others. There was a particularly relaxed sloth, for instance – an exquisite creature, I can vouch for it personally – which had scarcely got down to the foot of its tree before it was wiped out in the great wash of God's vengeance. What do you call that – natural selection? I'd call it professional incompetence.

The arrangements, frankly, were a shambles. Noah got behind with the building of the arks (it didn't help when the craftsmen realized there weren't enough berths for them to be taken along as well); with the result that insufficient attention was given to choosing the animals. The first normally present-able pair that came along was given the nod – this appeared to be the system; there was certainly no more than the scantiest examination of pedigree. And of course, while they *said* they'd take two of each species, when it came down to it . . . Some creatures were simply Not Wanted On Voyage. That was the case with us; that's why we had to stow away. And any number of beasts, with a perfectly good legal argument for being a separate species, had their claims dismissed. No, we've got two of you already, they were told. Well, what difference do a few extra rings round the tail make, or those bushy tufts down your backbone? We've got *you*. Sorry.

There were splendid animals that arrived without a mate and had to be left behind; there were families which refused to be separated from their offspring and chose to die together; there were medical inspections, often of a brutally intrusive nature; and all night long the air outside Noah's stockade was heavy with the wailings of the rejected. Can you imagine the atmos-phere when the news finally got out as to why we'd been asked to submit to this charade of a competition? There was much jealousy and bad behaviour, as you can imagine. Some of the nobler species simply padded away into the forest, declining to survive on the insulting terms offered them by God and Noah, preferring extinction and the waves. Harsh and envious words were spoken about fish; the amphibians began to look distinctly smug; birds practised staying in the air as long as possible. Certain types of monkey were occasionally seen trying to construct crude rafts of their own. One week there was a mysterious outbreak of food poisoning in the Compound of the Chosen, and for some of the less robust species the selection process had to start all over again.

There were times when Noah and his sons got quite hysterical. That doesn't tally with your account of things? You've always been led to believe that Noah was sage, righteous and God-fearing, and I've already described him as a hysterical rogue with a drink problem? The two views aren't entirely incompatible. Put it this way: Noah was pretty bad, but *you should have seen the others*. It came as little surprise to us that God decided to wipe the slate clean; the only puzzle was that he chose to preserve anything at all of this species whose creation did not reflect particularly well on its creator.

At times Noah was nearly on the edge. The Ark was behind schedule, the craftsmen had to be whipped, hundreds of terrified animals were bivouacking near his palace, and nobody knew when the rains were coming. God wouldn't even give him a date for that. Every morning we looked at the clouds: would it be a westerly wind that brought the rain as usual, or would God send his special downpour from a rare direction? And as the weather slowly thickened, the possibilities of revolt grew. Some of the rejected wanted to commandeer the Ark and save themselves, others wanted to destroy it altogether. Animals of a speculative bent began to propound rival selection principles, based on beast size or utility rather than mere number; but Noah loftily refused to negotiate. He was a man who had his little theories, and he didn't want anyone else's.

As the flotilla neared completion it had to be guarded round the clock. There were many attempts to stow away. A craftsman was discovered one day trying to hollow out a priest's hole among the lower timbers of the stores ship. And there were some pathetic sights: a young elk strung from the rail of Shem's ark; birds dive-bombing the protective netting; and so on. Stowaways, when detected, were immediately put to death; but these public spectacles were never enough to deter the desperate. Our species, I am proud to report, got on board without either bribery or violence; but then we are not as detectable as a young elk. How did we manage it? We had a parent with foresight. While Noah and his sons were roughly frisking the animals as they came up the gangway, running coarse hands through suspiciously shaggy fleeces and carrying out some of the earliest and most unhygienic prostate examinations, we were already well past their gaze and safely in our bunks. One of the ship's carpenters carried us to safety, little knowing what he did.

For two days the wind blew from all directions simultaneously; and then it began to rain. Water sluiced down from a bilious sky to purge the wicked world. Big drops exploded on the deck like pigeons' eggs. The selected representatives of each species were moved from the Compound of the Chosen to their allotted ark: the scene resembled some obligatory mass wedding. Then they screwed down the hatches and we all started getting used to the dark, the confinement and the stench. Not that we cared much about this at first: we were too exhilarated by our survival. The rain fell and fell, occasionally shifting to hail and rattling on the timbers. Sometimes we could hear the crack of thunder from outside, and often the lamentations of abandoned beasts. After a while these cries grew less frequent: we knew that the waters had begun to rise.

Eventually came the day we had been longing for. At first we thought it might be some crazed assault by the last remaining pachyderms, trying to force their way into the Ark, or at least knock it over. But no: it was the boat shifting sideways as the water began to lift it from the cradle. That was the high point of the Voyage, if you ask me; that was when fraternity among the

9

beasts and gratitude towards man flowed like the wine at Noah's table. Afterwards . . . but perhaps the animals had been naïve to trust Noah and his God in the first place.

Even before the waters rose there had been grounds for unease. I know your species tends to look down on our world, considering it brutal, cannibalistic and deceitful (though you might acknowledge the argument that this makes us closer to you rather than more distant). But among us there had always been, from the beginning, a sense of equality. Oh, to be sure, we ate one another, and so on; the weaker species knew all too well what to expect if they crossed the path of something that was both bigger and hungry. But we merely recognized this as being the way of things. The fact that one animal was capable of killing another did not make the first animal superior to the second; merely more dangerous. Perhaps this is a concept difficult for you to grasp, but there was a mutual respect amongst us. Eating another animal was not grounds for despising it; and being eaten did not instill in the victim – or the victim's family – any exaggerated admiration for the dining species.

Noah – or Noah's God – changed all that. If you had a Fall, so did we. But we were pushed. It was when the selections were being made for the Compound of the Chosen that we first noticed it. All this stuff about two of everything was true (and you could see it made a certain basic sense); but it wasn't the end of the matter. In the Compound we began to notice that some species had been whittled down not to a couple but to seven (again, this obsession with sevens). At first we thought the extra five might be travelling reserves in case the original pair fell sick. But then it slowly began to emerge. Noah – or Noah's God – had decreed that there were two classes of beast: the clean and the unclean. Clean animals got into the Ark by sevens; the unclean by twos.

There was, as you can imagine, deep resentment at the divisiveness of God's animal policy. Indeed, at first even the clean animals themselves were embarrassed by the whole thing; they knew they'd done little to deserve such special patronage.

Though being 'clean', as they rapidly realized, was a mixed
blessing. Being 'clean' meant that they could be eaten. Seven
animals were welcome on board, but five were destined for the
galley. It was a curious form of honour that was being done
them. But at least it meant they got the most comfortable
quarters available until the day of their ritual slaughter.

I could occasionally find the situation funny, and give vent to
the outcast's laugh. However, among the species who took
themselves seriously there arose all sorts of complicated
jealousies. The pig did not mind, being of a socially unambi-
tious nature; but some of the other animals regarded the notion
of uncleanliness as a personal slight. And it must be said that the
system – at least, the system as Noah understood it – made very
little sense. What was so special about cloven-footed rumi-
nants, one asked oneself? Why should the camel and the rabbit
be given second-class status? Why should a division be intro-
duced between fish that had scales and fish that did not? The
swan, the pelican, the heron, the hoopoe: are these not some of
the finest species? Yet they were not awarded the badge of
cleanness. Why round on the mouse and the lizard – which
had enough problems already, you might think – and under-
mine their self-confidence further? If only we could have seen
some glimpse of logic behind it all; if only Noah had explained
it better. But all he did was blindly obey. Noah, as you will have
been told many times, was a very God-fearing man; and given
the nature of God, that was probably the safest line to take. Yet
if you could have heard the weeping of the shellfish, the grave
and puzzled complaint of the lobster, if you could have seen the
mournful shame of the stork, you would have understood that
things would never be the same again amongst us.

And then there was another little difficulty. By some unhappy
chance, our species had managed to smuggle seven members
on board. Not only were we stowaways (which some resented),
not only were we unclean (which some had already begun to
despise), but we had also mocked those clean and legal species
by mimicking their sacred number. We quickly decided to lie
about how many of us there were – and we never appeared

together in the same place. We discovered which parts of the ship were welcoming to us, and which we should avoid.

So you can see that it was an unhappy convoy from the beginning. Some of us were grieving for those we had been forced to leave behind; others were resentful about their status; others again, though notionally favoured by the title of cleanness, were rightly apprehensive about the oven. And on top of it all, there was Noah and his family.

I don't know how best to break this to you, but Noah was not a nice man. I realize this idea is embarrassing, since you are all descended from him; still, there it is. He was a monster, a puffed-up patriarch who spent half his day grovelling to his God and the other half taking it out on us. He had a gopher-wood stave with which . . . well, some of the animals carry the stripes to this day. It's amazing what fear can do. I'm told that among your species a severe shock may cause the hair to turn white in a matter of hours; on the Ark the effects of fear were even more dramatic. There was a pair of lizards, for instance, who at the mere sound of Noah's gopher-wood sandals advancing down the companion-way would actually change colour. I saw it myself: their skin would abandon its natural hue and blend with the background. Noah would pause as he passed their stall, wondering briefly why it was empty, then stroll on; and as his footsteps faded the terrified lizards would slowly revert to their normal colour. Down the post-Ark years this has apparently proved a useful trick; but it all began as a chronic reaction to 'the Admiral'.

With the reindeer it was more complicated. They were always nervous, but it wasn't just fear of Noah, it was something deeper. You know how some of us animals have powers of foresight? Even *you* have managed to notice that, after millennia of exposure to our habits. 'Oh, look,' you say, 'the cows are sitting down in the field, that means it's going to rain.' Well, of course it's all much subtler than you can possibly imagine, and the point of it certainly isn't to act as a cheap weather-vane for human beings. Anyway . . . the reindeer were troubled with something deeper than Noah-angst, stranger than storm-

nerves; something . . . long-term. They sweated up in their
stalls, they whinnied neurotically in spells of oppressive heat;
they kicked out at the gopher-wood partitions when there was
no obvious danger – no subsequently proven danger, either –
and when Noah had been, for him, positively restrained in his
behaviour. But the reindeer sensed something. And it was
something beyond what we then knew. As if they were saying,
You think this is the worst? Don't count on it. Still, whatever it
was, even the reindeer couldn't be specific about it. Something
distant, major . . . long-term.

The rest of us, understandably enough, were far more
concerned about the short term. Sick animals, for instance, were
always ruthlessly dealt with. This was not a hospital ship, we
were constantly informed by the authorities; there was to be no
disease, and no malingering. Which hardly seemed just or
realistic. But you knew better than to report yourself ill.
A little bit of mange and you were over the side before you
could stick your tongue out for inspection. And then what do
you think happened to your better half? What good is fifty
per cent of a breeding pair? Noah was hardly the sentimentalist
who would urge the grieving partner to live out its natural
span.

Put it another way: what the hell do you think Noah and his
family ate in the Ark? They ate *us*, of course. I mean, if you look
around the animal kingdom nowadays, you don't think this is
all there ever was, do you? A lot of beasts looking more or less
the same, and then a gap and another lot of beasts looking more
or less the same? I know you've got some theory to make sense of
it all – something about relationship to the environment and
inherited skills or whatever – but there's a much simpler
explanation for the puzzling leaps in the spectrum of creation.
One fifth of the earth's species went down with Varadi; and as
for the rest that are missing, Noah's crowd ate them. They did.
There was a pair of Arctic plovers, for instance – very pretty
birds. When they came on board they were a mottled bluey-
brown in plumage. A few months later they started to moult.
This was quite normal. As their summer feathers departed,

their winter coat of pure white began to show through. Of course we weren't in Arctic latitudes, so this was technically unnecessary; still, you can't stop Nature, can you? Nor could you stop Noah. As soon as he saw the plovers turning white, he decided that they were sickening, and in tender consideration for the rest of the ship's health he had them boiled with a little seaweed on the side. He was an ignorant man in many respects, and certainly no ornithologist. We got up a petition and explained certain things to him about moulting and what-have-you. Eventually he seemed to take it in. But that was the Arctic plover gone.

Of course, it didn't stop there. As far as Noah and his family were concerned, we were just a floating cafeteria. Clean and unclean came alike to them on the Ark; lunch first, then piety, that was the rule. And you can't imagine what richness of wildlife Noah deprived you of. Or rather, you can, because that's precisely what you do: you imagine it. All those mythical beasts your poets dreamed up in former centuries: you assume, don't you, that they were either knowingly invented, or else they were alarmist descriptions of animals half-glimpsed in the forest after too good a hunting lunch? I'm afraid the explanation's more simple: Noah and his tribe scoffed them. At the start of the Voyage, as I said, there was a pair of behemoths in our hold. I didn't get much of a look at them myself, but I'm told they were impressive beasts. Yet Ham, Shem or the one whose name began with J apparently proposed at the family council that if you had the elephant and the hippopotamus, you could get by without the behemoth; and besides – the argument combined practicality with principle – two such large carcases would keep the Noah family going for months.

Of course, it didn't work out like that. After a few weeks there were complaints about getting behemoth for dinner every night, and so – merely for a change of diet – some other species was sacrificed. There were guilty nods from time to time in the direction of domestic economy, but I can tell you this: there was a lot of salted behemoth left over at the end of the journey.

The salamander went the same way. The real salamander, I

mean, not the unremarkable animal you still call by the same name; our salamander lived in fire. That was a one-off beast and no mistake; yet Ham or Shem or the other one kept pointing out that on a wooden ship the risk was simply too great, and so both the salamanders and the twin fires that housed them had to go. The carbuncle went as well, all because of some ridiculous story Ham's wife had heard about it having a precious jewel inside its skull. She was always a dressy one, that Ham's wife. So they took one of the carbuncles and chopped its head off; split the skull and found nothing at all. Maybe the jewel is only found in the female's head, Ham's wife suggested. So they opened up the other one as well, with the same negative result.

I put this next suggestion to you rather tentatively; I feel I have to voice it, though. At times we suspected a kind of system behind the killing that went on. Certainly there was more extermination than was strictly necessary for nutritional purposes – far more. And at the same time some of the species that were killed had very little eating on them. What's more, the gulls would occasionally report that they had seen carcases tossed from the stern with perfectly good meat thick on the bone. We began to suspect that Noah and his tribe had it in for certain animals simply for being what they were. The basilisk, for instance, went overboard very early. Now, of course it wasn't very pleasant to look at, but I feel it my duty to record that there was very little eating underneath those scales, and that the bird certainly wasn't sick at the time.

In fact, when we came to look back on it after the event, we began to discern a pattern, and the pattern began with the basilisk. You've never seen one, of course. But if I describe a four-legged cock with a serpent's tail, say that it had a very nasty look in its eye and laid a misshapen egg which it then employed a toad to hatch, you'll understand that this was not the most alluring beast on the Ark. Still, it had its rights like everyone else, didn't it? After the basilisk it was the griffon's turn; after the griffon, the sphinx; after the sphinx, the hippogriff. You thought they were all gaudy fantasies, perhaps? Not a bit of it. And do you see what they had in common? They were all cross-breeds. We think it was Shem – though it could well have been Noah himself – who had this thing about the purity of the species. Cock-eyed, of course; and as we used to say to one another, you only had to look at Noah and his wife, or at their three sons and their three wives, to realize what a genetically messy lot the human race would turn out to be. So why should they start getting fastidious about cross-breeds?

Still, it was the unicorn that was the most distressing. That business depressed us for months. Of course, there were the usual sordid rumours – that Ham's wife had been putting its horn to ignoble use – and the usual posthumous smear campaign by the authorities about the beast's character; but this only sickened us the more. The unavoidable fact is that Noah was jealous. We all looked up to the unicorn, and he couldn't stand it. Noah – what point is there in not telling you the truth? – was bad-tempered, smelly, unreliable, envious and cowardly. He wasn't even a good sailor: when the seas were high he would retire to his cabin, throw himself down on his gopher-wood bed and leave it only to vomit out his stomach into his gopher-wood wash-basin; you could smell the effluvia a deck away. Whereas the unicorn was strong, honest, fearless, impeccably groomed and a mariner who never knew a moment's queasiness. Once, in a gale, Ham's wife lost her footing near the rail and was about to go overboard. The unicorn – who had deck privileges as a result of popular lobbying – galloped across and stuck his horn through her trailing cloak, pinning it to the deck. Fine thanks he got for his valour; the Noahs had him casseroled one Embarkation Sunday. I can vouch for that. I spoke personally to the carrier-hawk who delivered a warm pot to Shem's ark.

You don't have to believe me, of course; but what do your own archives say? Take the story of Noah's nakedness – you remember? It happened after the Landing. Noah, not surprisingly, was even more pleased with himself than before – he'd saved the human race, he'd ensured the success of his dynasty, he'd been given a formal covenant by God – and he decided to take things easy in the last three hundred and fifty years of his life. He founded a village (which you call Arghuri) on the lower slopes of the mountain, and spent his days dreaming up new decorations and honours for himself: Holy Knight of the Tempest, Grand Commander of the Squalls and so on. Your sacred text informs you that on his estate he planted a vineyard. Ha! Even the least subtle mind can decode that particular euphemism: he was drunk all the time. One night, after a particularly hard session, he'd just finished undressing when he collapsed on the bedroom floor – not an unusual occurrence. Ham and his brothers happened to be passing his 'tent' (they still used the old sentimental desert word to describe their palaces) and called in to check that their alcoholic father hadn't done himself any harm. Ham went into the bedroom and . . . well, a naked man of six hundred and fifty-odd years lying in a drunken stupor is not a pretty sight. Ham did the decent, the filial thing: he got his brothers to cover their father up. As a sign of respect – though even at that time the custom was passing out of use – Shem and the one beginning with J entered their father's chamber backwards, and managed to get him into bed without letting their gaze fall on those organs of generation which mysteriously incite your species to shame. A pious and honourable deed all round, you might think. And how did Noah react when he awoke with one of those knifing new-wine hangovers? He cursed the son who had found him and decreed that all Ham's children should become servants to the family of the two brothers who had entered his room arse-first. Where is the sense in that? I can guess your explanation: his sense of judgment was affected by drink, and we should offer pity not censure. Well, maybe. But I would just mention this: *we* knew him on the Ark.

He was a large man, Noah – about the size of a gorilla, although there the resemblance ends. The flotilla's captain – he promoted himself to Admiral halfway through the Voyage – was an ugly old thing, both graceless in movement and indifferent to personal hygiene. He didn't even have the skill to grow his own hair except around his face; for the rest of his covering he relied on the skins of other species. Put him side by side with the gorilla and you will easily discern the superior creation: the one with graceful movement, superior strength and an instinct for delousing. On the Ark we puzzled ceaselessly at the riddle of how God came to choose man as His protégé ahead of the more obvious candidates. He would have found most other species a lot more loyal. If He'd plumped for the gorilla, I doubt there'd have been half so much disobedience – probably no need to have had the Flood in the first place.

And the smell of the fellow . . . Wet fur growing on a species which takes pride in grooming is one thing; but a dank, salt-encrusted pelt hanging ungroomed from the neck of a negligent species to whom it doesn't belong is quite another matter. Even when the calmer times came, old Noah didn't seem to dry out (I am reporting what the birds said, and the birds could be trusted). He carried the damp and the storm around with him like some guilty memory or the promise of more bad weather.

There were other dangers on the Voyage apart from that of being turned into lunch. Take our species, for instance. Once we'd boarded and were tucked away, we felt pretty smug. This was, you understand, long before the days of the fine syringe filled with a solution of carbolic acid in alcohol, before creosote and metallic naphthenates and pentachlorphenol and benzene and para-dichlor-benzene and ortho-di-chloro-benzene. We happily did not run into the family Cleridae or the mite Pediculoides or parasitic wasps of the family Braconidae. But even so we had an enemy, and a patient one: time. What if time exacted from us our inevitable changes?

It came as a serious warning the day we realized that time and nature were happening to our cousin *xestobium rufo-villosum*. That set off quite a panic. It was late in the Voyage, during calmer times, when we were just sitting out the days and waiting for God's pleasure. In the middle of the night, with the Ark becalmed and silence everywhere – a silence so rare and thick that all the beasts stopped to listen, thereby deepening it still further – we heard to our astonishment the ticking of *xestobium rufo-villosum*. Four or five sharp clicks, then a pause, then a distant reply. We the humble, the discreet, the disregarded yet sensible *anobium domesticum* could not believe our ears. That egg becomes larva, larva chrysalis, and chrysalis imago is the inflexible law of our world: pupation brings with it no rebuke. But that our cousins, transformed into adulthood, should choose this moment, this moment of all, to advertise their amatory intentions was almost beyond belief. Here we were, perilously at sea, final extinction a daily possibility, and all *xestobium rufo-villosum* could think about was sex. It must have been a neurotic response to fear of extinction or something. But even so . . .

One of Noah's sons came to check up on the noise as our stupid cousins, hopelessly in thrall to erotic publicity, struck their jaws against the wall of their burrows. Fortunately, the offspring of 'the Admiral' had only a crude understanding of the animal kingdom with which they had been entrusted, and he took the patterned clicks to be a creaking of the ship's timbers. Soon the wind rose again and *xestobium rufo-villosum* could make its trysts in safety. But the affair left the rest of us much more cautious. *Anobium domesticum*, by seven votes to none, resolved not to pupate until after Disembarkation.

It has to be said that Noah, rain or shine, wasn't much of a sailor. He was picked for his piety rather than his navigational skills. He wasn't any good in a storm, and he wasn't much better when the seas were calm. How would I be any judge? Again, I am reporting what the birds said – the birds that can stay in the air for weeks at a time, the birds that can find their way from one end of the planet to the other by navigational systems as elaborate as any invented by your species. And the *birds* said Noah didn't know what he was doing – he was all bluster and prayer. It wasn't difficult, what he had to do, was it? During the tempest he had to survive by running from the fiercest part of the storm; and during calm weather he had to ensure we didn't drift so far from our original map-reference that we came to rest in some uninhabitable Sahara. The best that can be said for Noah is that he survived the storm (though he hardly needed to worry about reefs and coastlines, which made things easier), and that when the waters finally subsided we

j

didn't find ourselves by mistake in the middle of some great ocean. If we'd done that, there's no knowing how long we'd have been at sea.

Of course, the birds offered to put their expertise at Noah's disposal; but he was too proud. He gave them a few simple reconnaissance tasks – looking out for whirlpools and tornadoes – while disdaining their proper skills. He also sent a number of species to their deaths by asking them to go aloft in terrible weather when they weren't properly equipped to do so. When Noah despatched the warbling goose into a Force Nine gale (the bird did, it's true, have an irritating cry, especially if you were trying to sleep), the stormy petrel actually volunteered to take its place. But the offer was spurned – and that was the end of the warbling goose.

All right, all right, Noah had his virtues. He was a survivor – and not just in terms of the Voyage. He also cracked the secret of long life, which has subsequently been lost to your species. But he was not a nice man. Did you know about the time he had the ass keel-hauled? Is that in your archives? It was in Year Two, when the rules had been just a little relaxed, and selected travellers were allowed to mingle. Well, Noah caught the ass trying to climb up the mare. He really hit the roof, ranted away about no good coming of such a union – which rather confirmed our theory about his horror of cross-breeding – and said he would make an example of the beast. So they tied his hooves together, slung him over the side, dragged him underneath the hull and up the other side in a stampeding sea. Most of us put it down to sexual jealousy, simple as that. What was amazing, though, was how the ass took it. They know all about endurance, those guys. When they pulled him over the rail, he was in a terrible state. His poor old ears looked like fronds of slimy seaweed and his tail like a yard of sodden rope and a few of the other beasts who by this time weren't too crazy about Noah gathered round him, and the goat I think it was butted him gently in the side to see if he was still alive, and the ass opened one eye, rolled it around the circle of concerned muzzles and said, 'Now I know what it's like to be a seal.' Not bad in the circumstances? But I have to tell you, that was nearly one more species you lost.

I suppose it wasn't altogether Noah's fault. I mean, that God of his was a really oppressive role-model. Noah couldn't do anything without first wondering what *He* would think. Now that's no way to go on. Always looking over your shoulder for approval – it's not adult, is it? And Noah didn't have the excuse of being a young man, either. He was six hundred-odd, by the way your species reckons these things. Six hundred years should have produced some flexibility of mind, some ability to see both sides of the question. Not a bit of it. Take the construction of the Ark. What does he do? He builds it in gopher-wood. *Gopher*-wood? Even Shem objected, but no, that was what he wanted and that was what he had to have. The fact that not much gopher-wood grew nearby was brushed aside. No doubt he was merely following instructions from his role-model; but even so. Anyone who knows anything about wood – and *I* speak with some authority in the matter – could have told him that a couple of dozen other tree-types would have done as well, if not better; and what's more, the idea of building all parts of a boat from a single wood is ridiculous. You should choose your material according to the purpose for which it is intended; everyone knows that. Still, this was old Noah for you – no flexibility of mind at all. Only saw one side of the question. Gopher-wood bathroom fittings – have you ever heard of anything more ridiculous?

He got it, as I say, from his role-model. What would God think? That was the question always on his lips. There was something a bit sinister about Noah's devotion to God; creepy, if you know what I mean. Still, he certainly knew which side his bread was buttered; and I suppose being selected like that as the favoured survivor, knowing that your dynasty is going to be the only one on earth – it must turn your head, mustn't it? As for his sons – Ham, Shem and the one beginning with J – it certainly didn't do much good for their egos. Swanking about on deck like the Royal Family.

You see, there's one thing I want to make quite clear. This

Ark business. You're probably still thinking that Noah, for all his faults, was basically some kind of early conservationist, that he collected the animals together because he didn't want them to die out, that he couldn't endure not seeing a giraffe ever again, that he was doing it for *us*. This wasn't the case at all. He got us together because his role-model told him to, but also out of self-interest, even cynicism. *He wanted to have something to eat after the Flood had subsided.* Five and a half years under water and most of the kitchen gardens were washed away, I can tell you; only rice prospered. And so most of us knew that in Noah's eyes we were just future dinners on two, four or however many legs. If not now, then later; if not us, then our offspring. That's not a nice feeling, as you can imagine. An atmosphere of paranoia and terror held sway on that Ark of Noah's. Which of us would he come for next? Fail to charm Ham's wife today and you might be a fricassee by tomorrow night. That sort of uncertainty can provoke the oddest behaviour. I remember when a couple of lemmings were caught making for the side of the ship – they said they wanted to end it once and for all, they couldn't bear the suspense. But Shem caught them just in time and locked them up in a packing-case. Every so often, when he was feeling bored, he would slide open the top of their box and wave a big knife around inside. It was his idea of a joke. But if it didn't traumatize the entire species I'd be very surprised.

And of course once the Voyage was over, God made Noah's dining rights official. The pay-off for all that obedience was the permission to eat whichever of us Noah chose for the rest of his life. It was all part of some pact or covenant botched together between the pair of them. A pretty hollow contract, if you ask me. After all, having eliminated everyone else from the earth, God had to make do with the one family of worshippers he'd got left, didn't he? Couldn't very well say, No you aren't up to scratch either. Noah probably realized he had God over a barrel (what an admission of failure to pull the Flood and then be obliged to ditch your First Family), and we reckoned he'd have eaten us anyway, treaty or no treaty. This so-called covenant had absolutely nothing in it for us – except our death-warrant. Oh yes, we were thrown one tiny sop – Noah and his crowd weren't permitted to eat any females that were in calf. A loophole which led to some frenzied activity around the beached Ark, and also to some strange psychological side-effects. Have you ever thought about the origins of the hysterical pregnancy?

Which reminds me of that business with Ham's wife. It was all rumour, they said, and you can see how such rumours might have started. Ham's wife was not the most popular person in the Ark; and the loss of the hospital ship, as I've said, was widely attributed to her. She was still very attractive – only about a hundred and fifty at the time of the Deluge – but she was also wilful and short-tempered. She certainly dominated poor Ham. Now the facts are as follows. Ham and his wife had two children – two male children, that is, which was the way they counted – called Cush and Mizraim. They had a third son, Phut, who was born on the Ark, and a fourth, Canaan, who arrived after the Landing. Noah and his wife had dark hair and brown eyes; so did Ham and his wife; so, for that matter, did Shem and Varadi and the one beginning with J. And all the children of Shem and Varadi and the one whose name began with J had dark hair and brown eyes. And so did Cush, and Mizraim, and Canaan. But Phut, the one born on the Ark, had red hair. Red hair and green eyes. Those are the facts.

At this point we leave the harbour of facts for the high seas of rumour (that's how Noah used to talk, by the way). I was not myself on Ham's ark, so I am merely reporting, in a dispassionate way, the news the birds brought. There were two main stories, and I leave you to choose between them. You remember the case of the craftsman who chipped out a priest's hole for himself on the stores ship? Well, it was said – though not officially confirmed – that when they searched the quarters of Ham's wife they discovered a compartment nobody had realized was there. It certainly wasn't marked on the plans. Ham's wife denied all knowledge of it, yet it seems one of her yakskin undervests was found hanging on a peg there, and a jealous examination of the floor revealed several red hairs caught between the planking.

The second story – which again I pass on without comment – touches on more delicate matters, but since it directly concerns a significant percentage of your species I am constrained to go on. There was on board Ham's ark a pair of simians of the most extraordinary beauty and sleekness. They were, by all accounts, highly intelligent, perfectly groomed, and had mobile faces which you could swear were about to utter speech. They also had flowing red fur and green eyes. No, such a species no longer exists: it did not survive the Voyage, and the circumstances surrounding its death on board have never been fully cleared up. Something to do with a falling spar . . . But what a coincidence, we always thought, for a falling spar to kill both members of a particularly nimble species at one and the same time.

The public explanation was quite different, of course. There were no secret compartments. There was no miscegenation. The spar which killed the simians was enormous, and also carried away a purple muskrat, two pygmy ostriches and a pair of flat-tailed aardvarks. The strange colouring of Phut was a sign from God – though what it denoted lay beyond human decipherability at the time. Later its significance became clear: it was a sign that the Voyage had passed its half-way mark. Therefore Phut was a blessed child, and no subject for alarm and punishment. Noah himself announced as much. God had come to him in a dream and told him to stay his hand against the infant, and Noah, being a righteous man as he pointed out, did so.

I don't need to tell you that the animals were pretty divided about what to believe. The mammals, for instance, refused to countenance the idea that the male of the red-haired, green-eyed simians could have been carnally familiar with Ham's wife. To be sure, we never know what is in the secret heart of even our closest friends, but the mammals were prepared to swear on their mammalhood that it would never have happened. They knew the male simian too well, they said, and could vouch for his high standards of personal cleanliness. He was even, they hinted, a bit of a snob. And supposing – just supposing – he had

24

wanted a bit of rough trade, there were far more alluring specimens on offer than Ham's wife. Why not one of those cute little yellow-tailed monkeys who were anybody's for a pawful of mashed nutmeg?

That is nearly the end of my revelations. They are intended – you must understand me – in a spirit of friendship. If you think I am being contentious, it is probably because your species – I hope you don't mind my saying this – is so hopelessly dogmatic. You believe what you want to believe, and you go on believing it. But then, of course, you all have Noah's genes. No doubt this also accounts for the fact that you are often strangely incurious. You never ask, for instance, this question about your early history: what happened to the raven?

When the Ark landed on the mountaintop (it was more complicated than that, of course, but we'll let details pass), Noah sent out a raven and a dove to see if the waters had retreated from the face of the earth. Now, in the version that has come down to you, the raven has a very small part; it merely flutters hither and thither, to little avail, you are led to conclude. The dove's three journeys, on the other hand, are made a matter of heroism. We weep when she finds no rest for the sole of her foot; we rejoice when she returns to the Ark with an olive leaf. You have elevated this bird, I understand, into something of symbolic value. So let me just point this out: the raven always maintained that *he* found the olive tree; that *he* brought a leaf from it back to the Ark; but that Noah decided it was 'more appropriate' to say that the dove had discovered it. Personally, I always believed the raven, who apart from anything else was much stronger in the air than the dove; and it would have been just like Noah (modelling himself on that God of his again) to stir up a dispute among the animals. Noah had it put about that the raven, instead of returning as soon as possible with evidence of dry land, had been malingering, and had been spotted (by whose eye? not even the upwardly mobile dove would have de-meaned herself with such a slander) gourmandising on carrion. The raven, I need hardly add, felt hurt and betrayed at this instant rewriting of history, and it is said – by those with a better ear than mine – that you can hear the sad croak of dissatisfaction in his voice to this day. The dove, by contrast, began sounding unbearably smug from the moment we disembarked. She could already envisage herself on postage stamps and letterheads.

Before the ramps were lowered, 'the Admiral' addressed the beasts on his Ark, and his words were relayed to those of us on other ships. He thanked us for our co-operation, he apologized for the occasional sparseness of rations, and he promised that since we had all kept our side of the bargain, he was going to get the best *quid pro quo* out of God in the forthcoming negotiations. Some of us laughed a little doubtingly at that: we remembered the keel-hauling of the ass, the loss of the hospital ship, the exterminatory policy with cross-breeds, the death of the unicorn . . . It was evident to us that if Noah was coming on all Mister Nice Guy, it was because he sensed what any clear-thinking animal would do the moment it placed its foot on dry land: make for the forests and the hills. He was obviously trying to soft-soap us into staying close to New Noah's Palace, whose construction he chose to announce at the same time. Amenities here would include free water for the animals and extra feed during harsh winters. He was obviously scared that the meat diet he'd got used to on the Ark would be taken away from him as fast as its two, four or however many legs could carry it, and that the Noah family would be back on berries and nuts once again. Amazingly, some of the beasts thought Noah's offer a fair one: after all, they argued, he can't eat all of us, he'll probably just cull the old and the sick. So some of them – not the cleverest ones, it has to be said – stayed around waiting for the Palace to be built and the water to flow like wine. The pigs, the cattle, the sheep, some of the stupider goats, the chickens . . . We warned them, or at least we tried. We used to mutter derisively, 'Braised or boiled?' but to no avail. As I say, they weren't very bright, and were probably scared of going back into the wild; they'd grown dependent on their gaol, and their gaoler. What happened over the next few generations was quite predictable: they became shadows of their former selves. The pigs and sheep you see walking around today are zombies compared to their effervescent ancestors on the Ark. They've had the stuffing knocked out of them. And some of them, like the turkey, have to endure the further indignity of having the stuffing put back into them – before they are braised or boiled.

And of course, what did Noah actually deliver in his famous Disembarkation Treaty with God? What did he get in return for the sacrifices and loyalty of his tribe (let alone the more considerable sacrifices of the animal kingdom)? God said – and this is Noah putting the best possible interpretation on the matter – that He promised not to send another Flood, and that as a sign of His intention He was creating for us the rainbow. The rainbow! Ha! It's a very pretty thing, to be sure, and the first one he produced for us, an iridescent semi-circle with a paler sibling beside it, the pair of them glittering in an indigo sky, certainly made a lot of us look up from our grazing. You could see the idea behind it: as the rain gave reluctant way to the sun, this flamboyant symbol would remind us each time that the rain wasn't going to carry on and turn into a Flood. But even so. It wasn't much of a deal. And was it legally enforceable? Try getting a rainbow to stand up in court.

The cannier animals saw Noah's offer of half-board for what it was; they took to the hills and the woods, relying on their own skills for water and winter feed. The reindeer, we couldn't help noticing, were among the first to take off, speeding away from 'the Admiral' and all his future descendants, bearing with them their mysterious forebodings. You are right, by the way, to see the animals that fled – ungrateful traitors, according to Noah – as the nobler species. Can a pig be noble? A sheep? A chicken? If only you had seen the unicorn . . . That was another contentious aspect of Noah's post-Disembarkation address to those still loitering at the edge of his stockade. He said that God, by giving us the rainbow, was in effect promising to keep the world's supply of miracles topped up. A clear reference, if ever I heard one, to the scores of original miracles which in the course of the Voyage had been slung over the side of Noah's ships or had disappeared into the guts of his family. The rainbow in place of the unicorn? Why didn't God just restore the unicorn? We animals would have been happier with that, instead of a big hint in the sky about God's magnanimity every time it stopped raining.

Getting off the Ark, I think I told you, wasn't much easier than getting on. There had, alas, been a certain amount of ratting by some of the chosen species, so there was no question of Noah simply flinging down the ramps and crying 'Happy land'. Every animal had to put up with a strict body-search before being released; some were even doused in tubs of water which smelt of tar. Several female beasts complained of having to undergo internal examination by Shem. Quite a few stow-aways were discovered: some of the more conspicuous beetles, a few rats who had unwisely gorged themselves during the Voyage and got too fat, even a snake or two. We got off – I don't suppose it need be a secret any longer – in the hollowed tip of a ram's horn. It was a big, surly, subversive animal, whose friendship we had deliberately cultivated for the last three years at sea. It had no respect for Noah, and was only too happy to help outsmart him after the Landing.

When the seven of us climbed out of that ram's horn, we were euphoric. We had survived. We had stowed away, survived and escaped – all without entering into any fishy covenants with either God or Noah. We had done it by ourselves. We felt ennobled as a species. That might strike you as comic, but we did: we felt ennobled. That Voyage taught us a lot of things, you see, and the main thing was this: that man is a very unevolved species compared to the animals. We don't deny, of course, your cleverness, your considerable potential. But you are, as yet, at an early stage of your development. We, for instance, are always ourselves: that is what it means to be evolved. We are what we are, and we know what that is. You don't expect a cat suddenly to start barking, do you, or a pig to start lowing? But this is what, in a manner of speaking, those of us who made the Voyage on the Ark learned to expect from your species. One moment you bark, one moment you mew; one moment you wish to be wild, one moment you wish to be tame. We knew where we were with Noah only in this one respect: that we never knew where we were with him.

You aren't too good with the truth, either, your species. You keep forgetting things, or you pretend to. The loss of Varadi and his ark – does anyone speak of that? I can see there might be a positive side to this wilful averting of the eye: ignoring the bad things makes it easier for you to carry on. But ignoring the bad things makes you end up believing that bad things never happen. You are always surprised by them. It surprises you that guns kill, that money corrupts, that snow falls in winter. Such naïvety can be charming; alas, it can also be perilous.

For instance, you won't even admit the true nature of Noah, your first father – the pious patriarch, the committed conservationist. I gather that one of your early Hebrew legends asserts that Noah discovered the principle of intoxication by watching a goat get drunk on fermented grapes. What a brazen attempt to shift responsibility on to the animals; and all, sadly, part of a pattern. The Fall was the serpent's fault, the honest raven was a slacker and a glutton, the goat turned Noah into an alkie. Listen: you can take it from me that Noah didn't need any cloven-footed knowledge to help crack the secret of the vine.

Blame someone else, that's always your first instinct. And if you can't blame someone else, then start claiming the problem isn't a problem anyway. Rewrite the rules, shift the goalposts. Some of those scholars who devote their lives to your sacred texts have even tried to prove that the Noah of the Ark wasn't the same man as the Noah arraigned for drunkenness and indecent exposure. How could a drunkard possibly be chosen by God? Ah, well, he wasn't, you see. Not *that* Noah. Simple case of mistaken identity. Problem disappears.

How could a drunkard possibly be chosen by God? I've told you – because all the other candidates were a damn sight worse. Noah was the pick of a very bad bunch. As for his drinking: to tell you the truth, it was the Voyage that tipped him over the edge. Old Noah had always enjoyed a few horns of fermented liquor in the days before Embarkation: who didn't? But it was the Voyage that turned him into a soak. He just couldn't handle the responsibility. He made some bad navigational decisions, he lost four of his eight ships and about a third of the species entrusted to him — he'd have been court-martialled if there'd been anyone around to sit on the bench. And for all his bluster, he felt guilty about losing half the Ark. Guilt, immaturity, the constant struggle to hold down a job beyond your capabilities — it makes a powerful combination, one which would have had the same ruinous effect on most members of your species. You could even argue, I suppose, that God drove Noah to drink. Perhaps this is why your scholars are so jumpy, so keen to separate the first Noah from the second: the consequences are awkward. But the story of the 'second' Noah — the drunkenness, the indecency, the capricious punishment of a dutiful son — well, it didn't come as a surprise to those of us who knew the 'first' Noah on the Ark. A depressing yet predictable case of alcoholic degeneration, I'm afraid.

As I was saying, we were euphoric when we got off the Ark. Apart from anything else, we'd eaten enough gopher-wood to last a lifetime. That's another reason for wishing Noah had been less bigoted in his design of the fleet: it would have given some of us a change of diet. Hardly a consideration for Noah, of course, because we weren't meant to be there. And with the hindsight of a few millennia, this exclusion seems even harsher than it did at the time. There were seven of us stowaways, but had we been admitted as a seaworthy species only two boarding-passes would have been issued; and we would have accepted that decision. Now, it's true Noah couldn't have predicted how long his Voyage was going to last, but considering how little we seven ate in five and a half years, it surely would have been worth the risk letting just a pair of us on board. And after all, it's not our fault for being woodworm.

2

THE VISITORS

FRANKLIN HUGHES HAD come on board an hour earlier to extend some necessary bonhomie towards those who would make his job easier over the next twenty days. Now, he leaned on the rail and watched the passengers climb the gangway: middle-aged and elderly couples for the most part, some bearing an obvious stamp of nationality, others, more decorous, preserving for the moment a sly anonymity of origin. Franklin, his arm lightly but unarguably around the shoulder of his travelling companion, played his annual game of guessing where his audience came from. Americans were the easiest, the men in New World leisure-wear of pastel hues, the women unconcerned by throbbing paunches. The British were the next easiest, the men in Old World tweed jackets hiding short-sleeved shirts of ochre or beige, the women sturdy-kneed and keen to tramp any mountain at the sniff of a Greek temple. There were two Canadian couples whose towelling hats bore a prominent maple-leaf emblem; a rangy Swedish family with four heads of blond hair; some confusable French and Italians whom Franklin identified with a simple mutter of *baguette* or *macaroni*; and six Japanese who declined their stereotype by not displaying a single camera among them. With the exception of a few family groups and the occasional lone aesthetic-looking Englishman, they came up the gangway in obedient couples.

'The animals came in two by two,' Franklin commented. He was a tall, fleshy man somewhere in his forties, with pale gold hair and a reddish complexion which the envious put down to drink and the charitable to an excess of sun; his face seemed familiar in a way which made you forget to ask whether or not

33

you judged it good-looking. His companion, or assistant, but not, she would insist, secretary, was a slim, dark girl displaying clothes newly bought for the cruise. Franklin, ostentatiously an old hand, wore a khaki bush-shirt and a pair of rumpled jeans. While it was not quite the uniform some of the passengers expected of a distinguished guest lecturer, it accurately suggested the origin of such distinction as Franklin could command. If he'd been an American academic he might have dug out a seersucker suit; if a British academic, perhaps a creased linen jacket the colour of ice-cream. But Franklin's fame (which was not quite as extensive as he thought it) came from television. He had started as a mouthpiece for other people's views, a young man in a corduroy suit with an affable and unthreatening way of explaining culture. After a while he realized that if he could speak this stuff there was no reason why he shouldn't write it as well. At first it was no more than 'additional material by Franklin Hughes', then a co-script credit, and finally the achievement of a full 'written and presented by Franklin Hughes'. What his special area of knowledge was nobody could quite discern, but he roved freely in the worlds of archaeology, history and comparative culture. He specialized in the contemporary allusion which would rescue and enliven for the average viewer such dead subjects as Hannibal's crossing of the Alps, or Viking treasure hoards in East Anglia, or Herod's palaces. 'Hannibal's elephants were the panzer divisions of their age,' he would declare as he passionately straddled a foreign landscape; or, 'That's as many foot-soldiers as could be fitted into Wembley Stadium on Cup Final Day'; or, 'Herod wasn't just a tyrant and a unifier of his country, he was also a patron of the arts – perhaps we should think of him as a sort of Mussolini with good taste.'

Franklin's television fame soon brought him a second wife, and a couple of years later a second divorce. Nowadays, his contracts with Aphrodite Cultural Tours always included the provision of a cabin for his assistant; the crew of the *Santa Euphemia* noted with admiration that the assistants tended not to last from one voyage to the next. Franklin was generous towards the stewards, and popular with those who had paid a couple of thousand pounds for their twenty days. He had the engaging habit of sometimes pursuing a favourite digression so fervently that he would have to stop and look around with a puzzled smile before reminding himself where he was meant to be. Many of the passengers commented to one another on Franklin's obvious enthusiasm for his subject, how refreshing it was in these cynical times, and how he really made history come alive for them. If his bush-shirt was often carelessly buttoned and his denim trousers occasionally stained with lobster, this was no more than corroboration of his beguiling zeal for the job. His clothes hinted, too, at the admirable democracy of learning in the modern age: you evidently did not have to be a stuffy professor in a wing-collar to understand the principles of Greek architecture.

'The Welcome Buffet's at eight,' said Franklin. 'Think I'd better put in a couple of hours on my spiel for tomorrow morning.'

'Surely you've done that lots of times before?' Tricia was half-hoping he would stay on deck with her as they sailed out into the Gulf of Venice.

'Got to make it different each year. Otherwise you go stale.' He touched her lightly on the forearm and went below. In fact, his opening address at ten the next morning would be exactly the same as for the previous five years. The only difference – the only thing designed to prevent Franklin from going stale – was the presence of Tricia instead of . . . of, what was that last girl's name? But he liked to maintain the fiction of working on his lectures beforehand, and he could easily pass up the chance of seeing Venice recede yet again. It would still be there the following year, a centimetre or two nearer the waterline, its pinky complexion, like his own, flaking a little more.

On deck, Tricia gazed at the city until the campanile of San Marco became a pencil-stub. She had first met Franklin three months ago, when he'd appeared on the chat-show for which she was a junior researcher. They'd been to bed a few times, but not much so far. She had told the girls at the flat she was going away with a schoolfriend; if things went well, she'd let on when she got back, but for the moment she was a little superstitious. Franklin Hughes! And he'd been really considerate so far, even allotting her some nominal duties so that she wouldn't look too much like just a girlfriend. So many people in television struck her as a bit fake – charming, yet not altogether honest. Franklin was just the same offscreen as on: outgoing, jokey, eager to tell you things. You believed what he said. Television critics made fun of his clothes and the tuft of chest-hair where his shirt parted, and sometimes they sneered at what he said, but that was just envy, and she'd like to see some of those critics get up and try to perform like Franklin. Making it look easy, he had explained to her at their first lunch, was the hardest thing of all. The other secret about television, he said, was how to know when to shut up and let the pictures do the work for you – 'You've got to get that fine balance between word and image.' Privately, Franklin was hoping for the ultimate credit: 'Written, narrated and produced by Franklin Hughes'. In his dreams he sometimes choreographed for himself a gigantic walking shot in the Forum which would take him from the Arch of Septimius Severus to the Temple of Vesta. Where to put the camera was the only problem.

The first leg of the trip, as they steamed down the Adriatic, went much as usual. There was the Welcome Buffet, with the crew sizing up the passengers and the passengers warily circling one another; Franklin's opening lecture, in which he flattered his audience, deprecated his television fame and announced that it was a refreshing change to be addressing real people instead of a glass eye and a cameraman shouting 'Hair in the gate, can we do it again, love?' (the technical reference would be lost on most of his listeners, which was intended by Franklin: they were allowed to be snobbish about TV, but not to assume it was idiots' business); and then there was Franklin's other opening lecture, one just as necessary to bring off, in which he explained to his assistant how the main thing they must remember was to have a good time. Sure he'd have to work – indeed, there'd be times when much as he didn't want to he'd be forced to shut himself away in his cabin with his notes – but mostly he felt they should treat it as three weeks' holiday from the filthy English weather and all that backstabbing at Television Centre. Tricia nodded agreement, though as a junior researcher she had not yet witnessed, let alone endured, any backstabbing. A more worldly-wise girl would have readily understood Franklin to mean 'Don't expect anything more out of me than this'. Tricia, being placid and optimistic, glossed his little speech more mildly as 'Let's be careful of building up false expectations' – which to do him credit was roughly what Franklin Hughes intended. He fell lightly in love several times each year, a tendency in himself which he would occasionally deplore but regularly indulge. However, he was far from heartless, and the moment he felt a girl – especially a nice girl – needing him more than he needed her a terrible flush of apprehension would break out in him. This rustling panic would usually make him suggest one of two things – either that the girl move into his flat, or that she move out of his life – neither of which he exactly wanted. So his address of welcome to Jenny or Cathy or in this case Tricia came more from prudence than cynicism, though when things subsequently went awry it was unsurprising if Jenny or Cathy or in this case Tricia remembered him as more calculating than in fact he had been.

The same prudence, murmuring insistently at him across numerous gory news reports, had made Franklin Hughes acquire an Irish passport. The world was no longer a welcoming place where the old dark-blue British job, topped up with the words 'journalist' and 'BBC', got you what you wanted. 'Her Britannic Majesty's Secretary of State,' Franklin could quote from memory, 'Requests and requires in the Name of Her Majesty all those whom it may concern to allow the bearer such assistance and protection as may be necessary.' Wishful thinking. Nowadays Franklin travelled on a green Irish passport with a gold harp on the cover, which made him feel like a Guinness rep every time he produced it. Inside, the word 'journalist' was also missing from Hughes's largely honest self-description. There were countries in the world which didn't welcome

journalists, and who thought that white-skinned ones pretending interest in archaeological sites were obviously British spies.
The less compromising 'Writer' was also intended as a piece of
self-encouragement. If Franklin described himself as a writer,
then this might nudge him into becoming one. Next time
round, there was a definite chance for a book-of-the-series; and
beyond that he was toying with something serious but sexy —
like a personal history of the world — which might roost for
months in the bestseller lists.

The *Santa Euphemia* was an elderly but comfortable ship with
a courtly Italian captain and an efficient Greek crew. These
Aphrodite Tours brought a predictable clientèle, disparate in
nationality but homogeneous in taste. The sort of people who
preferred reading to deck quoits, and sun-bathing to the disco.
They followed the guest lecturer everywhere, took most of the
supplementary trips and disdained straw donkeys in the souvenir shops. They had not come for romance, though a string
trio occasionally incited some old-fashioned dancing. They took
their turn at the captain's table, were inventive when it came
to fancy-dress night, and dutifully read the ship's newspaper,
which printed their daily route alongside birthday messages
and non-controversial events happening on the European
continent.

The atmosphere seemed a little torpid to Tricia, but it was a
well-organized torpor. As in the address to his assistant,
Franklin had emphasized in his opening lecture that the purpose
of the next three weeks was pleasure and relaxation. He hinted
tactfully that people had different levels of interest in classical
antiquity, and that he for one wouldn't be keeping an attendance book and marking down absentees with a black X.
Franklin engagingly admitted that there were occasions when
even he could tire of yet another row of Corinthian columns
standing against a cloudless sky; though he did this in a way
which allowed the passengers to disbelieve him.

The tail end of the Northern winter had been left behind; and
at a stately pace the *Santa Euphemia* took its contented passengers into a calm Mediterranean spring. Tweed jackets gave way

to linen ones, trouser-suits to slightly outdated sun-dresses. They passed through the Corinth Canal at night, with some of the passengers jammed against a porthole in their nightclothes, and the hardier ones on deck, occasionally letting off ineffectual bursts of flash from their cameras. From the Ionian to the Aegean: it was a little fresher and choppier in the Cyclades, but nobody minded. They went ashore at chichi Mykonos, where an elderly headmaster twisted his ankle while climbing among the ruins; at marbled Paros and volcanic Thira. The cruise was ten days old when they stopped at Rhodes. While the passengers were ashore the *Santa Euphemia* took on fuel, vegetables, meat and more wine. It also took on some visitors, although this did not become apparent until the following morning.

They were steaming towards Crete, and at eleven o'clock Franklin began his usual lecture on Knossos and Minoan Civilization. He had to be a little careful, because his audience tended to know about Knossos, and some of them would have their personal theories. Franklin liked people asking questions; he didn't mind pieces of obscure and even correct information being added to what he had already imparted – he would offer thanks with a courtly bow and a murmur of 'Herr Professor', implying that as long as some of us have an overall grasp of things, it was fine for others to fill their heads with recondite detail; but what Franklin Hughes couldn't stand were bores with pet ideas they couldn't wait to try out on the guest lecturer. Excuse me, Mr Hughes, it looks very Egyptian to me – how do we know the Egyptians didn't build it? Aren't you assuming that Homer wrote when people think he (a little laugh) – or she – did? I don't have any actual expert knowledge, yet surely it would make more sense if . . . There was always at least one of them, playing the puzzled yet reasonable amateur; unfooled by received opinion, he – or she – knew that historians were full of bluff, and that complicated matters were best understood using zestful intuition untainted by any actual knowledge or research. 'I appreciate what you're saying, Mr Hughes, but surely it would be more logical . . .' What Franklin occasionally wanted to say, though never did, was that

39

these brisk guesses about earlier civilizations seemed to him to have their foundation as often as not in Hollywood epics starring Kirk Douglas or Burt Lancaster. He imagined himself hearing out one of these jokers and replying, with a skirl of irony on the adverb, 'Of course, you realize that the film of Ben Hur isn't *entirely* reliable?' But not this trip. In fact, not until he knew it was going to be his last trip. Then he could let go a little. He could be franker with his audience, less careful with the booze, more receptive to the flirting glance.

The visitors were late for Franklin Hughes's lecture on Knossos, and he had already done the bit in which he pretended to be Sir Arthur Evans when they opened the double doors and fired a single shot into the ceiling. Franklin, still headily involved in his own performance, murmured, 'Can I have a translation of that?' but it was an old joke, and not enough to recapture the passengers' attention. They had already forgotten Knossos and were watching the tall man with a moustache and glasses who was coming to take Franklin's place at the lectern. Under normal circumstances, Franklin might have yielded him the microphone after a courteous inquiry about his credentials. But given that the man was carrying a large machine-gun and wore one of those red check head-dresses which used to be shorthand for lovable desert warriors loyal to Lawrence of Arabia but in recent years had become shorthand for baying terrorists eager to massacre the innocent, Franklin simply made a vague 'Over to you' gesture with his hands and sat down on his chair.

Franklin's audience — as he still thought of them in a brief proprietorial flurry — fell silent. Everyone was avoiding an incautious movement; each breath was discreetly taken. There were three visitors, and the other two were guarding the double doors into the lecture room. The tall one with the glasses had an almost scholarly air as he tapped the microphone in the manner of lecturers everywhere: partly to see if it was working, partly to attract attention. The second half of this gesture was not strictly necessary.

'I apologize for the inconvenience,' he began, setting off a nervous laugh or two. 'But I am afraid it is necessary to interrupt your holiday for a while. I hope it will not be a long interruption. You will all stay here, sitting exactly where you are, until we tell you what to do.'

A voice, male, angry and American, asked from the middle of the auditorium, 'Who are you and what the hell do you want?' The Arab swayed back to the microphone he had just left, and with the contemptuous suavity of a diplomat, replied, 'I am sorry, I am not taking questions at this juncture.' Then, just to make sure he was not mistaken for a diplomat, he went on. 'We are not people who believe in unnecessary violence. However, when I fired the shot into the ceiling to attract your attention, I had set this little catch here so that the gun only fires one shot at a time. If I change the catch' – he did so while holding the weapon half-aloft like an arms instructor with an exceptionally ignorant class – 'the gun will continue to fire until the magazine is empty. I hope that is clear.'

The Arab left the hall. People held hands; there were occasional sniffs and sobs, but mostly silence. Franklin glanced across to the far left of the auditorium at Tricia. His assistants were allowed to come to his lectures, though not to sit in direct line of sight – 'Mustn't start me thinking about the wrong thing.' She didn't appear frightened, more apprehensive about what the form was. Franklin wanted to say, 'Look, this hasn't happened to me before, it isn't normal, I don't know what to do,' but settled instead for an indeterminate nod. After ten minutes of stiff-necked silence, an American woman in her mid-fifties stood up. Immediately one of the two visitors guarding the door shouted at her. She took no notice, just as she ignored the whispers and grabbing hand of her husband. She walked down the central aisle to the gunmen, stopped a couple of yards short and said in a clear, slow voice suppurating with panic, 'I have to go to the goddam bathroom.'

The Arabs neither replied nor looked her in the eye. Instead, with a small gesture of their guns, they indicated as surely as such things can be that she was currently a large target and that any further advance would confirm the fact in an obvious and final way. She turned, walked back to her seat and began to cry. Another woman on the right of the hall immediately started sobbing. Franklin looked across at Tricia again, nodded, got to his feet, deliberately didn't look at the two guards, and went across to the lectern. 'As I was saying . . . ' He gave an authoritative cough and all eyes reverted to him. 'I was saying that the Palace of Knossos was not by any means the first human settlement on the site. What we think of as the Minoan strata reach down to about seventeen feet, but below this there are signs of human habitation down to twenty-six feet or so. There was life where the palace was built for at least ten thousand years before the first stone was laid . . . '

It seemed normal to be lecturing again. It also felt as if some feathered cloak of leadership had been thrown over him. He decided to acknowledge this, glancingly at first. Did the guards understand English? Perhaps. Had they ever been to Knossos? Unlikely. So Franklin, while describing the council chamber at the palace, invented a large clay tablet which, he claimed, had probably hung over the gypsum throne. It read – he looked towards the Arabs at this point – 'We are living in difficult times'. As he continued describing the site, he unearthed more tablets, many of which, as he now fearlessly began to point out, had a universal message. 'We must above all not do anything rash', one said. Another: 'Empty threats are as useless as empty scabbards'. Another: 'The tiger always waits before it springs' (Hughes wondered briefly if Minoan Civilization knew about tigers). He was not sure how many of his audience had latched on to what he was doing, but there came an occasional assenting growl. In a curious way, he was also enjoying himself. He ended his tour of the palace with one of the least typically Minoan of his many inscriptions: 'There is a great power where the sun sets which will not permit certain things'. Then he shuffled his notes together and sat down to warmer applause than usual. He looked across at Tricia and winked. She had tears in her eyes. He glanced towards the two Arabs and thought, that's shown you, now you can see what we're made of, there's some stiff upper lip for you. He rather wished he'd made up some Minoan aphorism about people who wore red tea-towels on their heads, but recognized he wouldn't have had the nerve. He'd keep that one for later, after they were all safe.

They waited for half an hour in a silence that smelt of urine before the leader of the visitors returned. He had a brief word with the guards and walked up the aisle to the lectern. 'I understand that you have been lectured on the palace of Knossos,' he began, and Franklin felt sweat burst into the palms of his hands. 'That is good. It is important for you to understand other civilizations. How they are great, and how' – he paused meaningfully – 'they fall. I hope very much that you will enjoy your trip to Knossos.'

He was leaving the microphone when the same American voice, this time more conciliatory in tone, as if heedful of the Minoan tablets, said, 'Excuse me, would you be able to tell us roughly who you are and roughly what you want?'

The Arab smiled. 'I am not sure that would be a good idea at this stage.' He gave a nod to indicate he had finished, then paused, as if a civil question at least deserved a civil answer. 'Let me put it this way. If things go according to plan, you will soon be able to continue your explorations of the Minoan Civilization. We shall disappear just as we came, and we shall seem to you simply to have been a dream. Then you can forget us. You will remember only that we were a small delay. So there is no need for you to know who we are or where we come from or what we want.'

He was about to leave the low podium when Franklin, rather to his own surprise, said, 'Excuse me.' The Arab turned. 'No more questions.' Hughes went on, 'This is not a question. I just think . . . I'm sure you've got other things on your mind . . . if we're going to have to stay here you ought to let us go to the lavatory.' The leader of the visitors frowned. 'The bathroom,' Franklin explained; then again, 'the toilet.'

'Of course. You will be able to go to the toilet when we move you.'

'When will that be?' Franklin felt himself a little carried away by his self-appointed role. For his part the Arab noted some

43

unacceptable lack of compliance. He replied brusquely, 'When we decide.'

He left. Ten minutes later an Arab they had not seen before came in and whispered to Hughes. He stood up. 'They are going to move us from here to the dining-room. We are to be moved in twos. Occupants of the same cabin are to identify themselves as such. We will be taken to our cabins, where we will be allowed to go to the lavatory. We are also to collect our passports, but nothing else.' The Arab whispered again. 'And we are not allowed to lock the lavatory door.' Without being asked, Franklin went on, 'I think these visitors to the ship are quite serious. I don't think we should do anything which might upset them.'

Only one guard was available to move the passengers, and the process took several hours. As Franklin and Tricia were being taken to C deck, he remarked to her, in the casual tone of one commenting on the weather, 'Take the ring off your right hand and put it on your wedding finger. Turn the stone round so that you can't see it. Don't do it now, do it when you're having a pee.'

When they reached the dining-room their passports were examined by a fifth Arab. Tricia was sent to the far end, where the British had been put in one corner and the Americans in another. In the middle of the room were the French, the Italians, two Spaniards and the Canadians. Nearest the door were the Japanese, the Swedes and Franklin, the solitary Irishman. One of the last couples to be brought in were the Zimmermanns, a pair of stout, well-dressed Americans. Hughes had at first placed the husband in the garment business, some master cutter who had set up on his own; but a conversation on Paros had revealed him to be a recently retired professor of philosophy from the Midwest. As the couple passed Franklin's table on their way to the American quarter, Zimmermann muttered lightly, 'Separating the clean from the unclean.'

When they were all present, Franklin was taken off to the purser's office, where the leader was installed. He found himself wondering if the slightly bulbous nose and the moustache were by any chance attached to the glasses; perhaps they all came off together.

'Ah, Mr Hughes. You seem to be their spokesman. At any event, now your position is official. You will explain to them the following. We are doing our best to make them comfortable, but they must realize that there are certain difficulties. They will be allowed to talk to one another for five minutes at each hour. At the same time those who wish to go to the toilet will be allowed to do so. One person at a time. I can see that they are all sensible people and would not like them to decide not to be sensible. There is one man who says he cannot find his passport. He says he is called Talbot.'

'Mr Talbot, yes.' A vague, elderly Englishman who tended to ask questions about religion in the Ancient World. A mild fellow with no theories of his own, thank God.

'He is to sit with the Americans.'

'But he's British. He comes from Kidderminster.'

'If he remembers where his passport is and he is British he can sit with the British.'

'You can tell he's British. I can vouch for him being British.' The Arab looked unimpressed. 'He doesn't talk like an American, does he?'

'I have not talked to him. Still, talking is not proof, is it? You, I think, talk like a British but your passport says you are not a British.' Franklin nodded slowly. 'So we will wait for the passport.'

'Why are you separating us like this?'

'We think you will like to sit with one another.' The Arab made a sign for him to go.

'There's one other thing. My wife. Can she sit with me?'

'Your wife?' The man looked at a list of passengers in front of him. 'You have no wife.'

'Yes I do. She's travelling as Tricia Maitland. It's her maiden name. We were married three weeks ago.' Franklin paused, then added in a confessional tone, 'My third wife, actually.'

But the Arab seemed unimpressed by Franklin's harem. 'You

were married three weeks ago? And yet it seems you do not share the same cabin. Are things going so badly?'

'No, I have a separate cabin for my work, you see. The lecturing. It's a luxury, having another cabin, a privilege.'

'She is your wife?' The tone gave nothing away.

'Yes she is,' he replied, mildly indignant.

'But she has a British passport.'

'She's Irish. You become Irish if you marry an Irishman. It's Irish law.'

'Mr Hughes, she has a British passport.' He shrugged as if the dilemma were insoluble, then found a solution. 'But if you wish to sit with your wife, then you may go and sit with her at the British table.'

Franklin smiled awkwardly. 'If I'm the passengers' spokesman, how do I get to see you to pass on the passengers' demands?'

'The passengers' demands? No, you have not understood. The passengers do not have demands. You do not see me unless I want to see you.'

After Franklin had relayed the new orders, he sat at his table by himself and thought about the position. The good part was that so far they had been treated with reasonable civility; no-one had yet been beaten up or shot, and their captors didn't seem to be the hysterical butchers they might have expected. On the other hand, the bad part lay quite close to the good part: being unhysterical, the visitors might also prove reliable, efficient, hard to divert from their purpose. And what was their purpose? Why had they hijacked the *Santa Euphemia*? Who were they negotiating with? And who was steering the sodding ship, which as far as Franklin could tell was going round in large, slow circles?

From time to time, he would nod encouragingly to the Japanese at the next table. Passengers at the far end of the dining-room, he couldn't help noting, would occasionally look up in his direction, as if checking that he was still there. He'd become the liaison man, perhaps even the leader. That Knossos lecture, in the circumstances, had been little short of brilliant; a

lot more ballsy than he'd imagined possible. It was the sitting
alone like this that got him down; it made him brood. His
initial burst of emotion – something close to exhilaration – was
seeping away; in its place came lethargy and apprehension.
Perhaps he should go and sit with Tricia and the Brits. But then
they might take his citizenship away from him. This dividing-
up of the passengers: did it mean what he feared it might mean?

Late that afternoon they heard a plane fly over, quite low.
There was a muted cheer from the American section of the
dining-room; then the plane went away. At six o'clock one of
the Greek stewards appeared with a large tray of sandwiches;
Franklin noted the effect of fear on hunger. At seven, as he went
for a pee, an American voice whispered, 'Keep up the good
work.' Back at his table, he tried to look soberly confident. The
trouble was, the more he reflected, the less cheerful he felt. In
recent years Western governments had been noisy about terror-
ism, about standing tall and facing down the threat; but the
threat never seemed to understand that it was being faced down,
and continued much as before. Those in the middle got killed;
governments and terrorists survived.

At nine Franklin was summoned again to the purser's office.
The passengers were to be moved for the night: the Americans
back to the lecture hall, the British to the disco, and so on.
These separate encampments would then be locked. It was
necessary: the visitors had to get their sleep as well. Passports
were to be held ready for inspection at all times.

'What about Mr Talbot?'

'He has become an honorary American. Until he finds his
passport.'

'What about my wife?'

'Miss Maitland. What about her?'

'Can she join me?'

'Ah. Your British wife.'

'She's Irish. You marry an Irishman you become Irish. It's the
law.'

'The law, Mr Hughes. People are always telling *us* what is the
law. I am often puzzled by what they consider is lawful and what

is unlawful.' He looked away to a map of the Mediterranean on the wall behind Franklin. 'Is it lawful to drop bombs on refugee camps, for instance? I have often tried to discover the law which says this is permissible. But it is a long argument, and sometimes I think argument is pointless, just as the law is pointless.' He gave a dismissive shrug. 'As for the matter of Miss Maitland, let us hope that her nationality does not become, how shall I put it, relevant.'

Franklin tried to damp down a shudder. There were times when euphemism could be much more frightening than direct threat. 'Are you able to tell me when it might become . . . relevant?'

'They are stupid, you see. They are stupid because they think we are stupid. They lie in the most obvious way. They say they do not have the authority to act. They say arrangements cannot be made quickly. Of course they can. There is such a thing as the telephone. If they think they have learned something from previous incidents of this kind, they are stupid not to realize that we have too. We know about their tactics, the lying and the delays, all this establishing of some kind of relationship with the freedom fighters. We know all that. And we know about the limits of the body for taking action. So we are obliged by your governments to do what we say we will do. If they started negotiating at once, there would be no problem. But they only start when it is too late. It is on their heads.'

'No,' said Franklin. 'It's on our heads.'

'You, Mr Hughes, I think, do not have to worry so soon.'

'How soon is soon?'

'Indeed, I think you may not have to worry at all.'

'How soon is soon?'

The leader paused, then made a regretful gesture. 'Tomorrow some time. The timetable, you see, is fixed. We have told them from the beginning.'

Part of Franklin Hughes could not believe he was having this conversation. Another part wanted to say he had always supported the cause of his captors – whatever that cause might be – and incidentally the Gaelic on his passport meant that he was a member of the IRA, and for Christ's sake could he please go to his cabin and lie down and forget all about it. Instead, he repeated, 'Timetable?' The Arab nodded. Without thinking, Franklin said, 'One an hour?' Immediately, he wished he hadn't asked. For all he knew he was giving the fellow ideas.

The Arab shook his head. 'Two. A pair every hour. Unless you raise the stakes they do not take you seriously.'

'Christ. Just coming on board and killing people just like that. Just like that?'

'You think it would be better if we explained to them why we were killing them?' The tone was sarcastic.

'Well, yes, actually.'

'Do you think they would be sympathetic?' Now there was more mockery than sarcasm. Franklin was silent. He wondered when the killing was due to start. 'Goodnight, Mr Hughes,' said the leader of the visitors.

Franklin was put for the night in a stateroom with the Swedish family and the three Japanese couples. They were, he deduced, the safest group among the passengers. The Swedes because their nation was famously neutral; Franklin and the Japanese presumably because in recent times Ireland and Japan had produced terrorists. How ludicrous. The six Japanese who had come on a cultural cruise in Europe hadn't been asked whether they supported the various political killers in their own country; nor had Franklin been quizzed about the IRA. A Guinness passport awarded through some genealogical fluke suggested the possibility of sympathy with the visitors, and this was his protection. In fact, Franklin hated the IRA, just as he hated any political group which interfered, or might interfere, with the fulltime job of being Franklin Hughes. For all he knew – and in accordance with his annual policy he had not asked – Tricia was far more sympathetic to the various worldwide groups of homicidal maniacs indirectly committed to interrupting the career of Franklin Hughes. Yet she was herded in with the diabolic British.

There was little talk in the stateroom that night. The Japanese kept to themselves; the Swedish family spent the time trying to distract their children by talking of home and Christmas and British football teams; while Franklin felt burdened by what he knew. He was scared and sickened; but isolation seemed to breed complicity with his captors. He tried thinking of his two wives and the daughter who must be — what? — fifteen now: he always had to remember the year of her birth and work it out from there. He should get down to see her more often. Perhaps he could take her with him when they filmed the next series. She could watch his famous walking shot in the Forum; she'd like that. Now where could he place the camera? Or perhaps a tracking shot. And some extras in toga and sandals — yes, he liked it . . .

Next morning Franklin was taken to the purser's office. The leader of the visitors waved him to sit down. 'I have decided to take your advice.'

'My advice?'

'The negotiations, I fear, are going badly. That is to say, there are no negotiations. We have explained our position but they are extremely unwilling to explain their position.'

'They?'

'They. So, unless things change very quickly, we shall be forced to put some pressure on them.'

'Pressure?' Even Franklin, who could not have made a career in television without skill in trading euphemisms, was enraged. 'You mean killing people.'

'That is the only pressure, sadly, which they understand.'

'What about trying other sorts?'

'But we have. We have tried sitting on our hands and waiting for world opinion to come to our help. We have tried being good and hoping that we would be rewarded by getting our land back. I can assure you that these systems do not work.'

'Why not try something in between?'

'An embargo on American goods, Mr Hughes? I do not think they would take us seriously. A lack of Chevrolets being imported to Beirut? No, regrettably there are people who only understand certain kinds of pressure. The world is only advanced . . .'

'. . . by killing people? A cheerful philosophy.'

'The world is not a cheerful place. I would have thought your investigations into the ancient civilizations would have taught you that. But anyway . . . I have decided to take your advice. We shall explain to the passengers what is happening. How they are mixed up in history. What that history is.'

'I'm sure they'll appreciate that.' Franklin felt queasy. 'Tell them what's going on.'

'Exactly. You see, at four o'clock it will become necessary to . . . to start killing them. Naturally we hope it will not be necessary. But if it is . . . You are right, things must be explained to them if it is possible. Even a soldier knows why he is fighting. It is fair that the passengers be told as well.'

'But they're not fighting.' The Arab's tone, as much as what he said, riled Franklin. 'They're civilians. They're on holiday. They're not fighting.'

'There are no civilians any more,' replied the Arab. 'Your governments pretend, but that is not the case. Those nuclear weapons of yours, they are only to be let off against an army? The Zionists, at least, understand this. All their people are fighting. To kill a Zionist civilian is to kill a soldier.'

'Look, there aren't any Zionist civilians on the ship, for Christ's sake. They're people like poor old Mr Talbot who's lost his passport and has been turned into an American.'

'All the more reason why things must be explained.'

'I see,' said Franklin, and he let the sneer come through. 'So you're going to assemble the passengers and explain to them how they're all really Zionist soldiers and that's why you've got to kill them.'

'No, Mr Hughes, you misunderstand. I am not going to explain anything. They would not listen. No, Mr Hughes, *you* are going to explain things to them.'

'Me?' Franklin didn't feel nervous. Indeed, he felt decisive. 'Certainly not. You can do your own dirty work.'

'But Mr Hughes, you are a public speaker. I have heard you, if only for a short time. You do it so well. You could introduce a historical view of the matter. My second-in-command will give you all the information you require.'

'I don't require any information. Do your own dirty work.'

'Mr Hughes, I really cannot negotiate in two directions at the same time. It is nine-thirty. You have half an hour to decide. At ten you will say that you do the lecture. You will then have two hours, three hours if that is required, with my second-in-command for the briefing.' Franklin was shaking his head, but the Arab continued regardless. 'Then you have until three o'clock to prepare the lecture. I suggest that you make it last forty-five minutes. I shall listen to you, of course, with the greatest interest and attention. And at three-forty-five, if I am satisfied with how you explain matters, we shall in return accept the Irish nationality of your recently married wife. That is all I have to say, you will send me your reply at ten o'clock.'

Back in the stateroom with the Swedes and the Japanese, Franklin remembered a TV series about psychology he'd once been asked to present. It had folded directly after the pilot, a loss nobody much regretted. One item in that show reported an experiment for measuring the point at which self-interest takes over from altruism. Put like this, it sounded almost respectable; but Franklin had been revolted by the actual test. The researchers had taken a female monkey who had recently given birth and put her in a special cage. The mother was still feeding and grooming her infant in a way presumably not too dissimilar from the maternal behaviour of the experimenters' wives. Then they turned a switch and began heating up the metal floor of the monkey's cage. At first she jumped around in discomfort, then squealed a lot, then took to standing on alternate legs, all the while holding her infant in her arms. The floor was made hotter, the monkey's pain more evident. At a certain point the heat from the floor became unbearable, and she was faced with a choice, as the experimenters put it, between altruism and self-interest. She either had to suffer extreme pain and perhaps death in order to protect her offspring, or else place her infant on the floor and stand on it to keep herself from harm.

In every case, sooner or later self-interest had triumphed over altruism.

Franklin had been sickened by the experiment, and glad the TV series hadn't got beyond the pilot, if that was what he would have had to present. Now he felt a bit like that monkey. He was being asked to choose between two equally repellent ideas: that of abandoning his girlfriend while retaining his integrity, or rescuing his girlfriend by justifying to a group of innocent people why it was right that they should be killed. And would that rescue Trish? Franklin hadn't even been promised his own safety; perhaps the pair of them, reclassified as Irish, would merely be moved to the bottom of the killing list, but still remain on it. Who would they start with? The Americans, the British? If they started with the Americans, how long would that delay the killing of the British? Fourteen, sixteen Americans – he translated that brutally into seven or eight hours. If they started at four, and the governments stood firm, by midnight they would start killing the British. What order would they do it in? Men first? Random? Alphabetical? Trish's surname was Maitland. Right in the middle of the alphabet. Would she see the dawn?

He imagined himself standing on Tricia's body to protect his own burning feet and shuddered. He would have to do the lecture. That was the difference between a monkey and a human being. In the last analysis, humans were capable of altruism. This was why he was not a monkey. Of course, it was more than probable that when he gave the lecture his audience would conclude the exact opposite – that Franklin was operating out of self-interest, saving his own skin by a foul piece of subservience. But this was the thing about altruism, it was always liable to be misunderstood. And he could explain everything to them all afterwards. If there was an afterwards. If there was a them all.

When the second-in-command arrived, Franklin asked to see the leader again. He intended demanding safe-conduct for Tricia and himself in exchange for the lecture. However, the second-in-command had only come for a reply, not for renewed conversation. Dully, Franklin nodded his head. He'd never been much good at negotiating anyway.

At two-forty-five Franklin was taken to his cabin and allowed to wash. At three o'clock he entered the lecture hall to find the most attentive audience he had ever faced. He filled a glass from the carafe of stale water that nobody had bothered to change. He sensed below him the swell of exhaustion, a rip-tide of panic. After only a day the men seemed almost bearded, the women crumpled. They had already begun not to look like themselves, or the selves that Franklin had spent ten days with. Perhaps this made them easier to kill.

Before he got his own writing credit Franklin had become expert at presenting the ideas of others as plausibly as possible. But never had he felt such apprehension at a script; never had a director imposed such conditions; never had his fee been so bizarre. When first agreeing to the task he had persuaded himself that he could surely find a way of tipping off his audience that he was acting under duress. He would think up some ploy like that of the false Minoan inscriptions; or he would make his lecture so exaggerated, pretend such enthusiasm for the cause thrust upon him, that nobody could possible miss the irony. No, that wouldn't work. 'Irony,' an ancient TV producer had once confided to him, 'may be defined as what people miss.' And the passengers certainly wouldn't be on the lookout for it in their present circumstances. The briefing had made things yet harder: the second-in-command had given precise instructions, and added that any deviation from them would result not just in Miss Maitland remaining British, but in Franklin's Irish passport no longer being recognized. They certainly knew how to negotiate, these bastards.

'I had been hoping,' he began, 'that the next time I addressed you I would be taking up again the story of Knossos. Unfortunately, as you are aware, the circumstances have changed. We have visitors amongst us.' He paused and looked down the aisle at the leader, who stood before the double doors with a guard on each side. 'Things are different. We are in the hands of others. Our . . . destiny is no longer our own.' Franklin coughed. This wasn't very good. Already he was straying into euphemism. The one duty, the one intellectual duty he had, was to speak as directly as he could. Franklin would freely admit he was a showman and would stand on his head in a bucket of herrings if that would raise viewing figures a few thousand; but there was a residual feeling in him – a mixture of admiration and shame – which made him hold in special regard those communicators who were deeply unlike him: the ones who spoke quietly, in their own simple words, and whose stillness gave them authority. Franklin, who knew he could never be like them, tried to acknowledge their example as he spoke.

'I have been asked to explain things to you. To explain how you – we – find ourselves in the position we are now in. I am not an expert on the politics of the Middle East, but I shall try to make things as clear as I can. We should perhaps begin by going back to the nineteenth century, long before the establishment of the state of Israel . . . ' Franklin found himself back in an easy rhythm, a bowler pitching on a length. He felt his audience begin to relax. The circumstances were unusual, but they were being told a story, and they were offering themselves to the story-teller in the manner of audiences down the ages, wanting to see how things turned out, wanting to have the world explained to them. Hughes sketched in an idyllic nineteenth century, all nomads and goat-farming and traditional hospitality which allowed you to stay in someone else's tent for three days before being asked what the purpose of your visit might be. He talked of early Zionist settlers and Western concepts of land-ownership. The Balfour Declaration. Jewish immigration from Europe. The Second World War. European guilt over the Holocaust being paid for by the Arabs. The Jews having learned from their persecution by the Nazis that the only way to survive was to be like Nazis. Their militarism, expansionism, racism. Their pre-emptive attack on the Egyptian air force at the start of the Six Day War being the exact moral equivalent of Pearl Harbor (Franklin deliberately did not look at the Japanese – or the Americans – at this moment, nor for some time thereafter). The refugee camps. The theft of land. The artificial support of the Israeli economy by the dollar. The atrocities committed against the dispossessed. The Jewish lobby in America. The Arabs only asking from the Western powers for the same justice in the Middle East as had already been accorded to the Jews. The regrettable necessity of violence, a lesson taught the Arabs by the Jews, just as it had been taught the Jews by the Nazis.

Franklin had used up two thirds of his time. If he could feel a brooding hostility in some parts of the audience, there was also, strangely, a wider drowsiness, as if they'd heard this story before and had not believed it then either. 'And so we come to the here and now.' That brought them back to full attention; despite the circumstances, Franklin felt a bubble of pleasure. He was the hypnotist who snaps his fingers. 'In the Middle East, we must understand, there are no civilians any more. The Zionists understand this, the Western governments do not. We, alas, are not civilians. The Zionists have made this happen. You – we – are being held hostage by the Black Thunder group to secure the release of three of their members. You may remember' (though Franklin doubted it, since incidents of this kind were frequent, almost interchangeable) 'that two years ago a civilian aircraft carrying three members of the Black Thunder group was forced down by the American air force in Sicily, that the Italian authorities in contravention of international law compounded this act of piracy by arresting the three freedom fighters, that Britain defended America's action at the United Nations, and that the three men are now in prison in France and Germany. The Black Thunder group does not turn the other cheek, and this legitimate . . . hijack' – Franklin used the word carefully, with a glance at the leader as if to demonstrate how he disdained euphemism – 'is in response to that act of piracy. Unfortunately the Western governments do not show the same concern for their citizens as the Black Thunder group shows for its freedom fighters. Unfortunately they are so far declining to release the prisoners. Regrettably the Black Thunder group has no alternative but to carry out its intended threat which was made very clear from the beginning to the Western governments . . .'

At this moment a large, unathletic American in a blue shirt

got to his feet and started running down the aisle towards the Arabs. Their guns had not been set to fire only one shot at a time. The noise was very loud and immediately there was a lot of blood. An Italian sitting in the line of fire received a bullet in the head and fell across his wife's lap. A few people got up and quickly sat down again. The leader of the Black Thunder group looked at his watch and waved at Hughes to continue. Franklin took a long swig of stale water. He wished it were something stronger. 'Because of the stubbornness of the Western governments,' he went on, trying to sound now more like an official spokesman than Franklin Hughes, 'and their reckless disregard for human life, it is necessary for sacrifices to be made. You will have understood the historical inevitability of this from what I have said before. The Black Thunder group has every confidence that the Western governments will swiftly come to the negotiating table. In a final effort to make them do so it will be necessary to execute two of you . . . of us . . . every hour until that point. The Black Thunder group finds this course of action regrettable, but the Western governments leave them no alternative. The order of executions has been decided according to the guilt of the Western nations for the situation in the Middle East.' Franklin could no longer look at his audience. He dropped his voice, yet could not avoid being heard as he went on. 'Zionist Americans first. Then other Americans. Then British. Then French, Italians and Canadians.'

'What the fuck has Canada ever done in the Middle East? What the fuck?' shouted a man still wearing a towelling maple-leaf hat. He was restrained from getting up by his wife. Franklin, who felt the heat from the metal floor of his cage to be unendurable, shuffled his notes together automatically, stepped off the podium without looking at anyone, walked up the aisle, getting blood on his crêpe soles as he stepped past the dead American, ignored the three Arabs, who could shoot him if they wanted to, and went without escort or opposition to his cabin. He locked the door and lay down on his bunk.

Ten minutes later there came the noise of shooting. From five o'clock to eleven o'clock, punctually on the hour like some terrible parody of a municipal clock, gunfire pealed. Splashes followed, as the bodies were flung over the rail in pairs. Shortly after eleven, twenty-two members of the American Special Forces, who had been trailing the *Santa Euphemia* for fifteen hours, managed to get on board. In the battle six more passengers, including Mr Talbot, the honorary American citizen from Kidderminster, were shot dead. Out of the eight visitors who had helped load supplies at Rhodes, five were killed, two after they had surrendered.

Neither the leader nor the second-in-command survived, so there remained no witness to corroborate Franklin Hughes's story of the bargain he had struck with the Arabs. Tricia Maitland, who had become Irish for a few hours without realizing it, and who in the course of Franklin Hughes's lecture had returned her ring to the finger where it originally belonged, never spoke to him again.

3

THE WARS OF RELIGION

Source: *the Archives Municipales de Besançon (section CG, boîte 377a). The following case, hitherto unpublished, is of particular interest to legal historians in that the* procureur pour les insectes *was the distinguished jurist Bartholomé Chassenée (also Chassanée and Chasseneux), later first president of the Parlement de Provence. Born in 1480, Chassenée made his name before the ecclesiastical court of Autun defending rats which had been charged with feloniously destroying a crop of barley. The following documents, from the opening* pétition des habitans *to the final judgment of the court, do not represent the entire proceedings — for instance, the testimony of witnesses, who might be anything from local peasants to distinguished experts on the behavioural patterns of the defendants, has not been recorded — but the legal submissions embody and often specifically refer to the evidence, and thus there is nothing absent from the essential structure and argument of the case. As was normal at the time, the pleas and the* conclusions du procureur épiscopal *were made in French, while the sentence of the court was solemnly delivered in Latin.*

(Translator's note: *The manuscript is continuous and all in the same hand. Thus we are not dealing with the original submissions as penned by each lawyer's clerk, but with the work of a third party, perhaps an official of the court, who may have omitted sections of the pleas. Comparison with the contents of boîtes 371—379 suggests that the case as it exists in this form was perhaps part of a set of exemplary or typical proceedings used in the training of jurists. This conjecture is supported by the fact that only Chassenée among the participants is identified by name, as if students were being directed to examine the instructive dexterity of a distinguished defence counsel, regardless of the result of the case. The handwriting belongs to the first half of the sixteenth century, so that if, as may be, the document is a copy of someone*

61

else's version of the trial, it is still contemporary. I have done my best to render the sometimes extravagant style of pleading – especially of the unnamed procureur des habitans – into a comparable English.)

Pétition des habitans

We, the inhabitants of Mamirolle in the diocese of Besançon, being fearful of Almighty God and humbly dutiful to his spouse the Church, and being furthermore most regular and obedient in the payment of our tithes, do hereby on this twelfth day of August 1520 most pressingly and urgently petition the court to relieve and disburden us of the felonious intervention of those malefactors which have infested us already for many seasons, which have brought upon us God's wrath and a shameful libel upon our habitation, and which threaten all of us, God-fearing and obedient in our duties to the Church as we are, with immediate and catastrophic death being flung down at us from above like clamorous thunder, which will surely come to pass unless the court in its solemn wisdom do not speedily and justly expel these malefactors from our village, conjuring them to depart, hateful and intolerable as they are, under pain of condemnation, anathema and excommunication from the Holy Church and the Dominion of God.

Plaidoyer des habitans

Gentlemen, these poor and humble petitioners, wretched and distressed, come before you as once did the inhabitants of the isles of Minorca and Majorca before the mighty Augustus Caesar, begging him in his justice and power to rid their islands of those rabbits which were destroying their crops and ruining their livelihood. If Augustus Caesar was able to help those dutiful subjects, how much more easily may this court lift the oppressive burden which lies upon the shoulders of your petitioners as heavily as when the great Aeneas did carry his father Anchises from the burning city of Troy. The old Anchises was blinded by a bolt of lightning, and these your petitioners are even now as if blinded, cast into darkness out of the light of the Lord's blessing, by the felonious behaviour of those who stand accused in this case, and yet who have not even appeared before the court to answer the charges, being contemptuous of this tribunal and blaspheming towards God, preferring instead to bury themselves in sinful darkness rather than face the truth of light.

Know, gentlemen, what has already been put before you by witnesses of humble faith and unimpeachable honesty, simple petitioners too trepid of this court to let anything but the clear fountain of truth flow from their mouths. They have testified to the events of the twenty-second day of the month of April in this year of Our Lord, which being the day of the annual pilgrimage of Hugo, Bishop of Besançon, to the humble church of Saint-Michel in their village. They have described to you, in detail which burns in your memory like the fiery furnace from which Shadrach, Meshach and Abednego came unscathed, how as in every year they had adorned and beautified their church to make it worthy for the eye of the Bishop to behold, how they had caused flowers to be placed upon the altar and the door to be made freshly safe against the irruption of animals, but how, though they might bar the door to the pig and the cow, they were unable to bar the door to those diabolic *bestioles* which crawl through the smallest hole even as David found the chink in Goliath's armour. They have told you how they lowered by rope from the rafters the Bishop's throne, which is tethered there from one year's end to the next and is descended only for the day of the Bishop's pilgrimage, lest any child or stranger might by chance sit on it and thereby profane it, this being a humble and devout tradition, fully worthy of the praise of God and of this court. How the throne, being lowered, was placed before the altar as it has been every year since the oldest Methuselah in the habitation can remember, and how the prudent villagers set a guard upon it through the night before the arrival of the Bishop, so heedful were they that the throne be not defiled. And how the next day Hugo, Bishop of Besançon, did come in his annual pilgrimage, like Gracchus coming among his beloved people, to the humble church of Saint-Michel, and was pleased by their devotion and true faith. And how, having first as was his custom given his general blessing to the villagers of Mamirolle from the step of the church, he went in procession up the nave of the church, followed at subservient distance by his flock, and prostrated himself, even in the finery of his apparel, before the altar, just as Jesus Christ prostrated himself before his Almighty Father. Then he rose, ascended the simple step to the altar, turned to face the congregation and lowered himself upon his throne. Oh malevolent day! Oh malevolent invaders! And how the Bishop fell, striking his head upon the altar step and being hurled against his will into a state of imbecility. And how, when the Bishop and his retinue had departed, bearing off the Bishop in a state of imbecility, the terrified petitioners did examine the Bishop's throne and discover in the leg that had tumbled down like the walls of Jericho a vile and unnatural infestation of woodworm, and how these woodworm, having secretly and darkly gone about their devilish work, had so devoured the leg that the Bishop did fall like mighty Daedalus from the heavens of light into the darkness of imbecility. And how, being much fearful of the wrath of God, the petitioners did climb up to the roof of the church of Saint-Michel and examine the cradle in which the throne had rested for three hundred and sixty-four days of the year, and how they found that woodworm had also infested the cradle so that it broke apart when they touched it and fell sacrilegiously down upon the altar steps, and how the timbers of the roof were all found to be vilely tainted by those diabolic *bestioles*, which made the petitioners apprehensive for their own lives, since they are both poor and devout, and their poverty would not permit them to build a new church, while their devotion commands them to worship their Holy Father as fervently as they have always done and in a sacred place not among the fields and woods.

Hear, Gentlemen, therefore, the petition of these humble villagers, wretched as the grass beneath the foot. They are accustomed to many plagues, to the locusts that darken the sky like the hand of God passing over the sun, to the ravages of rats that lay waste as did the boar to the environs of Calydon as narrated by Homer in the first book of the Iliad, to the weevil which devours the grain in their winter storehouse. How much more vile and malevolent, therefore, is this plague which attacks the grain which the villagers have stored up in Heaven by their humble piety and their payment of tithes. For these malefactors, disrespectful even to this day of your court, have offended God by attacking his House, they have offended his spouse the Church by casting Hugo, Bishop of Besançon, into the darkness of imbecility, they have offended these petitioners by threatening to bring the framework and fabric of their church tumbling down upon the innocent heads of children and infants even as the village is at prayer, and it is therefore right and reasonable and necessary for the court to injunct and enjoin these animals to quit their habitation, to withdraw from the House of God, and for the court to pronounce upon them the necessary anathemata and excommunications prescribed by our Holy Mother, the Church, for which your petitioners do ever pray.

Plaidoyer des insectes

Since, Gentlemen, it has pleased you to appoint me procurator for the *bestioles* in this case, I shall endeavour to explain to the court how the charges against them are null and void, and how the case must be non-suited. To begin with, I confess I am astonished that my clients, who have committed no crime, have been treated as if they were the worst criminals known to this court, and that my clients, though notoriously dumb, have been summoned to explain their behaviour as if they were accustomed to employ the human tongue while going about their daily business. I shall, in all humility, attempt to make my speaking tongue do service for their silent tongue.

Since you have permitted me to speak on behalf of these unfortunate animals, I will state, in the first place, that this court lacks the jurisdiction to try the defendants, and that the summons issued against them has no validity, for it implies that the recipients are endowed with reason and volition, being thereby capable both of committing a crime and of answering a summons for the trial of the said crime. Which is not the case, since my clients are brute beasts acting only from instinct, and which is confirmed by the first book of the *Pandects*, at the paragraph *Si quadrupes*, where it is written *Nec enim potest animal injuriam fecisse, quod sensu caret.*

In the second place, additionally and alternatively, I will submit that even if the court were to have jurisdiction over the *bestioles*, it would be unreasonable and unlawful for the present tribunal to consider their case, for it is a well-known and long-established principle that the accused may not be tried *in absentia*. It has been stated that the woodworm have been formally summoned by writ to appear before this court on this particular day, and have insolently refused to appear, thereby forfeiting their normal rights and permitting them to be tried *in absentia*. Against this argument I propose two counter-arguments. First, that while the summons for attendance was properly issued, have we any proof that it was accepted by the *bestioles*? For it is established that a writ must not just be issued but delivered, and the procurator *pour les habitans* has failed to indicate in what manner the woodworm did acknowledge the writ. Secondly, and further, it is a principle even more firmly established in the annals of the law that a defendant may be excused default or non-appearance if it can be shown that the length or difficulty or danger of the journey renders it impossible for attendance at the court safely to be made. If you summoned a rat before you, would you expect it to proceed to your court while passing through a town full of cats? And on this point, not only is the distance from the abode of the *bestioles* to the court a monstrous league for them to travel, it is also one which they would accomplish under mortal threat from those predators which attend on their humble lives. They may, therefore, in safety and in legality and with all respect to this tribunal courteously refuse to obey the writ.

In the third place, the summons is incorrectly drawn, since it refers to the woodworm who currently have their habitation in the church of Saint-Michel in the village of Mamirolle. Does this mean every single *bestiole* that is in the church? But there are many who live peaceable lives offering no threat whatsoever to the *habitans*. Must a whole village be summoned to court because there is a gang of robbers living within it? This is no sound law. Further, it is an established principle that defendants should be identified to the court. We have under examination two particular felonious acts, the injury to the leg of the Bishop's throne, and the injury to the roof of the church, and it is plain from any scant knowledge of the nature of the animals being charged that those woodworm which currently make their habitation in the leg could not possibly have had anything to do with the roof, and that those woodworm which make their habitation in the roof cannot possibly have had anything to do with the leg. Thus it is that two parties are charged with two crimes without separation in the writ of party and crime, which renders the summons invalid for failure of specificity.

In the fourth place, and without prejudice to the aforesaid, I will argue that not only, as we have proposed, is it contrary to Man's law and the Church's law to try the *bestioles* in this fashion, it is also contrary to God's law. For whence came these tiny creatures against whom the solemn might of this court is being flung? Who created them? None other than Almighty God who created us all, the highest and the lowest. And do we not read in the first chapter of the sacred book of Genesis that God made the beast of the earth after his kind, the cattle after their kind, and every living thing that creepeth upon the earth after his kind, and God saw that it was good? And further did not God give unto the beasts of the earth and unto every creeping thing every seed upon the face of the earth, and every tree upon the face of the earth, and every fruit of every tree as meat? And yet further, did he not give order unto them all to be fruitful and multiply and replenish the earth? The Creator would not have instructed the beasts of the earth and every creeping thing to multiply had He not, in His infinite wisdom, provided them with food, which He did so, expressly giving the seeds and the fruit and the trees as meat. What have these humble *bestioles* done since the

67

day of Creation but exercise the inalienable rights conferred on them at that time, rights which Man has no power to curtail or abrogate? That the woodworm make their habitation where they do may prove inconvenient to Man, but that is not sufficient reason to seek to rebel against the rules of Nature laid down at the Creation, such rebellion being a direct and insolent disobedience to the Creator. The Lord breathed life into the woodworm, and gave him the trees of the earth for meat: how presumptuous and how perilous it would be for us to seek to countermand the will of God. No, rather, I submit to the court that we should direct our attention not to the supposed felonies of God's humblest creation, but to the felonies of man himself. God does nothing without a purpose, and the purpose in permitting the *bestioles* to take up their habitation in the church of Saint-Michel can have been none other than as a warning and a punishment against the wickedness of mankind. That the woodworm were allowed to infest the church rather than any other building is, I further submit, an even more severe warning and punishment. Are those who come before the court as petitioners so certain of their obedience to God, so sure of their humility and Christian virtue that they would accuse the humblest animal before accusing themselves? Beware the sin of pride, I tell those petitioners. Cast out the beam from your own eye before you seek to extract the mote from the eye of another.

In the fifth and final place, the procurator *pour les habitans* asks the court to hurl against the *bestioles* that bolt of lightning known as excommunication. It is my duty to submit to you, and without prejudice to any of the aforesaid, that such a punishment is both inappropriate and unlawful. Excommunication being the separation of the sinner from communion with God, a refusal to permit him to eat of the bread and drink of the wine that are the body and blood of Christ, a casting-out from the Holy Church and its light and its warmth, how therefore can it be lawful to excommunicate a beast of the field or a creeping thing from upon the earth which has never been a communicant of the Holy Church? It cannot be a fit and proper punishment to deprive a defendant of that which he has never possessed in the first place. This makes bad law. And secondly, excommunication is a process of great terror, a casting of the sinner into fearsome darkness, an eternal separation of the sinner from the light and from the goodness of God. How can this be an appropriate punishment for a *bestiole* which does not possess an immortal soul? How is it possible to condemn a defendant to eternal torment when he does not have eternal life? These animals cannot be expelled from the Church since they are not members of it, and as the Apostle Paul says, 'Ye judge them that are within and not them also that are without.'

I ask, therefore, that the case be rejected and non-suited, and without prejudice to the foregoing, that the defendants be acquitted and exempted from all further prosecution.

Bartholomé Chassenée, Jurist

Réplique des habitans

Gentlemen, it does me honour to appear again before your solemn court, to plead for justice as did that poor offended mother who appeared before Solomon to claim her child. Like Ulysses against Ajax I shall fight the procurator for the *bestioles*, who has produced before you many arguments as bedizened as Jezebel.

In the first place, he contends that this court has no power and jurisdiction to try the bestial felonies that have taken place at Mamirolle, and towards this end argues that we are no better in God's eye than the woodworm, no higher and no lower, therefore we do not have the right to sit in judgment on them like Jupiter, whose temple was on the Tarpeian rock from whence were traitors flung. But I shall refute this as Our Lord turned the moneylenders out of the Temple at Jerusalem, and in this way. Is man not higher than the animals? Is it not clear from the holy book of Genesis that the animals, which were created before man, were so created in order to be subservient to his use? Did not the Lord give unto Adam dominion over the fish of the sea, and over the fowl of the air, and over every living thing that moveth upon the earth? Did not Adam give the names to all the cattle, and to the fowl of the air, and every beast of the field? Was not the dominion of man over the animals asserted by the Psalmist and reiterated by the apostle Paul? And how may man have dominion over the animals and such dominion not include the right to punish them for their misdeeds? Furthermore, this right to sit in judgment over the animals, which the procurator for the *bestioles* so actively denies, is specifically given to man by God himself, as appears in the sacred book of Exodus. Did not the Lord lay down unto Moses the sacred law of an eye for an eye and a tooth for a tooth? And did he not continue thus, if an ox gore a man or a woman, that they die, then the ox shall be surely stoned, and his flesh shall not be eaten? Does the holy book of Exodus not thus make clear the law? And does it not go on further, that if one man's ox hurt another's, that he die, then they shall sell the live ox, and divide the money of it, and the dead ox also they shall divide? Has not the Lord laid it down thus, and given man the judgment over the animals?

In the second place, that the woodworm are to be excused trial because of their failure to attend court. But they have been correctly summoned in accordance with all due process. They have been summoned as the Jews were summoned to be taxed by Augustus Caesar. And did not the Israelites obey? Which among those present here would prevent the *bestioles* from coming to court? My humble petitioners might have wished to do so, and to this end they might have sought to burn in the flames the leg of the throne that cast Hugo, Bishop of Besançon, into a state of imbecility by striking his head on the altar step, but like Christians stayed their hand, preferring instead to submit the matter to your solemn judgment. What enemy, therefore, might the accused *bestioles* encounter? The distinguished procurator has made reference to cats eating rats. I was not aware, Gentlemen, that cats had taken to devouring woodworm on their way to court, yet no doubt I shall be corrected if I am in error. No, there is only one explanation of the refusal of the accused to appear before you, and that is a blind and most wilful disobedience, a hateful silence, a guilt that blazes as the burning bush which did appear unto Moses, a bush which blazed but was not consumed, even as their guilt continues to blaze with every hour that they obstinately refuse to appear.

In the third place, it is argued that God created the wood-worm even as he created Man, and that he gave him the seeds and the fruit and the trees as meat, and that whatever they might choose to eat therefore has the blessing of God. Which is indeed the main and essential pleading of the procurator for the *bestioles*, and I hereby refute it thus. The sacred book of Genesis tells us that God in his infinite mercy and generosity gave unto the beasts of the field and unto the creeping things all the seeds and the fruit and the trees as meat. He gave the trees unto those creatures which have the instinct to devour trees, even though this might be a hindrance and a discomfort to Man. But He did not give them the cut wood. Where in the Holy Book of Genesis is it allowed that the creeping things of the earth may inhabit the cut wood? Did the Lord intend when He permitted a creature to burrow within the oak tree that the same creature had the right to burrow within the House of the Lord? Where in the Holy Scripture does the Lord give unto the animals the right to devour His temples? And does the Lord instruct His servants to pass by on the other side while His temples are devoured and His Bishops reduced to a state of imbecility? The pig that eats the holy sacramental wafer is hanged for its blasphemy, and the *bestiole* that makes his own habitation in the habitation of the Lord is no less blasphemous.

Furthermore, and without prejudice to the foregoing, it has been argued that the Lord created the woodworm even as He created Man, and that therefore everything the Lord might do has the Lord's blessing, however pestilential and maleficent it might be. But did the Almighty Lord, in His matchless wisdom and beneficence, create the weevil in order that it destroy our crops, and the woodworm in order that it destory the Lord's house? The wisest doctors of our Church for many centuries have examined every verse of the Holy Scripture just as Herod's soldiers searched for innocent children, and they have found no chapter, no line, no phrase wherein there is mention of the woodworm. Therefore the question which I lay before the court as the essential question in this case is the following: was the woodworm ever upon Noah's Ark? Holy writ makes no mention of the woodworm embarking upon or disembarking from the mighty vessel of Noah. And indeed how could it have been so, for was not the Ark constructed of wood? How can the Lord in his eternal wisdom have allowed on board a creature whose daily habits might cause the shipwreck and disastrous death of Man and all the beasts of the Creation? How could such a thing be so? Therefore, it follows that the woodworm was not upon the Ark, but is an unnatural and imperfect creature which did not exist at the time of the great bane and ruin of the Deluge. Whence its generation came, whether from some foul spontaneity or some malevolent hand, we know not, yet its hateful malice is evident. This vile creature has given over its body to the Devil and thereby put itself beyond the protection and shelter of the Lord. What greater proof could there be but the manner of its desecrations, the cunning odiousness with which it hurled Hugo, Bishop of Besançon, into imbecility? Was this not the work of the Devil, to proceed thus in darkness and secrecy for many years, and then make triumph of his foul purpose? Yet the procurator for the *bestioles* argues that the woodworm have the blessing of the Lord in all that they do and all that they eat. He contends, therefore, that what they did in devouring the leg of the Bishop's throne had the blessing of the Lord. He contends further that the Lord by his own hand smote down one of the Bishops of his own Holy Church just as He smote down Belshazzar, as He smote down Amalek, as He smote down the Midianites, as He smote down the Canaanites, as He smote down Sihon the Amorite. Is this not a vile blasphemy which the court must extirpate even as Hercules did cleanse the stables of Augeas?

And in the fourth place, it is contended that the court does not have the power and the right to pronounce the decree of excommunication. But this is to deny the very authority conferred by God upon his dear spouse, the Church, whom He has made sovereign of the whole world, having put all things under Her feet, as the Psalmist affirms, all sheep and oxen, the beasts of the field, the fowl of the air, the fish of the sea, and whatsoever passeth through the paths of the seas. Guided by the Holy Spirit, the Church can do nothing wrong. Indeed, do we not read in our sacred texts of serpents and poisonous reptiles whose venom has been conjured from them? Do we not read in the sacred book of Ecclesiastes that 'Surely the serpent will bite without enchantment'? Therefore it is in holy concord with God's teaching that the Church has for centuries used its mighty but righteous power to hurl anathemata and excommunication against those noxious animals whose foul presence is an offence to the eye of the Lord. Did not David's maledictions on the mountains of Gilboa cause the rain and the dew to cease there? Did not Jesus Christ the son of God ordain that every tree that bringeth not forth good fruit should be hewn down and cast into the fire? And if an irrational thing shall be destroyed because it does not produce fruit, how much more is it permitted to curse it, since the greater penalty includes the less: *cum si liceat quid est plus, debet licere quid est minus.* Was not the serpent cursed in the Garden of Eden, making it to crawl upon its belly for the rest of its life? And when the town of Aix was infested by serpents which inhabited the warm baths and killed many of the inhabitants by biting them, did not the holy Bishop of Grenoble excommunicate the serpents, whereupon they departed? And thus did the Bishop of Lausanne free Lake Leman from the infestation of eels. And thus did the same Bishop expel from the waters of the same lake those blood-suckers which fed on the salmon which the devout were wont to consume on fast-days. And did not Egbert, Bishop of Trier, anathematize the swallows whose chirping interrupted the prayers of the devout? And did not St Bernard likewise and for like reason excommunicate swarms of flies, which on the morrow, like Sennacherib's host, were all dead corpses? And did not the crozier of St Magnus, the apostle of Algau, expel and exterminate all manner of rats, mice and cockchafers? Therefore is it not right and established that this court may cast the bolt of excommunication upon these defilers and assassins of God's holy temple? The procurator for the *bestioles* argues that since a woodworm has no immortal soul it cannot be excommunicated. But have we not shown, firstly, that the woodworm is no natural beast, having not been on the Ark of Noah, and secondly, that the actions for which it has been summoned to appear before the court are clear evidence that it has been taken over by a malign spirit, namely that of Lucifer? How much more necessary, therefore, is the order of excommunication which I hereby beg and demand from this court.

Réplique des insectes

Gentlemen, we have been treated to many points of argument thus far, some blown away by the wind like the winnowed chaff, some resting on the ground before you like the valuable grain. I hereby prevail upon your patience a little further to make rejoinder to the contentions of the procurator *des habitans*, whose arguments will fall like the walls of Jericho before the trumpet of truth.

In the first place, the procurator makes mention of the length of time the *bestioles* had been making their habitation in the leg of the Bishop's throne, storing up their dark purpose, and offers this as proof that the work was diabolically inspired. It was for this reason that I called before you the good Brother Frolibert, who is wise in the ways of the creeping things of the earth, and indeed you know he makes the honey at the Abbey of St Georges. And did he not assert that wise men believe the *bestioles* do not live for more than a few brief summers? Yet we all know that an infestation of woodworm may proceed for many human generations before it cause the wood to break apart as it did under Hugo, Bishop of Besançon, reducing him to a condition of imbecility. From which we must conclude that the wood-worm summoned before this court are merely the descendants of many generations of woodworm who have made their habitation in the church of Saint-Michel. If malign intent is to be ascribed to the *bestioles*, it is surely only to be ascribed to the first generation of *bestioles* and not to their innocent posterity who without fault find themselves living where they do? On this ground, therefore, I apply again for the case to be non-suited. And further, there has been no evidence from the prosecution as to the occasion and date upon which the woodworm are alleged to have entered the wood. The procurator has attempted to maintain that the *bestioles* are not granted by Holy Scripture the right to inhabit cut wood. To which we reply, firstly, that the Scripture does not in any patent form forbid them from so doing, secondly, that if God had not intended them to eat the cut wood He would not have given them the instinct to do so, and thirdly, that in the absence of evidence to the contrary, an accused being innocent until proved guilty, an assumption of priority of possession in the matter of the wood must be granted to the *bestioles*, namely that they were in the wood when it was cut by the woodsman who sold it to the joiner who fashioned it into the throne. Far from the woodworm infesting what Man has constructed, it is Man who has wilfully destroyed the woodworm's habitation and taken it for his own purpose. On which ground also we ask that the case be non-suited.

In the second place, it is argued that the woodworm did not have passage on the Ark of Noah and therefore must be diabolically possessed. To which we reply, firstly, that the Holy Scripture does not list every species of God's creation, and that the legal presumption should be that any creature was upon the Ark unless it be specifically stated that he was not. And secondly, that if as the procurator alleges the woodworm was not upon the Ark, then it is even more evident that Man has not been given dominion over this creature. God sent the baneful Flood to purge the world, and when the waters receded and the world was new-born, He gave Man dominion over the animals. But where is it written that He also gave him dominion over any animals which had not travelled upon the Ark?

In the third place, it is a monstrous libel upon our pleading to claim that Hugo, Bishop of Besançon, according to our allegation, was thrust into the darkness of imbecility by God's own hand. We make no such allegation, for it would be the contention of a blasphemer. But indeed is it not the case that the ways of God are often most mysteriously hid from our gaze? When the Bishop of Grenoble fell from his horse and was killed we did not blame either the Lord or the horse or the woodworm. When the Bishop of Constance was lost overboard in the lake we did not conclude that God had hurled him into the water or that woodworm had destroyed the keel of the boat. When the pillar in the cloister of Saint Théodoric collapsed on the foot of the Bishop of Lyons causing him to walk ever thereafter with a staff, we did not blame the Lord or the pillar or the woodworm. The Lord's ways are indeed frequently hidden from us, but is it not also the case that the Lord has called down many plagues upon the unworthy? Did He not send a plague of frogs against Pharaoh? Did He not send lice and grievous swarms of flies upon the land of Egypt? Did He not, against that Pharaoh, send also a plague of boils, and thunder and hail, and a grievous plague of locusts? Did He not send hailstones against the Five Kings? Did He not strike even his own servant Job with boils? And it was for this reason that I called before you Father Godric and enquired of him for the records of the payment of tithes by the inhabitants of Mamirolle. And were there not many excuses proferred about the inclemency of the weather, and the crops that had failed, and the sickness there had been in the village, and the band of soldiers who had passed by and murdered several of the strong young men of the village? But for all this it was evident and plain that the tithes have not been paid as the Church lays down, that there has been wilful neglect amounting to disobedience of the Lord God and his spouse on earth the Church. And is it not therefore the case that, just as He sent a plague of locusts to scourge Pharaoh and grievous swarms of flies upon the land of Egypt, so he sent woodworm into the church to scourge the inhabitants for their disobedience? How can this have been done without the Lord's permission? Do we think Almighty God is so weak and timorous a creature that He is unable to protect His temple against these tiny *bestioles*? Surely it is a blasphemy to doubt God's power to do this. And therefore we must conclude that the infestation was either divinely ordered or divinely

permitted, that God sent the woodworm to punish the disobedient sinners and that the sinners should cower before His rage
and scourge themselves for their sins and pay their tithes as they
have been commanded. Truly, this is a matter for prayer and
fasting and scourging and the hope of God's mercy rather than
one for anathemata and excommunication against the agents,
the very conduits of the Lord's purpose and intent.

In the fourth place, therefore, acknowledging as we do that
the woodworm are God's creatures and as such are entitled to
sustenance even as man is entitled to sustenance, and acknowledging also that Justice shall be tempered by mercy, we
submit, without prejudice to the foregoing, that the court
demand of the *habitans* of Mamirolle, who have been so tardy in
their payment of tithes, to nominate and set aside for the said
bestioles alternative pasture, where they may graze peacefully
without future harm to the church of Saint-Michel, and that the
bestioles be commanded by the court, which has all such powers,
to move to the said pasture. For what do my humble clients
hope for and demand except to be allowed to live peaceably and
in the dark without interference and wrongful accusation.
Gentlemen, I make my final plea that the case be non-suited,
and without prejudice that the *bestioles* be declared innocent,
and without prejudice again that they be required to move to
fresh pasture. I submit on their behalf to the judgment of the
court.

Bartholemé Chassenée, Jurist

Conclusions du procureur épiscopal

The arguments offered by the counsel for the defence have been
truly and weightily delivered, and must be accorded great and
serious thought, for it is not lightly or at random that the court
should hurl the bolt of excommunication, for being lightly or at
random hurled, it may, by reason of its particular energy and
force, if it fails to strike the object at which it is aimed, return
against him who hurled it. The arguments offered by the

counsel for the prosecution have also been delivered with much learning and education, and it is truly a deep sea in which it is impossible to touch bottom.

In the matter raised by the procurator for the *bestioles* regarding the many generations of woodworm and whether this generation of woodworm summoned before us was the generation who committed the crime, we have this to say. Firstly, that it is stated in Holy Scripture in the book of Exodus that the Lord shall visit the iniquities of the fathers upon the children unto the third and fourth generation, and therefore in this matter the court has the power most piously to bring to judgment several generations of woodworm all of whom have offended against the Lord, which would indeed be a mighty act of justice to perform. And secondly, that if we accept the argument of the procurator *pour les habitans* that the *bestioles* are diabolically possessed, what could be more natural – in this case more foully unnatural – than that such possession should allow the woodworm to outlive their normal span of years, and thus it might be that only a single generation of creeping things have wrought all the damage unto the throne and the roof. In either case we have been much swayed by the argument of the procurator *pour les habitans* that the woodworm could not have been upon the Ark of Noah – for what prudent sea captain in his wisdom would permit such agents of shipwreck to board his vessel? – and therefore are not to be numbered among God's prime creations. What their status in the mighty hierarchy shall be – whether they be partly natural, whether they be living corruption, or whether they be creations of the devil – is a matter for those great doctors of the Church who weigh such matters.

Neither can we know all of the myriad reasons why God should have permitted a plague of woodworm to infest this humble church. Perhaps beggars have been turned away from the door. Perhaps the tithes have not been paid regularly. Perhaps there has been frivolity inside the church, and the mansion of the Lord has been turned into a place of assignation, whereupon God sent the insects. We must never forget the duty of charity and the requirement to give alms, and did not

Eusebius liken hell to a cold place where the wailing and gnashing of teeth are caused by the dreadful frost, not the everlasting fire, and is not charity one of the means by which we throw ourselves upon the mercy of the Lord? Therefore, in recommending the sentence of excommunication on these *bestioles* who have so vilely and viciously ravaged the temple of the Lord, we do also recommend that all the penances and prayers customary in such cases be required of the *habitans*.

Sentence du juge d'Église

In the name and by virtue of God, the omnipotent, Father, Son and Holy Spirit, and of Mary, the most blessed Mother of our Lord Jesus Christ, and by the authority of the Holy Apostles Peter and Paul, as well as by that which has made us a functionary in this case, having fortified ourselves with the Holy Cross, and having before our eyes the fear of God, we admonish the aforesaid woodworm as detestable vermin and command them, under pain of malediction, anathema and excommunication, to quit within seven days the church of Saint-Michel in the village of Mamirolle in the diocese of Besançon and to proceed without delay or hindrance to the pasture offered to them by the *habitans*, there to have their habitation and never again to infest the church of Saint-Michel. In order to make lawful this sentence, and to render effective any malediction, anathema and excommunication that may at any time be pronounced, the *habitans* of Mamirolle are hereby instructed to pay heedful attention to the duty of charity, to yield up their tithes as commanded by the Holy Church, to refrain from any frivolity in the House of the Lord, and once a year, on the anniversary of that hateful day when Hugo, Bishop of Besançon, was cast down into the darkness of imbecility . . .

Here the manuscript in the Archives Municipales de Besançon breaks off, without giving details of the annual penance or remembrance imposed by the court. It appears from the condition of the parchment that in the course of the last four and a half centuries it has been attacked, perhaps on more than one occasion, by some species of termite, which has devoured the closing words of the juge d'Église.

4

THE SURVIVOR

In fourteen hundred and ninety-two
Columbus sailed the ocean blue.

And then what? She couldn't remember. All those years ago,
obedient ten-year-olds with arms crossed, they had chanted it
back to the mistress. All except Eric Dooley, who sat behind her
and chewed her pigtail. Once she'd been asked to get up and
recite the next two lines but she was only a few inches out of her
seat when her head snapped back and the class laughed. Eric was
hanging on to her plait with his teeth. Perhaps that was why she
could never remember the next two lines.

She remembered the reindeer well enough, though. It all
began with the reindeer, which flew through the air at Christmas. She was a girl who believed what she was told, and the
reindeer flew.

She must have seen them first on a Christmas card. Six, eight,
ten of them, harnessed side by side. She always imagined that
each pair was man and wife, a happy couple, like the animals
that went into the Ark. That would be right wouldn't it, that
would be natural? But her Dad said you could tell from the
antlers that the reindeer pulling the sleigh were stags. At first
she only felt disappointed, but later resentment grew. Father
Christmas ran an all-male team. Typical. Absolutely bloody
typical, she thought.

They flew, that was the point. She didn't believe that Father
Christmas squeezed down the chimney and left presents at the
end of your bed, but she did believe that the reindeer flew.
People tried to argue her out of it, they said if you believe that
you'll believe anything. However, she was fourteen now,

short-haired and stubborn, and she always had her reply ready. No, she would say, if only you could believe that the reindeer can fly, then you'd realize anything is possible. Anything.

Around that time she went to the zoo. It was their horns that fascinated her. They were all silky, as if they'd been covered with some posh material from a smart shop. They looked like branches in some forest where nobody had trodden for centuries; soft, sheeny, mossy branches. She imagined a sloping bit of wood with a gentle light and some fallen nuts cracking beneath her foot. Yeah, and a cottage made out of gingerbread at the end of the path, said her best friend Sandra when she told her. No, she thought, the antlers turn into branches, the branches into antlers. Everything's connected, and the reindeer *can* fly.

She saw them fighting once, on television. They butted and raged at one another, charged headlong, tangled horns. They fought so hard they rubbed the skin off their antlers. She thought that underneath there'd be just dry bone, and their horns would look like winter branches stripped of their bark by hungry animals. But it wasn't like that. Not at all. They bled. The skin was torn off and underneath was blood as well as bone. The antlers turned scarlet and white, standing out in the soft greens and browns of the landscape like a tray of bones at the butcher's. It was horrible, she thought, yet we ought to face it. Everything *is* connected, even the parts we don't like, especially the parts we don't like.

*

She watched the television a lot after the first big accident. It wasn't a very serious accident, they said, not really, not like a bomb going off. And anyway it was a long way away, in Russia, and they didn't have proper modern power stations over there like we do, and even if they did their safety standards were obviously much lower so it couldn't happen here and there wasn't anything to worry about, was there? It might even teach the Russians a lesson, people said. Make them think twice about dropping the big one.

In a strange way people were excited by it. Something bigger than the latest unemployment figures or the price of a stamp. Besides, most of the nasty things were happening to other people. There was a cloud of poison, and everyone tracked its course like they'd follow the drift of quite an interesting area of low pressure on the weather map. For a while people stopped buying milk, and asked the butcher where the meat came from. But soon they stopped worrying, and forgot about it all.

At first the plan had been to bury the reindeer six feet down. It wasn't much of a news story, just an inch or two on the foreign page. The cloud had gone over where the reindeer grazed, poison had come down in the rain, the lichen became radioactive, the reindeer had eaten the lichen and got radioactive themselves. What did I tell you, she thought, everything is connected.

People couldn't understand why she got so upset. They said she shouldn't be sentimental, and after all it wasn't as if she had to live off reindeer meat, and if she had some spare sympathy going shouldn't she save it for human beings? She tried to explain, but she wasn't very good at explaining and they didn't understand. The ones who thought they understood said, Yes, we see, it's all about your childhood and the silly romantic ideas you had when you were a kid, but you can't go on having silly romantic ideas all your life, you've got to grow up in the end, you've got to be realistic, please don't cry, no maybe that's a good idea, here, have a good cry, it'll probably be good for you in the long run. No, it's not like that, she said, it's not like that at all. Then cartoonists started making jokes, about how the reindeer were so gleaming with radioactivity that Father Christmas didn't need headlights on his sleigh, and Rudolf the Red-Nosed Reindeer had a very shiny nose because he came from Chernobyl; but she didn't think it was funny.

Listen, she'd tell people. The way they measure the level of radioactivity is in something called becquerels. When the accident happened the Norwegian government had to decide what amount of radiation in meat was safe, and they came up with a figure of 600 becquerels. But people didn't like the idea of their meat being poisoned, and the Norwegian butchers didn't do such good business, and the one sort of meat no-one would buy was reindeer, which was hardly surprising. So this is what the government did. They said that as people obviously weren't going to eat reindeer very often because they were so scared, then it would be just as safe for them to eat meat that was more contaminated every once in a while as to eat less contaminated meat more often. So they raised the permitted limit for reindeer meat to 6,000 becquerels. Hey presto! One day it's harmful to eat meat with 600 becquerels in it, the next day it's safe with ten times that amount. This only applied to reindeer, of course. At the same time it's still officially dangerous to eat a pork chop or scrag end of lamb with 601 becquerels in it.

One of the TV programmes showed a couple of Lapp farmers bringing a reindeer corpse in for inspection. This was just after the limit had been raised ten times. The official from the Department of whatever it was, Agriculture or something, chopped up the little bits of reindeer innards and did the usual tests on them. The reading came out at 42,000 becquerels. Forty-two *thousand*.

At first the plan was to bury them, six feet down. Still, there's nothing like a good disaster to get people thinking clever thoughts. *Bury* the reindeer? No, that makes it look as if there's been a problem, like something's actually gone wrong. There must be a more useful way of disposing of them. You couldn't feed the meat to humans, so why not feed it to animals? That's a good idea – but which animals? Obviously not the sort which end up getting eaten by humans, we've got to protect number one. So they decided to feed it to the mink. What a clever idea. Mink aren't supposed to be very nice, and anyway the sort of people who can afford mink coats probably don't mind a little dose of radioactivity on top of it. Like a dash of scent behind the ears or something. Rather chic, really.

Most people had stopped paying attention to what she was telling them by now, but she always carried on. Listen, she said, so instead of burying the reindeer they're now painting a big blue stripe down the carcases and feeding them to mink. I think they should have buried them. Burying things gives you a proper sense of shame. Look what we've done to the reindeer, they'd say as they dug the pit. Or they might, at least. They might think about it. Why are we always punishing animals? We pretend we like them, we keep them as pets and get soppy if we think they're reacting like us, but we've been punishing animals from the beginning, haven't we? Killing them and torturing them and throwing our guilt on to them?

*

She gave up eating meat after the accident. Every time she found a slice of beef on her plate or a spoonful of stew she thought of reindeer. The poor beasts with their horns stripped bare and all bloody from fighting. Then the row of carcases each with a stripe of blue paint down its back, clanking past on a row of shiny hooks.

That, she explained, was when she first came here. Down south, that is. People said she was silly, she was running away, wasn't being realistic, if she felt that strongly about things she ought to stay and argue against them. But it depressed her too much. People didn't listen enough to her arguments. Besides, you should always go where you believe the reindeer can fly: *that* was being realistic. They couldn't fly up in the north any more.

*

I wonder what's happened to Greg. I wonder if he's safe. I wonder what he thinks about me, now he knows I was right. I hope he doesn't hate me for it. Men often hate you for being right. Or perhaps he'll pretend nothing has even happened; that way he can be sure he was right. Yes, it wasn't what you thought, it was just a comet burning out in the sky, or a summer storm, or a hoax on TV. Silly cow.

Greg was an ordinary bloke. Not that I wanted anything different when I met him. He went to work, came home, sat around, drank beer, went out with his mates and drank some more beer, sometimes slapped me around a bit on pay-night. We got on fair enough. Argued about Paul, of course. Greg said

87

I ought to get him fixed so he'd be less aggressive and stop scratching the furniture. I said it wasn't anything to do with that, all cats scratched the furniture, maybe we should get him a scratching pole. Greg said how did I know that wouldn't encourage him, like giving him permission to scratch everything a whole lot more? I said don't be daft. He said it was scientifically proved that if you castrate cats they're less aggressive. I said wasn't the opposite more likely — that if you mutilated them it'd make them angry and violent? Greg picked up this big pair of scissors and said well why don't we bloody find out then? I screamed.

I wouldn't let him have Paul fixed, even if he did mess up the furniture quite a bit. Later I remembered something. They castrate reindeer, you know. The Lapps do. They pick out a big stag and castrate it and that makes it tame. Then they hang a bell round its neck and this bell-bull as they call it leads the rest of the reindeer around, wherever the herdsmen decide they want them to go. So the idea probably does work, but I still think it's wrong. It's not a cat's fault that it's a cat. I didn't tell any of this to Greg of course, about the bell-bulls. Sometimes, when he slapped me around, I'd think, maybe we ought to get you fixed first, that might make you less aggressive. But I never did say it. It wouldn't have helped.

We used to row about animals. Greg thought I was soft. Once I told him they were turning all the whales into soap. He laughed and said that was a bloody good way of using them up. I burst into tears. I suppose as much because he could think of something like that as because he said it.

We didn't row about the Big Thing. He just said politics was men's business and I didn't know what I was talking about. That was as far as our conversations about the extinction of the planet went. If I said I was worried what America might do if Russia didn't back down or vice versa, or the Middle East or whatever, he said did I think it might be pre-menstrual tension. You can't talk to anyone like that, can you? He wouldn't even discuss it, wouldn't row about it. Once I said maybe it *was* pre-menstrual tension, and he said yes I thought so. I said no, listen, maybe women are more in touch with the world. He said what did I mean, and I said, well, everything's connected, isn't it, and women are more closely connected to all the cycles of nature and birth and rebirth on the planet than men, who are only impregnators after all when it comes down to it, and if women are in tune with the planet then maybe if terrible things are going on up in the north, things which threaten the whole existence of the planet, then maybe women get to feel these things, like the way some people know earthquakes are coming, and perhaps that's what sets off PMT. He said silly cow, that's just why politics is men's business, and got another beer out of the fridge. A few days later he said to me, what happened about the end of the world? I just looked at him and he said, as far as I can see all that pre-menstrual tension you had was about the fact that you were getting your period. I said you make me so angry I almost want the end of the world to come just so you'll be proved wrong. He said he was sorry, but what did he know, after all he was just an impregnator as I'd pointed out, and he reckoned those other impregnators up in the north would sort something out.

Sort something out? That's what the plumber says, or the man who comes to nail the roof back on. 'Reckon we'll be able to sort something out,' they say with one of those confident winks. Well, they didn't sort something out on this occasion, did they? They bloody didn't. And in the last days of the crisis, Greg didn't always come home at nights. Even he'd finally noticed and decided to have some fun before it was all over. In a way I couldn't blame him, except for the fact that he wouldn't admit it. He said he was staying out because he couldn't stand coming home and getting nagged at by me. I told him I understood and it was all right, yet when I explained he got very uptight. He said if he wanted a bit on the side then it wouldn't be because of the world situation but because I was on his back all the time. They just don't see the connections, do they? When men in dark-grey suits and striped ties up there in the north start taking certain strategic precautions as they term it, men like Greg in thongs and T-shirts down here in the south begin staying out late in bars trying to pick up girls. They should understand that, shouldn't they? They should admit it.

So when I knew what had happened, I didn't wait for Greg to come home. He was out there knocking back another beer, saying how those fellows up there would sort something out, and in the meantime why don't you come and sit on my knee, darling? I just took Paul and put him in his basket and got on the bus with as much tinned food as I could carry and some bottles of water. I didn't leave a note because there wasn't anything to say. I got off at the terminal on Harry Chan Avenue and started walking towards the Esplanade. Then guess what I saw, sunning herself on the roof of a car? A sleepy, friendly, tortoiseshell cat. I stroked her, she purred, I sort of scooped her up in my arm, one or two people stopped to look but I was round the corner into Herbert Street before they could say anything.

Greg would have been angry about the boat. Still, he only had a quarter share in her, and if the four of them were going to spend their last days drinking in bars and picking up girls because of the men in dark-grey suits who in my opinion should have been fixed themselves years ago, then they weren't going to miss the boat, were they? I filled her up, and as I cast off I saw that the tortoiseshell I'd put down just anywhere was sitting on top of Paul's basket, looking at me. 'You'll be Linda,' I said.

*

She left the world behind from a place called Doctor's Gully. At the end of the Esplanade at Darwin, behind the modern YMCA building, a zig-zag road runs down to a disused boat ramp. The big hot car-park is mostly empty, except when tourists come to watch the fish feed. Nothing else goes on nowadays at Doctor's Gully. Every day at high tide hundreds, thousands of fish come right up to the water's edge to be fed.

She thought how trusting the fish were. They must think these huge two-legged creatures are giving them food out of the kindness of their hearts. Maybe that's how it started, but now it's $2.50 admission for adults, $1.50 for children. She wondered why none of the tourists who stayed in the big hotels along the Esplanade thought it odd. But nobody stops to think about the world any more. We live in a world where they make children pay to see the fish eat. Nowadays even fish are exploited, she thought. Exploited, and then poisoned. The ocean out there is filling up with poison. The fish will die too.

Doctor's Gully was deserted. Hardly anyone sailed from there any more; they'd all moved off to the marina years ago. But there were still a couple of boats pulled up on the rocks, looking abandoned. One of them, pink and grey, with not much of a mast, had NOT FOR SALE painted along its side. This always made her laugh. Greg and his friends kept their little boat behind this one, away from the fish-feeding place. The rocks over here were strewn with discarded bits of metal – engines, boilers, valves, pipes, all turning orangey-brown with rust. As she walked, she stirred up flocks of orangey-brown butterflies which had started to live among the scrap metal, using it as camouflage. What have we done to the butterflies, she thought; look where we've made them live. She gazed out to sea, across the scrubby bits of mangrove pushing up by the shore, towards a line of small tankers, and beyond them low, humpy islands on the horizon. This was the place from which she left the world behind.

Past Melville Island, through Dundas Strait, and out into the Arafura Sea; after that she let the wind govern her direction. Mostly they seemed to be heading east, but she didn't attend too carefully. You only followed where you were going if you wanted to get back to where you had started from, and she knew that was impossible.

She hadn't expected neat mushroom clouds on the horizon. She knew it wouldn't be like it was in the films. Sometimes there was a shifting of the light, sometimes a distant rumbling noise. Such things could have meant nothing at all; but somewhere it had happened, and the winds that circled the planet were doing the rest. At night she slackened sail and went below to the little cabin, leaving the deck to Paul and Linda. At first Paul had wanted to fight the newcomer – all the old territorial stuff. But after a day or two the cats became accustomed to one another.

*

She thought she might have caught the sun a little. She'd been out in the heat all day with only one of Greg's old baseball caps for protection. He had this collection of stupid caps with silly slogans on them. This one was red with white lettering on it, an advertisement for a restaurant somewhere. It read UNTIL YOU'VE ATE AT BJ'S YOU AIN'T SHIT. Some drinking mate of Greg's had given it him for a birthday, and Greg could never tire of the joke. He'd sit there on the boat with a can of beer in his hand and his cap on his head and just start chuckling to himself. Then he'd laugh a lot more until everyone was watching, and finally announce 'Until you've ate at BJ's you ain't shit.' That would crack him up, time and again. She hated the cap but it made sense to wear it. She'd forgotten the zinc cream and all the other tubes of stuff.

She knew what she was doing. She knew probably nothing would come of what Greg would have referred to as her little venture. Whenever she had a plan of any sort – especially something that didn't involve him – he would always refer to it as her little venture. She didn't think she was going to land on some undamaged island where you only had to throw a bean over your shoulder for a row of them to spring up and wave their pods at you. She didn't expect a coral reef, a strip of sand from the holiday brochures and a nodding palm. She didn't imagine some good-looking fellow turning up after a couple of weeks in a dinghy with two dogs on board; then a girl with two chickens, a bloke with two pigs, and so on. Her expectations were not high. She just thought you had to try it, whatever the result. It was your duty. You weren't allowed to get out of it.

*

I couldn't tell last night. I was coming out of a dream, or maybe I was still in it, but I heard the cats, I swear I did. Or rather, the sound of a cat in heat, calling. Not that Linda would have had far to call. By the time I was fully awake there was only the sound of the waves against the hull. I went up the steps and pushed open the doors. In the moonlight I could see the pair of them, sitting smugly on their paws, side by side, looking back at me. Just like a couple of kids who'd almost got caught necking by the girl's mum. A cat in heat sounds like a baby crying, doesn't it? That ought to tell us something.

I don't keep count of the days. There isn't any point, is there? We aren't going to measure things in days any more. Days and weekends and holidays – that's how the men in grey suits measure things. We'll have to go back to some older cycle, sunrise to sunset for a start, and the moon will come into it, and the seasons, and the weather – the new, terrible weather we shall have to live under. How do tribes in the jungle measure the days? It's not too late to learn from them. People like that have the key to living with nature. They wouldn't castrate their cats. They might worship them, they might even eat them, but they wouldn't have them fixed.

I just eat enough to keep me going. I'm not going to calculate how long I might be at sea and then divide the rations into forty-eight portions or anything like that. That's the old sort of thinking, the thinking that led us into all this. I eat enough to keep going, that's all. I fish, of course. I'm sure it's safe. But when I catch something I can't help giving it to Paul and Linda. Still tins for me, while the cats grow plump.

*

I must be more careful. Must have passed out in the sun. Came to lying on my back with the cats licking my face. Felt very parched and feverish. Too much tinned food, perhaps. Next time I catch a fish I'd better eat it myself, even if it makes me unpopular.

I wonder what Greg's up to. Is he up to anything? I sort of see him there, with a beer in his hand, laughing and pointing. 'Until you've ate at BJ's you ain't shit,' he says. He's reading it off my cap, staring at me. He's got a girl on his knee. My life

with Greg seems as far away from me now as my life in the
north.

I saw a flying fish the other day. I'm sure I did. I couldn't have
made it up, could I? It made me happy. Fish can fly, and so can
reindeer.

*

Definitely got some fever. Managed to catch a fish and even cook
it. Big trouble from Paul and Linda. Dreams, bad dreams. Still
heading more or less east, I think.

I'm sure I'm not alone. I mean, I'm sure everywhere in the
world there are people like me. It can't be just me, just me alone
in a boat with two cats and everyone else on dry land shouting
silly cow. I bet there are hundreds, thousands of boats with
people in and animals doing what I'm doing. Abandon ship,
that was the old cry. Now it's abandon land. There's danger
everywhere, but more on land. We all crawled out of the sea
once, didn't we? Maybe that was a mistake. Now we're going
back to it.

I imagine all the other people doing what I'm doing and that
gives me hope. It must be an instinct in the human race,
mustn't it? When threatened, scatter. Not just running away
from the danger, but raising our chances of survival as a species.
If we spread out over the whole globe, the poison won't be able
to harm everyone. Even if they fired off all their poison, there
must be a chance.

In the night I hear the cats. A hopeful sound.

*

Bad dreams. Nightmares, I suppose. When does a dream
become a nightmare? These dreams of mine go on after I've
woken up. It's like having a hangover. The bad dreams won't let
the rest of life go on.

*

She thought she saw another boat on the horizon, and steered
towards it. She didn't have any flares, and it was too far away for

shouting, so she just steered towards it. It was sailing parallel to the horizon, and she had it in view for half an hour or so. Then it went away. Perhaps it wasn't a boat anyway, she said to herself; but whatever it was, its disappearance left her feeling depressed.

She remembered a terrible thing she'd once read in a newspaper story about life on board a supertanker. Nowadays the ships had got bigger and bigger, while the crew had got smaller and smaller, and everything was done by technology. They just programmed a computer in the Gulf or wherever, and the ship practically sailed itself all the way to London or Sydney. It was much nicer for the owners, who saved lots of money, and much nicer for the crew, who only had to worry about the boredom. Most of the time they sat around below deck drinking beer like Greg, as far as she could make out. Drinking beer and watching videos.

There was one thing she couldn't ever forget from the article. It said that in the old days there was always someone up in the crow's nest or on the bridge, watching for trouble. But nowadays the big ships didn't have a lookout any more, or at least the lookout was just a man staring from time to time at a screen with a lot of blips on it. In the old days if you were lost at sea in a raft or a dinghy or something, and a boat came along, there was a pretty good chance of being rescued. You waved and shouted and fired off any rockets you had; you ran your shirt up to the top of the mast; and there were always people keeping an eye out for you. Nowadays you can drift in the ocean for weeks, and a supertanker finally comes along, and it goes right past. The radar won't pick you up because you're too small, and it's pure luck if anybody happens to be hanging over the rail being sick. There had been lots of cases where castaways who would have been rescued in the old days simply weren't picked up; and even incidents of people being run down by the ships they thought were coming to rescue them. She tried to imagine how awful it would be, the terrible wait, and then the feeling as the ship goes past and there's nothing you can do, all your shouts drowned by the engines. That's what's wrong with the world, she thought. We've given up having lookouts. We don't think about saving other people, we just sail on by relying on our machines. Everyone's below deck, having a beer with Greg.

So maybe that ship on the horizon wouldn't have spotted her anyway. Not that she wanted to be rescued or anything. There just might have been some news about the world, that was all.

*

She began to have more nightmares. The bad dreams hung over longer into the day. She felt she was on her back. There was a pain in her arm. She was wearing white gloves. She was in a sort of cage, as far as she could tell: on either side of her metal bars rose vertically. Men came and saw her, always men. She thought she must write down the nightmares, write them down as well as the true things that were happening. She told the men in the nightmares that she was going to write about them. They smiled and said they would give her a pencil and paper. She refused. She said she would use her own.

*

She knew the cats were getting a good diet of fish. She knew they didn't get much exercise and were putting on weight. But it just seemed to her that Linda was putting on more weight than Paul. She didn't like to believe it was happening. She didn't dare.

One day she saw land. She started the engine and steered towards it. She got close enough to see mangroves and palms, then the fuel ran out and the winds carried her away. It was a surprise to find no sadness or disappointment within her as the island receded. In any case, she thought, it would have been cheating to find the new land with the help of a diesel engine. The old ways of doing things had to be rediscovered: the future lay in the past. She would allow the winds to guide and guard her. She threw the empty fuel cans overboard.

*

I'm crazy. I should have got pregnant before I left. Of course. How didn't I see that was the answer? All these jokes from Greg about him being just an impregnator and I couldn't see what was obvious. That was what he was there for. That's why I met him. All that side of things seems odd now. Bits of rubber and tubes to squeeze and pills to swallow. There won't be any of that any more. We're going to give ourselves back to nature now.

I wonder where Greg is; *whether* Greg is. He could be dead. I've always wondered about that phrase the survival of the fittest. Anyone would think, looking at us, that Greg was the fitter to survive: he's bigger, stronger, more practical in our terms anyway, more conservative, more easy-going. I'm a worrier, I've never done carpentry, I'm not so good at being on my own. But I'm the one that's going to survive, or have the chance to anyway. The Survival of the Worriers – is that what it means? People like Greg will die out like the dinosaurs. Only those who can see what's happening will survive, that must be the rule. I bet there were animals who sensed the Ice Age was coming and set off on some long and dangerous journey to find a safer, warmer climate. And I bet the dinosaurs thought they were neurotic, put it down to pre-menstrual tension, said silly cow. I wonder if the reindeer saw what was going to happen to them. Do you think they ever sensed it somehow?

*

They say I don't understand things. They say I'm not making the right connections. Listen to them, listen to them and their connections. This happened, they say, and as a consequence that happened. There was a battle here, a war there, a king was deposed, famous men – always famous men, I'm sick of famous men – made events happen. Maybe I've been out in the sun too long, but I can't see their connections. I look at the history of the world, which they don't seem to realize is coming to an end, and I don't see what they see. All I see is the old connections, the ones we don't take any notice of any more because that makes it easier to poison the reindeer and paint stripes down their backs and feed them to mink. Who made that happen? Which famous man will claim the credit for that?

*

97

It's laughable. Listen to this dream. I was in bed, and I couldn't move. Things were a bit blurry. I didn't know where I was. There was a man. I don't remember what he looked like – just a man. He said, 'How are you feeling?'

I said, 'I'm fine.'

'Are you really?'

'Of course I am. Why shouldn't I be?'

He didn't reply, just nodded, and seemed to be looking up and down my body, which was under the bedclothes of course. Then he said, 'None of these urges?'

'What urges?'

'You know what I'm talking about.'

'Excuse me,' I replied – it's funny how you come over all formal in dreams, where you wouldn't in real life – 'Excuse me, but I really haven't the faintest notion of what it is you are referring to.'

'You've been attacking men.'

'Oh, yes? What was I after, their wallets?'

'No. It seems you were after sex.'

I began to laugh. The man frowned; I can remember the frown even if the rest of his face has gone. 'This really is too transparent,' I said, a frosty actress in an old film. I laughed some more. You know that moment, like a break in the cloud, when you realize inside a dream that you're only dreaming? He frowned again. I said, 'Don't be so obvious.' He didn't like that, and went away.

I woke up grinning to myself. Thinking about Greg and the cats and whether I should have got pregnant, and I have a sex-dream. The mind can be pretty straightforward, can't it? What made it think it could get away with something like that?

*

I'm stuck with this rhyme as we head in whatever direction we're heading:

> In fourteen hundred and ninety-two
> Columbus sailed the ocean blue

And then what? They always make it sound so simple. Names, dates, achievements. I hate dates. Dates are bullies, dates are know-alls.

*

She was always confident of reaching the island. She was asleep when the wind brought her there. All she had to do was steer between two knuckles of rock and run the boat aground on some pebbles. There was no perfect sweep of sand ready for the tourist's footprint, no coral breakwater, not even a nodding palm. She was relieved and grateful about this. It was better that the sand was rock, the lush jungle a scrub, the fertile soil a dustheap. Too much beauty, too much verdure might make her forget the rest of the planet.

Paul jumped ashore, but Linda waited to be carried. Yes, she thought, it was time we found land. She decided to sleep in the boat at first. You were supposed to start building a log cabin as soon as you arrived, but that was silly. The island might not prove suitable.

*

She thought that landing on the island would make the nightmares stop.

*

It was very hot. Anyone would think the place had central heating, she said to herself. There were no breezes, no change in the weather. She watched over Paul and Linda. They were her consolation.

She wondered if the nightmares were caused by sleeping in the boat, by being cooped up all night after having the freedom to walk around all day. She thought her mind could be protesting, asking to be let out. So she made a little shelter above the tideline and began sleeping there.

This didn't make any difference.

Something terrible was happening to her skin.

*

The nightmares got worse. She decided this was normal, as far as you could use the word *normal* any more. At least, it was to be expected, given her condition. She had been poisoned. How bad the poison was she didn't know. In her dreams the men were always very polite, even gentle. This was how she knew not to trust them: they were tempters. The mind was producing its own arguments against reality, against itself, what it knew. There was obviously something chemical behind it all, like antibodies or whatever. The mind, being in a state of shock because of what had happened, was creating its own reasons for denying what had happened. She should have expected something like that.

*

I'll give you an example. I'm quite cunning in my nightmares. When the men come I pretend not to be surprised. I act as if it's normal that they should be there. I call their bluff. Last night we had the following exchange. Make of it what you will.

'Why am I wearing white gloves?' I asked.

'Is that what you think they are?'

'What do you think they are?'

'We had to put a drip in your arm.'

'Is that why I have to wear white gloves? This isn't the opera.'

'They aren't gloves. They're bandages.'

'I thought you said I had a drip in my arm.'

'That's right. The bandages are to hold the drip in place.'

'But I can't move my fingers.'

'That's normal.'

'*Normal?*' I said. 'What's normal nowadays?' He couldn't find an answer to that, so I carried on. 'Which arm is the drip in?'

'The left. You can see that for yourself.'

'Then why have you bandaged my right arm as well?'

He had to think about that for a long time. Finally he said, 'Because you were trying to pull the drip out with your free arm.'

'Why should I want to do that?'

'I should think only you can tell us.'

I shook my head. He went away defeated. But I gave as good as I got, didn't I? And the next night I took them on again. My mind obviously thought I'd seen off that tempter too easily, so it produced a different one, who kept calling me by name.

'How are you tonight, Kath?'

'I thought you always said *we*. That is, if you're who you pretend you are.'

'Why should I say *we*, Kath? I know how I am. I was asking about you.'

'*We*,' I said sarcastically, 'we in the zoo are fine, thank you very much.'

'What do you mean, the zoo?'

'The bars, stupid.' I didn't really think it was a zoo; I wanted to find out what they thought it was. Fighting your own mind isn't always an easy business.

'The bars? Oh, they're just part of your bed.'

'My bed? Excuse me, so it isn't a cot and I'm not a baby?'

'It's a special bed. Look.' He flicked a catch and folded one set of bars down and out of my sight. Then he pulled them up again and latched them shut.

'Oh, I see, you're locking me up, is that the idea?'

'No, no, no, Kath. We just don't want you to fall asleep and roll out of bed. If you had a nightmare, for instance.'

That was a crafty tactic. *If you had a nightmare* . . . But it would take a lot more than this to trick me. I think I know what my mind is doing. It *is* a sort of zoo I'm imagining, because a zoo is the only place I've seen reindeer. Live, I mean. So I associate them with bars. My mind knows that for me it all started with the reindeer; that's why it invented this deception. It's very plausible, the mind.

'I don't *have* nightmares,' I said firmly, as if they were spots or something. I thought that was good, telling him he didn't exist.

'Well, in case you started sleep-walking or something.'

'Have I been sleep-walking?'

'We can't watch everybody, Kath. There are many others in the same boat as you.'

'I know!' I shouted. 'I know!' I was shouting because I felt triumphant. He was clever, that one, but he'd given himself away. *In the same boat*. Naturally he meant *in other boats*, but he – or rather my mind – had tripped up.

I slept well that night.

*

She had a terrible thought. What if the kittens weren't all right? What if Linda gave birth to freaks, to monsters? Could it happen this soon? What winds had blown them all here, what poison was in those winds?

She seemed to sleep a lot. The flat heat continued. She felt parched much of the time, and drinking from the stream didn't help. Perhaps there was something wrong with the water. Her skin was falling off. She held up her hands and her fingers looked like the antlers of a fighting stag. Her depressions continued. She tried to cheer herself up with the thought that at least she didn't have a boyfriend on the island. What would Greg say if he saw her like this?

*

It was the mind, she decided; that was the cause of it all. The mind simply got too clever for its own good, it got carried away. It was the mind that invented these weapons, wasn't it? You couldn't imagine an animal inventing its own destruction, could you?

She told herself the following story. There was a bear in the forest, an intelligent, lively bear, a . . . *normal* bear. One day it started digging a great pit. When it had finished it broke a branch from a tree, pulled off the leaves and twigs, gnawed one end to a sharp point and planted this stake in the bottom of the pit, sticking upwards. Then the bear covered the hole it had dug with branches and undergrowth so that it looked like any other part of the forest floor, and went away. Now where do you think the bear had dug its pit? Right in the middle of one of its own favourite trails, a spot it regularly crossed on its way to drink honey from the trees, or whatever it is bears do. So the next day the bear lolloped along the path, fell into the pit and got impaled on the stake. As it died it thought, My, my, this is a surprise, what a curious way things have turned out. Perhaps it was a mistake to dig a trap where I did. Perhaps it was a mistake to dig a trap in the first place.

You can't imagine a bear doing that, can you? But that's what it's like with us, she reflected. The mind just got carried away. Never knew when to stop. But then the mind never does. It's the same with these nightmares – the sleeping mind just gets carried away. She wondered if primitive people had nightmares. She bet they didn't. Or at least, not the sort we have.

She didn't believe in God, but now she was tempted. Not because she was afraid of dying. It wasn't that. No, she was tempted to believe in someone watching what was going on, watching the bear dig its own pit and then fall into it. It wouldn't be such a good story if there was no-one around to tell it. Look what they went and did – they blew themselves up. Silly cows.

*

The one I had the argument with about the gloves was here again. I caught him out.

'I've still got my gloves on,' I said.

'Yes,' he replied, humouring me but getting it wrong.

'I haven't got a drip in my arm.'

He obviously wasn't prepared for that. 'Ah, no.'

'So why am I wearing my white gloves?'

'Ah.' He paused while deciding which lie to tell. It wasn't a bad one he came up with. 'You were pulling your hair out.'

'Nonsense. It's falling out. It falls out every day.'

'No, I'm afraid you were pulling it out.'

'Nonsense. I only have to put my hand to it and it falls out in great hanks.'

'I'm afraid not,' he said patronizingly.

'Go away,' I shouted. 'Go away, go away.'

'Of course.'

And he went. It was a very devious thing he came up with

about my hair, a lie as close to the truth as possible. Because I have been touching my hair. Well, that's not surprising, is it?

Still, it was a good sign that I told him to go and he went. I feel I'm getting on top of things, I'm beginning to control my nightmares. This is just a period I've been going through. I'll be glad when it ends. The next period may be worse, of course, but at least it'll be different. I wish I knew how much I was poisoned. Enough to put a blue stripe down my back and feed me to the mink?

*

The mind got carried away, she found herself repeating. Everything was connected, the weapons and the nightmares. That's why they'd had to break the cycle. Start making things simple again. Begin at the beginning. People said you couldn't turn the clock back, but you could. The future was in the past.

She wished she could put a stop to the men and their temptations. She thought they would stop when she reached the island. She thought they would stop when she gave up sleeping in the boat. But they only became more persistent and more cunning. At night she was afraid to fall asleep because of the nightmares; yet she needed rest so much, and each morning she woke later and later. The flat heat continued, a stale, institutional heat; it was like being surrounded by radiators. Would it ever end? Perhaps the seasons had been killed off by what had happened, or at least reduced from four to two – that special winter they'd all been warned about, and this unbearable summer. Maybe the world had to earn the spring and autumn back by good behaviour over many centuries.

*

I don't know which of the men it was. I've started closing my eyes. That's harder than you think. If you've already got your eyes closed in sleep, try closing them again to shut out a nightmare. It's not easy. But if I can learn this, then perhaps I'll be able to learn putting my hands over my ears as well. That would help.

'How are you feeling this morning?'

'Why do you say *morning?* It's always night when you call.' You see how I don't let them get away with anything?

'If you say so.'

'What do you mean, if I say so?'

'You're the boss.' That's right, I am the boss. You've got to keep control of your own mind, otherwise it'll run away with you. And that's what's caused the peril we're in at the moment. Keep the mind under control.

So I answer, 'Go away.'

'You keep saying that.'

'Well if I'm the boss I'm allowed to, aren't I?'

'You'll have to talk about it one day.'

'*Day.* There you go again.' I kept my eyes closed. 'What's *it,* anyway?' I thought I was still pursuing him, but this may have been a tactical mistake.

'*It?* Oh, everything . . . How you got yourself into this situation, how we're going to help you get out of it.'

'You really are a very ignorant man, you know that?'

He ignored this. I hate the way they pretend not to have heard the things they can't deal with. 'Greg,' he said, clearly changing the subject. 'Your feelings of guilt, rejection, things like that . . . '

'Is Greg alive?' The nightmare was so real I somehow thought the man might know the answer.

'Greg? Yes, Greg's fine. But we thought it wouldn't help . . . '

'Why should I have guilt feelings? I'm not guilty about taking the boat. He just wanted to drink beer and get off with girls. He didn't need a boat for that.'

'I don't think the boat's central to the matter.'

'What do you mean, not central? I wouldn't be here without the boat.'

'I mean you're offloading a lot on to the boat. So that you can avoid thinking about what happened before the boat. Do you think that's what you might be doing?'

'How would I know? *You*'re meant to be the expert.' This was very sarcastic of me, I know, but I couldn't resist it. I was angry with him. As if *I* was ignoring what had happened before I took the boat. *I* was one of the few people that noticed, after all. The rest of the world behaved like Greg.

'Well, I think we seem to be making some progress.'

'Go away.'

*

I knew he'd be back. In a way I was sort of waiting for him to return. Just to get it over with, I suppose. And he had me intrigued, I'll admit that. I mean, I know exactly what's happened, and more or less why and more or less how. But I wanted to see how clever his – well, my own, really – explanation would be.

'So you think you might be ready to talk about Greg.'

'*Greg?* What's it got to do with Greg?'

'Well, it seems to us, and we'd like your confirmation on this one, that your . . . your break-up with Greg has a lot to do with your present . . . problems.'

'You really are a very ignorant man.' I liked saying that.

'Then help cure me of my ignorance, Kath. Explain things to me. When did you first notice things were going wrong with Greg?'

'Greg, Greg. There's been a bloody nuclear war and all you want to talk about is *Greg*.'

'Yes, the war, of course. But I thought we'd better take one thing at a time.'

'And Greg is more important than the war? You certainly have an odd system of priorities. Perhaps Greg caused the war. You know he's got a baseball cap that says MAKE WAR NOT LOVE on it? Perhaps he sat there drinking beer and pressed the button just for something to do.'

'That's an interesting approach. I think we could get somewhere with that.' I didn't respond. He went on, 'Would we be right in thinking that with Greg you sort of were putting all your eggs in one basket? You thought he was your last chance? Perhaps you were laying too many expectations on him?'

I'd had enough of this. 'My name is Kathleen Ferris,' I said, as much to myself as to anybody else. 'I'm thirty-eight years old. I left the north and came to the south because I could see what was happening. But the war pursued me. It came anyway. I got in the boat, I let the winds carry me. I took two cats, Paul and Linda. I found this island. I am living here. I don't know what will happen to me, but I know it's the duty of those of us who care about the planet to go on living.' When I stopped I found I'd burst into tears without realizing. The tears ran down the sides of my face and into my ears. I couldn't see, I couldn't hear. I felt I was swimming, drowning.

Eventually, very quietly – or was it just that my ears were full of water? – the man said, 'Yes, we thought you might be seeing things like that.'

'I have been through the bad winds. My skin is falling off. I am thirsty all the time. I don't know how serious it is, but I know I have to go on. If only for the cats. They might need me.'

'Yes.'

'What do you *mean*, Yes?'

'Well, psychosomatic symptoms can be very convincing.'

'Can't you get it into your head? There's been a bloody nuclear war.'

'Hmmm,' said the man. He was being deliberately provocative.

'All right,' I replied. 'I may as well listen to your version. I can feel you wanting to tell me.'

'Well, we think it goes back to your break-up with Greg. And to your relationship of course. The possessiveness, the violence. But the break-up . . . '

Though I'd been meaning to play along with him, I couldn't help interrupting. 'It wasn't really a break-up. I just took the boat when the war started.'

'Yes, of course. But things between you . . . you wouldn't say they were going well?'

'No worse than with other blokes. He's just a bloke, Greg. He's normal for a bloke.'

'Precisely.'

'What do you mean, *precisely?*'

'Well, we called in your files from the north, you see. There does seem to be a pattern. You like putting all your eggs in one basket. With the same type of man. And that's always a bit dangerous, isn't it?' When I didn't reply, he went on, 'We call it the persistent victim syndrome. PVS.'

I decided to ignore that too. For a start, I didn't know what he was talking about. Spinning some tale or other.

'There's a lot of denial in your life, isn't there? You . . . deny a lot of things.'

'Oh no I don't,' I said. This was ridiculous. I made up my mind to force him out into the open. 'Are you telling me, are you telling me there hasn't been a war?'

'That's right. I mean, it was very worrying. It looked as if there might well be one. But they sorted something out.'

'They sorted something out!' I said it in a sarcastic shout, because this proved everything. My mind had been remembering that phrase of Greg's which I'd found so complacent. I enjoyed shouting, I wanted to shout something else, so I did. 'Until you've ate at BJ's you ain't shit!" I yelled. I was feeling triumphant, but the man didn't seem to understand, and he laid a hand on my arm as if I needed comforting.

'Yes, they really sorted something out. It never happened.'

'I see,' I replied, still victorious. 'So of course I'm not on the island?'

'Oh no.'

'I imagined it.'

'Yes.'

'And so of course the boat doesn't exist either?'

'Oh yes, you went on the boat.'

'But there weren't any cats on it.'

'Yes, you had two cats with you when they found you. They were terribly thin. They only just survived.'

It was cunning of him not to contradict me entirely. Cunning, but predictable. I decided on a switch of tactics. I'd be puzzled, and a bit pathetic. 'I don't understand,' I said, reaching out and taking his hand. 'If there wasn't any war, why was I in the boat?'

'Greg,' he said, with a sort of nasty confidence, as if I'd finally admitted something. 'You were running away. We find that those with persistent victim syndrome often experience acute guilt when they finally take flight. Then there was the bad news from the north. That was your excuse. You were exteriorizing things, transferring your confusion and anxiety on to the world. It's normal,' he added patronizingly, though it was obvious he didn't think so. 'Quite normal.'

'I'm not the only persistent victim around here,' I replied. 'The whole bloody world's a persistent victim.'

'Of course.' He agreed without really listening.

'They said there was going to be a war. They said the war had started.'

'They're always saying that. But they sorted something out.'

'So you keep saying. Well. So, in your *version*' — I stressed the word — 'where did they find me?'

'About a hundred miles east of Darwin. Going round in circles.'

'Going round in circles,' I repeated. 'That's what the world does.' First he tells me I'm projecting myself on to the world, then he tells me I'm doing what we all know the world does all the time. This really wasn't very impressive.

'And how do you explain my hair falling out?'

'You've been pulling it out, I'm afraid.'

'And my skin falling off?'

'It's been a bad time for you. You've been under severe stress. It's not unusual. But it'll get better.'

'And how do you explain that I remember very clearly everything that's happened from the news of the war breaking out in the north to my time here on the island?'

'Well, the technical term is fabulation. You make up a story to cover the facts you don't know or can't accept. You keep a few true facts and spin a new story round them. Particularly in cases of double stress.'

'Meaning?'

'Severe stress in the private life coupled with a political crisis in the world outside. We always get an increase in admissions when things are going badly in the north.'

'You'll be telling me next there were dozens of crazy people going round in circles in the sea.'

'A few. Four or five maybe. Most of the admissions didn't make it as far as a boat, though.' He sounded as if he was impressed by my tenacity.

'And how many . . . admissions have you had this time?'

'A couple of dozen.'

'Well, I admire your fabulation,' I said, using the technical term back to him. That put him in his place. 'I really think it's quite clever.' He'd given himself away, of course. *You keep a few true facts and spin a new story round them* – exactly what he'd done.

'I'm glad we're making some progress, Kath.'

'Go away and sort something out,' I said. 'By the way, is there any news of the reindeer?'

'What sort of news did you want?'

'Good news!' I shouted. 'Good news!'

'I'll see what I can do.'

*

She felt tired when the nightmare left; tired but victorious. She had drawn out the worst the tempter had to offer. She would be safe now. Of course, he'd made a whole series of blunders. *I'm glad we're making some progress*: he should never have said that. Nobody likes to be patronized by their own mind. The one that really gave him away was about the cats getting thin. That had been the most noticeable thing about the whole voyage, the way the cats got fatter, the way they loved the fish she caught.

She made a decision not to speak to the men again. She couldn't stop them coming – and she was sure they would visit her for many more nights – but she wouldn't speak to them. She had learnt how to shut her eyes in her nightmares; now she would learn to stop her ears and her mouth. She wouldn't be tempted. She wouldn't.

If she had to die then she would. They must have come

through some very bad winds; how bad she would only find out when she either recovered or died. She worried about the cats, but believed they'd be able to fend for themselves. They would return to nature. They already had. When the food from the boat ran out they took to hunting. Or rather Paul did: Linda was too fat to hunt. Paul brought back small creatures for her, things like voles and mice. Tears bubbled into Kath's eyes when he did so.

It was all about her mind being afraid of its own death, that's what she finally decided. When her skin got bad and her hair started falling out, her mind tried to think up an alternative explanation. She even knew the technical term for it now: fabulation. Where had she picked that up from? She must have read it in a magazine somewhere. Fabulation. You keep a few true facts and spin a new story round them.

She remembered an exchange she'd had the previous night. The man in the dream said you deny a lot of things in your life don't you, and she'd answered oh no I don't. That was funny, looking back; but it was also serious. You mustn't fool yourself. That's what Greg did, that's what most people did. We've got to look at things how they are; we can't rely on fabulation any more. It's the only way we'll survive.

*

The next day, on a small, scrubby island in the Torres Strait, Kath Ferris woke up to find that Linda had given birth. Five tortoiseshell kittens, all huddling together, helpless and blind, yet quite without defect. She felt such love. The cat wouldn't let her touch the kittens, of course, but that was all right, that was normal. She felt such happiness! Such hope!

5

SHIPWRECK

I

I T BEGAN WITH a portent.

They had doubled Cape Finisterre and were sailing south before a fresh wind when a school of porpoises surrounded the frigate. Those on board crowded the poop and the breastwork, marvelling at the animals' ability to circle a vessel already gaily proceeding at nine or ten knots. As they were admiring the sports of the porpoises, a cry was raised. A cabin boy had fallen through one of the fore portholes on the larboard side. A signal gun was fired, a life-raft thrown out, and the vessel hove to. But these manoeuvres were cumbrously done, and by the time the six-oared barge was let down, it was in vain. They could not find the raft, let alone the boy. He was only fifteen years old, and those who knew him maintained that he was a strong swimmer; they conjectured that he would most probably have reached the raft. If so, he doubtless perished upon it, after having experienced the most cruel sufferings.

The expedition for Senegal consisted of four vessels: a frigate, a corvette, a flute and a brig. It had set sail from the Island of Aix on 17th June 1816 with 365 people on board. Now it continued south with its complement reduced by one. They provisioned at Tenerife, taking on precious wines, oranges, lemons, banian figs and vegetables of all kinds. Here they noted the depravity of the local inhabitants: the women of Saint Croix stood at their doors and urged the Frenchmen to enter, confident that their husbands' jealousies would be cured by the monks of the Inquisition who would speak disapprovingly of conjugal mania as the blinding gift of Satan. Reflective passengers ascribed such behaviour to the southern sun, whose power, it is known, weakens both natural and moral bonds.

From Tenerife they sailed south-south-west. Fresh winds and navigational ineptitude scattered the flotilla. Alone, the frigate passed the tropic and rounded Cape Barbas. It was running close to the shore, at times no more than half a cannon shot away. The sea was strewn with rocks; brigantines could not frequent these seas at low water. They had doubled Cape Blanco, or so they believed, when they found themselves in shallows; the lead was cast every half-hour. At daybreak Mr Maudet, ensign of the watch, made out the reckoning upon a chicken coop, and judged that they were on the edge of the Arguin reef. His advice was discounted. But even those un-schooled in the sea could observe that the water had changed colour; weed was apparent at the ship's side, and a great many fish were being taken. In calm seas and clear weather, they were running aground. The lead announced eighteen fathoms, then shortly afterwards six fathoms. The frigate luffing, almost immediately gave a heel; a second and third, then stopped. The sounding line showed a depth of five metres and sixty centimetres.

By misfortune, they had struck the reef at high tide; and the seas growing violent, attempts to free the ship failed. The frigate was assuredly lost. Since the boats it carried were not capacious enough to contain the whole personnel, it was decided to build a raft and embark upon it those who could not be put into the boats. The raft would then be towed to the shore and all would be saved. This plan was perfectly well-laid; but as two of the company were later to affirm, it was traced upon loose sand, which was dispersed by the breath of egotism.

The raft was made, and well made, places in the boats allotted, provisions made ready. At daybreak, with two metres and seventy centimetres of water in the hold and the pumps failing, the order was given to abandon ship. Yet disorder quickly embraced the well-laid plan. The allotment of places was ignored, and the provisions were carelessly handled, forgotten or lost in the waters. One hundred and fifty was to be the complement of the raft: one hundred and twenty soldiers including officers, twenty-nine men sailors and passengers, one

woman. But scarcely had fifty men got on board this machine –
whose extent was twenty metres in length and seven in breadth
– than it sank to at least seventy centimetres under water. They
cast off the barrels of flour which had been embarked, whereupon the level of the raft rose; the remaining people descended
upon it, and it sank again. When the machine was fully laden, it
was a metre beneath the surface, and those on board so crowded
that they could not take a single step; at the back and front, they
were in water up to the waist. Loose flour barrels were cast
against them by the waves; a twenty-five pound bag of biscuit
was thrown down to them, which the water converted at once
into a paste.

It had been intended that one of the naval officers should take
command of the raft; but this officer declined to come on board.
At seven o'clock in the morning the signal for departure was
given, and the little flotilla pulled away from the abandoned
frigate. Seventeen persons had refused to leave the vessel, or had
concealed themselves away, and thus remained on board to
discover their fate.

The raft was towed by four boats in line astern, preceded by a
pinnace, which made soundings. As the boats took up their
positions, cries of *Vive le roi!* arose from the men on the raft, and
a small white flag was raised upon the end of a musket. But it
was at this instant of greatest hope and expectation for those
upon the raft that the breath of egotism was added to the normal
winds of the seas. One by one, whether for reason of self-
interest, incompetence, misfortune or seeming necessity, the
tow-ropes were cast aside.

The raft was barely two leagues from the frigate when it was
abandoned. Those on board had wine, a little brandy, some
water and a small portion of sodden biscuit. They had been
given no compass or chart. With neither oars nor rudder, there
was no means of controlling the raft, and little means either of
controlling those upon it, who were constantly flung against
one another as the waters rolled over them. In the first night, a
storm got up and threw the machine with great violence; the
cries of those on board mingled with the roaring of the billows.

Some attached ropes to the timbers of the craft, and held fast to these; all were buffeted without mercy. By daybreak the air was filled with lamentable cries, vows which could never be fulfilled were offered up to Heaven, and all prepared themselves for imminent death. It was impossible to form an idea of that first night which was not below the truth.

The next day the seas were calm, and for many hope was rekindled. Nevertheless, two young lads and a baker, convinced that there was no escape from death, bade farewell to their companions and willingly embraced the sea. It was during this day that those on the raft began to experience their first delusions. Some fancied that they saw land, others espied vessels come to save them, and the dashing of these deceptive hopes upon the rocks provoked greater despondency.

The second night was more terrible than the first. The seas were mountainous and the raft constantly near to being overthrown; the officers, clustered by the short mast, ordered the soldiery from one side of the machine to the other to counterbalance the energy of the waves. A group of men, certain that they were lost, broke open a cask of wine and resolved to soothe their last moments by abandoning the power of reason; in which they succeeded, until the sea water coming in through the hole they had made in the cask spoiled the wine. Thus doubly maddened, these disordered men determined to send all to a common destruction, and to this end attacked the ropes that bound the raft together. The mutineers being resisted, a pitched battle took place amid the waves and the darkness of the night. Order was restored, and there was an hour of tranquillity upon that fatal machine. But at midnight the soldiery rose again and attacked their superiors with knives and sabres; those without weapons were so deranged that they attempted to tear at the officers with their teeth, and many bites were endured. Men were thrown into the sea, bludgeoned, stabbed; two barrels of wine were thrown overboard and the last of the water. By the time the villains were subdued, the raft was laden with corpses.

During the first uprising, a workman by the name of

Dominique, who had joined the mutineers, was cast into the sea. On hearing the piteous cries of this treacherous underling, the engineer in charge of the workmen threw himself into the water, and taking the villain by the hair, succeeded in dragging him back on board. Dominique's head had been split open by a sabre. In the darkness the wound was bound up and the wretch restored to life. But no sooner was he so revived than, ungrateful as he was, he rejoined the mutineers and rose with them again. This time he found less fortune and less mercy; he perished that night.

Delirium now menaced the unhappy survivors. Some threw themselves into the sea; some fell into torpor; some unfortunate wretches rushed at their comrades with sabres drawn demanding to be given *the wing of a chicken*. The engineer whose bravery had saved the workman Dominique pictured himself travelling the fine plains of Italy, and one of the officers saying to him, 'I remember that we have been deserted by the boats; but fear nothing; I have just written to the governor, and in a few hours we shall be saved.' The engineer, calm in his delirium, responded thus: 'Have you a pigeon to carry your orders with as much celerity?'

Only one cask of wine remained for the sixty still on board the raft. They collected tags from the soldiers and fashioned them into fish-hooks; they took a bayonet and bent it into such shape as to catch a shark. Whereupon a shark arrived, and seized the bayonet, and with a savage twist of its jaw straightened it fully out again, and swam away.

An extreme resource proved necessary to prolong their miserable existence. Some of those who had survived the night of the mutiny fell upon the corpses and hacked pieces from them, devouring the flesh on the instant. Most of the officers refused this meat; though one proposed that it should first be dried to make it more palatable. Some tried chewing swordbelts and cartouche boxes, and the leather trimmings to their hats, with little benefit. One sailor attempted to eat his own excrements, but he could not succeed.

The third day was calm and fine. They took repose, but cruel dreams added to the horrors already inflicted by hunger and thirst. The raft, which now carried less than one half its original complement, had risen up in the water, an unforeseen benefit of the night's mutinies. Yet those on board remained in water to the knees, and could only repose standing up, pressed against one another in a solid mass. On the fourth morning they perceived that a dozen of their fellows had died in the night; the bodies were given to the sea, except for one that was reserved against their hunger. At four o'clock that afternoon a shoal of flying fish passed over the raft, and many became ensnared in the extremities of the machine. That night they dressed the fish, but their hunger was so great and each portion so exiguous, that many of them added human flesh to the fish, and the flesh being dressed was found less repugnant. Even the officers began to eat it when presented in this form.

It was from this day onwards that all learned to consume human flesh. The next night was to bring a fresh supply. Some Spaniards, Italians and Negroes, who had remained neutral during the first mutinies, conspired together with the plan of throwing their superiors overboard and escaping to the shore, which they believed to be at hand, with those valuables and possessions which had been placed into a bag and hung upon the mast. Once more, a terrible combat ensued, and blood washed over the fatal raft. When this third mutiny was finally suppressed, there remained no more than thirty on board, and the raft had risen yet again in the water. Barely a man lay without wounds, into which salt water constantly flowed, and piercing cries were heard.

On the seventh day two soldiers concealed themselves behind the last barrel of wine. They struck a hole in it and began to drink the wine through a straw. On being discovered, the two trespassers were instantly cast into the water, in accordance with the necessary law that had been promulgated.

It was now that the most terrible decision came to be taken. On counting their numbers, it was found that they were twenty-seven. Fifteen of these were likely to live for some days; the rest, suffering from large wounds and many of them delirious, had but the smallest chance of survival. In the time that might elapse before their deaths, however, they would surely diminish further the limited supply of provisions. It was calculated that they could well drink between them as many as thirty or forty bottles of wine. To put the sick on half allowance was but to kill them by degrees. And thus, after a debate in which the most dreadful despair presided, it was agreed among the fifteen healthy persons that their sick comrades must, for the common good of those who might yet survive, be cast into the sea. Three sailors and a soldier, their hearts now hardened by the constant sight of death, performed these repugnant but necessary executions. The healthy were separated from the unhealthy like the clean from the unclean.

After this cruel sacrifice, the last fifteen survivors threw all their arms into the water, reserving only a sabre lest some rope or wood might need cutting. There was sustenance left for six days while they awaited death.

There came a small event which each interpreted according to his nature. A white butterfly, of a species common in France, appeared over their heads fluttering, and settled upon the sail. To some, crazed with hunger, it seemed that even this could make a morsel. To others, the ease with which their visitor moved appeared a very mockery when they lay exhausted and almost motionless beneath it. To yet others, this simple butterfly was a sign, a messenger from Heaven as white as Noah's dove. Even those sceptical ones who declined to recognize a divine instrument knew with cautious hope that butterflies travel little distance from the dry land.

Yet no dry land appeared. Under the burning sun a raging thirst consumed them, until they began to moisten their lips with their own urine. They drank it from little tin cups which first they placed in water to cool their inner liquid the quicker. It happened that a man's cup might be stolen and restored to him later, but without the urine it had previously held. There was one who could not bring himself to swallow it, however thirsty he might be. A surgeon amongst them remarked that the urine of some men was more agreeable to swallow than that of others. He further remarked that the one immediate effect of drinking urine was an inclination to produce urine anew.

An officer of the army discovered a lemon, which he intended to reserve entirely for himself; violent entreaties persuaded him of the perils of selfishness. Thirty cloves of garlic were also found, from which arose further disputation; had all weapons but a sabre not been discarded, blood might have been shed once more. There were two phials filled with spirituous liquor for cleaning the teeth; one or two drops of this liquor, dispensed with reluctance by its possessor, produced on the tongue a delightful sensation which for a few seconds cast out thirst. Some pieces of pewter on being placed in the mouth effected a kind of coolness. An empty phial which had once contained essence of roses was passed among the survivors; they inhaled, and the remnants of perfume made a soothing impression.

On the tenth day several of the men, upon receiving their allotment of wine, conceived the plan of becoming intoxicated and then destroying themselves; they were with difficulty persuaded from this notion. Sharks surrounded the raft, and some soldiers, in their derangement, openly bathed within sight of the great fish. Eight of the men, reckoning that land could not be far distant, constructed a second raft upon which to escape. They built a narrow machine with a low mast and a hammock cloth for a sail; but as they made a trial of it, the frailty of the craft proved to them the temerity of their enterprise, and they abandoned it.

On the thirteenth day of their ordeal, the sun rose entirely free from clouds. The fifteen wretches had put up their prayers to the Almighty, and divided amongst them their portion of wine, when a captain of infantry, looking towards the horizon, descried a ship and announced it with an exclamation. All offered thanks to the Lord and gave way to transports of joy. They straightened barrel hoops and attached handkerchiefs to the end; one of their number mounted to the top of the mast and waved these little flags. All watched the vessel on the horizon and guessed at its progress. Some estimated that it was coming closer by the minute; others asserted that its course lay in a contrary direction. For half an hour they lay suspended between hope and fear. Then the ship disappeared from the sea.

From joy they fell into despondency and grief; they envied the fate of those who had died before them. Then, to find some consolation from their despair in sleep, they rigged a piece of cloth as shelter from the sun, and lay down beneath it. They proposed to write an account of their adventures, which they would all sign, and nail it to the top of the mast, hoping that it might by some means reach their families and the Government.

They had passed two hours among the most cruel reflections when the master gunner, wishing to go to the front of the raft, went out of the tent and saw the *Argus* half a league distant, carrying a full press of sail, and bearing down upon them. He could scarcely breathe. His hands stretched towards the sea. 'Saved!' he said. 'See the brig close upon us!' All rejoiced; even the wounded made to crawl towards the back part of the machine, the better to see their saviours approaching. They embraced one another, and their delight redoubled when they saw that they owed their deliverance to Frenchmen. They waved handkerchiefs and thanked Providence.

The *Argus* clewed up her sails and lay on to their starboard, half a pistol shot away. The fifteen survivors, the strongest of whom could not have lived beyond the next forty-eight hours, were taken up on board; the commander and officers of the brig, by their reiterated care, rekindled in the survivors the flame of life. Two who later wrote their account of the ordeal concluded that the manner in which they were saved was truly miraculous, and that the finger of Heaven was conspicuous in the event.

The voyage of the frigate had begun with a portent, and it ended with an echo. When the fatal raft, towed by its attendant vessels, had put to sea, there were seventeen persons left behind. Thus abandoned by their own choice, they straightaway examined the ship for everything that the departing had not taken and the sea had not penetrated. They found biscuit, wine, brandy and bacon, enough to subsist for a while. At first tranquillity prevailed, for their comrades had promised to return to their rescue. But when forty-two days had passed without relief, twelve of the seventeen determined to reach land. To this end they constructed a second raft from some of the frigate's remaining timbers, which they bound together with strong ropes, and they embarked upon it. Like their predecessors, they lacked oars and navigational equipment, and possessed no more than a rudimentary sail. They took with them a small supply of provisions and what hope there was remaining. But many days later some Moors who live beside the Saharan coast and are subjects of King Zaide discovered the vestiges of their craft, and came to Andar with this information. It was believed that the men on this second raft were doubtless the prey of those sea-monsters which are found in great numbers off the shores of Africa.

And then finally, as if in mockery, there came the echo of an echo. Five men remained upon the frigate. Several days after the second raft had departed, a sailor who had refused to go upon it also attempted to reach the shore. Unable to construct a third raft for himself, he put to sea in a chicken coop. Perhaps it was the very cage upon which Mr Maudet had verified the frigate's fatal course on that morning when they had struck the reef. But the chicken coop sank and the sailor perished when no more than half a cable's length from the *Medusa*.

HOW DO YOU turn catastrophe into art?
Nowadays the process is automatic. A nuclear plant explodes? We'll have a play on the London stage within a year. A President is assassinated? You can have the book or the film or the filmed book or the booked film. War? Send in the novelists. A series of gruesome murders? Listen for the tramp of the poets. We have to understand it, of course, this catastrophe; to understand it, we have to imagine it, so we need the imaginative arts. But we also need to justify it and forgive it, this catastrophe, however minimally. Why did it happen, this mad act of Nature, this crazed human moment? Well, at least it produced art. Perhaps, in the end, that's what catastrophe is *for*.

He shaved his head before he started the picture, we all know that. Shaved his head so he wouldn't be able to see anyone, locked himself in his studio and came out when he'd finished his masterpiece. Is that what happened?

The expedition set off on 17th June 1816.
The *Medusa* struck the reef in the afternoon of 2nd July 1816.
The survivors were rescued from the raft on 17th July 1816.
Savigny and Corréard published their account of the voyage in November 1817.
The canvas was bought on 24th February 1818.
The canvas was transferred to a larger studio and restretched on 28th June 1818.
The painting was finished in July 1819.
On 28th August 1819, three days before the opening of the Salon, Louis XVIII examined the painting and addressed to the artist what the *Moniteur Universel* called 'one of those

felicitous remarks which at the same time judge the work and encourage the artist.' The King said, 'Monsieur Géricault, your shipwreck is certainly no disaster.'

It begins with truth to life. The artist read Savigny and Corréard's account; he met them, interrogated them. He compiled a dossier of the case. He sought out the carpenter from the *Medusa*, who had survived, and got him to build a scale model of his original machine. On it he positioned wax models to represent the survivors. Around him in his studio he placed his own paintings of severed heads and dissected limbs, to infiltrate the air with mortality. Recognizable portraits of Savigny, Corréard and the carpenter are included in the final picture. (How did they feel about posing for this reprise of their sufferings?)

He was perfectly calm when painting, reported Antoine Alphonse Montfort, the pupil of Horace Vernet; there was little perceptible motion of the body or the arms, and only a slight flushing of the face to indicate his concentration. He worked directly on to the white canvas with only a rough outline to guide him. He painted for as long as there was light with a remorselessness which was also rooted in technical necessity: the heavy, fast-drying oils he used meant that each section, once begun, had to be completed that day. He had, as we know, had his head shaved of its reddish-blond curls, as a Do Not Disturb sign. But he was not solitary: models, pupils and friends continued coming to the house, which he shared with his young assistant Louis-Alexis Jamar. Among the models he used was the young Delacroix, who posed for the dead figure lying face down with his left arm extended.

Let us start with what he did not paint. He did not paint:

1) The *Medusa* striking the reef;
2) The moment when the tow-ropes were cast off and the raft abandoned;
3) The mutinies in the night;
4) The necessary cannibalism;
5) The self-protective mass murder;

6) The arrival of the butterfly;

7) The survivors up to their waists, or calves, or ankles in water;

8) The actual moment of rescue.

In other words his first concern was not to be 1) political; 2) symbolic; 3) theatrical; 4) shocking; 5) thrilling; 6) sentimental; 7) documentational; or 8) unambiguous.

Notes

1) The *Medusa* was a shipwreck, a news story and a painting; it was also a cause. Bonapartists attacked Monarchists. The behaviour of the frigate's captain illuminated a) the incompetence and corruption of the Royalist Navy; b) the general callousness of the ruling class towards those beneath them. Parallels with the ship of state running aground would have been both obvious and heavy-handed.

2) Savigny and Corréard, survivors and co-authors of the first account of the shipwreck, petitioned the government, seeking compensation for the victims and punishment for the guilty officers. Rebuffed by institutional justice, they applied to the wider courts of public opinion with their book. Corréard subsequently set up as a publisher and pamphleteer with a shop called At the Wreck of the Medusa; it became a meeting-place for political malcontents. We can imagine a painting of the moment when the tow-ropes are loosed: an axe, glittering in the sun, is being swung; an officer, turning his back on the raft, is casually slipping a knot . . . It would make an excellent painted pamphlet.

3) The Mutiny was the scene that Géricault most nearly painted. Several preliminary drawings survive. Night, tempest, heavy seas, riven sail, raised sabres, drowning, hand-to-hand combat, naked bodies. What's wrong with all this? Mainly that it looks like one of those saloon-bar fights in B-Westerns where every single person is involved – throwing a punch, smashing a chair, breaking a bottle over an enemy's

head, swinging heavy-booted from the chandelier. Too much is going on. You can tell more by showing less.

The sketches of the Mutiny that survive are held to resemble traditional versions of the Last Judgment, with its separation of the innocent from the guilty, and with the fall of the mutinous into damnation. Such an allusion would have been misleading. On the raft, it was not virtue that triumphed, but strength; and there was little mercy to be had. The sub-text of this version would say that God was on the side of the officer-class. Perhaps he used to be in those days. Was Noah officer-class?

4) There is very little cannibalism in Western art. Prudishness? This seems unlikely: Western art is not prudish about gouged eyes, severed heads in bags, sacrificial mastectomy, circumcision, crucifixion. What's more, cannibalism was a heathen practice which could be usefully condemned in paint while surreptitiously enflaming the spectator. But some subjects just seem to get painted more than others. Take officer-class Noah, for instance. There seem to be surprisingly few pictures of his Ark around. There is the odd jocular American primitive, and a murky Giacomo Bassano in the Prado, yet not much else springs to mind. Adam and Eve, the Expulsion, the Annunciation, the Last Judgment – you can have all these by major artists. But Noah and his Ark? A key moment in human history, a storm at sea, picturesque animals, divine intervention in human affairs: surely the necessary elements are there. What could account for this iconographical deficiency? Perhaps the lack of a single Ark painting great enough to give the subject impetus and popularity. Or is it something in the story itself: maybe artists agreed that the Flood doesn't show God in the best possible light?

Géricault made one sketch of cannibalism on the raft. The spotlit moment of anthropophagy shows a well-muscled survivor gnawing the elbow of a well-muscled cadaver. It is almost comic. Tone was always going to be the problem here.

5) A painting is a moment. What would we think was happening in a scene where three sailors and a soldier were throwing people off a raft into the sea? That the victims were

already dead? Or if not, that they were being murdered for their jewellery? Cartoonists having trouble explaining the background to their jokes often give us newsvendors standing by billboards on which some convenient headline is inscribed. With painting, the equivalent information would have to be given in the title: A GRIEVOUS SCENE ABOARD THE RAFT OF THE MEDUSA IN WHICH DESPERATE SURVIVORS, WRACKED BY CONSCIENCE, REALIZE THAT PROVISIONS ARE INSUFFICIENT AND TAKE THE TRAGIC BUT NECESSARY DECISION TO SACRIFICE THE WOUNDED IN ORDER THAT THEY THEMSELVES MIGHT HAVE A GREATER CHANCE OF SURVIVAL. That should just about do it.

The title of 'The Raft of the Medusa', incidentally, is not 'The Raft of the Medusa'. The painting was listed in the Salon catalogue as *Scène de naufrage* – 'Scene of Shipwreck'. A cautious political move? Perhaps. But it's equally a useful instruction to the spectator: this is a painting, not an opinion.

6) It's not hard to imagine the arrival of the butterfly as depicted by other painters. But it sounds fairly coarse in its emotional appeal, doesn't it? And even if the question of tone could be overcome, there are two major difficulties. First, it wouldn't look like a true event, even though it was; what is true is not necessarily convincing. Second, a white butterfly six or eight centimetres across, alighting on a raft twenty metres long by seven metres broad, does give serious problems of scale.

7) If the raft is under water, you can't paint the raft. The figures would all be sprouting from the sea like a line-up of Venus Anadyomenes. Further, the lack of a raft presents formal problems: with everyone standing up because if they lay down they would drown, your painting is stiff with verticals; you have to be extra-ingenious. Better to wait until more on board have died, the raft has risen out of the water, and the horizontal plane becomes fully available.

8) The boat from the *Argus* pulling alongside, the survivors holding out their arms and clambering in, the pathetic contrast between the condition of the rescued and that of the rescuers, a

scene of exhaustion and joy – all very affecting, no doubt about it. Géricault made several sketches of this moment of rescue. It could make a strong image; but it's a bit . . . straightforward. That's what he didn't paint.

What did he paint, then? Well, what does it look as if he painted? Let us reimagine our eye into ignorance. We scrutinize 'Scene of Shipwreck' with no knowledge of French naval history. We see survivors on a raft hailing a tiny ship on the horizon (the distant vessel, we can't help noticing, is no bigger than that butterfly would have been). Our initial presumption is that this is the moment of sighting which leads to a rescue. This feeling comes partly from a tireless preference for happy endings, but also from posing ourselves, at some level of consciousness, the following question: how would we know about these people on the raft if they had *not* been rescued?

What backs up this presumption? The ship is on the horizon; the sun is also on the horizon (though unseen), lightening it with yellow. Sunrise, we deduce, and the ship arriving with the sun, bringing a new day, hope and rescue; the black clouds overhead (very black) will soon disappear. However, what if it were sunset? Dawn and dusk are easily confused. What if it were sunset, with the ship about to vanish like the sun, and the castaways facing hopeless night as black as that cloud overhead? Puzzled, we might look at the raft's sail to see if the machine was being blown towards or away from its rescuer, and to judge if that baleful cloud is about to be dispelled; but we get little help – the wind is blowing not up and down the picture but from right to left, and the frame cuts us off from further knowledge of the weather to our right. Then, still undecided, a third possibility occurs: it could be sunrise, yet even so the rescuing vessel is not coming towards the shipwrecked. This would be the plainest rebuff of all from fate: the sun is rising, *but not for you*.

The ignorant eye yields, with a certain testy reluctance, to the informed eye. Let's check 'Scene of Shipwreck' against Savigny and Corréard's narrative. It's clear at once that Géricault hasn't painted the hailing that led to the final rescue: that happened differently, with the brig suddenly close upon the raft and everyone rejoicing. No, this is the first sighting, when the *Argus* appeared on the horizon for a tantalizing half hour. Comparing paint with print, we notice at once that Géricault has not represented the survivor up the mast holding straightened-out barrel-hoops with handkerchiefs attached to them. He has opted instead for a man being held up on top of a barrel and waving a large cloth. We pause over this change, then acknowledge its advantage: reality offered him a monkey-up-a-stick image; art suggested a solider focus and an extra vertical.

But let us not inform ourselves too quickly. Return the question to the tetchy ignorant eye. Forget the weather; what can be deduced from the personnel on the raft itself? Why not start with a head-count. There are twenty figures on board. Two are actively waving, one actively pointing, two vigorously supplicating, plus one offering muscular support to the hailing figure on the barrel: six in favour of hope and rescue. Then there are five figures (two prone, three supine) who look either dead or dying, plus an old greybeard with his back to the sighted *Argus* in a posture of mourning: six against. In between (we measure space as well as mood) there are eight more figures: one half-supplicating, half-supporting; three watching the hailer with non-committal expressions; one watching the hailer agonizingly; two in profile examining, respectively, waves past and waves to come; plus one obscure figure in the darkest, most damaged part of the canvas, with head in hands (and clawing at his scalp?). Six, six and eight: no overall majority.

(Twenty? queries the informed eye. But Savigny and Corréard said there were only fifteen survivors. So all those five figures who might only be unconscious are definitely dead? Yes. But then what about the culling which took place, when the last fifteen healthy survivors pitched their thirteen wounded comrades into the sea? Géricault has dragged some of them back from the deep to help out with his composition. And should the dead lose their vote in the referendum over hope versus despair? Technically, yes; but not in assessing the mood of the picture.)

So the structure is balanced, six for, six against, eight don't knows. Our two eyes, ignorant and informed, squintily roam. Increasingly, they are drawn back from the obvious focus of attention, the hailer on the barrel, towards the mourning figure front left, the only person looking out at us. He is supporting on his lap a younger fellow who is – we have done our sums – certainly dead. The old man's back is turned against every living person on the raft: his pose is one of resignation, sorrow, despair; he is further marked out by his grey hair and the red cloth worn as a neck-protector. He might have strayed in from a different genre – some Poussin elder who had got lost, perhaps. (Nonsense, snaps the informed eye. Poussin? Guérin and Gros, if you must know. And the dead 'Son'? A medley of Guérin, Girodet and Prud'hon.) What is this 'Father' doing? a) lamenting the dead man (his son? his chum?) on his lap; b) realizing they will never be rescued; c) reflecting that even if they are rescued it doesn't matter a damn because of the death he holds in his arms? (By the way, says the informed eye, there really are handicaps to being ignorant. You'd never, for instance, guess that the Father and Son are an attentuated cannibalistic motif, would you? As a group they first appear in Géricault's only surviving sketch of the Cannibalism scene; and any educated contemporary spectator would be assuredly reminded of Dante's description of Count Ugolino sorrowing in his Pisan tower among his dying children – whom he ate. Is that clear now?)

Whatever we decide that the old man is thinking, his presence becomes as powerful a force in the painting as that of the hailer. This counterbalance suggests the following deduction: that the picture represents the mid-point of that first sighting of the *Argus*. The vessel has been in view for a quarter of an hour and has another fifteen minutes to offer. Some believe it is still coming towards them; some are uncertain and waiting to see what happens; some – including the wisest head on board – know that it is heading away from them, and that they will not be saved. This figure incites us to read 'Scene of Shipwreck' as an image of hope being mocked.

Those who saw Géricault's painting on the walls of the 1819

Salon knew, almost without exception, that they were looking at the survivors of the *Medusa*'s raft, knew that the ship on the horizon did pick them up (if not at the first attempt), and knew that what had happened on the expedition to Senegal was a major political scandal. But the painting which survives is the one that outlives its own story. Religion decays, the icon remains; a narrative is forgotten, yet its representation still magnetizes (the ignorant eye triumphs — how galling for the informed eye). Nowadays, as we examine 'Scene of Shipwreck', it is hard to feel much indignation against Hugues Duroy de Chaumareys, captain of the expedition, or against the minister who appointed him captain, or the naval officer who refused to skipper the raft, or the sailors who loosed the tow-ropes, or the soldiery who mutinied. (Indeed, history democratizes our sympathies. Had not the soldiers been brutalized by their wartime experiences? Was not the captain a victim of his own pampered upbringing? Would we bet on ourselves to behave heroically in similar circumstances?) Time dissolves the story into form, colour, emotion. Modern and ignorant, we reimagine the story: do we vote for the optimistic yellowing sky, or for the grieving greybeard? Or do we end up believing both versions? The eye can flick from one mood, and one interpretation, to the other: is this what was intended?

8a) He very nearly painted the following. Two oil studies of 1818, which in composition are closest of any preparatory sketches to the final image, show this significant difference: the vessel which is being hailed is much closer. We can see its outline, sails and masts. It is in profile, on the extreme right of the canvas, and has just begun a painful voyage across the painted horizon. It has clearly not yet seen the raft. The impact of these preliminary sketches is more active, kinetic: we feel as if the frantic waving by those on the raft might have some effect over the next few minutes, and that the picture, instead of being an instant of time, propels itself into its own future, asking the question, Will the ship sail off the edge of the canvas without seeing the raft? In contrast, the final version of 'Shipwreck' is less active, offers a less articulated question. The signalling seems more futile, and the hazard on which the survivors' fate depends more terrifying. What is their chance of rescue? A drop in the ocean.

He was eight months in his studio. Around this time he drew a self-portrait, from which he stares out at us with the sullen, rather suspicious gaze that painters often assume when faced by a mirror; guiltily, we assume that the disapproval is aimed at us, whereas in fact it is mostly directed back at the sitter. His beard is short, and a tasselled Greek cap covers his shorn hair (we only hear of it being cropped when he began the picture, but hair grows a long way in eight months: how many extra trims did he need?). He strikes us as a piratical figure, determined and ferocious enough to take on, to board his enormous Shipwreck. The width of his brushes, by the way, was surprising. From the breadth of his manner, Montfort supposed that Géricault used very thick brushes; yet they were small compared to those of other artists. Small brushes, and heavy, fast-drying oils.

We must remember him at work. It is a normal temptation to schematize, reducing eight months to a finished picture and a series of preliminary sketches; but we must resist this. He is tallish, strong and slender, with admirable legs which were compared to those of the ephebe restraining the horse in the centre of his 'Barberi Race'. Standing before the Shipwreck, he works with an intensity of concentration and a need for absolute silence: the scratch of a chair was enough to break the invisible thread between eye and brush-tip. He is painting his large figures directly on to the canvas with only an outline drawing for assistance. When the work is half done it looks like a row of sculptures hanging on a white wall.

We must remember him in the confinement of his studio, at work, in motion, making mistakes. When we know the final result of his eight months, his progress towards it seems irresistible. We start with the masterpiece and work backwards through the discarded ideas and near-misses; but for him the discarded ideas began as excitements, and he saw only at the very end what we take for granted at the beginning. For us the conclusion was inevitable; not for him. We must try to allow for hazard, for lucky discovery, even for bluff. We can only explain it in words, yet we must also try to forget words. A painting may be represented as a series of decisions labelled 1) to 8a), but we should understand that these are just the annotations of feeling. We must remember nerves and emotions. The painter isn't carried fluently downstream towards the sunlit pool of that finished image, but is trying to hold a course in an open sea of contrary tides.

Truth to life, at the start, to be sure; yet once the process gets under way, truth to art is the greater allegiance. The incident never took place as depicted; the numbers are inaccurate; the cannibalism is reduced to a literary reference; the Father and Son group has the thinnest documentary justification, the barrel group none at all. The raft has been cleaned up as if for the state visit of some queasy-stomached monarch: the strips of human flesh have been housewifed away, and everyone's hair is as sleek as a painter's new-bought brush.

As Géricault approaches his final image, questions of form predominate. He pulls the focus, crops, adjusts. The horizon is raised and lowered (if the hailing figure is below the horizon, the whole raft is gloomily engulfed by the sea; if he breaks the horizon, it is like the raising of hope). Géricault cuts down the surrounding areas of sea and sky, hurling us on to the raft whether we like it or not. He stretches the distance from the shipwrecked to the rescuing vessel. He readjusts the positions of his figures. How often in a picture do so many of the chief participants have their backs to the spectator?

And what splendidly muscular backs they are. We feel embarrassed at this point, yet we shouldn't be. The naïve question often proves to be the central one. So go on, let's ask. *Why do the survivors look so healthy?* We admire the way Géricault sought out the *Medusa*'s carpenter and had him build a scale model of the raft . . . but . . . but if he bothered to get the raft right, why couldn't he do the same with its inhabitants? We can understand why he fiddled the hailing figure into a separate vertical, why he added some supernumerary corpses to assist the formal structure. But why does everyone – even the corpses – look so muscled, so . . . healthy? Where are the wounds, the scars, the haggardness, the disease? These are men who have drunk their own urine, gnawed the leather from their hats, consumed their own comrades. Five of the fifteen did not survive their rescue very long. So why do they look as if they have just come from a body-building class?

When television companies make drama-docs about concentration camps, the eye – ignorant or informed – is always drawn to those pyjamaed extras. Their heads may be shaven, their shoulders hunched, all nail varnish removed, yet still they throb with vigour. As we watch them queue on screen for a bowl of gruel into which the camp guard contemptuously spits, we imagine them offscreen gorging themselves at the catering van. Does 'Scene of Shipwreck' prefigure this anomaly? With some painters we might pause and wonder. But not with Géricault, the portrayer of madness, corpses and severed heads. He once stopped a friend in the street who was yellow with jaundice and told him how handsome he was looking. Such an artist would hardly shrink from flesh at the limit of its endurance.

So let's imagine something else he didn't paint – 'Scene of Shipwreck' with the casting redistributed among the emaciated. Shrivelled flesh, suppurating wounds, Belsen cheeks: such details would move us, without trouble, to pity. Salt water would gush from our eyes to match the salt water on the canvas. But this would be precipitate: the painting would be acting on us too directly. Withered castaways in tattered rags are in the same emotional register as that butterfly, the first impelling us to an easy desolation as the second impels us to an easy consolation. The trick is not hard to work.

Whereas the response Géricault seeks is one beyond mere pity and indignation, though these emotions might be picked up *en route* like hitchhikers. For all its subject-matter, 'Scene of Shipwreck' is full of muscle and dynamism. The figures on the raft are like the waves: beneath them, yet also through them, surges the energy of the ocean. Were they painted in lifelike exhaustion they would be mere dribbles of spume rather than formal conduits. For the eye is washed – not teased, not persuaded, but tide-tugged – up to the peak of the hailing figure, down to the trough of the despairing elder, across to the recumbent corpse front right who links and leaks into the real tides. It is because the figures are sturdy enough to transmit such power that the canvas unlooses in us deeper, submarinous emotions, can shift us through currents of hope and despair, elation, panic and resignation.

What has happened? The painting has slipped history's anchor. This is no longer 'Scene of Shipwreck', let alone 'The Raft of the Medusa'. We don't just imagine the ferocious miseries on that fatal machine; we don't just become the sufferers. They become us. And the picture's secret lies in the pattern of its energy. Look at it one more time: at the violent waterspout building up through those muscular backs as they reach for the speck of the rescuing vessel. All that straining – to what end? There is no formal response to the painting's main surge, just as there is no response to most human feelings. Not merely hope, but any burdensome yearning: ambition, hatred, love (especially love) – how rarely do our emotions meet the object they seem to deserve? How hopelessly we signal; how dark the sky; how big the waves. We are all lost at sea, washed between hope and despair, hailing something that may never come to rescue us. Catastrophe has become art; but this is no reducing process. It is freeing, enlarging, explaining. Catastrophe has become art: that is, after all, what it is for.

And what of that earlier catastrophe, the Flood? Well, the iconography of officer-class Noah begins as we might imagine. For the first dozen or more Christian centuries the Ark (usually represented as a mere box or sarcophagus to indicate that Noah's salvation was a premonstration of Christ's escape from his sepulchre) appears widely in illuminated manuscripts, stained-glass windows, cathedral sculpture. Noah was a very popular fellow: we can find him on the bronze doors of San Zeno in Verona, on Nîmes cathedral's west façade and Lincoln's east; he sails into fresco at the Campo Santo in Pisa and Santa Maria

Novella in Florence; he anchors in mosaic at Monreale, the Baptistery in Florence, St Mark's in Venice.

But where are the great paintings, the famous images that these are leading up to? What happens – does the Flood dry up? Not exactly; but the waters are diverted by Michelangelo. In the Sistine Chapel the Ark (now looking more like a floating bandstand than a ship) for the first time loses its compositional pre-eminence; here it is pushed right to the back of the scene. What fills the foreground are the anguished figures of those doomed antediluvians left to perish when the chosen Noah and his family were saved. The emphasis is on the lost, the abandoned, the discarded sinners, God's detritus. (Should we allow ourselves to postulate Michelangelo the rationalist, moved by pity to subtle condemnation of God's heartlessness? Or Michelangelo the pious, fulfilling his papal contract and showing us what might happen if we failed to mend our ways? Perhaps the decision was purely aesthetic – the artist preferring the contorted bodies of the damned to yet another dutiful representation of yet another wooden Ark.) Whatever the reason, Michelangelo reoriented – and revitalized – the subject. Baldassare Peruzzi followed him, Raphael followed him; painters and illustrators increasingly concentrated on the forsaken rather than the saved. And as this innovation became a tradition, the Ark itself sailed farther and farther away, retreating towards the horizon just as the *Argus* did when Géricault was approaching his final image. The wind continues to blow, and the tides to run: the Ark eventually reaches the horizon, and disappears over it. In Poussin's 'The Deluge' the ship is nowhere to be seen; all we are left with is the tormented group of non-swimmers first brought to prominence by Michelangelo and Raphael. Old Noah has sailed out of art history.

Three reactions to 'Scene of Shipwreck':
  a) Salon critics complained that while they might be familiar with the events the painting referred to, there was no internal evidence from which to ascertain the nationality of the victims, the skies under which the tragedy was taking place, or the date

at which it was all happening. This was, of course, the point.

b) Delacroix in 1855 recalled his reactions nearly forty years earlier to his first sight of the emerging Medusa: 'The impression it gave me was so strong that as I left the studio I broke into a run, and kept running like a madman all the way back to the rue de la Planche, where I then lived, at the far end of the faubourg Saint-Germain.'

c) Géricault, on his death-bed, in reply to someone who mentioned the painting: 'Bah, une vignette!'

And there we have it – the moment of supreme agony on the raft, taken up, transformed, justified by art, turned into a sprung and weighted image, then varnished, framed, glazed, hung in a famous art gallery to illuminate our human condition, fixed, final, always there. Is that what we have? Well, no. People die; rafts rot; and works of art are not exempt. The emotional structure of Géricault's work, the oscillation between hope and despair, is reinforced by the pigment: the raft contains areas of bright illumination violently contrasted with patches of the deepest darkness. To make the shadow as black as possible, Géricault used quantities of bitumen to give him the shimmeringly gloomy black he sought. Bitumen, however, is chemically unstable, and from the moment Louis XVIII examined the work a slow, irreparable decay of the paint surface was inevitable 'No sooner do we come into this world,' said Flaubert, 'than bits of us start to fall off.' The masterpiece, once completed, does not stop: it continues in motion, downhill. Our leading expert on Géricault confirms that the painting is 'now in part a ruin'. And no doubt if they examine the frame they will discover woodworm living there.

6

THE MOUNTAIN

Tick, tick, tick, tick. Tock. Tick, tick, tick, tick. Tock. It sounded like a clock gently misfiring, time entering a delirium. This might have been appropriate, the Colonel reflected, but it wasn't the case. It was important to stick to what you knew, right to the end, especially at the end. He knew it wasn't the case. It wasn't time, it wasn't even a distant clock.

Colonel Fergusson lay in the cold square bedroom of his cold square house three miles outside Dublin and listened to the clicking overhead. It was one o'clock in the morning on a windless November night of 1837. His daughter Amanda sat at his bedside in stiff, pout-lipped profile, reading some piece of religious mumbo-jumbo. At her elbow the candle burned with a steady flame, which was more than that perspiring fool of a doctor with letters after his name had been able to say about the Colonel's heart.

It was a provocation, that's what it was, thought the Colonel. Here he was on his deathbed, preparing for oblivion, and she sits over there reading Parson Noah's latest pamphlet. Actively disagreeing right to the end. Colonel Fergusson had long since given up trying to understand the business. How could the child he loved most have failed to inherit either his instincts or the opinions he had with such difficulty acquired? It was vexing. If he hadn't adored her he would have treated her as a credulous imbecile. And still, despite it all, despite this living, fleshly rebuttal, he believed in the world's ability to progress, in man's ascent, in the defeat of superstition. It was all finally very puzzling.

Tick, tick, tick, tick. Tock. The clicking continued overhead. Four, five loud ticks, a silence, then a fainter echo. The Colonel

143

could tell that the noise was distracting Amanda from her pamphlet, though she gave no outward sign. It was simply that he could judge such things after living so closely with her for however many years. He could tell she hadn't really got her nose in the Reverend Abraham. And it was her fault that he could tell, that he knew her so thoroughly. He'd told her to go off and get married when that lieutenant whose name he could never recall had asked her. She'd argued about that, too. She'd said she loved her father more than her uniformed claimant. He'd replied that this wasn't a sound reason, and anyway he'd only die on her. She'd wept and said he wasn't to talk like that. But he'd been right, hadn't he? He was bound to be, wasn't he?

Amanda Fergusson now rested her book on her lap and looked at the ceiling in alarm. The beetle was a harbinger. Everyone knew that its sound portended the death of someone in the house within the year. It was the wisdom of ages. She looked across to see if her father was still awake. Colonel Fergusson had his eyes closed and was breathing out through his nose in long smooth puffs like a bellows. But Amanda knew him well enough to suspect that he might be bluffing. It would be just like him. He had always played tricks on her.

Like that time he'd taken her to Dublin, one blustery day in February of 1821. Amanda was seventeen, and everywhere carried with her a sketching book as she now carried her religious pamphlets. She had lately been excited by reports of the exhibition at Bullock's Egyptian Hall in Piccadilly, London, of Monsieur Jerricault's Great Picture, 24 feet long by 18 feet high, representing the Surviving Crew of the Medusa French Frigate on the Raft. Admission 1s, Description 6d, and 50,000 spectators had paid to see this new masterpiece of foreign art, shown alongside such permanent displays as Mr Bullock's magnificent collection of 25,000 fossils and his Pantherion of stuffed wild beasts. Now the canvas had come to Dublin, where it was put on view at the Rotunda: Admission 1s 8d, Description 5d.

Amanda had been chosen above her five siblings by reason of her precocity with water-colour — at least, this was Colonel

Fergusson's official excuse for indulging his natural preference once again. Except that they did not go, as promised, to the Rotunda, but went instead to a rival attraction advertised in *Saunder's News-Letter & Daily Advertiser*: one, indeed, which ensured that Monsieur Jerricault's Great Picture did not triumph in Dublin as it had done in London. Colonel Fergusson took his daughter to the Pavilion, where they witnessed Messrs Marshall's Marine Peristrephic Panorama of the Wreck of the Medusa French Frigate and the Fatal Raft: Admission front seats 1s 8d, back seats 10d, children in the front seats at half price. 'The Pavilion is always rendered perfectly comfortable by patent stoves'.

Whereas the Rotunda displayed a mere twenty-four feet by eighteen of stationary pigment, here they were offered some 10,000 square feet of mobile canvas. Before their eyes an immense picture, or series of pictures, gradually unwound: not just one scene, but the entire history of the shipwreck passed before them. Episode succeeded episode, while coloured lights played upon the unreeling fabric, and an orchestra emphasized the drama of events. The audience was constantly moved to applause by the spectacle, and Colonel Fergusson would nudge his daughter heavily at some particularly felicitous aspect of the display. In the sixth scene those poor French wretches on the raft were represented in very much the same posture as that in which they had been first delineated by Monsieur Jerricault. But how much grander, Colonel Fergusson observed, to picture their tragic plight with movement and coloured lights, accompanied by music which he identified quite unnecessarily to his daughter as 'Vive Henrico!'

'That is the way forward,' remarked the Colonel with enthusiasm as they left the Pavilion. 'Those painters will have to look to their brushes.'

Amanda did not reply, but the following week she returned to Dublin with one of her five siblings and this time visited the Rotunda. There she greatly admired Monsieur Jerricault's canvas, which though static contained for her much motion and lighting and, in its own way, music – indeed, in some fashion it contained more of these things than did the vulgar Panorama. Upon her return she told her father as much.

Colonel Fergusson nodded indulgently at such pertness and obstinacy, but held his peace. On the 5th of March, however, he jauntily indicated to his favourite daughter a fresh advertisement in *Saunder's News-Letter* announcing that Mr Bullock had reduced – had clearly been *obliged* to reduce, the Colonel interpreted – the price of admission into his immobile spectacle to a mere ten pence. At the end of that month Colonel Fergusson imparted the news that the Frenchy picture at the Rotunda had closed for lack of spectators, whereas Messrs Marshall's Peristrephic Panorama was still being shown three times a day to audiences rendered perfectly comfortable by patent stoves.

'It is the way forward,' the Colonel repeated in June of that year, after attending by himself the farewell performance at the Pavilion.

'Mere novelty is no proof of value,' his daughter had replied, sounding a little too smug for one so young.

Tick, tick, tick, tick. Tock. Colonel Fergusson's faked sleep became more choleric. God damn it, he was thinking, this dying business is difficult. They just won't let you get on with it, not on your own terms, anyway. You have to die on other people's terms, and that's a bore, love them as you might. He opened his eyes and prepared to correct his daughter for the several hundredth occasion in their lives together.

'It's love,' he said suddenly. 'That's all it is.' Amanda's gaze was surprised from the ceiling, and she looked across with brimming eyes. 'It's the love-call of *xestobium rufo-villosum*, for God's sake, girl. Simple as that. Put one of the little fellows in a box and tap on the table with a pencil and he behaves in exactly the same way. Thinks you're a female and butts his head against the box trying to get to you. Speaking of which, why didn't you marry that lieutenant when I told you to? Sheer damn insubordination.' He reached across and took her hand.

But his daughter didn't reply, her eyes continued to overflow, the ticking carried on overhead, and Colonel Fergusson was duly buried before the year's end. On this prediction the doctor and the death-watch beetle had managed to agree.

Amanda's grief for her father was compounded by anxiety over his ontological status. Did his obstinate refusal to acknowledge the divine plan – and his careless use of the Almighty's name even on his deathbed – mean that he was now consigned to outer darkness, to some chilly region unheated by patent stoves? Miss Fergusson knew the Lord to be just, yet merciful. Those who accepted his commandments were to be judged in punctilious accordance with the law, whereas the ignorant savage in the darkened jungle who could not possibly have known the light would be treated with gentleness and given a second chance. But did the category of ignorant savage extend to occupants of cold square houses outside Dublin? Was the pain which unbelievers bore all their lives at the prospect of oblivion to be extended into further pain inflicted for having denied the Lord? Miss Fergusson feared that it might be.

How could her father have failed to recognize God, His eternal design, and its essential goodness? The proof of this plan and of this benevolence lay manifest in Nature, which was provided by God for Man's enjoyment. This did not mean, as some had assumed, that Man might recklessly pillage Nature for what he sought; indeed, Nature was deserving of the more respect because it was a divine creation. But God had created both Man and Nature, placing Man into that Nature as a hand is placed into a glove. Amanda frequently reflected upon the fruits of the field, how various they were, and yet how perfectly each was adapted for Man's enjoyment. For instance, trees bearing edible fruits were made easy to climb, being much lower than forest trees. Fruits which were soft when ripe, such as the apricot, the fig or the mulberry, which might be bruised by falling, presented themselves at a small distance from the ground; whereas hard fruit, which ran no risk of sustaining an injury by a fall, like the cocoa, the walnut or the chestnut, presented themselves at a considerable height. Some fruit – like the cherry and the plum – were moulded for the mouth; others – the apple and the pear – for the hand; others still, like the melon, were made larger, so as to be divided among the family circle. Yet others, like the pumpkin, were made of a size to be shared amongst the whole neighbourhood, and many of these larger fruits were marked on their outer rind with vertical divisions, so as to make apportionment the easier.

Where Amanda discovered in the world divine intent, benevolent order and rigorous justice, her father had seen only chaos, hazard and malice. Yet they were both examining the same world. In the course of their many arguments, Amanda once asked him to consider the domestic condition of the Fergusson family, who lived together with strong bonds of affection, and declare whether they too were the consequence of chaos, hazard and malice. Colonel Fergusson, who could not quite bear to inform his daughter that the human family sprang from the same impulse which animated a beetle striking its head against the walls of its box, replied that in his view the Fergussons were a happy accident. His daughter replied that there were too many happy accidents in the world for them to be accidental.

In part, Amanda reflected, it was a matter of how you perceived things. Her father saw in a vulgar simulacrum of coloured lights and trilling music a true portrayal of a great maritime tragedy; whereas for her the reality was best conveyed by a simple, static canvas adorned with pigment. Mainly, however, it was a question of faith. A few weeks after their visit to the Peristrephic Panorama, her father was rowing her slowly across the serpentine lake on the neighbouring estate of Lord F——. Some connection having been made in his mind, he began to rebuke her for a belief in the reality of Noah's Ark, which he referred to sarcastically as the Myth of the Deluge. Amanda was not discountenanced by the accusation. She replied by asking her father if he believed in the reality of Mr Bullock's Pantherion of stuffed wild beasts at his Egyptian Hall in Piccadilly, London. The Colonel, taken aback, responded that naturally he did; whereupon his daughter exhibited a humorous astonishment. She believed in the reality of something ordained by God and described in a book of Holy Scripture read and remembered for thousands of years; whereas he believed in the reality of something described in the pages of *Saunder's News-Letter & Daily Advertiser*, which people were unlikely to remember the very next morning. Which of them, she insisted upon knowing, with a continuing and unnecessary mockery in her eye, was the more credulous?

It was in the autumn of 1839, after long meditation, that Amanda Fergusson proposed to Miss Logan the expedition to Arghuri. Miss Logan was a vigorous and seemingly practical woman some ten years older than Miss Fergusson, and had been fond of the Colonel without any zephyr of indiscretion arising. More to the point, she had travelled to Italy a few years previously while in the employment of Sir Charles B——.

'I regret that I am unacquainted with the place,' replied Miss Logan when first interviewed. 'Is it far beyond Naples?'

'It is on the lower slopes of Mount Ararat,' Miss Fergusson responded. 'The name Arghuri is derived from two Armenian words signifying *he planted the vine*. It is where Noah returned to his agricultural labours after the Flood. An ancient vine stock planted by the Patriarch's own hands still flourishes.'

Miss Logan concealed her astonishment at this curious lecture, but felt bound to enquire further. 'And why might we be going there?'

'To intercede for the soul of my father. There is a monastery upon the mountain.'

'It is a long way to go.'

'I believe it to be appropriate.'

'I see.' Miss Logan was pensive at first, but then brightened. 'And shall we drink the wine there?' She was remembering her travels in Italy.

'It is forbidden,' replied Miss Fergusson. 'Tradition forbids it.'

'Tradition?'

'Heaven, then. Heaven has forbidden it, in memory of the fault into which the grapes betrayed the Patriarch.' Miss Logan, who would complaisantly allow the Bible to be read to her but was not diligent in turning the pages herself, exhibited a momentary confusion. 'Drunkenness,' explained Miss Fergusson. 'Noah's drunkenness.'

'Of course.'

'The monks of Arghuri are permitted to eat the grapes, but not to ferment them.'

'I see.'

'There is also an ancient willow tree, sprung from one of the planks of Noah's Ark, which grows there.'

'I see.'

And thus it was agreed. They would depart in the spring, to avoid the malarial menace of the later seasons. Each would require a portable bedstead, an air mattress and a pillow; they would take some Oxley's essence of ginger, some good opium, quinine and Sedlitz powders; a portable inkstand, a match-box and supply of German tinder; umbrellas against the sun and flannel belts to ward off cramps of the stomach during the night. After some discussion they decided not to travel with either a portable bath or a patent coffee-machine. But they counted as necessary a pair of iron-pointed walking sticks, a clasp-knife, stout hunting-whips to beat off the legions of dogs they were prepared to encounter and a policeman's small lantern, since they had been warned that Turkish paper lanterns were useless in a hurricane. They took mackintoshes and heavy greatcoats, anticipating that Lady Mary Wortley Montagu's dream of perennial sunshine was unlikely to be fulfilled for lesser voyagers. Miss Logan understood gunpowder to be the most acceptable offering for the Turkish peasant, and writing-paper for the superior classes. A common box-compass, she had further been advised, would afford pleasure by directing the Mussulman to the point of his prayers; but Miss Fergusson was disinclined to assist the heathen in his false adorations. Finally, the ladies packed two small glass bottles, which they intended to fill with grape juice crushed from the fruit of Noah's vineyard.

They travelled by Government steam-packet from Falmouth to Marseilles, thereafter entrusting themselves to the French conveyances. In early May they were received by the British Ambassador in Constantinople. As Miss Fergusson explained the extent and purpose of their journey, the diplomat studied her: a dark-haired woman in early middle age, with protuberant black eyes and rather full, reddish cheeks which pushed her lips forward into a pout. Yet she was in no wise a flirt: her natural expression appeared to mix prudishness with certainty, a combination which left the Ambassador indifferent. He grasped most of what she was saying without ever quite bestowing upon her his full attention.

'Ah,' he said at the finish, 'there was a rumour a few years ago that some Russo had managed to get to the top of the mountain.'

'Parrot,' replied Miss Fergusson without a smile. 'Not a Russo, I think. Dr Friedrich Parrot. Professor in the University of Dorpat.'

The Ambassador gave a diagonal nod of the head, as if it were slightly impertinent to know more than he did about local matters.

'It seems to me appropriate and just,' went on Miss Fergusson, 'that the first traveller to ascend the mountain upon which the Ark rested should bear the name of an animal. No doubt part of the Lord's great design for us all.'

'No doubt,' replied the Ambassador, looking away to Miss Logan for some clue as to the personality of her employer. 'No doubt.'

They remained a week in the Ottoman capital, by no means long enough for Miss Logan to become accustomed to the coarse stares she received at the *tables d'hôte*. Then the two ladies gave themselves up to the Favaid-i-Osmaniyeh, a Turkish company running steamers to Trebizond. The accommodation was crowded and to Miss Logan's mind far filthier than anything she had previously encountered. She ventured upon deck the first morning, and was approached by not one but three potential beaux, each with his hair curled and exuding a powerful odour of bergamot. Thereafter Miss Logan, despite having been engaged for her experience, confined herself to the cabin. Miss Fergusson professed not to notice such inconveniences and to be positively intrigued by the scrum of third-class passengers on board; she would occasionally return with an observation or a question designed to stir Miss Logan from her dismal state of mind. Why, her employer wished to know, were the Turkish women all accommodated on the left-hand side of the quarter-deck? Was there some purpose, be it of society or of religion, behind such positioning? Miss Logan was unable to furnish a reply. Now that they had left Naples way behind them she felt increasingly less secure. At the faintest whiff of bergamot she shuddered.

When Miss Logan had permitted herself to become engaged for the voyage to Asiatic Turkey, she had under-estimated Miss Fergusson's pertinacity. The absconding muleteer, the swindling innkeeper and the devious customs-house officer were all treated to the same display of unthwartable will. Miss Logan lost count of the times their luggage was detained, or they were told that a *buyurulda* or special permit would be necessary in addition to the *tezkare* they had already procured; but Miss Fergusson, with assistance from a dragoman whose own brief display of independent thought had been snuffed out early on, harried, demanded and succeeded. She was tirelessly willing to discuss things in the manner of the country; to sit down with a landlord, for example, and answer such questions as whether England was smaller than London, and which of the two belonged to France, and how much larger the Turkish navy was than those of England, France and Russia put together.

Miss Logan had further imagined that their journey, while devotional in its final purpose, might afford pleasant opportunities for sketching, the activity which had first established a bond between employer and companion. But antiquities held no charm for Amanda Fergusson; she had no desire to examine heathen temples to Augustus, or half-surviving columns supposedly erected in honour of the apostate Emperor Julian. At least she evinced an interest in the natural landscape. As they rode inland from Trebizond, hunting-whips at the ready against the expected dog-packs, they viewed mohair goats on hillsides of dwarf oak, dull yellow vines, lush apple orchards; they heard grasshoppers whose ringing note seemed sharper and more insistent than that of their British cousins; and they witnessed sunsets of the rarest purple and rose. There were fields of corn, opium and cotton; bursts of rhododendron and yellow azalea; red-legged partridge, hoopoes and blue crows. In the Zirgana mountains large red deer softly returned their gaze from an apprehensive distance.

At Erzerum Miss Logan prevailed upon her employer to visit the Christian church. The impulse proved at first a happy one, for in the graveyard Miss Fergusson discovered tombstones and crosses whose Celtic air recalled those of her native Ireland; a smile of approval crossed her dutiful features. But this unexpected lenity was short-lived. Leaving the church, the two ladies noticed a young peasant woman placing a votive offering in a crevice by the main door. It proved to be a human tooth, no doubt her own. The crevice, upon further examination, was found to be stuffed full of yellowing incisors and weathered molars. Miss Fergusson expressed herself forcibly on the subject of popular superstition and the responsibility of the clergy. Those who preached the word of God, she maintained, should be judged according to the word of God, and punished the more severely if found wanting.

They crossed into Russia, engaging at the frontier post a new guide, a large and bearded Kurd who claimed familiarity with the requirements of foreigners. Miss Fergusson addressed him in what seemed to Miss Logan a mixture of Russo and Turk. The days when Miss Logan's fluent Italian had been of use to them were long past; having begun the journey as guide and interpreter, she felt she had dwindled into a mere hanger-on, with little greater status than the discarded dragoman or the newly appointed Kurd.

As the three of them proceeded into Caucasia, they disturbed flocks of pelican, whose earthbound ungainliness was miraculously transfigured by flight. Miss Fergusson's irritation over the incident in Erzerum began to calm. Passing the eastern spur of Mount Alageuz, they gazed intently as the broad bulk of Great Ararat slowly revealed itself. The summit was hidden, enfolded in a circle of white cloud which glittered brilliantly in the sun.

'It has a halo,' exclaimed Miss Logan. 'Like an angel.'

'You are correct,' Miss Fergusson replied, with a little nod. 'People like my father would not agree, of course. They would tell us that such comparisons are all hot air. Literally.' She gave a pursed smile and Miss Logan, with an enquiring glance, invited her to continue. 'They would explain that the halo of cloud is a perfectly natural phenomenon. During the night and for several hours after dawn the summit remains clearly visible, but as the plain warms up in the morning sun, the hot air rises and becomes vapour at a given height. At the day's end, when everything cools down again, the halo disappears. It comes as no surprise to . . . science,' she said with a disapproving emphasis upon the final word.

'It is a magic mountain,' commented Miss Logan.

Her employer corrected her. 'It is a *holy* mountain.' She gave an impatient sigh. 'There always appear to be two explanations of everything. That is why we have been given free will, in order that we may choose the correct one. My father failed to comprehend that his explanations were based as much upon faith as mine. Faith in nothing. It would be all vapour and clouds and rising air to him. But who created the vapour, who created the clouds? Who ensured that Noah's mountain of all mountains would be blessed each day with a halo of cloud?'

'Exactly,' said Miss Logan, not entirely in agreement.

That day they encountered an Armenian priest who informed them that the mountain towards which they were heading had never been ascended and, moreover, never would be. When Miss Fergusson politely suggested the name of Dr Parrot, the priest assured her that she was mistaken. Perhaps she was confusing Massis – as he referred to Great Ararat – with the volcano far to the south which the Turks called Sippan Dagh. The Ark of Noah, before it found its final resting-place, had struck the summit of Sippan Dagh and removed its cap, thereby exposing the inner fires of the earth. That mountain, he understood, was accessible to man, but not Massis. On this subject, if on nothing else, Christian and Mussulman agreed. And furthermore, went on the priest, was it not so proven by Holy Scripture? The mountain before them was the birthplace of mankind; and he referred the ladies, while excusing himself with an ingratiating laugh for mentioning an indelicate subject, to the authority of Our Saviour's words to Nicodemus, where it is stated that a man cannot enter a second time into his mother's womb and be born once more.

As they were parting, the priest drew from his pocket a small black amulet, worn smooth over many centuries. It was, he claimed, a piece of bitumen which assuredly had once formed part of the hull of Noah's Ark, and had great value in the averting of mischief. Since the ladies had expressed such interest in the mountain of Massis, then perhaps . . .

Miss Fergusson courteously responded to the suggested transaction by pointing out that if indeed it was impossible to ascend the mountain, then the likelihood of their believing that the amulet could be a piece of bitumen from the Patriarch's vessel was not very great. The Armenian, however, saw no incompatibility between his two propositions. Perhaps a bird had carried it down, as the dove had borne the olive branch. Or it might have been brought by an angel. Did not tradition relate how Saint James had three times attempted to ascend Massis, and on the third occasion been told by an angel that it was forbidden, but that the angel had given him a plank of wood from the Ark, and there where he had received it was founded the monastery of Saint James?

They parted without a bargain being struck. Miss Logan, embarrassed by Our Lord's words to Nicodemus, was instead thinking about bitumen: was that not the material used by artists to blacken the shadows in their paintings? Miss Fergusson, on the other hand, had merely been put into a temper: first by the attempt to thrust some foolish meaning on to the scriptural verse; and secondly by the priest's brazen commercial behaviour. She had yet to be impressed by the Eastern clergy, who not only countenanced belief in the miraculous powers of human teeth, but actually traded in bogus religious relics. It was monstrous. They should be punished for it. No doubt they would be. Miss Logan examined her employer apprehensively.

The next day they crossed a relentless plain of reeds and coarse grass, relieved only by colonies of bustard and the black tents of Kurdish tribesmen. They stopped for the night in a small village a day's ride from the foot of the mountain. After a meal of cream cheese and salted salmon trout from the Gokchai, the two women stood in the dark air scented with apricot and looked towards the mountain of Noah. The range before them contained two separate crescendi: Great Ararat, a bulky, broad-shouldered mass like a buttressed dome, and Little Ararat, some four thousand feet lower, an elegant cone with smooth and regular sides. Miss Fergusson did not think it fanciful to perceive in the comparative design and height of the two Ararats a bodying-forth of that primal divide in the human race between the two sexes. She did not communicate this reflection to Miss Logan, who had so far proved dismally unreceptive to the transcendental.

As if to confirm her pedestrian turn of mind, Miss Logan at this point revealed that it had been a matter of curiosity to her since childhood how the Ark had succeeded in resting upon the top of a mountain. Had the peak risen up from the waters and punctured the keel, thereby skewering the vessel in place? For if not, how otherwise had the Ark avoided a precipitous descent as the waters had retreated?

'Others before you have had similar reflections,' replied Miss Fergusson with distinct lack of indulgence. 'Marco Polo insisted that the mountain was made in the shape of a cube, which would certainly have explained the matter. My father would probably have agreed with him, had he given the subject his attention. But we can see that this is not the case. Those who have ascended to the peak of Great Ararat inform us that close below the summit there is a gently sloping valley. It is', she specified, as if Miss Logan could not otherwise understand the matter, 'approximately half the size of Green Park in London. As a place of disembarkation it would be both natural and safe.'

'So the Ark did not land on the very summit?'

'Scripture makes no such claim.'

As they approached Arghuri, which lay at a height of more than six thousand feet above sea level, the temperature of the air became more genial. Three miles below the village they came upon the first of the hallowed plantations of Father Noah. The vines had just finished flowering, and tiny dark green grapes hung intermittently among the foliage. A peasant put down his rough hoe and conducted the unexpected party to the village elder, who received their offering of gunpowder with formal thanks yet little surprise. Miss Logan was sometimes irked by such civility. The elder was behaving as if parties of white women were constantly presenting him with gunpowder.

Miss Fergusson, however, remained her dutiful and efficient self. It was arranged that later in the afternoon they would be conducted to the Monastery of Saint James; they would be lodged that night in the village, and would return again to the church the following day for their devotions.

The monastery lay beside the Arghuri rivulet in the lower part of a great chasm which extended almost to the very summit of the mountain. It consisted of a cruciform church whose stone was hewn from hardened lava. Various small dwellings pressed against its sides like the farrow of a sow. As the party entered the courtyard a middle-aged priest stood waiting for them, the cupola of Saint James rising behind him. He was dressed in a plain gown of blue serge, with a pointed Capuchin cowl; his beard was long, its blackness intertwined with grey; on his feet he wore woollen Persian socks and common slippers. One hand bore the rosary; the other was folded across his chest in a gesture of welcome. Something urged Miss Logan to kneel before the pastor of Noah's church; but the presence and certain disapproval of Miss Fergusson, who dismissed as 'Romish' a large category of religious behaviour, prevented her.

The courtyard spoke less of a monastery than a farm. Sacks of corn were piled loosely against a wall; three sheep had wandered in from the nearby pasture and had not been expelled; there was a rank smell from underfoot. Smiling, the Archimandrite invited them to his cell, which proved to be one of the tiny dwellings built hard against the outer wall of the church. As he was conducting them across the dozen or so yards, the Archimandrite appeared to touch Miss Fergusson's elbow by way of courteous but strictly unnecessary guidance.

The monk's cell had stout clay walls and a plaster roof supported by a sturdy central prop. There was a rough icon of some unidentifiable saint hanging above a straw pallet; the courtyard odours continued here. To Miss Logan it seemed admirably simple, to Miss Fergusson squalid. The behaviour of the Archimandrite also provoked differing interpretations: Miss Logan discerned an amiable candour where Miss Fergusson saw only sly obsequiousness. It seemed to Miss Logan that her employer had perhaps exhausted her stock of civility on the long journey to Mount Ararat, and had now retreated into a stony carelessness. When the Archimandrite suggested that the two ladies might like to lodge at the monastery that night, she was briefly dismissive; when he pressed his offer of hospitality further, she was brusque.

The Archimandrite continued to smile, and his mood still appeared to Miss Logan a gracious one. At this point a servant appeared bearing a rough tray on which were set three horn beakers. Water from the Arghuri brook, thought Miss Logan; or perhaps that sourish milk which they had already received many times on their travels from obliging shepherds. But the servant returned with a wineskin, and at a signal poured a liquor from it into the horn vessels. The Archimandrite raised his beaker towards the women, and drank fully; whereupon his servant poured for him again.

Miss Fergusson sipped. Then she put questions to the Archimandrite which provoked a severe apprehension in Miss Logan. This feeling was exacerbated by waiting for the guide to translate.

'This is wine?'

'Indeed.' The priest smiled, as if encouraging the women to indulge in this local taste which was still clearly unknown in their distant land.

'It is made from grapes?'

'You are correct, lady.'

'Tell me, the grapes from which this wine has been made, where are they grown?'

The Archimandrite spread both hands and circled to indicate the neighbouring countryside.

'And the vines from which the grapes were plucked, who first planted them?'

'Our great ancestor and forefather, parent of us all, Noah.'

Miss Fergusson summed up the exchange so far, needless as this seemed to her companion. 'You are serving us the fermented grapes from Noah's vines?'

'It is my honour, Madam.' He smiled again. He seemed to expect if not especial thanks, at least some expression of wonder. Instead, Miss Fergusson stood up, took the untasted wine from Miss Logan, and returned both beakers to the servant. Without a word she left the Archimandrite's cell, swept from the courtyard in a manner which made three sheep instinctively follow her and started down the mountainside. Miss Logan made indeterminate gestures to the priest, then set off in pursuit of her employer. They traversed lush apricot orchards without comment; they ignored a shepherd holding out a bowl of milk; wordlessly they returned to the village, where Miss Fergusson, her calculated civility now restored to her, asked the elder if lodgings could be supplied to them without delay. The old man proposed his own house, the largest in Arghuri. Miss Fergusson thanked him, and offered in return a small parcel of sugar, which was gravely accepted.

That evening in their room a low table no bigger than a music stool was set with food. They were given *losh*, the thin local bread, cold mutton cut in pieces, hard-boiled eggs taken from their shells and halved, and the fruit of the arbutus. They were served no wine, either because such was the custom of the house, or because intelligence of their visit to the monastery had reached the elder. Instead, they drank sheep's milk once more.

'It is a blasphemy,' said Miss Fergusson eventually. 'A blasphemy. On Noah's mountain. He lives like a farmer. He invites women to stay with him. He ferments the grape of the Patriarch. It is a blasphemy.'

Miss Logan knew better than to reply, let alone plead the cause of the amiable Archimandrite. She recalled to herself that the circumstances of their visit had deprived them of an opportunity to examine the ancient willow tree sprung from a plank of Noah's Ark.

'We shall ascend the mountain,' said Miss Fergusson.

'But we do not know how to do such a thing.'

'We shall ascend the mountain. Sin must be purged with water. The sin of the world was purged by the waters of the flood. It is a double blasphemy that the monk commits. We shall fill our bottles with snow from the holy mountain. The pure juice of Noah's vine we came in search of has been rendered impure. We shall bring back purging water instead. That is the only way to salvage the journey.'

Miss Logan nodded, in startled acquiescence rather than agreement.

They set off from the village of Arghuri on the morning of June 20th, in the year of Our Lord 1840, accompanied only by their Kurdish guide. The elder regretfully explained the villagers' belief that the mountain was sacred, and that no-one should venture upon it higher than the Monastery of Saint James. He himself shared these beliefs. He did not try to dissuade the party from their ascent, but he did insist on loaning Miss Fergusson a pistol. This she displayed at her belt, though she had neither the intention nor the resource to use it. Miss Logan carried a small bag of lemons, which had also been advised.

The ladies rode with white umbrellas raised against the morning sun. Looking upwards, Miss Fergusson observed the halo of cloud beginning to form itself around the summit of the mountain. A daily miracle, she noted to herself. For several hours they appeared to make little progress; they were traversing a barren region of fine sand and yellowish clay, broken only by a few stunted, prickly bushes. Miss Logan observed several butterflies and numerous lizards, but was secretly disappointed that so few of the creatures which had descended from the Ark were manifesting themselves. She had, she admitted to herself, foolishly pictured the slopes of the mountain as a kind of zoological garden. But the animals had been told to go forth and multiply. They must have obeyed.

They dipped into rocky ravines, none of which contained the smallest stream. It seemed an arid mountain, as dry as a chalk down in Sussex. Then, a little higher, it surprised them, suddenly unveiling green pasture and rose bushes with delicate pink blossom. They rounded a spur and came upon a small encampment – three or four rude tents, with matting walls and black roofs made from goats' hair. Miss Logan was slightly alarmed by the sudden presence of this group of nomads, whose flock could be seen lower down the slope, but Miss Fergusson directed her horse straight towards them. A ferocious-looking man whose tangled hair resembled the roof of his own tent held up to them a rough bowl. It contained sourish milk mixed with water, and Miss Logan drank somewhat nervously. They nodded, smiled and continued on their way.

'Did you judge that a natural gesture of hospitality?' asked Amanda Fergusson suddenly.

Miss Logan considered this strange question. 'Yes,' she responded, for they had previously come across many similar instances of such behaviour.

'My father would have said it was merely an animal bribe to turn away the wrath of strangers. It would be an article of faith with him to believe that. He would have said those nomads were just like beetles.'

'Like beetles?'

'My father was interested in beetles. He told me that if you put one in a box and tapped on the lid, it would knock back, thinking you were another beetle offering itself in marriage.'

'I do not consider that they were behaving like beetles,' said Miss Logan, while carefully indicating by her tone that this was only her private opinion and in no way derogatory of Colonel Fergusson.

'Nor do I.'

Miss Logan did not fully understand her employer's condition of mind. Having come this great distance to intercede for her father, she now seemed instead to be constantly arguing with his shade.

At the first steep slope of Great Ararat they tethered their horses to a thorn tree and hobbled them. They were to proceed from here on foot. Miss Fergusson, umbrella aloft and pistol at her belt, led the way with the certain tread of the righteous; Miss Logan, dangling her bag of lemons, struggled to keep up as the terrain grew more precipitous; their Kurdish guide, weighed down with baggage, brought up the rear. They would be obliged to spend two nights on the mountain if they were to reach the snowline.

They had climbed hard all afternoon, and shortly before seven o'clock, with the sky softening towards apricot, were resting on a rocky outcrop. At first they did not identify the noise, or what it signified. They were aware of a low rumble, a granite growl, though whence it came, whether from above or below them, was not evident. Then the ground beneath their feet began to vibrate, and there came a noise like thunder – but internal, suppressed, terrifying thunder, the sound of a primeval, subterranean god raging against his confinement. Miss Logan glanced fearfully at her employer. Amanda Fergusson was directing her field-glasses at the Monastery of Saint James, and her face bore an expression of prim pleasure which shocked her companion. Miss Logan was near-sighted, and consequently it was from Miss Fergusson's features rather than from personal observation that she grasped what was happening. When the field-glasses were finally passed to her she was able to confirm that every roof and every wall of the monastery church and of the little community they had left only that morning had been thrown down by the violent commotion.

Miss Fergusson got to her feet and briskly began to continue the ascent.

'Are we not to help the survivors?' asked Miss Logan in perplexity.

'There will not be any,' replied her employer. Adding in a

sharper tone, 'It was a punishment they should have foreseen.'

'A punishment?'

'For disobedience. For fermenting the fruit of Noah's vine. For building a church and then blaspheming within it.' Miss Logan looked at Amanda Fergusson cautiously, unsure how to express the view that to her humble and ignorant mind the punishment seemed excessive. 'This is a holy mountain,' said Miss Fergusson coldly. 'The mountain upon which Noah's Ark rested. A small sin is a great sin in this place.'

Miss Logan did not break her alarmed silence; she merely followed her employer, who was pushing on ahead up a gully of rock. At the top Miss Fergusson waited and then turned to her. 'You expect God to be like the Lord Chief Justice in London. You expect a whole speech of explanation. The God of this mountain is the God who saved only Noah and his family out of the whole world. Remember that.'

Miss Logan grew seriously perturbed at these observations. Was Miss Fergusson comparing the earthquake which had thrown down the village of Arghuri to the great Flood itself? Was she likening the salvation of two white women and a Kurd to that of Noah's family? When preparing for their expedition they had been told that the magnetic compass was useless on such mountains as these, for the rocks were loaded with iron. It seemed evident that you could lose your bearing here in other ways as well.

What was she doing on Noah's mountain alongside a pilgrim turned fanatic and a bearded peasant with whom she could not communicate, while the rock below them exploded like the gunpowder they had brought to ingratiate themselves with the local chieftains? Everything urged them to go down, yet they were continuing upwards. The Kurd, whom she had expected to flee at the first shaking of the ground, was staying with them. Perhaps he intended to slit their throats while they slept.

They rested that night and continued climbing as soon as the sun rose. Their white umbrellas stood out vividly against the harsh terrain of the mountain. Here was only bare rock and gravel; nothing grew but lichen; all was utterly dry. They might have been upon the surface of the moon.

They climbed until they reached the first pocket of snow, which lay in a long, dark slash on the mountain's side. They were three thousand feet from the peak, just below a cornice of ice which encircled Great Ararat. It was here that the rising air from the plain turned to vapour and formed the miraculous halo. The sky above them was beginning to turn a brightish green, scarcely blue at all any more. Miss Logan felt very cold.

The two bottles were filled with snow and entrusted to the guide. Later, Miss Logan would try picturing to herself her employer's curious serenity of face and confidence of carriage as they started down the mountain; she exhibited contentment bordering on smugness. They had travelled no more than a few hundred yards – the Kurd leading, Miss Logan bringing up the rear – and were crossing a patch of rough scree, a descent more tiring than dangerous, when Miss Fergusson fell. She pitched forwards and sideways, sliding a dozen yards down the slope before the Kurd was able to arrest her progress. Miss Logan halted, initially in surprise, for it appeared that Miss Fergusson had lost her footing on a little stretch of solid rock which should have afforded no peril.

She was smiling when they reached her, apparently unconcerned by the blood. Miss Logan would not allow the Kurd to bandage Miss Fergusson; she accepted pieces of his shirt for the purpose, but then insisted that he turn his back. After half an hour or so, the two of them restored their employer to her feet, and they set off again, Miss Fergusson leaning on the guide's arm with a strange nonchalance, as if she were being conducted round a cathedral or a zoological garden.

They made only a short distance in the remainder of that day, for Miss Fergusson demanded frequent rests. Miss Logan calculated how far away their horses were tethered, and was not encouraged. Towards nightfall they came upon a pair of small caves, which Miss Fergusson compared to the pressing of God's thumb into the mountainside. The Kurd entered the first of them cautiously, sniffing for wild beasts, then beckoned them in. Miss Logan prepared the bedding and administered some opium; the guide, after making gestures incomprehensible to her, vanished. He returned an hour later with a few stunted bushes he had managed to prise from the rock. He made a fire; Miss Fergusson lay down, took some water, and slept.

When she awoke she pronounced herself feeble, and said her bones were stiff in her skin. She had neither strength nor hunger. They waited through that day in the cave, trusting that Miss Fergusson's condition would improve by the next morning. Miss Logan began to reflect upon the changes in her employer since they had arrived on the mountain. Their purpose in coming here had been to intercede for the soul of Colonel Fergusson. Yet so far they had not prayed; Amanda Fergusson appeared still to be arguing with her father; while the God she had taken to proclaiming did not sound the kind of God who would lightly forgive the Colonel's obstinate sinning against the light. Had Miss Fergusson realized, or at least decided, that her father's soul was lost, cast out, condemned? Is that what had happened?

As evening fell, Miss Fergusson told her companion to leave the cave while she spoke to the guide. This seemed unnecessary, for Miss Logan had not a word of Turk or Russo or Kurdish or whatever mixture it was the other two communicated in; but she did as she was told. She stood outside looking up at a creamy moon, fearful lest some bat might fly into her hair.

'You are to move me so that I may see the moon.' They lifted her gently, as if she were an old lady, and placed her nearer the mouth of the cave. 'You are to set off at first light tomorrow. Whether you return or not is immaterial.' Miss Logan nodded. She did not argue because she knew she would not win; she did not weep because she knew she would be rebuked. 'I shall remember the Holy Scripture and wait for God's will. On this mountain God's will is quite manifest. I cannot imagine a happier place from which to be taken unto Him.'

Miss Logan and the Kurd took turns watching over her that night. The moon, now almost full, illuminated the floor of the cave where Amanda Fergusson lay. 'My father would have

wanted music with it,' she said at one point. Miss Logan smiled
an agreement which irritated her employer. 'You cannot possibly know to what I am referring.' Miss Logan immediately
agreed a second time.

There was a silence. The dry cold air was scented with
woodsmoke. 'He thought pictures should move. With lights
and music and patent stoves. He thought that was the future.'
Miss Logan, little better informed than before, considered it
safest not to respond. 'But it was not the future. Look at the
moon. The moon does not require music and coloured lights.'

Miss Logan did win one small, final argument – by forceful
gesture rather than words – and Miss Fergusson was left with
both bottles of molten snow. She also accepted a couple of
lemons. At daybreak Miss Logan, now wearing the pistol at her
belt, set off down the mountain with the guide. She felt resolved
in spirit but uncertain how best to proceed. She imagined, for
instance, that if the inhabitants of Arghuri had been unwilling
to venture on to the mountain before the earthquake, any
survivors would scarcely be ready to do so now. She might be
compelled to seek help in a more distant village.

The horses were gone. The Kurd made a long noise in his
throat which she presumed to indicate disappointment. The
tree to which they had been tethered was still there, but the
horses had disappeared. Miss Logan imagined them panicking
as the ground raged beneath them, tearing themselves free and
violently bearing away their hobbles as they fled from the
mountain. Later, as she trudged behind the Kurd towards the
village of Arghuri, Miss Logan envisaged an alternative explanation: the horses being stolen by those hospitable nomads
encountered that first morning.

The Monastery of Saint James had been quite destroyed, and
they passed it without halting. As they neared the ruins of
Arghuri, the Kurd indicated that Miss Logan was to wait for
him while he investigated the village. Twenty minutes later he
returned, shaking his head in a universal gesture. As they
skirted the wrecked houses, Miss Logan could not help observ-
ing to herself that the earthquake had killed all the inhabitants

while leaving intact those vines which — if Miss Fergusson should be believed — were the very source of their temptation and their punishment.

It took them two days before they reached human habitation. In a hill village to the south-west, the guide delivered her to the house of an Armenian priest who spoke passable French. She explained the need to raise an immediate rescue party and return to Great Ararat. The priest replied that no doubt the Kurd was organizing the relief at that very moment. Something in his demeanour indicated that perhaps he did not quite believe her story of having climbed most of the way up Massis, which peasants and holy men alike knew to be inaccessible.

She waited all day for the Kurd to return, but he failed to do so; and when she made enquiries the next morning she was told that he had left the town within minutes of conducting her to the priest's house. Miss Logan was angry and distressed at such Judas-like behaviour, and expressed herself forcibly on the subject to the Armenian priest, who nodded and offered to say prayers for Miss Fergusson. Miss Logan accepted, while wondering about the efficacy of mere unadorned prayer in a region where people yielded up their teeth as votive offerings.

Only several weeks later, as she lay stifling in her cabin on a filthy steamer from Trebizond, did she reflect that the Kurd, in the whole time he had been with them, had executed Miss Fergusson's commands with punctiliousness and honour; further, that she had no means of knowing what had passed between the two of them that last night in the cave. Perhaps Miss Fergusson had instructed the guide to lead her companion to a place of safety, and then desert.

Miss Logan also reflected upon Miss Fergusson's fall. They had been crossing a scree; there had been many loose stones, and footing was difficult, but surely at that point they had been traversing a gentler slope, and her employer had actually been standing on a flattish stretch of granite when she had fallen. It was a magnetic mountain where a compass did not work, and it was easy to lose your bearing. No, that was not it. The question she was avoiding was whether Miss Fergusson might not have been the instrument of her own precipitation, in order to achieve or confirm whatever it was she wanted to achieve or confirm. Miss Fergusson had maintained, when they first stood before the haloed mountain, that there were two explanations of everything, that each required the exercise of faith, and that we had been given free will in order that we might choose between them. This dilemma was to preoccupy Miss Logan for years to come.

7

THREE SIMPLE
STORIES

I

I WAS A NORMAL eighteen-year-old: shuttered, self-conscious, untravelled and sneering; violently educated, socially crass, emotionally blurting. At least, all the other eighteen-year-olds I knew were like this, so I presumed it was normal. I was waiting to go up to university and had just got a job as a prep-school master. The fiction I had read predicted gaudy roles for me — as private tutor at the old stone mansion where peacocks roost in the yew hedges and chalky bones are discovered in the sealed-up priest's hole; as gullible ingénu at an eccentric private establishment on the Welsh borders stuffed with robust drunkards and covert lechers. There would be careless girls and unimpressable butlers. You know the social moral of the story: the meritocrat becomes infected with snobbery.

Reality proved more local. I taught for a term at a crammer half a mile from my home, and instead of passing lazy days with charming children whose actively hatted mothers would smile, condescend and yet flirt during some endless pollen-spattered sports day, I spent my time with the son of the local bookmaker (he lent me his bike: I crashed it) and the daughter of the suburb's solicitor. Yet half a mile is a fine distance to the untravelled; and at eighteen the smallest gradations of middle-class society thrill and daunt. The school came with a family attached; the family lived in a house. Everything here was different and therefore better: the stiff-backed brass taps, the cut of the banister, the genuine oil paintings (we had a genuine oil painting too, but not as genuine as that), the library which somehow was more than just a roomful of books, the furniture old enough to have woodworm in it, and the casual acceptance of inherited things. In the hall hung the amputated blade of an oar: inscribed in gold lettering on its black scoop were the names of a college eight, each of whom had been awarded such a trophy in sun-ridden pre-war days; the item seemed impossibly exotic. There was an air-raid shelter in the front garden which at home would have provoked embarrassment and been subjected to vigorous camouflage with hardy perennials; here it evoked no more than amused pride. The family matched the house. The father was a spy; the mother had been an actress; the son wore tab collars and double-breasted waistcoats. Need I say more? Had I read enough French novels at the time, I would have known what to expect; and of course it was here that I fell in love for the first time. But that is another story, or at least another chapter.

It was the grandfather who had founded the school, and he still lived on the premises. Although in his mid-eighties, he had only recently been written out of the curriculum by some crafty predecessor of mine. He was occasionally to be seen wandering through the house in his cream linen jacket, college tie – Gonville and Caius, you were meant to know – and flat cap (in our house a flat cap would have been common; here it was posh and probably indicated that you used to go beagling). He was searching for 'his class', which he never found, and talked about 'the laboratory', which was no more than a back kitchen with a bunsen burner and running water. On warm afternoons he would sit outside the front door with a Roberts portable radio (the all-wood construction, I learned, gave better sound quality than the plastic or metal bodies of the transistors I admired), listening to the cricket commentary. His name was Lawrence Beesley.

Apart from my great-grandfather, he was the oldest man I had ever met. His age and status induced in me the normal mixture of deference, fear and cheek. His decrepitude – the historically stained clothes, that dangle of egg-white slobber from the chin – set off in me a general adolescent anger against life and its inevitable valedictory condition; a feeling which smoothly translated itself into hatred of the person undergoing that condition. His daughter fed him on tins of baby food, which again confirmed for me the sour joke of existence and the particular contemptibility of this old man. I used to tell him invented cricket scores. '84 for 2, Mr Beesley,' I would shout as I passed him snoozing in the sun beneath the gangling wisteria. 'West Indies 790 for 3 declared,' I would insist as I delivered him his child's dinner on a tray. I would tell him scores from matches that were not being played, scores from matches that could never have been played, fanciful scores, impossible scores. He would nod in reply, and I would creep away, sniggering at my tiny cruelty, pleased that I was not such a nice young man as he might have imagined.

Fifty-two years before I met him, Lawrence Beesley had been a second-class passenger on the maiden voyage of the *Titanic*. He was thirty-five, had recently given up his job as science master at Dulwich College and was crossing the Atlantic – according to subsequent family legend, at least – in half-hearted pursuit of an American heiress. When the *Titanic* struck its iceberg, Beesley escaped in the underpopulated Lifeboat 13, and was picked up by the *Carpathia*. Among the souvenirs this octogenarian survivor kept in his room was a blanket embroidered with the name of the rescuing ship. The more sceptical members of his family maintained that the blanket had acquired its lettering at a date considerably later than 1912. They also amused themselves with the speculation that their ancestor had escaped from the *Titanic* in women's clothing. Was it not the case that Beesley's name had been omitted from the initial list of those saved, and actually included among the drowned in the final casualty bulletin? Surely this was solid confirmation of the hypothesis that the false corpse turned mystery survivor had taken to petticoats and a high voice until safely landed in New York, where he surreptitiously discarded his drag in a subway toilet?

I supported this theory with pleasure, because it confirmed my view of the world. In the autumn of that year I was to wedge into the mirror of my college bedsitting-room a piece of paper bearing the following lines: 'Life's a cheat and all things shew it/I thought so once and now I know it.' Beesley's case offered corroboration: the hero of the *Titanic* was a blanket-forger and transvestite imposter; how just and appropriate, therefore, that I fed him false cricket scores. And on a wider scale, theorists maintained that life amounted to the survival of the fittest: did not the Beesley hypothesis prove that the 'fittest' were merely the most cunning? The heroes, the solid men of yeoman virtue, the good breeding stock, even the captain (especially the captain!) – they all went down nobly with the ship; whereas the cowards, the panickers, the deceivers found reasons for skulking in a lifeboat. Was this not deft proof of how the human gene-pool was constantly deteriorating, how bad blood drove out good?

Lawrence Beesley made no mention of female dress in his book *The Loss of the Titanic*. Installed at a Boston residential club by the American publishers Houghton Mifflin, he wrote the account in six weeks; it came out less than three months after the sinking it describes, and has been reprinted at intervals ever since. It made Beesley one of the best-known survivors of the disaster, and for fifty years – right up to the time I met him – he was regularly consulted by maritime historians, film researchers, journalists, souvenir hunters, bores, conspiracy theorists and vexatious litigants. When other ships were sunk by icebergs he would be telephoned by newsmen eager for him to imagine the fate of the victims.

Forty or so years after his escape he was engaged as a consultant on the film *A Night to Remember*, made at Pinewood. Much of the movie was shot after dark, with a half-size replica of the vessel poised to sink into a sea of ruckled black velvet. Beesley watched the action with his daughter on several successive evenings, and what follows is based upon the account she gave to me. Beesley was – not surprisingly – intrigued by the reborn and once-again-teetering *Titanic*. In particular, he was keen to be among the extras who despairingly crowded the rail as the ship went down – keen, you could say, to undergo in fiction an alternative version of history. The film's director was equally determined that this consultant who lacked the necessary card from the actors' union should not appear on celluloid. Beesley, adept in any emergency, counterfeited the pass required to let him board the facsimile *Titanic*, dressed himself in period costume (can echoes prove the truth of the thing being echoed?) and installed himself among the extras. The film lights were turned on and the crowd briefed about their imminent deaths in the ruckled black velvet. Right at the last minute, as the cameras were due to roll, the director spotted that Beesley had managed to insinuate himself to the ship's rail; picking up his megaphone, he instructed the amateur imposter kindly to disembark. And so, for the second time in his life, Lawrence Beesley found himself leaving the *Titanic* just before it was due to go down.

Being a violently educated eighteen-year-old, I was familiar with Marx's elaboration of Hegel: history repeats itself, the first time as tragedy, the second time as farce. But I had yet to come across an illustration of this process. Years later I have still to discover a better one.

II

WHAT WAS JONAH doing inside the whale in the first place? It's a fishy story, as you might expect.

It all began when God instructed Jonah to go and preach against Nineveh, a place which, despite God's substantial record of annihilating wicked cities, was still – obstinately, unaccountably – a wicked city. Jonah, disliking the task for unexplained reasons which might have had something to do with a fear of being stoned to death by the partying Ninevites, ran away. At Joppa he embarked on a boat to the farthest end of the known world: Tarshish, in Spain. He failed to understand, of course, that the Lord knew exactly where he was, and what's more had operative control over the winds and waters of the

Eastern Mediterranean. When a storm of rare violence blew up, the mariners, being superstitious folk, cast lots to determine which of those on board was the cause of the evil, and the short straw, broken domino or queen of spades was drawn by Jonah. He was promptly pitched overboard and just as promptly swallowed by a great fish or whale which the Lord had directed through the waters for this especial purpose.

Inside the whale, for three days and three nights, Jonah prayed to the Lord and swore his future obedience so convincingly that God ordered the fish to vomit up the penitent. Not surprisingly, the next time the Almighty posted him to Nineveh, Jonah did as he was told. He went and denounced the wicked city, saying that like all other wicked cities of the Eastern Mediterranean it was about to be annihilated. Whereupon the partying Ninevites, just like Jonah inside the whale, repented; whereupon God decided after all to spare the city; whereupon Jonah became incredibly irritated, which was only normal in one who'd been put to a lot of trouble to bring the message of destruction, only for the Lord, despite a well-known, indeed historic, taste for wrecking cities, to turn round and change his mind. As if this wasn't enough, God, tireless to prove himself top dog, now pulled a fancy parable on his minion. First he made a gourd spring up to protect Jonah from the sun (by 'gourd' we are to understand something like the castor-oil plant or *Palma Christi*, with its rapid growth and all-sheltering leaves); then, with no more than a wave of the silk handkerchief, he sent a maggot to destroy the said gourd, leaving Jonah painfully exposed to the heat. God's explanation of this little piece of street theatre ran as follows: you didn't punish the gourd when it failed you, did you; and in the same way I'm not going to punish Nineveh.

It's not much of a story, is it? As in most of the Old Testament, there's a crippling lack of free will around – or even the illusion of free will. God holds all the cards and wins all the tricks. The only uncertainty is how the Lord is going to play it this time: start with the two of trumps and lead up to the ace, start with the ace and run down to the two, or mix them around.

And since you never can tell with paranoid schizophrenics, this element does give the narrative some drive. But what do we make of that gourd business? It's not very convincing as a logical argument: anyone can see there's a world of difference between a castor-oil plant and a city of 120,000 people. Unless, of course, this is the whole point, and the God of the Eastern Mediterranean values his creation no higher than vegetable matter.

If we examine God not as protagonist and moral bully but as author of this story, we have to mark him down for plot, motivation, suspense and characterization. Yet in his routine and fairly repellent morality there is one sensational stroke of melodrama – the business with the whale. Technically, the cetacean side of things isn't at all well handled: the beast is evidently as much of a pawn as Jonah; its providential appearance just as the sailors are tossing Jonah overboard smacks far too heavily of a *deus ex machina*; and the great fish is casually dismissed from the story the moment its narrative function has been fulfilled. Even the gourd comes off better than the poor whale, who is no more than a floating prison where Jonah spends three days purging his contempt of court. God finger-flips the blubbery jail hither and thither like a war-game admiral nudging his fleet across maps of the sea.

And yet, despite all this, the whale steals it. We forget the allegorical point of the story (Babylon engulfing disobedient Israel), we don't much care whether or not Nineveh was saved, or what happened to the regurgitated penitent; but we remember the whale. Giotto shows him chomping on Jonah's thighs, with only the knees and the flailing feet to go. Brueghel, Michelangelo, Correggio, Rubens and Dali emblazoned the tale. In Gouda there is a stained-glass window of Jonah leaving the fish's mouth like a foot-passenger stepping from the jaws of a car-ferry. Jonah (portrayed as everything from muscular faun to bearded elder) has an iconography whose pedigree and variety would make Noah envious.

What is it about Jonah's escapade that transfixes us? Is it the moment of swallowing, the oscillation between danger and salvation, when we imagine ourselves miraculously rescued

from the peril of drowning only to be cast into the peril of being
eaten alive? Is it the three days and three nights in the whale's
belly, that image of enclosure, smothering, live burial? (Once,
taking the night train from London to Paris, I found myself in
the locked sleeping compartment of a locked coach in a locked
hold beneath the waterline on a cross-channel ferry; I didn't
think of Jonah at the time, but perhaps my panic was related to
his. And is a more textbook fear involved: does the image of
pulsing blubber set off some terror of being transported back to
the womb?) Or are we most struck by the third element in the
story, the deliverance, the proof that there is salvation and
justice after our purgatorial incarceration? Like Jonah, we are all
storm-tossed by the seas of life, undergo apparent death and
certain burial, but then attain a blinding resurrection as the
car-ferry doors swing open and we are delivered back into the
light and into a recognition of God's love. Is this why the myth
swims through our memory?

Perhaps: or perhaps not at all. When the film *Jaws* came out,
there were many attempts to explain its hold over the audience.
Did it draw on some primal metaphor, some archetypal dream
known the world over? Did it exploit the clashing elements of
land and water, feeding on our anxiety at the concept of
amphibianism? Did it relate in some way to the fact that
millions of years ago our gill-bearing ancestors crawled out of
the pond, and ever since we have been paralyzed by the thought
of a return to it? The English novelist Kingsley Amis, considering the film and its possible interpretations, came to the
following conclusion: 'It's about being bloody frightened of
being eaten by a bloody great shark.'

At bottom, this is the grip which the story of Jonah and the
whale still has on us: fear of being devoured by a large creature,
fear of being chomped, slurped, gargled, washed down with a
draught of salt water and a school of anchovies as a chaser; fear of
being blinded, darkened, suffocated, drowned, hooded with
blubber; fear of sensory deprivation, which we know drives
people mad; fear of being dead. Our response is as vivid as that of
every other death-dreading generation since the tale was first

invented by some sadistic mariner keen to terrify the new cabin-boy.

Of course, we recognize that the story can't have any basis in truth. We are sophisticated people, and we can tell the difference between reality and myth. A whale might swallow a man, yes, we can allow that as plausible; but once inside he could not possibly live. For a start he would drown, or if he didn't drown he would suffocate; and most probably he would have died of a heart attack when he felt the great mouth gape for him. No, it is impossible for a man to survive in a whale's belly. We know how to distinguish myth from reality. We are sophisticated people.

On 25th August 1891, James Bartley, a thirty-five-year-old sailor on the *Star of the East*, was swallowed by a sperm whale off the Falkland Islands:

I remember very well from the moment that I fell from the boat and felt my feet strike some soft substance. I looked up and saw a big-ribbed canopy of light pink and white descending over me, and the next moment I felt myself drawn downward, feet first, and I realised that I was being swallowed by a whale. I was drawn lower and lower; a wall of flesh surrounded me and hemmed me in on every side, yet the pressure was not painful and the flesh easily gave way like soft india-rubber before my slightest movement.

Suddenly I found myself in a sack much larger than my body, but completely dark. I felt about me; and my hands came in contact with several fishes, some of which seemed to be still alive, for they squirmed in my fingers, and slipped back to my feet. Soon I felt a great pain in my head and my breathing became more and more difficult. At the same time I felt a terrible heat; it seemed to consume me, growing hotter and hotter. My eyes became coals of fire in my head, and I believed every moment that I was condemned to perish in the belly of a whale. It tormented me beyond all endurance, while at the same time the awful silence of the terrible prison weighed me down. I tried to rise, to move my arms and legs, to cry out. All action was now impossible, but

my brain seemed abnormally clear; and with a full comprehension of my awful fate, I finally lost all consciousness.

The whale was later killed and taken alongside the *Star of the
East*, whose crewmen, unaware of the proximity of their lost
comrade, spent the rest of the day and part of the night flensing
their capture. The next morning they attached lifting tackle to
the stomach and hauled it on deck. There seemed to be a light,
spasmodic movement from within. The sailors, expecting a
large fish or perhaps a shark, slit open the paunch and discovered
James Bartley: unconscious, his face, neck and hands bleached
white by the gastric fluids, but still alive. For two weeks he was
in a delirous condition, then began to recover. In due course he
was returned to normal health, except that the acids had
removed all the pigmentation from his exposed skin. He
remained an albino until the day he died.

M. de Parville, scientific editor of the *Journal des Débats*,
examined the case in 1914 and concluded that the account given
by captain and crew was 'worthy of belief'. Modern scientists
tell us that Bartley could not have survived more than a few
minutes in the whale's belly, let alone the half-day or more it
took the unwitting sailors on the mother ship to release this
modern Jonah. But do we believe modern scientists, none of
whom has actually been inside a whale's belly? Surely we can
make compromise with professional scepticism by suggesting
air pockets (do whales suffer from wind like everyone else?) or
stomach juices whose efficacy was hindered by some cetacean
ailment.

And if you are a scientist, or infected by gastric doubt, look at
it this way. Many people (including me) believe the myth of
Bartley, just as millions have believed the myth of Jonah. You
may not credit it, but what has happened is that the story has
been retold, adjusted, updated; it has shuffled nearer. For Jonah
now read Bartley. And one day there will be a case, one which
even you will believe, of a sailor lost in a whale's mouth and
recovered from its belly; maybe not after half a day, perhaps
after only half an hour. And then people will believe the myth of

Bartley, which was begotten by the myth of Jonah. For the point is this: not that myth refers us back to some original event which has been fancifully transcribed as it passed through the collective memory; but that it refers us forward to something that will happen, that must happen. Myth will become reality, however sceptical we might be.

III

A T 8 PM ON Saturday, 13th May 1939, the liner *St Louis* left its home port of Hamburg. It was a cruise ship, and most of the 937 passengers booked on its transatlantic voyage carried visas confirming that they were 'tourists, travelling for pleasure'. The words were an evasion, however, as was the purpose of their voyage. All but a few of them were Jews, refugees from a Nazi state which intended to dispossess, transport and exterminate them. Many, indeed, had already been dispossessed, since emigrants from Germany were permitted to take with them no more than a nominal ten Reichsmarks. This enforced poverty made them easier targets for propaganda: if they left with no more than their allowance, they could be portrayed as shabby *Untermenschen* scuttling away like rats; if they managed to outwit the system, then they were economic criminals fleeing with stolen goods. All this was normal.

The *St Louis* was flying the swastika flag, which was normal; its crew included half-a-dozen Gestapo agents, which was also normal. The shipping line had instructed the captain to lay in cheaper cuts of meat for this voyage, to remove luxury goods from the shops and free postcards from the public rooms; but the captain largely circumvented such orders, decreeing that this journey should resemble other cruises by the *St Louis* and be, as far as possible, normal. So when the Jews arrived on board from a mainland where they had been despised, systematically humiliated and imprisoned, they discovered that although this ship was legally still part of Germany, flew the swastika and had large portraits of Hitler in its public rooms, the Germans with whom they had dealings were courteous, attentive and even obedient. This was abnormal.

None of these Jews – half of whom were women and children – had any intention of revisiting Germany in the near future. Nevertheless, in accordance with the regulations of the shipping company, they had all been obliged to buy return tickets. This payment, they were told, was designed to cover 'unforeseen eventualities'. When the refugees landed in Havana, they would be given by the Hamburg-Amerika line a receipt for the unused part of the fare. The money itself had been lodged in a special account in Germany: if ever they returned there, they could collect it. Even Jews who had been released from concentration camps on strict condition that they leave the Fatherland immediately were obliged to pay for the round trip.

Along with their tickets the refugees had bought landing permits from the Cuban director of immigration, who had given a personal guarantee that they would face no difficulties entering his country. It was he who had classed them as 'tourists, travelling for pleasure'; and in the course of the voyage some passengers, particularly the younger ones, were able to make the remarkable transition from despised *Untermensch* to pleasure-seeking tourist. Perhaps their escape from Germany felt as miraculous as that of Jonah from the whale. Every day there was food, drink and dancing. Despite a warning to crew members from the Gestapo cell about contravention of the Law for the Protection of German Blood and Honour, sexual activity continued as normal on a cruise. Towards the end of the Atlantic crossing, the traditional costume ball took place. The band played Glenn Miller; Jews appeared as pirates, sailors and Hawaiian dancers. Some high-spirited girls came as harem women, with Arab dress made from bedsheets – a transformation which struck the more orthodox on board as unseemly.

On Saturday, 27th May, the *St Louis* anchored in Havana Harbour. At 4 am the klaxon for reveille sounded, and half an hour later the breakfast gong. Small boats came out to the liner, some bearing vendors of coconuts and bananas, others containing friends and relatives who shouted up names to the rail. The ship was flying a quarantine flag, which was normal. The captain had to certify to the Port of Havana medical officer that no-one on board was 'an idiot, or insane, or suffering from a loathsome or contagious disease'. When this had been done, immigration officers began to process the passengers, examining their papers and indicating whereabouts on the pier to expect their luggage. The first fifty refugees gathered at the top of the ladder, waiting for the boat to take them ashore.

Immigration, like emigration, is a process in which money is no less important than principles or laws, and often sounder than either of them. Money reassures the host country – or, in the case of Cuba, the transit country – that the new arrivals will not be a charge on the state. Money also serves to bribe the officials who have to take this decision. The Cuban director of immigration had made a great deal of money from previous boatloads of Jews; the President of Cuba had not made enough money from them. The President had therefore issued a decree on 6th May revoking the validity of tourist visas when the true purpose of travel was immigration. Did this decree apply to those on board the St Louis or not? The ship had sailed from Hamburg after the law had been promulgated; on the other hand, the landing permits had been issued earlier. It was a question on which much argument and money could be spent. The number of the presidential decree was 937, which the superstitious might have noticed was also the number of passengers on board when the St Louis left Europe.

A delay developed. Nineteen Cubans and Spaniards were allowed to disembark, plus three passengers with authentic visas; the remaining 900 or so Jews waited for news of the negotiations which involved, variously, the Cuban President, his director of immigration, the shipping line, the local relief committee, the ship's captain and a lawyer flown in from the New York headquarters of the Joint Distribution Committee. These talks lasted several days. Factors to be considered were money, pride, political ambition and Cuban public opinion. The captain of the *St Louis*, while distrustful of both local politicians and his own shipping line, was convinced at least of one thing: that if Cuba proved inaccessible, the United States, to which most of his passengers had the right of eventual entry, would surely accept them earlier than promised.

Some of the marooned passengers were less confident, and became unnerved by the uncertainties, the delay, the heat. They had spent so long reaching a place of safety, and were now so near. Friends and relatives continued to circle the liner in small boats; a fox terrier, sent on ahead from Germany, was rowed out each day and held up towards the rail and its distant owners. A passengers' committee had been formed, to whom the shipping company gave free cabling facilities; appeals for intercession were despatched to influential people, including the wife of the Cuban president. It was during this time that two passengers attempted suicide, one with a syringe and tranquillizers, another by slashing his wrists and jumping into the sea; both survived. Thereafter, to prevent further suicide attempts, there were security patrols at night; the lifeboats were always ready, and the ship was lit up by floodlights. These measures reminded some Jews of the concentration camps they had recently left.

The *St Louis* was not meant to leave Havana empty after dropping its 937 emigrants. Some 250 passengers were booked on the return trip to Hamburg via Lisbon. One suggestion was that 250 of the Jews could at least be disembarked to make room for those on shore. But how would you choose the 250 who were to be allowed off the Ark? Who would separate the clean from the unclean? Was it to be done by casting lots?

The predicament of the *St Louis* was not a disregarded, local issue. The voyage was being logged by the German, British and American press. *Der Stürmer* commented that if the Jews chose to take up their return passages to Germany, they should be accommodated at Dachau and Buchenwald. Meanwhile, in Havana harbour, American reporters managed to get on board what they nicknamed, perhaps too easily, 'the ship that shamed the world'. Such publicity does not necessarily help refugees. If the shame belongs to the whole world, then why should one particular country – which had already accepted many Jewish refugees – be so frequently expected to bear it? The world, apparently, did not feel its shame so strongly that it moved its hand to its wallet. The Cuban government accordingly voted to exclude the immigrants and ordered the *St Louis* to leave the island's territorial waters. This did not mean, the President added, that he had closed the door on negotiations; merely that he would not consider further offers until the ship had left harbour.

How much are refugees? It depends how desperate they are, how rich their patrons, how greedy their hosts. In the world of entry permits and panic it is always a seller's market. Prices are arbitrary, speculative, evanescent. The lawyer from the Joint Distribution Committee put forward an opening offer of $50,000 for the safe landing of the Jews, and was told that the sum might usefully be trebled. But if trebled, why not trebled again? The director of immigration – who had already received $150 a head for the landing permits which had not been honoured – suggested to the shipping line a fee of $250,000 to help get decree number 937 rescinded. A purported intermediary of the President seemed to think that the Jews could be landed for $1,000,000. In the end, the Cuban government was to fix on a bond of $500 for each Jew. This price had a certain logic, being the amount of surety which each official immigrant into the country had to post. So the 907 passengers on board, who had already paid their outward and return fares, who had bought their permits and then been reduced to an official ten Deutschmarks each, would cost $453,500.

As the liner started its engines, a group of women charged the accommodation ladder; they were repelled by Cuban police with pistols. During its six days in Havana harbour the *St Louis* had become a tourist attraction, and its departure was watched by an estimated crowd of 100,000. The captain had been given permission by his superiors in Hamburg to sail for any port which would accept his passengers. At first he steamed idly in ever-widening circles, waiting to be recalled to Havana; then headed north for Miami. When the ship reached the American coast it was greeted by a U.S. Coast Guard cutter. But this apparent welcome was a rebuff: the cutter was there to see that the *St Louis* did not enter territorial waters. The State Department had already decided that if the Jews were turned down by Cuba, they would not be granted entry into the United States. Money was a less direct factor here: high unemployment and reliable xenophobia were sufficient justifications.

The Dominican Republic offered to accept the refugees for the standardized market price of $500 a head; but this merely duplicated the Cuban tariff. Venezuela, Ecuador, Chile, Colombia, Paraguay and Argentina were all approached; each declined to bear the world's shame single-handed. In Miami the immigration inspector announced that the *St Louis* would not be allowed to dock in any U.S. port.

The liner, denied entry to the whole American continent, continued steaming northwards. Those on board were aware that they were approaching the point at which it would have to swing east and head inevitably back to Europe. Then, at 4.50 on the afternoon of Sunday, 4th June, a news flash was picked up. The President of Cuba had apparently given permission for the Jews to be landed on the Isle of Pines, a former penal colony. The captain turned the *St Louis* round and headed south again. Passengers brought their luggage up on deck. That evening, over dinner, the spirits of the gala evening returned.

The next morning, three hours' sailing away from the Isle of Pines, the ship received a cable: permission to disembark had not yet been confirmed. The passenger committee, who throughout the crisis had been sending telegrams to prominent Americans asking them to intercede, could think of no one else to contact. Someone suggested the Mayor of St Louis, Missouri, thinking that the consonance of names might perhaps evoke sympathy. A cable was duly despatched.

The Cuban President had asked for a $500 surety per refugee, plus a subsidiary guarantee to cover food and lodging during the period of transit on the Isle of Pines. The American lawyer had offered (according to the Cuban government) a total of

$443,000, but further stipulated that this sum was to cover not just the refugees on the *St Louis* but also 150 Jews on two other ships. The Cuban government found itself unable to accept this counter-proposal and withdrew its own offer. The lawyer for the Joint Committee responded by agreeing in full to the original Cuban demand. The government in return regretted that its offer had already been terminated and could not now be revived. The *St Louis* turned round and headed north for a second time.

As the ship began its return voyage to Europe, the British and French governments were informally sounded out to see if their countries might take the Jews. The British answer was that they would prefer to view the present difficulty in the wider context of the general European refugee situation, but that they might be prepared to consider possible subsequent entry of the Jews to Britain after their return to Germany.

There had been unconfirmed or impracticable offers from the President of Honduras, from an American philanthropist, even from a quarantine station in the Panama Canal Zone; the ship steamed on. The passenger committee addressed its appeals to political and religious leaders throughout Europe; though its messages now had to be shorter, since the shipping line had withdrawn free cabling facilities. One suggestion made at this time was that the strongest swimmers among the Jews should jump overboard at intervals, thus forcing the *St Louis* to stop and turn round. This would slow its progress towards Europe and allow more time for negotiations. The idea was not taken up.

German radio announced that since no country would agree to accept the boat-load of Jews, the Fatherland would be obliged to take them back and support them. It was not difficult to guess where they might be supported. What's more, if the *St Louis* was forced to unload its cargo of degenerates and criminals back in Hamburg, this would prove that the world's supposed concern was mere hypocrisy. Nobody wanted the shabby Jews, and nobody therefore had any right to criticize whatever welcome the Fatherland might extend to the filthy parasites on their return.

It was at this time that a group of younger Jews attempted to hijack the ship. They invaded the bridge, but were dissuaded from further action by the captain. For his part, he conceived a plan of setting fire to the *St Louis* off Beachy Head, which would compel the rescuing nation to take his passengers in. This desperate scheme might even have been tried. Finally, when many had given up hope and the liner was nearing Europe, the Belgian government announced that it would admit 200 of the passengers. In the days that followed, Holland agreed to take 194, Britain 350, and France 250.

After a voyage of 10,000 miles, the *St Louis* docked at Antwerp, 300 miles from its port of departure. Relief workers from the four countries involved had already met to decide the distribution of the Jews. Most of those on board possessed the right of eventual entry into the United States, and had therefore been ascribed a number on the U.S. quota list. It was observed that the relief workers competed for passengers with low numbers, since these refugees would leave their countries of transit the soonest.

In Antwerp a pro-Nazi youth organization had distributed handbills bearing the slogan: 'We too want to help the Jews. If they call at our offices each will receive gratis a length of rope and a long nail.' The passengers were disembarked. Those admitted to Belgium were put on a train whose doors were locked and windows nailed shut; they were told that such measures were necessary for their own protection. Those admitted to Holland were immediately transferred to a camp surrounded by barbed wire and guard dogs.

On Wednesday, 21st June, the British contingent from the *St Louis* docked at Southampton. They were able to reflect that their wanderings at sea had lasted precisely forty days and forty nights.

On 1st September the Second World War began, and the passengers from the *St Louis* shared in the fate of European Jewry. Their chances rose or fell depending upon the country to which they had been allotted. Estimates of how many survived vary.

8

UPSTREAM!

Darling —

Just time for a card — we leave in half an hour — had our last night on the Johnny Walker now it's local firewater or nothing — remember what I said on the phone and don't have it cut too short. Love you — your Circus Strongman.

My own darling —

Just spent 24 hours on a bus with the dashboard covered in St Christophers or whatever the local version hereabouts is. Wouldn't have minded if the driver had gone in for some stronger magic — the old Christianity didn't seem to be having much effect on his driving. When not thinking about puking your guts up round every hairpin bend, scenery magnificent. Great big trees, mountains — that sort of thing — I've got some postcards. Crew all a bit over-excited at the moment — if I hear another joke about 'I was going Caracas back there' I think I'll strangle someone. Still, that's normal on a job like this. Not that I've ever done a job like this before, should be great fun. It'd better be after all those needles they stuck in me so I won't get beri-beri and co.

It's a relief to get away from people recognizing you as well. You know, even with the beard and glasses they still copped the face in Caracas. At the airport, of course, but that's normal anyway. No, it was funny. Guess what they'd seen me in? Not your upmarket angst number with the Pinter script that got the

Palme d'Or, none of that. No, that filthy little American soap I did for Hal Screwyouupalotodos. It's STILL playing here. Kids come up in the street and say, 'Hey Mista Rick, how ya doin'?' What about that? The poverty here is something else. Still, after India nothing will surprise me. Now what have you done about your hair? I hope you haven't gone and done anything silly to it just to get your own back for me going away. I know what you girls are like, you say you'll just have it short to see what it looks like, and then you say Pedro at the salon won't let you grow it just for the moment, and then you say you've got to look your best for some wedding or other and you can't go with it straggly and then you end up not growing it again and if I don't mention it every week you think I've learned to like it and if I do mention it every week you think I'm nagging so I don't mention it and I'm stuck with it. And it's not fair to say it's because of the beard because the beard's not my fault, they just didn't shave in the jungle in whatever century it's going to be when we get there and I *know* I grew it early but that's the way I am, I like to start thinking myself into the part as soon as possible. You know what Dirk says, how he starts with the shoes, once he gets the shoes right he knows what the rest of the character's like, well with me it's the face. Sorry if it's the first thing you see in the morning, still it's not everyone who can say they've been sleeping with a Jesuit. A very old Jesuit too. Weather very hot, laundry problems I expect. Still taking those tummy tablets. Had a word with Vic about the script and he says not to worry but they always say that at this stage, don't they? I told him what I said to you on the phone about shouldn't he be given a bit more obvious humanity because priests aren't great box-office nowadays and Vic said we'd talk about it nearer the time. Getting on well with Matt — obviously there's going to be some competition once we start work but he's not half as paranoid as I thought he'd be, a bit back-slapping, still I guess that's Yanks for you. I told him my Vanessa story and he told me his and we'd both heard them before! Got stinko paralytico together on our last night in town and ended up doing the Zorba dance in a restaurant! Matt tried plate-smashing but they said it wasn't the local custom and threw us out! Charged us for the plates, too.

You know what they call post offices out here? Our Lady of Communications. You probably have to get down on your knees for next-day delivery. Not that we've seen one of them for miles. God knows if I'll be able to post this before the Jungle starts. Maybe we'll come across a friendly native with a forked stick going in the right direction and I'll give him the big-screen smile and hand it over. (Joke.) Don't worry about me. Love you.

– Charlie

Letter 2

Darling –

If you look in your photo album for our flat-smouldering party you'll see there's something missing. Don't worry – I've got it. It's the one where you've got your chipmunk face on. You've got a bit wet out here – terrible downpour couple of days ago – but you still don't mind being kissed last thing at night. You might get a bit crumpled from here on in as we've seen our last hotel for a bit. Now it's all Boy Scout stuff and bivouacs and tents. Hope I get the sleep I need. It's so hard to work on full glow when you've only had a couple of hours kip. Anyway we're well into the Jungle now. Lots of delays. Usual stuff – you arrange that on such-and-such a day you'll turn up with so many people and so much luggage and he'll transport you to the next place and when you turn up he pretends things have changed and you didn't say fifty but fifteen and anyway the price has gone up and so on and so bloody on until he gets the backhander he wants. God, when things like that happen I just feel like shouting I Want To Work in a very loud voice. I did that one day when things got hairier than usual, went down to where some bandit was trying to rip us off and practically rubbed beards with him and shouted into his face I Want To Work For Christ's Sake Let Me Work, but Vic said that wasn't being helpful.

Later. Matt was peeing in the river when one of the sparks came up and told him it wasn't a good idea. Apparently they've got this tiny fish which is attracted by the heat or whatever and can swim up your pee as you're peeing. Didn't sound likely at first but think of salmon I suppose. Then what it does is swim straight into your dick and once it gets there it sticks out a couple of spines sideways and just stays there. Ouch in spades, to say the least of it. The sparks says you can't get it out, it's like having an umbrella opened up in there, you have to have the whole doings chopped off in hospital. Matt didn't know whether to believe him but can you risk it? No one's peeing in the river at the moment, anyway.

Later. We were puttering upriver late in the afternoon and the sun was beginning to go down over these huge trees and a flight of big birds, herons or something, were taking off like pink seaplanes as someone said and the second assistant suddenly stood up and yelled out This is paradise, this is fucking paradise. Actually, feeling a bit depressed, love. Sorry to lay this on you, not fair I know as I'll probably be right as rain by the time you get this. Bloody Matt getting me down. What an ego. You'd think no-one else had ever made a film except him and you can see him coming on all good mates with the crew so they'll make things easier for him when he gets in front of camera, so he looks five years younger and I get the shiny nose. Vic's not tough enough for this job, to be frank. You need one of those slave-driving old studio bosses if you ask me, not a sensitive graduate who went into movies because he liked the clouds in Antonioni and then turned himself into a nouvelle vague Deutscher all hot for Truthspiel. I ask you, forty of us slogging into the Jungle all because we bought his line about needing to work our way into the reality of a couple of deeply dead Jesuit priests. How this applies to the crew as well I don't know but I expect Vic's got some theory to cover it. Us going in on foot and then the equipment being airlifted in is about as arsy-versy as you can get. He won't even let us use the radio-telephone until after we've made the rendez-vous. The focus-puller's girlfriend is having a baby and he wanted to call

headquarters in Caracas to see if there was any news but Vic said
no.

Bloody weather. Bloody hot all the time. Sweating like a pig,
comme un porco. Still worrying about the script. Think I'll have to
do some rewrites on my part. No chance of getting any laundry
done unless we meet some tribe of washerwomen waiting for
custom outside one of those zinc shacks like we saw in that
village in Provence do you remember? Bloody tin sign for
Coca-Cola at a trading post this morning. I ask you, hundreds of
miles from bloody anywhere and the Coke reps have been there
before you and shat on the landscape. Or some chum of Matt's
put it there to make him feel at home. Sorry about this.

Love Charlie

Letter 3

Hey Good Looking!

Sorry about that whingeing on at the end of the last letter.
Everything much better now. For one thing we've all started
peeing in the river again. We were asking Fish Sparks as we call
him how he knew about the fish that swims up your pee and he
said he'd seen some fat explorer fellow on the box going on about
it, which sounded likely enough. But then we asked him a bit
more about it and he made his fatal mistake. He said this
explorer had said he'd had some special underpants made so that
he could pee in the river safely. He got a cricket protector, the
sparks says, and cut the front bit out and stuck a tea-strainer
down it. Well I ask you. If you're telling fibs, keep them
simple, that's the rule, isn't it? Never over-egg the pudding. So
we all had a good laugh at the sparks and all of us unzipped our
flies and peed in the river whether we wanted to or not. The only
person that didn't was Fish, who had to save face and went on
claiming it was true.

So that cheered us up a bit as you can imagine but what really
cheered us up was making contact with the Indians. I mean, if
the bandits on the way here were anything to go by ('here', if you

195

want to look it up in your schoolgirl atlas, is somewhere near the Mocapra) why should the Indians keep their word? Matt said afterwards he'd half expected the whole thing would turn out to be a wild goose chase and I told him I thought the same. But there they were, four of them, just where they said they'd be, in a clearing on a bend in the river, naked as nature intended, standing very upright which still didn't make them very tall and looking at us without any fear. Without any curiosity either, in a funny sort of way, which was odd. You expect they'll want to prod you or something. But they just stood there as if we were the odd ones not them, which when you come to think about it is dead right. They watched us unpack everything and then we set off. Didn't offer to help carry anything which was a bit of a surprise but then I suppose they're not Sherpas are they? It's about two days march apparently to the rest of the tribe and the river we're looking for. We couldn't see the track they were following at all – amazing sense of direction they must have in the Jungle. You'd be lost here I can tell you angel, especially given you don't know how to get from Shepherd's Bush to Hammersmith without a police escort.* We marched for about two hours then stopped for the night and ate fish the Indians had caught in the river while they were waiting for us. Very tired, but quite a day. Kiss you.

*Joke (not serious)

Later. A whole day on the move. Glad I did all that training in the gym. Some of the crew puffing after only half an hour or so, which isn't surprising as the only exercise they take in the normal run of things is putting their legs under a table and aiming their snouts at the trough. Oh yes and putting their hands up to order another bottle. Matt's pretty fit from all those outdoor movies where they put olive oil on his pectorals (though not as fit as he ought to be) and the two of us gave the crew a bit of a hard time, said union rules didn't apply in the Jungle, and so on. They certainly didn't want to get left behind! Fish Sparks, who's been a bit down in the mouth since we rumbled his story, thought it was terrifically funny to start calling the Indians things like Sitting Bull and Tonto, but of course they didn't understand and anyway the rest of us sort of froze him out. It just wasn't funny, anyway. They're incredible, these Indians. Walking starkers through the forest, incredibly agile, never get tired, killed a monkey in a tree with a blowpipe. Had it for dinner, well some of us did, the squeamish ones had a tin of corned beef. I had the monkey. Tasted a bit like oxtail only much redder. A bit stringy but delicious.

Tuesday. God knows how the post system's going to work. At the moment we just give it to Rojas – he's the fourth assistant and a local and he's been appointed postman. All that means is that he puts the letters into a plastic bag so they won't get eaten by beetles or woodworm or whatever. Then when we meet up with the copter he'll take the mail out. So God knows when you'll get this.

Miss you (pause while I do my Circus Strongman howl). Today we should have met up with the rest of the tribe but we aren't as fit as we might be. I bet some of the crew thought there'd be wheels right into the Jungle and food trucks parked every few miles and they'd get burgers and chips served by girls wearing flower garlands round their necks. Fat Dick the sound man probably packed a Hawaiiiiiian shirt.

You have to hand it to Vic in a way. Smallest crew-to-budget ratio in years. Me and Matt doing our own stunts (good old Norman really screwed the dollars up for me on that clause). Not even daily rushes either – the copter's only coming in every three days because Vic thinks it'll break our concentration or something no doubt posher intellectually than that. Lab report over the radio-telephone, the rushes with the copter. And the studio went along with it all. Amazing, isn't it?

No it isn't amazing, as you well know sweetie. The studio thinks Vic's a genius and gave him as much as they could until the insurance boys dug their heels in over big-name leads falling out of a canoe and then they went down the list and found a couple of guys the industry could afford to lose.* So I've been a bad boy at times but they reckon I can't walk out on a job if I'm in the Jungle and Matt's temperamental which means he doesn't normally work unless they give him a hamper full of white

powder but he seems to have kicked it and there aren't too many
dealers swinging through the trees like Tarzan out here. And we
agree to Vic's conditions because we bloody need to and deep
down we probably think Vic's a genius too.

*Joke. Well, sort of. No real danger, I'm sure.

Wondering if it was a mistake to have the monkey last night.
It certainly slowed me down a bit today, and Matt was behind a
bush a lot as well.

Later. Sorry, Wednesday. Met the tribe. The greatest day of
my life. Except for meeting you, babe, of course. They were
just there, suddenly, as we came over a hill and saw a river below
us. The lost river and the lost people side by side – amazing.
They're quite short, and you'd think they were plump except
it's all muscle, and they don't have a stitch on. The girls are
pretty, too (don't worry, angel – riddled with diseases). The
funny thing is there don't seem to be any old folks. Or maybe
they've left them behind somewhere. But we did have this idea
that the whole tribe went around together. Puzzling. Also, I've
run out of mosquito stuff – the really powerful one anyway.
Getting bitten quite a lot. Vic says not to worry – did I think
Father Firmin had insect repellent all those years ago? I said
authenticity was one thing but did my devoted fans really want
to see me on the big screen with spots a foot across all over my
face? Vic told me I had to suffer for my art. I told Vic to fuck off.
Bloody Truthspiel.

Thursday. We've set up camp now on the bank. A couple of
camps actually, one for whites (most of whom are brown with
red spots) and one for Indians. I said why didn't we have one big
camp, for Christ's sake. Some of the crew were against this
because they thought they'd get their watches stolen (I ask you)
and some in favour so that they could get a closer look at the
women (I ask you). Vic said he thought two camps were a good
idea because there would have been two originally and it would
psychologically prepare the Indians for playing their ancestors,
which I said was just a rationalisation of elitism. Anyway things
got quite hot and eventually one of the guides was sent over to
talk to the Indians and the word came back that they wouldn't

share their camp with us anyway, which is quite funny I suppose.

Here comes the copter so I'll end now.

Love Charlie

Dear Pips,

First rendez-vous! They coptered in the genny and the rest of the equipment. Great excitement (except for the Indians who ignored it all). Food, ciggies. No mosquito stuff on board – can you believe it? Another thing – Vic wouldn't let them bring in newspapers, which pissed me off. I mean we're not kids are we? Reading a two-week-old copy of The Independent isn't likely to screw up my acting, is it? Or is it? I'm amazed Vic allowed us letters. None for Charlie. I know I told you not to write except in emergency but I didn't mean it. Hope you guessed.

Friday. Look, I know you don't want to talk about it, but I think this spell of being apart will do us lots of good. In lots of ways. Really. I'm getting too old for hellraising anyway. 'MY HELLRAISING DAYS ARE OVER' SAYS TV'S 'BAD-BOY' CHARLIE. Love you.

Pippa love, I really think it's the effect of the Indians (oh, Saturday). They're so open, so direct. There they are, not a stitch on them, they say what they mean, do what they want, eat when they're hungry, make love as if it's the most natural thing in the world*, and lie down to die when they reach the end of their lives. It's really something. I don't mean I could do it myself, not straight away, I just mean I get a great sense of comradeship with these people. I almost feel I've been sent here so they can teach me a lesson about life. Does that make sense? It's all right, sweetie, I'm not coming back with a bone through my nose, but I might come back with a bit less of a bone in my head. All that business about Linda – I know we agreed not to talk about it – but I feel such a shit out here. Hurting you. Not telling the truth. Out here, with the lost river running past my feet, learning the names of birds I don't even know the names of in English, I feel good about us.

*Not personal experience. Charlie's nose clean.

Sunday. It's not just distance lends enchantment or whatever. It's something about being *here*. You remember the American astronauts, how they went to the moon and came back totally changed by looking at the earth and seeing it like just any old planet all small and a long way away? Some of them got religious or went barmy I seem to remember, but the point is they were all different when they came back. It's a bit like that with me, except that instead of going into the technological future I had to go back in time. Actually, I don't really mean that, back in time. All the crew here think the Indians are fantastically primitive just because they don't have radios. I think they're fantastically advanced and mature because they don't have radios. They're teaching me something without knowing they're doing it. I'm beginning to see things a lot more in perspective. God I'm damn sorry about Linda.

Monday. A long time setting up, then it rained. One of the girls is teaching me the language. Don't worry, chipmunk, riddled with diseases I'm sure.* Tried to find out what they call themselves, you know, name of the tribe. Guess what, THEY DON'T HAVE A NAME FOR THEMSELVES!!! and they don't have a name for their language either. Isn't that amazing!! Incredibly mature. It's like, nationalism out of the window.

*Sort of catch-phrase with the crew. If anyone starts talking about sex or looking at the Indian women, someone always says, 'Riddled with diseases I'm sure.' Probably not so funny in London.

Tuesday. There's a really good feeling now we've started. Everyone pulling together. None of this silly bloody union rules. Everyone *contributing*. I'm sure it's the influence of the Indians. It's how things should be.

Wednesday. I think my accent's improving. There's a big white stork sort of bird called a *thkarni*. I think that's how you write it down. Anyway, I say *thkarni* when one takes off or lands on the water, and the Indians think this is jolly funny. They fall about laughing. Well they aren't any better at saying Charlie.

Thursday. Not much. Bitten by 80000000000000 mosquitoes. Matt makes stupid joke. If you look closely, he's bandy-legged, I swear.

Friday. It's amazing when you think about it. Here's this tribe of Indians, totally obscure, don't even have a name for themselves. A couple of hundred years ago two Jesuit missionaries trying to find their way back to the Orinoco stumble across them, get them to build a raft and then pole the two Godmen several hundred miles south while the said Godmen preach them the Gospel and try to get them to wear Levis. Just when they get near their destination the raft capsizes, the missionaries nearly drown and the Indians disappear. Melt into the Jungle and no-one sees them again until Vic's researchers track them down a year ago. Now they're helping us do exactly the same thing a couple of hundred years on. What I'm dying to know is does the tribe remember? Do they have ballads about transporting the two white men dressed as women up to the great watery anaconda to the south, or however they might put it? Or did the white men vanish from the tribe's memory as completely as the tribe vanished for the white man? So many things to think about. And what will happen when we've gone? Will they disappear again for another two or three hundred years? Or disappear forever wiped out by some killer bug and all that will be left of them is a film in which they're playing their own ancestors? I'm not sure I can get my head round that.

My blessings on thee, daughter, sin no more.*

Love, Charlie

*Joke!!
Nothing from you Sunday or Wednesday. Hope Rojas has something tomorrow. Didn't mean you not to write whatever I said. Will send this anyway.

Darling –

This priest outfit must be the most uncomfortable garment ever invented for Jungle travel. Makes you sweat like a pig, *comme un porco*. How did old Father Firmin keep his dignity, I ask myself. Still I suppose you could say he suffered for his religion in the same way I suffer for my art.

Sunday. My God, guess what? Fat Dick the sound man was peeing in the river last night when one of the Indians came up to him all agitated, making lots of gestures, sign language, sort of swimming with his hands and so on. Dick doesn't follow him – in fact he thinks the bloke is trying to get off with him which is a bit of a laugh if you've seen the Indian women, until the Indian runs off and fetches Miguel who's one of the guides. Lots more gestures and explanations and Dick zips up his trousers pretty smartish. Guess what? The Indian was telling him about this little fish that lives in the river and – you can guess the rest!!! Not much chance of this particular member of this particular tribe watching British telly the same night Fish Sparks was. And not much chance of Fishy learning enough of the local lingo to set up a sting like this. So we just had to accept he was right all along! Boy did he have the last laugh.

Monday. Here's a funny thing. While the Indians appear to understand roughly what we're doing – they're happy to do retakes and don't seem at all put out by this great big eye being pointed at them – they don't seem to understand about the idea of acting. I mean sure they're acting their ancestors and they're quite willing (in exchange for some Mickey Mouse presents) to build us a raft and transport us upstream on it and be filmed doing this. But they won't do anything else. If Vic says could you stand in a different way or use the pole like this and tries to demonstrate they simply won't. Absolutely refuse. This is how we pole a raft and just because a white man is watching through his funny machine we aren't going to do it any differently. The other thing is even more incredible. They actually think that when Matt and I are dressed up as Jesuits we actually are Jesuits! They think we've gone away and these two blokes in black dresses have turned up! Father Firmin is just as real a person for them as Charlie, though I'm glad to say they like Charlie more. But you can't persuade them about what's going on. The crew think this is pretty stupid of them but I wonder if it isn't fantastically mature. The crew think they're such a primitive civilization they haven't even discovered acting yet. I wonder if it's the opposite and they're a sort of post-acting civilization, maybe the first one on the earth. Like, they don't need it any more, so they've forgotten about it and don't understand it any longer. Quite a thought!

Wednesday. Ought to have said more about the job. Not going badly. Script isn't what I remembered, but then it never is, usually because they've changed it. Matt isn't too bad to work with. I asked Make-Up to give him a few mosquito bites but he refused point-blank. Said he wanted to be the pretty one for a change. Quite funny that – I mean it's obvious that deep down he thinks he's jolly good-looking! I suppose I'd better not tell him that thing you said about his face looking as if it was carved out of corned beef.

Thursday. Terrible thing happened. Quite terrible. One of the Indians fell off the raft and was drowned. Just swept away. We stared at the water which was pretty choppy and waited for the Indian to surface but he never did. Naturally we said we'd stop work for the day. Guess what? The Indians wouldn't hear of it. What good old troupers they are!

Friday. Thinking about yesterday's incident. We were much more upset about it than the Indians were. I mean, he must have been somebody's brother or husband or something, but there wasn't any crying or anything. I half expected that when we pitched camp for the night there'd be some sort of ceremony – I don't know, burning a bundle of clothes or whatever. Not so. Same old jolly camp-fire life went on as per usual. I wondered if they hadn't liked the fellow who went overboard, but that's too obvious. Maybe they don't distinguish between life and death in some way. Maybe they don't think he's 'gone' as we do – or at least not gone altogether. Gone to a nicer bit of the river. I tried this out on Matt who said, 'Hey man I didn't know you had hippie blood.' Matt is not exactly the most spiritual and sophisticated fellow you've ever met. Believes in making your own way through life, walking tall, shooting straight, balling chicks as he puts it and spitting in the eye of anyone who does you wrong. That at any rate seems to be the sum of his wisdom. He thinks the Indians are rather cute kids who haven't yet invented the video recorder. I must say it's pretty funny that a chap like him ends up playing a Jesuit priest having doctrinal disputes in the rain forest. The fact is, he's one of those perfectly efficient American actors whose careers are decided by their image makers. I told him about taking six months off and doing rep in the provinces just to get back in touch with live acting and live audiences and he reacted as if I told him I'd had a mental breakdown. Say what you like, I think the stage is the place you learn to act. Matt can twitch his face in any direction and crinkle up his eyes knowing that his jailbait fans will be sitting there wetting themselves. But can he act with his body? Call me old-fashioned, but I think a lot of American actors just do a sort of swagger and leave it at that. Tried to explain all this to Vic, who said I was doing fine and Matt was doing fine and he thought we'd gel together on screen. Sometimes I do wish he'd LISTEN to what I say. Here comes the post, or rather the copter. Nothing from you yet.

– love, Charlie

Letter 6

Pippa love –
   Look I know we said we wouldn't talk about it and maybe it's not fair cos I don't know what state you'll be in when you get this, but why don't we just move to the country and have babies? No I haven't fallen in the river or anything. You've no idea how good it's been for me out here. I've cut out coffee after lunch and almost don't smoke at all. Well the Indians don't, do they, I say to myself. The Indians don't need to support the mighty firm of Philip Morris Inc. of Richmond Va. When

things get tough they sometimes chew on a little green leaf, which I reckon is their equivalent of the occasional ciggy one takes when the director is behaving like a prize muffin. So why not cut it down like they do? And that Linda thing. I know you probably don't want to hear her name ever again and if that's what you want that's my promise, but it's all to do with London isn't it? Not really to do with *us* at all. Just bloody London with its grime and filthy streets and the booze. Well that's not really living, the way we do in cities, is it? Also I think cities make people lie to one another. Do you think that's possible? These Indians never lie, same as they don't know how to act. No pretence. Now I don't think that's primitive at all, I think it's bloody mature. And I'm sure it's because they live in the Jungle not in cities. They spend all their time surrounded by nature and the one thing nature doesn't do is lie. It just goes ahead and does its thing, as Matt would say. Walks tall and shoots straight. It may not be very nice some of the time but it doesn't tell lies. Which is why I think the country and babies is the answer. And when I say the country I don't mean one of those villages just off the motorway full of people just like us buying Australian Chardonnay from the local wine merchant and the only time you hear an ooo-aarr accent is when you're listening to the Archers in the bath. I mean the real country, somewhere hidden away – Wales maybe or Yorkshire.

Sunday. The baby thing. It's to do with the Indians in a funny sort of way. You know I said they're all fantastically healthy and yet there aren't any old folks even though we thought they travelled around together in a group? Well, I finally got Miguel to talk to them about it and it turns out the reason there aren't any old folk around is because they don't live much longer than about 35. So I was wrong when I thought they were fantastically healthy and a good advert for the Jungle. The truth is it's only the fantastically healthy ones who can get by at all. What a turnaround. But the point is, I'm now older than most of this tribe will ever be and that feels like a chill wind. And if we lived in the country then it wouldn't be me coming home every night whacked out and wanting to be looked after and having a squawking infant instead. If I only took the big parts and none of this TV crap I'd just go away to film, and then when I was around I'd really be around. See? I could make a playpen for him and buy him one of those big wooden Arks with all the animals in and I could get one of those bags you carry babies around in like the Indians have had for centuries. Then I'd go striding off across the moors to get the both of us out of your hair for a bit, what do you say? By the way, I really am sorry I hit Gavin.

Monday. Bit depressed, love. Had this ludicrous tiff with Vic about a line. Six bloody words, but I *knew* Firmin wouldn't say them. I mean, I've been *living* this guy for three weeks now and Vic starts telling me how to speak? He said OK rewrite them, so I held things up for an hour and at the end of it he said he wasn't convinced. We tried it out all the same, because I insisted, and guess what? Bloody Matt wasn't convinced either. I said he couldn't tell a line of dialogue from a line of coke and anyway his face was carved out of corned beef, and he threatened to punch me. Stupid bloody film.

Tuesday. Still boiling.

Wednesday. Amazing thing. You know I said about the Indians not understanding about acting. Well in the last 2 days Firmin and Antonio have been getting more and more hostile (which isn't hard to do given how Charlie and Matt are currently feeling about one another) and you could really sense the Indians getting involved, following it all from their part of the raft as if their lives depended on it – which in a way they did I suppose because we were arguing about whether they had the right to be baptised and have their souls saved or not. They sensed this somehow, I don't know. Anyway today we had the scene where Matt had to hit me with the paddle sort of semi-accidentally. It was best balsa wood of course, not that the Indians could know, but I duly went down poleaxed and Matt started pretending it was an accident. The Indians were supposed to look on at what was happening as if these two white men in skirts were barmy. That's what they'd been told to do. But they didn't. Lots of them came rushing over to me and started stroking my face and wetting my brow and making a sort of wailing noise, and then three of them turned on Matt looking really nasty. Incredible! What's more they might have done him an injury if he hadn't pulled off his cassock pretty smartish and turned back into Matt, which calmed them down. Amazing! It was only old Matt, and that nasty priest Antonio had gone away. Then I slowly got to my feet and they all started laughing happily as if I wasn't dead after all. The good thing was that Vic kept running so we didn't miss any of it. Now he thinks he can work it in, which I'm pleased about because if this is the way the Indians react to me and Matt then maybe that's a pointer to how the fans will go.

Thursday. Vic says the lab report on yesterday's scuffle wasn't too kosher. Bet bloody Matt's been getting at him – probably knew the camera had caught him looking shit-scared. I said let's wait and see how it prints and Vic agreed but I didn't get good vibes. So much for Truthspiel: when they get it, they don't use it.

Friday. I don't think the script's up to scratch, and the whole thing's underbudgeted, but one thing I will say for it is that it's ABOUT something. I mean, it isn't afraid of the big issues. Most films aren't about anything, are they, that's what I find more and more. 'Two Priests up the Jungle' (which is what Old Fish Sparks sings from time to time to the tune of Red Sails in the Sunset) – sure, but it's about the sort of conflict running through human life in every time and every civilization. Discipline v. permissiveness. Sticking to the letter of the law v. sticking to its spirit. Means and ends. Doing the right thing for the wrong reason v. doing the wrong thing for the right reason. How great ideas like the Church get bogged down in bureaucracy. How Christianity starts off as the religion of peace but ends up violent like other religions. You could say the same about Communism or anything else, any big idea. I think this film could be really quite subversive in Eastern Europe and not because it's about priests either. Whether they'd distribute it is another matter. I said to Fish the film has a message for the trade unions as well if they could find it and he said he'd keep looking.

Pippa love, think about the baby thing, won't you?

Your Charlie

P.S. Funny thing happened today. Not serious, but makes me wonder about the Indians.
P.P.S. Can't think why you haven't written.

Letter 7
Dearest Pippa –
    Bloody jungle. It just doesn't give up. Bloody clouds of flies and biting things and humming whatsits and for the first couple of weeks you think how extraordinary, well it doesn't matter getting bitten, everyone else is, except Matt with his NASA US-Govt issue personal mosquito repellent and corned-beef face-protector. But they just go on and on and bloody on. After a while you just want the Jungle to take a day off. Go on, Jungle, it's Sunday, knock it off, you want to shout as it rattles on 24 hrs per day. I don't know. Maybe it's not the Jungle it's the film. You can feel the tension mounting. Matt and me getting edgier with one another off camera as well as on. The film's all spilling over into the rest of the time. Even the Indians don't seem so sure that I'm not Firmin all the time and Matt's Antonio. It's as if they think I'm *really* Firmin and then from time to time I just pretend to be this white man called Charlie. Really upside down.
    Sunday. That thing about the Indians. To tell you the truth I was a bit miffed when I found out, but now I'm beginning to see it from their point of view. I told you I was learning the language – she's really very sweet and not a stitch on but as I said no need to worry, angel, riddled with diseases I'm sure, apart from anything else, I mean. It turns out that half the words she's been teaching me are all wrong. I mean, they're real words except they're not the right ones. The first thing I learned more or less was *thkarni* which means – well she said it meant – this white stork we've been seeing a lot of. So when we saw one go flapping by I used to shout *thkarni* and the Indians would all

laugh. Turns out – and I learned this not through Miguel but
our second guide who hasn't said much most of the trip – that
thkarni is the Indians' name – well, one of their many names, to
be precise – for you-know-what. The thing up which the little
fish in the river swims if you aren't careful. Same goes for about
half the words I've been learning from that little minx. I've
learned about 60 I suppose overall and half of them are duds –
naughty words or words for something completely different. I
was majorly unpleased as you can imagine at the time but I
think what it does show is that the Indians have got a terrific
sense of humour. So I was determined to show them I could take
a joke and the next time a big stork went over I pretended not to
know what it was called and asked my girl. *Thkarni* she said
with a straight face. I looked very puzzled and shook my head a
lot and said No it can't be *thkarni* because *this* is *thkarni* (no I
didn't pull it out or anything – just pointed). And then she
knew the game was up and started giggling, and so did I to
show there weren't any hard feelings.

Monday. Getting near the end now. Just the big scene to do.
Taking two days off first. I think that's a silly decision by Vic
but I expect he's got the unions on his back. He says it's a good
idea to recharge the batteries before the big scene. I think if
you're on a roll you better go with the flow. It's all right, honey,
I don't really talk like that, I do it to irritate Matt, though it
usually doesn't because he's so thick-skinned and thinks everyone else talks like that anyway, so I guess I do it for my own
private amusement. 'Hey, Matt,' I say to him, 'we're on a roll,
let's go with the flow,' and he nods like some old prophet in The
Ten Commandments. Anyway the plan is today and tomorrow
off, then two days rehearsal for the capsizing of the raft, then
Friday the big deal. Maybe Vic is right after all, we do need to
be at our best. It's not just doing it right it's covering all the
angles. We've got to have ropes on us as per contract in case
anything happens. Don't *worry* darling it's not really dangerous.
We're doing some covering footage on a stretch of the river
where there are some rapids, but the actual capsizing which is
meant to happen there doesn't really. The crew have got a

couple of machines which churn everything up to make white water and the chippie ran up some rocks which they anchor to the bottom of the river and look just like the real thing. So no need to worry. I'm quite looking forward to it though naturally we've had a few of the old arguments about it. What happens is that both the priests get tipped into the water, one of them hits his head on a rock and the other one rescues him. Point is, who does what? I mean, here are these two, fighting tooth and nail all the way upstream, there's this huge split of doctrine going on, one of them very authoritarian and hardline (Me) and the other very permissive and soft on the Indians (Matt). I think it would be much more effective if the one who was meant to be the hardhat and who might be expected to let the other one drown in fact saves the other one even though he thinks his ideas about the Indians and his plan to baptise them when they get to the Orinoco are blasphemous. But no, it has to be *Matt* who saves *me*. Vic says that's what's historically the case, and Matt says that's what was in the script he read back in Dudesville North Dakota or wherever he hangs his hat and that's what he's going to play. '*Nobody* rescues Matt Smeaton,' he said. He actually said it, can you imagine? '*Nobody* rescues Matt Smeaton.' I said I'd remember that if ever I found him dangling upside down by one toe from a ski-lift cable. So it's all going to go ahead as per the script.

Tuesday. Another rest day.

Later

Later

Later

— love Charlie

Letter 8

Jesus Pippa. Jesus. I just couldn't go on with that last letter. Jolly bits of news from each day's shooting. Couldn't go on with it, not after what happened. But I'm fine. Really I'm fine.

Later. Poor old Matt. Shit, he was a good bloke. Sure he

could get under your skin but so would St Francis of Assisi on a job like this. He'd have spent all his time looking at the bloody birds in the Jungle instead of reading his cue-cards. Sorry, love. Bad taste, I know. Just can't find the way to put things. Very low. Poor old Matt. I wonder how you'll hear the news and what you'll think.

Jesus those fucking Indians. I think I'm going to die. I can hardly hold this biro. Sweating like a pig, *comme un porco*. God I do love you, Pippa, I just hold on to that.

C

Letter 9

I get out your photo with the chipmunk face and kiss it. That's all that matters, you and me and having babies. Let's do it, Pippa. Your mum would be pleased, wouldn't she? I said to Fish do you have kids, he said yes they're the apple of my eye. I put my arm round him and gave him a hug just like that. It's things like that keep everything going, isn't it?

It's true what they say. Go into the Jungle and you really find out what people are like. Vic's a whinger, always knew it. Whingeing on about the sodding film. I said don't worry you can always sell your memoirs to the paper. He didn't like that.

Why did they do it? Why did they do it?

love C

P.S. Wish you'd written. Would have helped now.

Letter 10

It could have been me. It could just as easily have been me. Who decides? Does anyone decide? Hey you up there in the sky, is anyone home?

I've been having this thought all day. I said to Old Fishy do you have kids and he said yes they're the apple of my eye and we just hugged each other right there in front of everyone and ever since I've been wondering what it means. The apple of my eye. What does it mean? You say words like that and everyone knows what they mean but when you look at them you can't understand them. The film's like that, the whole trip's like that. You go along thinking you know exactly what everything is, and then you stop and look at it and it doesn't make any sense and you think maybe it only made any sense in the first place because everyone was pretending it did. Does this make any sense? I mean it's like the Indians and the fake rocks that the chippie ran up. They looked at them and looked at them and the more they did the less they understood. They started off knowing they were rocks and they ended up not knowing anything. You could see it in their faces.

I'm going to give this to Rojas now. He walked past a few minutes ago and said that's the third letter you've written today why don't you put them in the same envelope and save postage? I got up and you know I swear I turned into Firmin for a moment and I said, 'Listen, Our Lady of Communications, I shall write and you will transmit as many fucking letters per day as I happen to feel like writing.' Well Firmin wouldn't have said fuck of course, but his tone was there. Sort of austere and pissed off with anything less than perfection in the world. Oh well, better go and say sorry, otherwise he'll throw them all away.

– love C

Letter 11
Waiting for copter

Pippa love –
When we get out, I'm going to do the following things. Have the biggest fucking Scotch they can pour in Caracas. Have the biggest fucking bath they can pour in Caracas. Have the longest phone call I can have with you. I can just hear your voice answering the phone, as if I've been to the shop for some ciggies and I'm back late. Then I'm going to the British Embassy and get a copy of the Daily Telegraph and I don't care if it's weeks

old and I'm going to read something I never normally look at like the nature notes if they have them. I want to be told that the house-martins are nesting or you might see a badger if you're lucky. Ordinary things that go on all the time. I'll look at the cricket scores and pretend I'm some old member in from the shires with a striped blazer and a pink gin in his fist. Maybe I'll read the births column as well. To Emma and Nicholas, a daughter, Suzie, sister to Alexander and Bill. Good old Alexander and Bill, I'll say, now you've got little Suzie to play with. You must be gentle with her, you must protect her all your lives, she's your little sister, you must make her the apple of your eye. God I'm crying Pippa, the tears are just streaming down my face.

love C

Letter 12
Caracas 21st July

Pippa love, I don't believe it, I mean I just don't believe it. We finally reach what we laughingly call civilization, we finally reach a telephone which is capable of handling transatlantic calls, I finally get my turn in the queue, I finally get through to home, and you're out. 'Number no answer, sir.' Try again. 'Number sti no answer, sir.' Try again. 'OK sir, number sti no answer.' Where are you? I don't want to ring anyone else. I don't want to ring your mum and say look we had a spot of bother but now we're back in Caracas and Matt's dead, yes, you heard it on the news but I don't want to talk about it. I just want to talk to you, honey, and I can't.

Tried again.

Tried again.

All right, so I've got a bottle of Scotch which costs about 50 quid and if the studio doesn't pay for it I'll never work for them again, and a big pile of this flimsy hotel notepaper. The others have gone out on the town. I couldn't face it. I keep remembering the last night we were here – same hotel and all – and how Matt and I went out and got stinko-paralytico together and ended up doing the Zorba dance and got thrown out and Matt pointing at me and saying to the waiters Hey don't you recognize Mista Rick from Parkway Peninsula and they didn't and made us pay for the plates.

We'd had our rest days, just three days work left. The first morning we rehearsed in the white water, pretty gingerly I don't mind saying. Vic and the crew were on the bank, Matt and I were on the raft with about a dozen Indians paddling and poling. Just to be on the safe side we had a long rope attached to the raft and tied round a tree on the bank so that if the Indians lost control the rope would pull it to a stop. Matt and I had ropes on us as per contract. So we did a run-through in the morning which was OK, then had an afternoon in the shallows with the churning machine. I thought we didn't need another day of rehearsal but Vic insisted. So the second morning we all went out again only this time wearing radio mikes as well. Vic hadn't decided whether to dub or not. The rope was attached to the tree, the crew set up on the bank, and we got ready to do three or four runs past the camera with Matt and me so busy arguing about baptising the Indians that we couldn't see the danger behind us which the audience could see for themselves. I've thought about what happened next a million times and I still don't know the answer. It was on our third run. We got the thumbs-up, started our argument and then noticed something odd. Instead of a dozen Indians on the raft there were only two, each with just a pole at the back of the raft. I suppose we thought Vic must have said try it this way because Matt and I were already into our quarrel and it shows what a pro he was to his fingertips that he carried on as per normal. So did I for that matter. Then at the end of the scene we noticed the Indians weren't doing what they normally did which was stick their poles in to stop the raft. They were just poling away and Matt shouted 'Hey, fellers, cut' but they didn't take any notice and I remember thinking maybe they're testing the rope to see if it works, and Matt and I turned at just the same moment and saw where the Indians were heading us – straight into a pile of rocks and foaming water – and I knew the rope must have broken or something. We shouted but what with the noise of the water and not knowing their language of course it wasn't any use and then we were in the water. I thought of you as we capsized, Pippa, honest I did. Just saw your face and tried to think about you. Then I tried swimming, but what with the current and the fucking cassock – and then bang I got hit in the ribs like someone had kicked me and I thought I was a goner, it must be a rock I thought and I gave up and sort of passed out. What happened was that the rope they'd put on me suddenly pulled tight. I don't remember anything else until I was on the bank throwing up water and puking in the mud while the sound-man thumped on my back and put his fists in my stomach. My line held, Matt's line broke. That's how it was, that's my luck.

Everyone was in shock, as you can imagine. Some of the crew tried getting along the bank – you know how people are sometimes found clinging to the branches of trees overhanging the river a mile or so downstream. But it wasn't like that. That sort of thing is strictly for the movies. Matt was gone, and anyway the crew couldn't get more than 20 or 30 yards beyond where they'd set up because they don't exactly have towpaths in the Jungle. 'Why were there only two?' Vic kept saying. 'Why only two?' They looked around for the Indians who'd helped them set up but they weren't there. Then they went back to camp and the only person there was Miguel the interpreter, who'd been having a long conversation with one of the Indians and when he turned round all the other Indians had scarpered.

Then we went to see what had happened to the rope round the tree and there wasn't anything left, it had just gone. Which was pretty odd as it was fixed with one of those fancy knots which simply can't pull out. No doubt as per contract. Bloody suspicious. Then we talked to Miguel again and it turned out the Indian had started this long conversation with him before we could possibly have had the accident. So they presumably knew what was going to happen. And when we looked in the camp they'd taken everything – clothes, food, equipment.

What did they take the clothes for? They don't even wear them.

It was a bloody long wait for the copter, I can tell you. The Indians had taken the radio telephones (they'd have gone off with the genny if they'd had a crane) and Caracas thought they'd just broken down again so came as per normal. Two days waiting like two bloody months. Me thinking I'd probably got some filthy fever in spite of the jabs. Apparently when they pulled me out of the river and bashed the water out of my belly the first thing I said as I came round was, 'Riddled with diseases, I'm sure' and the crew broke up in this hysterical laughter. Don't remember, but it sounds like Charlie. Thought I might be in for beri-beri and co. Ouch in spades, I thought.

Why did they do it? That's what I keep coming back to. Why? Most of the others think they did it because they're primitive – you know, not white men, never trust a native and so on. That's no go. I never did think they were primitive and they always told the truth (except when they were teaching me the language) and were a damn sight more trustworthy than some of the white men we had on the job. The first thing I thought of was that we'd offended them in some way we didn't know – done a terrible insult to their gods or something. But I simply couldn't think of anything.

The way I'm looking at it, either there's some connection with what happened a couple of hundred years ago or there isn't. Perhaps it's just a chance coincidence. It so happens that the descendants of the original Indians whose raft capsized were also in charge of another raft that capsized at about the same point in the river. Maybe these Indians can only take so much of poling Jesuits upstream and just instinctively snap and turn nasty and shove them overboard. Not very likely is it? *Or* there is some connection between the two incidents. This is what I think anyway. It seems to me that the Indians – our Indians – knew what had happened to Father Firmin and Father Antonio all those years ago. It's the sort of thing that gets handed down as the women are pounding the manioc root or whatever. Those Jesuits were probably quite big in the Indians' history. Think of that story getting passed down the generations, each time they handed it on it became more colourful and exaggerated. And then we come along, another lot of white men who've also got two chaps in long black skirts with them, who also want to be poled up the river to the Orinoco. Sure, there are differences, they've got this one-eyed machine and so on, but basically it's the same thing, and we even tell them it's going to end in the same way with the raft capsizing. I mean, it's hard to think of an equivalent, but say you were an inhabitant of Hastings in the year 2066 and you went down to the beach one day and these longships were coming towards you and lots of people in chainmail and pointy helmets got out and said they'd come for the Battle of Hastings and would you rustle up King Harold so they could shoot him in the eye and here was a huge wallet full of money for you to play your part. First of all, you might be inclined to do it, wouldn't you? And then you'd get thinking about why *they* wanted you to do it. And one thing you might come up with – this is just my idea, Vic isn't so sure about it – is that they (i.e. us) have come back to re-enact the ceremony for some reason that's tremendously important to their tribe. Perhaps the Indians thought it was a religious thing, like celebrating the 500th anniversary of a cathedral or whatever.

And there's another possibility – that the Indians were actually following the argument between the Jesuits and under-standing it a lot better than we thought. They – Matt and me, that's to say – were arguing about baptising the Indians, and at the point the raft capsized it looked as if I was winning the argument. I was the senior priest, after all, and I was against baptism – at least until the Indians pulled their socks up and stopped some of their filthy practices. So maybe the Indians understood this and tipped up the raft because they were trying to kill Father Firmin (me!) so that Father Antonio would survive and baptise them. How about that? Except that the first time round the Indians saw that Firmin survived and they ran away because they were afraid, and the second time round they saw they'd killed Antonio, which was quite the wrong result for them so they ran away because it had all gone wrong.

Is that right? I just know it's more complicated than it's ever going to seem in the newspapers. I shouldn't be surprised if Hollywood sends a plane to bomb the Indians and punish them for the death of Matt. Or does a remake – yes, that'd be more bloody likely. Who gets the part of Matt? What a career opportunity. I ask you.

Seem to be stuck here for a week or so. That bloody studio and its bloody lawyers. Apparently the movie has to be officially called off in some way and that takes time.

Taking this down to Our Lady of Communications and expressing it. Makes a change to be giving it to a real postman.

all love, Charlie

Letter 13

Christ don't you do that to me, and I mean *ever*. Two days out of the fucking Jungle after nearly dying and you put the phone down on me. Look, as I was trying to explain to you, she was out here working, it was a complete coincidence. I know I've been behaving like a pig, *comme un porco*, for a bit, but please read all my letters from the Jungle and you'll see I'm a changed man. It's all over between Linda and me, I told you that before I left. And I can't control where the woman works, can I? Yes I did know she was going to be in Caracas and No I didn't tell you and Yes that was wrong but would it have been better if I'd told you? How on earth did you find out anyway? No she isn't here, as far as I know or care she's in the West Indies. For God's sake, Pippa, let's not throw away five years.

– your Charlie

P.S. Am expressing this.
P.P.S. Caracas filthy dump. Stuck here at least until the 4th.
P.P.P.S. Love you.

Telegram

PLEASE CALL CHARLIE HOTEL INTERCONTINENTAL
SOONEST STOP LOVE CHARLIE STOP

Telegram

FOR GS SAKE CALL INTERCONTINENTAL MUST TALK
SOONEST STOP LOVE CHARLIE

Telegram

WILL CALL NOON YOUR TIME THURSDAY MUCH TO
DISCUSS STOP CHARLIE

Telegram

DAMN YOU ANSWER THE PHONE OR CALL ME PIPPA
STOP CHARLIE

Letter 14

Dear Pippa –
   As you don't seem to be responding to telegrams for reasons
best known to yourself, I am writing to say that I am not coming
home immediately. I need time and space not just to get over
the appalling things which have happened to me in which you
do not seem to show much interest but also to think through
where the two of us are at. There seems no point in saying that I
love you in spite of everything because that only seems to irritate
you for reasons best known to yourself and which you choose
neither to explain nor comment on. I will be in touch when I
know where I'm at about all this.

Charlie

219

P.S. I'm expressing this.

P.P.S. If any of this is anything to do with that creep Gavin I will personally break his personal fucking neck. I should have hit him a lot harder in the first place. And in case you haven't noticed, he couldn't act his way out of a paper bag. No talent. No cojones.

Letter 15
St Lucia
Some bloody day or other

Listen bitch why don't you just get out of my life, go on just get out GET OUT. You always fucked things up didn't you that was your one great talent fucking things up. My friends said she's trouble and the last thing I should have done was let her move in and I was a bloody fool not to believe them. Christ if you think I'm an egotist you should look in the mirror baby. Of course I'm drunk what do you think it's one way of getting you out of my head. Now I'm going to get stinko bloody paralytico. In vino bloody veritas.

Charlie "the Hell-Raiser"

P.S. I'm expressing this.

Telegram

RETURNING LONDON MONDAY FIFTEENTH STOP KINDLY REMOVE SELF AND POSSESSIONS FROM FLAT BEFORE THEN STOP LEAVE KEY STOP ENDIT STOP

PARENTHESIS

Let me tell you something about her. It's that middle stretch of the night, when the curtains leak no light, the only street-noise is the grizzle of a returning Romeo, and the birds haven't begun their routine yet cheering business. She's lying on her side, turned away from me. I can't see her in the dark, but from the hushed swell of her breathing I could draw you the map of her body. When she's happy she can sleep for hours in the same position. I've watched over her in all those sewery parts of the night, and can testify that she doesn't move. It could be just down to good digestion and calm dreams, of course; but I take it as a sign of happiness.

Our nights are different. She falls asleep like someone yielding to the gentle tug of a warm tide, and floats with confidence till morning. I fall asleep more grudgingly, thrashing at the waves, either reluctant to let a good day depart or still bitching about a bad one. Different currents run through our spells of unconsciousness. Every so often I find myself catapulted out of bed with fear of time and death, panic at the approaching void; feet on the floor, head in hands, I shout a useless (and disappointingly uneloquent) 'No, no, *no*' as I wake. Then she has to stroke the horror away from me, like sluicing down a dog that's come barking from a dirty river.

Less often, it's her sleep that's broken by a scream, and my turn to move across her in a sweat of protectiveness. I am starkly awake, and she delivers to me through sleepy lips the cause of her outcry. 'A *very* large beetle,' she will say, as if she wouldn't have bothered me about a smaller one; or 'The steps were slippery'; or merely (which strikes me as cryptic to the point of tautology), 'Something nasty.' Then, having expelled this damp toad, this handful of gutter-muck from her system, she sighs and returns to a purged sleep. I lie awake, clutching a slimy amphibian, shifting a handful of sodden detritus from hand to hand, alarmed and admiring. (I'm not claiming grander dreams, by the way. Sleep democratizes fear. The terror of a lost shoe or a missed train is as great here as that of guerrilla attack or nuclear war.) I admire her because she's got this job of sleeping that we all have to do, every night, ceaselessly, until we die, much better worked out than I have. She handles it like a sophisticated traveller unthreatened by a new airport. Whereas I lie there in the night with an expired passport, pushing a baggage trolley with a squeaking wheel across to the wrong carousel.

Anyway . . . she's asleep, turned away from me on her side. The usual stratagems and repositionings have failed to induce narcosis in me, so I decide to settle myself against the soft zigzag of her body. As I move and start to nestle my shin against a calf whose muscles are loosened by sleep, she senses what I'm doing, and without waking reaches up with her left hand and pulls the hair off her shoulders on to the top of her head, leaving me her bare nape to nestle in. Each time she does this I feel a shudder of love at the exactness of this sleeping courtesy. My eyes prickle with tears, and I have to stop myself from waking her up to remind her of my love. At that moment, unconsciously, she's touched some secret fulcrum of my feelings for her. She doesn't know, of course; I've never told her of this tiny, precise pleasure of the night. Though I'm telling her now, I suppose . . .

You think she's really awake when she does it? I suppose it could sound like a conscious courtesy – an agreeable gesture, but hardly one denoting that love has roots below the gum of consciousness. You're right to be sceptical: we should be indulgent only to a certain point with lovers, whose vanities rival those of politicians. Still, I can offer further proof. Her hair falls, you see, to her shoulders. But a few years ago, when they promised us the summer heat would last for months, she had it cut short. Her nape was bare for kissing all day long. And in the dark, when we lay beneath a single sheet and I gave off a

Calabrian sweat, when the middle stretch of the night was shorter but still hard to get through – then, as I turned towards that loose S beside me, she would, with a soft murmur, try to lift the lost hair from the back of her neck.

'I love you,' I whisper into that sleeping nape, 'I love you.' All novelists know their art proceeds by indirection. When tempted by didacticism, the writer should imagine a spruce sea-captain eyeing the storm ahead, bustling from instrument to instrument in a catherine wheel of gold braid, expelling crisp orders down the speaking tube. But there is nobody below decks; the engine-room was never installed, and the rudder broke off centuries ago. The captain may put on a very good act, convincing not just himself but even some of the passengers; though whether their floating world will come through depends not on him but on the mad winds and sullen tides, the icebergs and the sudden crusts of reef.

Still, it's natural for the novelist sometimes to fret at the obliquities of fiction. In the lower half of El Greco's 'Burial of the Count of Orgaz' in Toledo there is a line-up of angular, ruffed mourners. They gaze this way and that in stagey grief. Only one of them looks directly out of the picture, and he holds us with a gloomy, ironical eye – an unflattered eye, as well, we can't help noticing. Tradition claims that the figure is El Greco himself. I did this, he says. I painted this. I am responsible, and so I face towards you.

Poets seem to write more easily about love than prose writers. For a start, they own that flexible 'I' (when I say 'I' you will want to know within a paragraph or two whether I mean Julian Barnes or someone invented; a poet can shimmy between the two, getting credit for both deep feeling and objectivity). Then again, poets seem able to turn bad love – selfish, shitty love – into good love poetry. Prose writers lack this power of admirable, dishonest transformation. We can only turn bad love into prose about bad love. So we are envious (and slightly distrustful) when poets talk to us of love.

And they write this stuff called love poetry. It's collected into books called *The Great Lovers' Valentine World Anthology of*

Love Poetry or whatever. Then there are love letters; these are collected into *The Golden Quill Treasury of Love Letters* (available by mail order). But there is no genre that answers to the name of love prose. It sounds awkward, almost self-contradictory. *Love Prose: A Plodder's Handbook.* Look for it in the carpentry section.

The Canadian writer Mavis Gallant put it like this: 'The mystery of what a couple *is*, exactly, is almost the only true mystery left to us, and when we have come to the end of it there will be no more need for literature – or for love, for that matter.' When I first read this, I gave it in the margin the chess marking '!?' indicating a move which, though possibly brilliant, is probably unsound. But increasingly the view convinces, and the marking is changed to '!!'

'What will survive of us is love.' This is the cautiously approached conclusion of Philip Larkin's poem 'An Arundel Tomb'. The line surprises us, for much of the poet's work was a squeezed flannel of disenchantment. We are ready to be cheered; but we should first give a prosey scowl and ask of this poetic flourish, Is it true? Is love what will survive of us? It would be nice to think so. It would be comforting if love were an energy source which continued to glow after our deaths. Early television sets, when you turned them off, used to leave a blob of light in the middle of the screen, which slowly diminished from the size of a florin to an expiring speck. As a boy I would watch this process each evening, vaguely wanting to hold it back (and seeing it, with adolescent melancholy, as the pinpoint of human existence fading inexorably in a black universe). Is love meant to glow on like this for a while after the set has been switched off? I can't see it myself. When the survivor of a loving couple dies, love dies too. If anything survives of us it will probably be something else. What will survive of Larkin is not his love but his poetry: that's obvious. And whenever I read the end of 'An Arundel Tomb' I'm reminded of William Huskisson. He was a politician and a financier, well-known in his time; but we remember him today because on the 15th of September 1830, at the opening of the Liverpool and Manchester Railway, he became the first person to be run down and killed by a train (that's what he *became*, was turned into). And did William Huskisson love? And did his love last? We don't know. All that has survived of him is his moment of final carelessness; death froze him as an instructive cameo about the nature of progress.

'I love you.' For a start, we'd better put these words on a high shelf; in a square box behind glass which we have to break with our elbow; in the bank. We shouldn't leave them lying around the house like a tube of vitamin C. If the words come too easily to hand, we'll use them without thought; we won't be able to resist. Oh, we say we won't, but we will. We'll get drunk, or lonely, or – likeliest of all – plain damn hopeful, and there are the words gone, used up, grubbied. We think we might be in love and we're trying out the words to see if they're appropriate? How can we know what we think till we hear what we say? Come off it; that won't wash. These are grand words; we must make sure we deserve them. Listen to them again: 'I love you.' Subject, verb, object: the unadorned, impregnable sentence. The subject is a short word, implying the self-effacement of the lover. The verb is longer but unambiguous, a demonstrative moment as the tongue flicks anxiously away from the palate to release the vowel. The object, like the subject, has no consonants, and is attained by pushing the lips forward as if for a kiss. 'I love you.' How serious, how weighted, how freighted it sounds.

I imagine a phonic conspiracy between the world's languages. They make a conference decision that the phrase must always sound like something to be earned, to be striven for, to be worthy of. *Ich liebe dich*: a late-night, cigarette-voiced whisper, with that happy rhyme of subject and object. *Je t'aime*: a different procedure, with the subject and object being got out of the way first, so that the long vowel of adoration can be savoured to the full. (The grammar is also one of reassurance: with the object positioned second, the beloved isn't suddenly going to turn out to be someone different.) *Ya tebya lyublyu*: the object once more in consoling second position, but this time – despite the hinting rhyme of subject and object – an implication of difficulty, obstacles to be overcome. *Ti amo*: it sounds perhaps a bit too much like an apéritif, but is full of structural conviction with subject and verb, the doer and the deed, enclosed in the same word.

Forgive the amateur approach. I'll happily hand the project over to some philanthropic foundation devoted to expanding the sum of human knowledge. Let them commission a research team to examine the phrase in all the languages of the world, to see how it varies, to discover what its sounds denote to those who hear them, to find out if the measure of happiness changes according to the richness of the phrasing. A question from the floor: are there tribes whose lexicon lacks the words *I love you*? Or have they all died out?

We must keep these words in their box behind glass. And when we take them out we must be careful with them. Men will say 'I love you' to get women into bed with them; women will say 'I love you' to get men into marriage with them; both will say 'I love you' to keep fear at bay, to convince themselves of the deed by the word, to assure themselves that the promised condition has arrived, to deceive themselves that it hasn't yet gone away. We must beware of such uses. *I love you* shouldn't go out into the world, become a currency, a traded share, make profits for us. It will do that if we let it. But keep this biddable phrase for whispering into a nape from which the absent hair has just been swept.

I'm away from her at the moment; perhaps you guessed. The transatlantic telephone gives off a mocking, heard-it-all-before echo. 'I love you,' and before she can answer I hear my metallic other self respond, 'I love you.' This isn't satisfactory; the echoing words have gone public. I try again, with the same result. *I love you I love you* – it's become some trilling song popular for a lurid month and then dismissed to the club circuit where pudgy rockers with grease in their hair and yearning in their voice will use it to unfrock the lolling front-row girls. *I love you I love you* while the lead guitar giggles and the drummer's tongue lies wetly in his opened mouth.

We must be precise with love, its language and its gestures.

If it is to save us, we must look at it as clearly as we should learn to look at death. Should love be taught in school? First term: friendship; second term: tenderness; third term: passion. Why not? They teach kids how to cook and mend cars and fuck one another without getting pregnant; and the kids are, we assume, much better at all of this than we were, but what use is any of that to them if they don't know about love? They're expected to muddle through by themselves. Nature is supposed to take over, like the automatic pilot on an aeroplane. Yet Nature, on to whom we pitch responsibility for all we cannot understand, isn't very good when set to automatic. Trusting virgins drafted into marriage never found Nature had all the answers when they turned out the light. Trusting virgins were told that love was the promised land, an ark on which two might escape the Flood. It may be an ark, but one on which anthropophagy is rife; an ark skippered by some crazy greybeard who beats you round the head with his gopher-wood stave, and might pitch you overboard at any moment.

Let's start at the beginning. Love makes you happy? No. Love makes the person you love happy? No. Love makes everything all right? Indeed no. I used to believe all this, of course. Who hasn't (who doesn't still, somewhere below decks in the psyche)? It's in all our books, our films; it's the sunset of a thousand stories. What would love be *for* if it didn't solve everything? Surely we can deduce from the very strength of our aspiration that love, once achieved, eases the daily ache, works some effortless analgesia?

A couple love each other, but they aren't happy. What do we conclude? That one of them doesn't really love the other; that they love one another a certain amount but not enough? I dispute that *really*; I dispute that *enough*. I've loved twice in my life (which seems quite a lot to me), once happily, once unhappily. It was the unhappy love that taught me most about love's nature – though not at the time, not until years later. Dates and details – fill them in as you like. But I was in love, and loved, for a long time, many years. At first I was brazenly happy, bullish with solipsistic joy; yet most of the time I was puzzlingly, naggingly unhappy. Didn't I love her enough? I knew I did – and put off half my future for her. Didn't she love me enough? I knew she did – and gave up half her past for me. We lived side by side for many years, fretting at what was wrong with the equation we had invented. Mutual love did not add up to happiness. Stubbornly, we insisted that it did.

And later I decided what it was I believed about love. We think of it as an active force. My love *makes* her happy; her love *makes* me happy: how could this be wrong? It is wrong; it evokes a false conceptual model. It implies that love is a transforming wand, one that unlooses the ravelled knot, fills the top hat with handkerchiefs, sprays the air with doves. But the model isn't from magic but particle physics. My love does not, cannot *make* her happy; my love can only release in her the capacity to be happy. And now things seem more understandable. How come I can't make her happy, how come she can't make me happy? Simple: the atomic reaction you expect isn't taking place, the beam with which you are bombarding the particles is on the wrong wavelength.

But love isn't an atomic bomb, so let's take a homelier comparison. I'm writing this at the home of a friend in Michigan. It's a normal American house with all the gadgets technology can dream (except a gadget for making happiness). He drove me here from the Detroit airport yesterday. As we turned into the driveway he reached into the glove pocket for a remote-control device; at a masterful touch, the garage doors rolled up and away. This is the model I propose. You are arriving home – or think you are – and as you approach the garage you try to work your routine magic. Nothing happens; the doors remain closed. You do it again. Again nothing. At first puzzled, then anxious, then furious with disbelief, you sit in the driveway with the engine running; you sit there for weeks, months, for years, waiting for the doors to open. But you are in the wrong car, in front of the wrong garage, waiting outside the wrong house. One of the troubles is this: the heart isn't heart-shaped.

'We must love one another or die,' wrote W. H. Auden,

bringing from E. M. Forster the declaration: 'Because he once wrote "We must love one another or die," he can command me to follow him.' Auden, however, was dissatisfied with this famous line from 'September 1, 1939.' 'That's a damned lie!' he commented. 'We must die anyway.' So when reprinting the poem he altered the line to the more logical 'We must love one another and die.' Later he suppressed it altogether.

This shift from *or* to *and* is one of poetry's most famous emendations. When I first came across it, I applauded the honest rigour with which Auden the critic revised Auden the poet. If a line sounds ringingly good but isn't true, out with it – such an approach is bracingly free of writerly self-infatuation. Now I am not so sure. *We must love one another and die* certainly has logic on its side; it's also about as interesting on the subject of the human condition, and as striking, as *We must listen to the radio and die* or *We must remember to defrost the fridge and die.* Auden was rightly suspicious of his own rhetoric; but to say that the line *We must love one another or die* is untrue because we die anyway (or because those who do not love do not instantly expire) is to take a narrow or forgetful view. There are equally logical, and more persuasive, ways of reading the *or* line. The first, obvious one is this: we must love one another because if we don't we are liable to end up killing one another. The second is: we must love one another because if we don't, if love doesn't fuel our lives, then we might as well be dead. This, surely, is no 'damned lie', to claim that those who get their deepest satisfactions from other things are living empty lives, are posturing crabs who swagger the sea-bed in borrowed shells.

This is difficult territory. We must be precise, and we mustn't become sentimental. If we are to oppose love to such wily, muscled concepts as power, money, history and death, then we mustn't retreat into self-celebration or snobby vagueness. Love's enemies profit from its unspecific claims, its grand capacity for isolationism. So where do we start? Love may or may not produce happiness; whether or not it does in the end, its primary effect is to energize. Have you ever talked so well, needed less sleep, returned to sex so eagerly, as when you were first in love? The anaemic begin to glow, while the normally healthy become intolerable. Next, it gives spine-stretching confidence. You feel you are standing up straight for the first time in your life; you can do anything while this feeling lasts, you can take on the world. (Shall we make this distinction: that love enhances the confidence, whereas sexual conquest merely develops the ego?) Then again, it gives clarity of vision: it's a windscreen wiper across the eyeball. Have you ever seen things so clearly as when you were first in love?

If we look at nature, do we see where love comes in? Not really. There are occasional species which apparently mate for life (though imagine the opportunities for adultery on all those long-distance migratory swims and night flights); but on the whole we see merely the exercise of power, dominance and sexual convenience. The feminist and the chauvinist interpret Nature differently. The feminist looks for examples of disinterested behaviour in the animal kingdom, sees the male here and there performing tasks which in human society might be characterized as 'female'. Consider the king penguin: the male is the one that incubates the egg, carrying it around on its feet and protecting it for months from the Antarctic weather with a fold of its lower belly . . . Yeah, replies the chauvinist, and what about the bull elephant seal? Just lies about on the beach all day and fucks every female in sight. It does regrettably seem true that the seal's behaviour is more standard than that of the male penguin. And knowing my sex as I do, I'm inclined to doubt the latter's motivation. The male penguin might just have calculated that if you're stuck in the Antarctic for years on end then the cleverest thing to do is stay at home minding the egg while you send the female off to catch fish in the freezing waters. He might just have worked things out to his own convenience.

So where does love come in? It's not strictly necessary, is it? We can build dams, like the beaver, without love. We can organize complex societies, like the bee, without love. We can travel long distances, like the albatross, without love. We can put our head in the sand, like the ostrich, without love. We can die out as a species, like the dodo, without love.

Is it a useful mutation that helps the race survive? I can't see it. Was love implanted, for instance, so that warriors would fight harder for their lives, bearing deep inside them the candlelit memory of the domestic hearth? Hardly: the history of the world teaches us that it is the new form of arrowhead, the canny general, the full stomach and the prospect of plunder that are the decisive factors in war, rather than sentimental minds drooling about home.

Then is love some luxury that sprang up in peaceful times, like quilt-making? Something pleasant, complex, but inessential? A random development, culturally reinforced, which just happens to be love rather than something else? I sometimes think so. There was once a tribe of Indians in the far north-west of the United States (I'm not inventing them) who lived an extraordinarily easy life. They were protected from enemies by their isolation and the land they cultivated was boundlessly fertile. They only had to drop a wizened bean over their shoulders for a plant to spurt from the ground and rain pods at them. They were healthy, content and had failed to develop any taste for internecine warfare. As a result, they had a lot of time on their hands. No doubt they excelled at things in which indolent societies specialize; no doubt their basketwork became rococo, their erotic skills more gymnastical, their use of crushed leaves to induce stupefying trances increasingly efficient. We don't know about such aspects of their lives, but we do know what was the main pursuit of their generous leisure hours. They stole from one another. That's what they liked to do, and that's what they celebrated. As they staggered out of their tepees and another faultless day came smooching in from the Pacific, they would sniff the honeyed air and ask one another what they'd got up to the previous night. The answer would be a shy confession – or smug boast – of theft. Old Redface had his blanket pilfered again by Little Grey Wolf. Well, did you ever? He's coming along, that Little Grey Wolf. And what did you get up to? Me? Oh, I just snitched the eyebrows from the top of the totem-pole. Oh, not that one again. Bo-*ring*.

Is this how we should think of love? Our love doesn't help us survive, any more than did the Indians' thieving. Yet it gives us our individuality, our purpose. Take away their joyful larcenies and those Indians would be able to define themselves less easily. So is it just a rogue mutation? We don't need it for the expansion of our race; indeed, it's inimical to orderly civilization. Sexual desire would be much easier if we didn't have to worry about love. Marriage would be more straightforward – and perhaps most lasting – if we were not itchy for love, exultant on its arrival, fearful of its departure.

If we look at the history of the world, it seems surprising that love is included. It's an excrescence, a monstrosity, some tardy addition to the agenda. It reminds me of those half-houses which according to normal criteria of map reading shouldn't exist. The other week I went to this North American address: 2041 ½ Yonge Street. The owner of 2041 must at some point have sold off a little plot, and this half-numbered, half-acknowledged house was put up. And yet people can live in it quite comfortably, people call it home . . . Tertullian said of Christian belief that it was true because it was impossible. Perhaps love is essential because it's unnecessary.

She is the centre of my world. The Armenians believed that Ararat was the centre of the world; but the mountain was divided between three great empires, and the Armenians ended up with none of it, so I shan't continue this comparison. *I love you*. I'm home again, and there's no mocking echo on the words. *Je t'aime*. *Ti amo* (with soda). And if you had no tongue, no celebrating language, you'd do this: cross your hands at the wrist with palms facing towards you; place your crossed wrists over your heart (the middle of your chest, anyway); then move your hands outwards a short distance, and open them towards the object of your love. It's just as eloquent as speech. And imagine all the tender modulations that are possible, the subtleties that can be constructed from kissing knuckles, matching palms and playful fingertips whose whorled pads bear the proof of our individuality.

But matching palms mislead. The heart isn't heart-shaped, that's one of our problems. We imagine, don't we, some neat bivalve whose shape encodes the way in which love fuses two halves, two separatenesses, into a whole? We imagine this crisp symbol scarlet with a powerful blush, scarlet also with the blood of tumescence. A medical textbook doesn't immediately disenchant us; here the heart is mapped like the London Underground. Aorta, left and right pulmonary arteries and veins, left and right subclavian arteries, left and right coronary arteries, left and right carotid arteries . . . it looks elegant, purposeful, a confident network of pumping tubes. Here the blood runs on time, you think.

Reverberent facts:

- the heart is the first organ to develop in the embryo; when we are no more than the size of a kidney bean, our heart is visible, pumping away;
- in a child, the heart is proportionately much larger than in an adult: 1/130th of total body weight, as opposed to 1/300th;
- during life the size, shape and position of the heart are subject to considerable variations;
- after death the heart assumes the shape of a pyramid.

The ox heart I bought at Corrigans weighed 2lbs 13oz and cost £2.42p. The biggest available animal specimen; but also one with human application. 'He had the heart of an ox': a phrase from the literature of Empire, of adventure, of childhood. Those pith-helmeted cavaliers who despatched rhinos with a single well-placed slug from an army pistol while the colonel's daughter cowered behind the baobab had simple natures but not, if this ox was anything to go by, simple hearts. The organ was heavy, squat, bloody, clamped tight like a violent fist. Unlike the railway map in the textbook, the real thing proved close and reluctant with its secrets.

I sliced it up with a radiologist friend. 'It hadn't got long to go, this ox,' she commented. Had the heart belonged to one of her patients, he wouldn't have pangaed his way through many more jungles. Our own small journey was effected with a Sabatier kitchen knife. We hacked our way into the left atrium and left ventricle, admiring the porterhouse heft of the muscles. We stroked the silky Rue de Rivoli lining, poked our fingers into exit wounds. The veins were stretch elastic, the arteries chunky squid. A post-mortal blood clot lay like a burgundy slug in the left ventricle. We frequently lost our way in this compacted meat. The two halves of the heart did not ease apart as I'd fancifully imagined, but clung desperately round one another like drowning lovers. We cut into the same ventricle twice, believing we'd found the other one. We admired the clever valve system, and the *chordae tendineae* which restrain each valve from opening too far: a tough little parachute harness preventing over-deployment of the canopy.

After we'd finished with it, the heart lay on a stained bed of newspaper for the rest of the day, reduced to an unpromising dinner. I went through cookbooks to see what I might do with it. I did find one recipe, for stuffed heart served with boiled rice and wedges of lemon, but it didn't sound very inviting. It certainly didn't merit the name given it by the Danes, who invented it. They call this dish Passionate Love.

Do you remember that paradox of love, of the first few weeks and months of Passionate Love (it's capitalized, like the recipe, to begin with) – the paradox about time? You are in love, at a point where pride and apprehension scuffle within you. Part of you wants time to slow down: for this, you say to yourself, is the best period of your whole life. I am in love, I want to savour it, study it, lie around in languor with it; may today last forever. This is your poetical side. However, there is also your prose side, which urges time not to slow down but hurry up. How do you know this is love, your prose side whispers like a sceptical lawyer, it's only been around for a few weeks, a few months. You won't know it's the real thing unless you (and she) still feel the same in, oh, a year or so at least; that's the only way to prove you aren't living a dragonfly mistake. Get through this bit, however much you enjoy it, as fast as possible; then you'll be able to find out whether or not you're *really* in love.

A photograph develops in a tray of liquid. Previously it's been just a blank sheet of printing paper shut up in a lightproof envelope; now it has a function, an image, a certainty. We slide the photo quickly into the tray of fixer to secure that clear, vulnerable moment, to make the image harder, unchippable, solid for at least a few years. But what if you plunge it into the fixer and the chemical doesn't work? This progress, this amorous motion you feel, might refuse to stabilize. Have you seen a picture go on relentlessly developing until its whole surface is black, its celebratory moment obliterated?

Is it normal, this state of love, or abnormal? Statistically, of course, it's abnormal. In a wedding photograph, the interesting faces are not those of the bride and groom, but of the encircling guests: the bride's younger sister (will it happen to me, the tremendous thing?), the groom's elder brother (will she let him down like that bitch did me?), the bride's mother (how it takes me back), the groom's father (if the lad knew what I know now — if only *I'd* known what I know now), the priest (strange how even the tongue-tied are moved to eloquence by these ancient vows), the scowling adolescent (what do they want to get *married* for?), and so on. The central couple are in a profoundly abnormal state; yet try telling them that. Their condition feels more normal than it has ever done before. *This* is normal, they say to one another; all that time before, which we thought was normal, wasn't normal at all.

And such conviction of normality, such certainty that their essence has been developed and fixed by love, and is now to be framed forever, gives them a touching arrogance. This is definitely abnormal: when else is arrogance touching? It is here. Look at the photo again: study, beneath the happy dentition, the serious self-satisfaction of the moment. How can you not be moved? Couples noisy with their love (for nobody has ever loved before — not properly — have they?) may irritate, but can't be mocked. Even when there's something to make an emotional conformist smirk — some thumping disparity of age, looks, education, pretension — the couple have for this moment a lacquer finish: laughter's bubbling spittle simply wipes off. The young man on the older woman's arm, the frump attached to the dandy, the hostess chained to an ascetic: they all feel profoundly

normal. And this should move us. *They* will be feeling indulgent towards us, because we are not so evidently, so rowdily in
love; yet we should be discreetly indulgent towards them.

Don't get me wrong. I'm not recommending one form of love
over another. I don't know if prudent or reckless love is the
better, monied or penniless love the surer, heterosexual or
homosexual love the sexier, married or unmarried love the
stronger. I may be tempted towards didacticism, but this isn't
an advice column. I can't tell you whether or not you're in love.
If you need to ask, then you probably aren't, that's my only
advice (and even this might be wrong). I can't tell you who to
love, or how to love: those school courses would be how-not-
not-to as much as how-to classes (it's like creative writing – you
can't teach them how to write or what to write, only usefully
point out where they're going wrong and save them time). But I
can tell you why to love. Because the history of the world, which
only stops at the half-house of love to bulldoze it into rubble, is
ridiculous without it. The history of the world becomes brutally
self-important without love. Our random mutation is essential
because it is unnecessary. Love won't change the history of the
world (that nonsense about Cleopatra's nose is strictly for
sentimentalists), but it will do something much more important: teach us to stand up to history, to ignore its chin-out strut.
I don't accept your terms, love says; sorry, you don't impress,
and by the way what a silly uniform you're wearing. Of course,
we don't fall in love to help out with the world's ego problem;
yet this is one of love's surer effects.

Love and truth, that's the vital connection, love and truth.
Have you ever told so much truth as when you were first in love?
Have you ever seen the world so clearly? Love makes us see the
truth, makes it our duty to tell the truth. Lying in bed: listen to
the undertow of warning in that phrase. *Lying in bed, we tell the
truth*: it sounds like a paradoxical sentence from a first-year
philosophy primer. But it's more (and less) than that: a description of moral duty. Don't roll that eyeball, give a flattering
groan, fake that orgasm. Tell the truth with your body even if –
especially if – that truth is not melodramatic. Bed is one of the

prime places where you can lie without getting caught, where you can holler and grunt in the dark and later boast about your 'performance'. Sex isn't acting (however much we admire our own script); sex is about truth. How you cuddle in the dark governs how you see the history of the world. It's as simple as that.

We get scared by history; we allow ourselves to be bullied by dates.

> In fourteen hundred and ninety-two
> Columbus sailed the ocean blue

And then what? Everyone became wiser? People stopped building new ghettoes in which to practise the old persecutions? Stopped making the old mistakes, or new mistakes, or new versions of old mistakes? (And does history repeat itself, the first time as tragedy, the second time as farce? No, that's too grand, too considered a process. History just burps, and we taste again that raw-onion sandwich it swallowed centuries ago.)

Dates don't tell the truth. They bawl at us – left, right, left, right, pick 'em up there you miserable shower. They want to make us think we're always progressing, always going forward. But what happened after 1492?

> In fourteen hundred and ninety-three
> He sailed right back across the sea

That's the sort of date I like. Let's celebrate 1493, not 1492; the return, not the discovery. What happened in 1493? The predictable glory, of course, the royal flattery, the heraldic promotions on the Columbus scutcheon. But there was also this. Before departure a prize of 10,000 maravedis had been promised to the first man to sight the New World. An ordinary sailor had won this bounty, yet when the expedition returned Columbus claimed it for himself (the dove still elbowing the raven from history). The sailor went off in disappointment to

Morocco, where, they say, he became a renegade. It was an interesting year, 1493.

History isn't what happened. History is just what historians tell us. There was a pattern, a plan, a movement, expansion, the march of democracy; it is a tapestry, a flow of events, a complex narrative, connected, explicable. One good story leads to another. First it was kings and archbishops with some offstage divine tinkering, then it was the march of ideas and the movements of masses, then little local events which mean something bigger, but all the time it's connections, progress, meaning, this led to this, this happened because of this. And we, the readers of history, the sufferers from history, we scan the pattern for hopeful conclusions, for the way ahead. And we cling to history as a series of salon pictures, conversation pieces whose participants we can easily reimagine back into life, when all the time it's more like a multi-media collage, with paint applied by decorator's roller rather than camel-hair brush.

The history of the world? Just voices echoing in the dark; images that burn for a few centuries and then fade; stories, old stories that sometimes seem to overlap; strange links, impertinent connections. We lie here in our hospital bed of the present (what nice clean sheets we get nowadays) with a bubble of daily news drip-fed into our arm. We think we know who we are, though we don't quite know why we're here, or how long we shall be forced to stay. And while we fret and writhe in bandaged uncertainty – are we a voluntary patient? – we fabulate. We make up a story to cover the facts we don't know or can't accept; we keep a few true facts and spin a new story round them. Our panic and our pain are only eased by soothing fabulation; we call it history.

There's one thing I'll say for history. It's very good at finding things. We try to cover them up, but history doesn't let go. It's got time on its side, time and science. However ferociously we ink over our first thoughts, history finds a way of reading them. We bury our victims in secrecy (strangled princelings, irradiated reindeer), but history discovers what we did to them. We lost the *Titanic*, forever it seemed, in the squid-ink depths, but they turned it up. They found the wreck of the *Medusa* not long ago, off the coast of Mauretania. There wasn't any hope of treasure, they knew that; and all they salvaged after a hundred and seventy-five years were a few copper nails from the frigate's hull and a couple of cannon. But they went and found it just the same.

What else can love do? If we're selling it, we'd better point out that it's a starting-point for civic virtue. You can't love someone without imaginative sympathy, without beginning to see the world from another point of view. You can't be a good lover, a good artist or a good politician without this capacity (you can get away with it, but that's not what I mean). Show me the tyrants who have been great lovers. By which I don't mean great fuckers; we all know about power as an aphrodisiac (an auto-aphrodisiac too). Even our democratic hero Kennedy serviced women like an assembly-line worker spraying car bodies.

There is an intermittent debate, in these last dying millennia of puritanism, about the connection between sexual orthodoxy and the exercise of power. If a President can't keep his pants on, does he lose the right to rule us? If a public servant cheats on his wife does this make him more likely to cheat on the electorate? For myself, I'd rather be ruled by an adulterer, by some sexual rogue, than by a prim celibate or zipped-up spouse. As criminals tend to specialize in certain crimes, so corrupt politicians normally specialize in their corruption: the sexual blackguards stick to fucking, the bribe-takers to graft. In which case it would make more sense to elect proven adulterers instead of discouraging them from public life. I don't say we should pardon them – on the contrary, we need to fan their guilt. But by harnessing this useful emotion we restrict their sinning to the erotic sphere, and produce a countervailing integrity in their governing. That's my theory, anyway.

In Great Britain, where most of the politicians are men, there's a tradition among the Conservative Party to interview the wives of potential candidates. This is, of course, a demeaning occasion, with the wife being vetted by the local members for normality. (Is she sane? Is she steady? Is she the right colour? Does she have sound views? Is she a tart? Will she look good in photos? Can we let her out canvassing?) They ask these wives, who dutifully vie with one another in supportive dullness, many questions, and the wives solemnly swear their joint commitment to nuclear weapons and the sanctity of the family. But they don't ask them the most important question: does your husband love you? The question shouldn't be misunderstood as being merely practical (is your marriage free from scandal?) or sentimental; it's an exact enquiry about the candidate's fitness to represent other people. It's a test of his imaginative sympathy.

We must be precise about love. Ah, you want descriptions, perhaps? What are her legs like, her breasts, her lips, what colour is that hair? (Well, sorry.) No, being precise about love means attending to the heart, its pulses, its certainties, its truth, its power – and its imperfections. After death the heart becomes a pyramid (it has always been one of the wonders of the world); but even in life the heart was never heart-shaped.

Put the heart beside the brain and see the difference. The brain is neat, segmented, divided into two halves as we imagine the heart should obviously be. You can deal with the brain, you think; it is a receptive organ, one that invites comprehension. The brain looks sensible. It's complicated, to be sure, with all those wrinkles and frowns and gulleys and pockets; it resembles coral, making you wonder if it might be surreptitiously on the move all the time, quietly adding to itself without your noticing. The brain has its secrets, though when cryptanalysts, maze-builders and surgeons unite, it will surely be possible to solve those mysteries. You can deal with the brain, as I say; it looks sensible. Whereas the heart, the human heart, I'm afraid, looks a fucking mess.

Love is anti-mechanical, anti-materialist: that's why bad love is still good love. It may make us unhappy, but it insists that the mechanical and the material needn't be in charge. Religion has become either wimpishly workaday, or terminally crazy, or merely businesslike – confusing spirituality with charitable donations. Art, picking up confidence from the decline of religion, announces its transcendence of the world (and it lasts, it lasts! art beats death!), but this announcement isn't accessible to all, or where accessible isn't always inspiring or welcome. So religion and art must yield to love. It gives us our humanity, and also our mysticism. There is more to us than us.

The materialist argument attacks love, of course; it attacks everything. Love boils down to pheromones, it says. This bounding of the heart, this clarity of vision, this energizing, this moral certainty, this exaltation, this civic virtue, this murmured *I love you*, are all caused by a low-level smell emitted by one partner and subconsciously nosed by the other. We are just a grander version of that beetle bashing its head in a box at the sound of a tapped pencil. Do we believe this? Well, let's believe it for the moment, because it makes love's triumph the greater. What is a violin made of? Bits of wood and bits of sheep's intestine. Does its construction demean and banalize the music? On the contrary, it exalts the music further.

And I'm not saying love will make you happy – above all, I'm not saying that. If anything, I tend to believe that it will make you unhappy: either immediately unhappy, as you are impaled by incompatibility, or unhappy later, when the woodworm has quietly been gnawing away for years and the bishop's throne collapses. But you can believe this and still insist that love is our only hope.

It's our only hope even if it fails us, although it fails us, because it fails us. Am I losing precision? What I'm searching for is the right comparison. Love and truth, yes, that's the prime connection. We all know objective truth is not obtainable, that when some event occurs we shall have a multiplicity of subjective truths which we assess and then fabulate into history, into some God-eyed version of what 'really' happened. This God-eyed version is a fake – a charming, impossible fake, like those medieval paintings which show all the stages of Christ's Passion happening simultaneously in different parts of the picture. But while we know this, we must still believe that objective truth is obtainable; or we must believe that it is 99 per cent obtainable; or if we can't believe this we must believe that

43 per cent objective truth is better than 41 per cent. We must do so, because if we don't we're lost, we fall into beguiling relativity, we value one liar's version as much as another liar's, we throw up our hands at the puzzle of it all, we admit that the victor has the right not just to the spoils but also to the truth. (Whose truth do we prefer, by the way, the victor's or the victim's? Are pride and compassion greater distorters than shame and fear?)

And so it is with love. We must believe in it, or we're lost. We may not obtain it, or we may obtain it and find it renders us unhappy; we must still believe in it. If we don't, then we merely surrender to the history of the world and to someone else's truth.

It will go wrong, this love; it probably will. That contorted organ, like the lump of ox meat, is devious and enclosed. Our current model for the universe is entropy, which at the daily level translates as: things fuck up. But when love fails us, we must still go on believing in it. Is it encoded in every molecule that things fuck up, that love will fail? Perhaps it is. Still we must believe in love, just as we must believe in free will and objective truth. And when love fails, we should blame the history of the world. If only it had left us alone, we could have been happy, we could have gone on being happy. Our love has gone, and it is the fault of the history of the world.

But that's still to come. Perhaps it will never come. In the night the world can be defied. Yes, that's right, it can be done, we can face history down. Excited, I stir and kick. She shifts and gives a subterranean, a subaqueous sigh. Don't wake her. It seems a grand truth now, though in the morning it may not seem worth disturbing her for. She gives a gentler, lesser sigh. I sense the map of her body beside me in the dark. I turn on my side, make a parallel zigzag, and wait for sleep.

9

PROJECT ARARAT

I T IS A FINE afternoon and you are driving the Outer Banks of
North Carolina – the Atlantic Coast's austere rehearsal for the
Florida Keys. You cross Currituck Sound from Point Harbor
to Anderson, then south on 158 and you soon reach Kitty
Hawk. Across the dunes you'll find the Wright Brothers
National Memorial; but maybe you take a raincheck on that,
and in any case this isn't the thing you remember from Kitty
Hawk. No, you remember this: on the right-hand side of the
road, the west side, its high prow pointing towards the ocean,
stands an ark. It's large as a barn, with slatted wooden sides, and
painted brown. As you turn an amused and passing head, you
realize that it is a church. Where you might normally see the
ship's name and port of registration perhaps, you read instead
the ark's function: WORSHIP CENTER, it says. You have
been warned to expect all manner of religious excrescence in the
Carolinas, and so this strikes you as a piece of fundamentalist
rococo, rather cute in a way, but no, you don't stop.

Later that evening, you take the seven o'clock ferry from
Hatteras to Ocracoke Island. It's chill, early spring, and you feel
a little cold and lost in the darkness, on the black water, with
the Plough hanging upside down above you in a blazing sky
rented from Universal Pictures. The ferry feels anxious too, its
huge searchlight charging the water twenty yards ahead; nois-
ily, but without conviction, it shrugs its course between the
marker lights, red, green and white. Only now, as you step out
on deck and your breath turns solid, do you think back to that
replica ark. It is there, of course, for a purpose, and had you
stopped to think instead of merely lifting your foot from the gas
pedal in a merry way, you might have felt its meaning. You had

247

driven to the place where Man first took to the air; and you are reminded instead of an earlier, more vital occasion, when Man first took to the sea.

The ark was not yet there back in 1943 when Spike Tiggler, only a year or two out of short pants, was taken to Kitty Hawk by his father. You remember Spike Tiggler? Hell, *everybody* remembers Spike Tiggler. The guy who threw the football on the moon. The guy who threw the god-damned football on the moon? That's right. Longest pass in the history of the NFL, four hundred fifty yards into the leaping hands of a volcanic crater. Touchdown! That's what he shouted, and it came crackling back to us, down here on earth. Touchdown Tiggler, that's what the crick-necked world knew him as, least for a summer or two. Touchdown Tiggler, the guy who snuck a football into the capsule (how'd he do that?). Remember when they asked him why he did it, and he just kept that poker face on him? 'Always wanted to try out for the Redskins,' he said. 'Sure hope the fellas were watching.' The fellas had been watching, just as they watched his press conference, and they wrote Touchdown asking if they could have the football, offering to pay what strikes us even now as a decent price. But Spike had left it far away in that ashen crater – in case some running-back from Mars or Venus happened by.

Touchdown Tiggler: they called him that on the banner across the street in Wadesville, North Carolina, a little one-bank town where the gas station had to double as a liquor store to make anything half-way near a profit. WADESVILLE PROUDLY WELCOMES ITS FINEST SON, TOUCH-DOWN TIGGLER. Everyone turned out that hot morning in 1971 as Tiggler rode through in a movie star's limousine with the top down. Even Mary-Beth, who twenty years earlier had allowed Spike certain liberties and spent a week or two worrying, and who'd scarcely had a good word to say about him until he was selected for Project Apollo, turned out for the occasion, and reminded those around her – she'd already refreshed their memory a couple of times before – that there'd been a time when she and Spike were, well, real close. Even then, she professed, she could see that he would go far. How far did he go with you, Mary-Beth, asked one of the sharper young wives of the town, and Mary-Beth smiled beatifically, like a Virgin in a coloring book, knowing that either way her status could only rise.

Meanwhile, Touchdown Tiggler had reached the end of Main Street and turned by the hairdresser called Shear Pleasure, which would care for your poodle too if you took him round the back, and while the public address endlessly played 'I am just a country boy/Who's always known the love and joy/Of coming home . . .' Spike Tiggler was welcomed three times from one direction and three times from the other. The convertible moved slowly, because after the first triumphal sweep Spike got perched up on the back so that everyone could see him, and each time the limo tortoised past the gas-station-cum-liquor-store its proprietor Buck Weinhart shouted 'Drive it or milk it!' in remembrance of Spike's habit of abusing slow drivers when the pair of them used to stir up the town all those years before. Six times Buck bellowed, 'Hey, Spike, drive it or milk it!' and Spike, a stocky, dark-haired figure, waved back with a good-ole-boy inclination of the head. Later, at a civic lunch in the Wadesville diner, which Spike had once thought very grand but which now reminded him of a funeral parlor, the returning hero, at first unfamiliar in his astronaut's crewcut and city suit which made him look like he was trying out for President Eisenhower, gave a speech about always remembering where you come from however far it is you go, which was accounted fine and dignified by those present, and one of those who spontaneously replied to his words even proposed that in honor of the achievement of their favorite son they should strike Wadesville and rename the town Moonsville, an idea which flourished for a few weeks and then quietly died, partly because of opposition from Old Jessie Wade, last surviving grand-daughter of Ruben Wade, a travelling man who way back at the start of the century had decided that pumpkins might grow well on the land hereabouts. The pumpkins failed, as it happened, but that was no reason to dishonor the man now.

Spike Tiggler had not always been as popular in Wadesville as he was that day in 1971, and it wasn't just Mary-Beth's mother who'd thought him wild and regretted that the war had ended too soon for them to ship young Tiggler out East and fight the Japs instead of fighting half the town. He was fifteen when they dropped the Hiroshima bomb, an event Mary-Beth's mother deplored for purely local reasons; but in due course Spike got his war, flying F-86s up to the Yalu River. Twenty-eight missions, two MiG-15s shot down. Reason enough for celebration in Wadesville, though Tiggler did not return at that time, or for a while afterwards. As he was to explain it in 1975, during his first appeal for funds at the Moondust Diner (a change of name approved even by Jessie Wade), the movement of a man's life, of every life, is marked by escape and return. Escape and return, escape and return, like the tides that play in Albermale Sound and up the Pasquotank River to Elizabeth City. We all go out with the tide, and then we all come back in on the tide. Some of the audience hadn't ever much left Wadesville in most of their lives, so couldn't be expected to have an opinion, and Jeff Clayton remarked afterwards that the other year when he'd driven through Fayetteville and around Fort Bragg to visit the World Golf Hall of Fame at Pinehurst and come home in time for his beer ration from Alma, it hadn't felt to him much like the tides in the Pasquotank River; still, what did Jeff Clayton know, and everyone agreed to give Spike the benefit of the doubt, since Spike had not just been out inta the world but – as old Jessie Wade herself so memorably put it – had been out outa the world as well.

Spike Tiggler dated the first ratchet-click of the escape-and-return cycle in his life to the day his father took him to Kitty Hawk, way back before the replica ark went up as a worship center. At this time, there was only the flat runway and the flat open sky above, and then, across an empty road with barely the glint of a distant truck, some flat dunes and the softly churning sea. Where other kids found allure in the lipstick and jazz of a brawling city, Spike found it in the calming simplicity of the land, sea and sky at Kitty Hawk. This, at any rate, was how he explained it at another of his fund-raising dinners, and they believed him, even though neither Mary-Beth nor Buck Weinhart had heard him talk like that back at the time. Spike Tiggler's home town was strong for the Democrats and even stronger for the Baptists. The Sunday after his trip to Kitty Hawk, Spike was heard displaying a rather too disrespectful sort of enthusiasm about the Wright Brothers outside the Church of the Holy Water, and old Jessie Wade opined to the thirteen-year-old that if God had intended us to fly, he'd have given us wings. 'But God intended us to drive, didn't he?' replied young Spike, a shade too quick for courtesy, and actually pointing at the freshly shined Packard in which his elderly detractor had ridden the two hundred yards to church; whereupon Spike's father reminded him that if it were not for the Sabbath, the Lord might very well have intended Spike to receive a whack upside the head. The exchange, rather than anything about land and sea and sky, was what the inhabitants of Wadesville recalled of Spike Tiggler's conversation, c. 1943.

A couple of years passed, the bomb fell on Hiroshima too soon for Mary-Beth's mother, and Spike discovered that if God hadn't given him wheels, then at least his father would occasionally loan him some. On warm evenings he and Buck Weinhart would play their game of picking out a slow automobile on a back road and trailing up behind it until their radiator grille was almost in the other fellow's trunk. Then, as they pulled softly out and swept past, the two of them would yell in unison, 'Drive it or milk it, fella!' It was in the same car and at about this time that Spike, his eyes bulging with hope, said to Mary-Beth, 'But if God didn't intend us to use it, what did he put it there for?' – a remark which set back his cause quite a few weeks, Mary-Beth being of a more church-obedient nature than young Spike, and this courting line of his in any case not being the most persuasive ever invented. A few weeks later, however, Spike found himself in the back seat murmuring, 'I really don't think I can live without you, Mary-Beth,' and this seemed to do the trick.

Spike left Wadesville not too long afterwards, and more or

less the next thing the town heard was that he was flying an F-86 Sabre jet out in Korea and stopping the Communist MiGs from crossing the Yalu River. It had taken a series of moments and emotions, not all of them logically linked, to get him there, and if Spike tried to reduce his life to a comic strip, as he sometimes did, he would first of all see himself standing on the dunes at Kitty Hawk, looking out to sea; then grabbing at Mary-Beth's breast without being rejected and thinking, 'God can't strike me dead for this, he can't'; and then driving at dusk with Buck Weinhart waiting for the early stars to come out. Love of machines was there too, of course, and patriotism, and a strong feeling that he looked pretty cute in his blue uniform; but in a way it was the earlier things he remembered the more vividly. That was what he meant, when he gave his first appeal for funds in 1975, about your life coming back to the place where it started. Wisely, no doubt, he didn't translate this general sentiment into particular memories, else he probably wouldn't have gotten a contribution out of Mary-Beth for one thing.

Along with his father's car and a resentful Mary-Beth, Spike had left his faith behind when he quit Wadesville. Though he dutifully filled in 'Baptist' on all the Navy forms, he didn't think about the Lord's commands, or the blessed grace, or being saved, not even on the bad days when one of his fellow-aviators – hell, one of his friends – bought the farm. That was a friend gone, but you didn't try to raise the Lord on the radio. Spike was a flier, a man of science, an engineer. You might acknowledge God on paper forms just as you deferred to senior officers around the base; yet the moment you were most you, when you were really Spike Tiggler, the kid who'd grown up from a borrowed car on a quiet road to a roaring fighter in an empty sky, was when you'd climbed hard and were levelling out your silver wings, high up in the clear air south of the Yalu River. Then you were wholly in charge, and you were also most alone. This was life, and the only person who could let you down was yourself. On the nose of his F-86 Spike had painted the slogan 'Drive It or Milk It!' as a warning to any MiG unlucky enough to catch Lieutenant Tiggler nearly up its ass.

After the war in Korea he transferred to the Navy's Test Pilot School at Patuxent River, Maryland. When the Russians launched their first Sputnik and Project Mercury got under way, Spike volunteered, even though something inside him – and quite a few aviators outside him – insisted that on the first flights they might as well use a chimpanzee, hell, they were *going* to use a chimpanzee. The job was just riding a rocket; you were a piece of cargo with wires sticking out, a lump of meat for the scientist to study. Part of him wasn't disappointed he didn't make the first seven to be chosen, yet part of him was; and next time around he put in again and got himself accepted. It was front-page on the *Fayetteville Observer* with a photo, which made Mary-Beth forgive him and write; but seeing as his new wife Betty was going through a jealous period he pretended he'd forgotten this particular girl from Wadesville and her letter received no reply.

In the summer of 1974 Spike Tiggler stood on the surface of the moon and threw a football pass four hundred and fifty yards. Touchdown! This was during a thirty-minute period when no specific tasks had been assigned and the two fellows on the surface were allowed to follow up anything that made them curious. Well, Spike had always been curious to see how far you could throw a football up there in the thin atmosphere, and now he knew. Touchdown! The voice at Mission Control sounded indulgent, and so did fellow-astronaut Bud Stomovicz when Spike said he was going to hop on over and get his ball back. He set off across the dead landscape like a jack rabbit with tubes. The moon looked pretty rough and beat-up to Spike, and the dust he stirred, which settled back in slow motion, was like sand from a dirty beach. His football lay beside a small crater. He kicked it gently into the arid hollow, then turned around to examine the distance he had come. The lunar module, almost out of sight, seemed tiny and precarious, a toy spider with a wheezing battery. Spike was not much given to private thinking on a mission – in any case, the work schedule was devised to discourage introspection – but it struck him that he and Bud (plus Mike still circling above in the command module) were as

far as you could currently get from the rest of the human species.
Yesterday they had watched the earth rise, and for all their
bagful of jokes it had been an awesome sight which turned your
head upside down. Now, right here, he felt at the very edge of
things. If he walked another ten yards, he might just fall off the
world's wingtip and spin boots over helmet into deepest space.
Though he knew such an occurrence to be scientifically impossible, that was how it felt to Spike Tiggler.

At this exact moment a voice said to him, 'Find Noah's Ark.'

'Don't read you,' he replied, thinking it must be Bud.

'Didn't say a word.' This time it was Bud's voice. Spike
recognized it, and in any case it came through his earphones in
the usual way. The other voice had seemed to come direct, to be
around him, inside him, close to him, loud yet intimate.

He'd made it a dozen or so yards back towards the LM when
the voice repeated its command. 'Find Noah's Ark.' Spike
carried on doing his aerated moon-hop, wondering if this was
somebody's joke. But nobody could have put a recorder in his
helmet − there wasn't room for it, he'd have noticed, they
wouldn't have allowed it. You could drive someone nutsy with a
trick like that, and though one or two of his fellow-astronauts
had a pretty curveball sense of humor, it mainly stopped at
hollowing out a plug in your melon slice, slipping mustard into
the hole and replacing the plug. Nothing as big-league as this.

'You'll find it on Mount Ararat, in Turkey,' the voice went
on. 'Find it, Spike.'

There were electrodes monitoring most of Spike's physical
reactions, and he guessed they'd see the needles jumping all
over the graphs when this part of the mission was reviewed. If
so, it wouldn't be beyond him to dream up a cover story. For the
moment, he just wanted to think about what he'd heard, what it
might mean. So when he returned to the LM he made a crack
about a fumble by the wide receiver, and went back to being a
normal astronaut, that's to say test pilot turned chimpanzee
turned national hero turned stuntman turned prospective con-
gressman or if not that then future decorative board member of a
dozen corporations. He hadn't been the first man to stand on the

moon, but there were never going to be so many that he'd stop
being a rarity, a cause for celebrity and reward. Spike Tiggler
knew a few of the angles, and Betty a whole lot more, which had
helped their marriage along on several occasions. He thought he
was getting a tall, athletic girl with a good figure, who read *The
Joy of Cooking* on their honeymoon and kept her fear to herself when
he was late returning to base; but she turned out a sight more
familiar with the reproductive habits of the dollar than he was.
'You do the flying and I'll do the thinking,' she'd occasionally
say to him, which sounded like a tease, or at any rate both of
them mostly pretended that it was only a tease. So Spike Tiggler
went back to his mission and fulfilled his work schedule and let
no-one suspect that anything had changed, that everything had
changed.

After splashdown came the personal how-de-do from the
White House, then the medical, the debriefing, the first call to
Betty, the first *night* again with Betty . . . and the fame. In the
throbbing cities he'd always distrusted – smug Washington,
cynical New York, nutsy San Francisco – Spike Tiggler was big;
in North Carolina he was huge. Tickertape was upended on his
head like bowls of spaghetti; his right hand discovered the
fatigue of congratulation; he was kissed, hugged, pawed,
slapped, punched. Small boys would dig in his vest pocket and
shamelessly beg for moondust. Most of all, people just wanted
to be *with* him, beside him for a few minutes, breathe in the air
that he was breathing out, wonder at the man from outer space
who was also the man from the neighboring county. It was after
some months of fevered coast-to-coast coddling that the North
Carolina state legislature, proud of its boy and a little jealous
that he seemed to have somehow become a general property of
the nation, announced that they were striking a medal to be
awarded at a special ceremony. What more appropriate place,
everyone agreed, than at Kitty Hawk, on the flat land beneath
the flat sky?

Appropriate words were pronounced that afternoon, yet
Spike could only half apprehend them; Betty had on a new outfit
with even a hat and needed reassurance that she was looking

terrific, which she was, but she didn't get it. A large gold medal, with the Kitty Hawk on one side and the Apollo capsule on the other, was hung around his neck; Spike's hand was battered several dozen more times; and all the while, as he gave out the polite smile and the inclination of the head, he was thinking about that moment on the drive, the moment that told him.

It had been cordial, not to say flattering, in the back of the Governor's limousine, and Betty had been looking so good he thought he should tell her only was shy of doing so in front of the Governor and his wife. There was the usual conversation about gravity and moon-hopping and earth-rise and tell me, what about going to the bathroom, when suddenly, just as they were nearing Kitty Hawk, he saw the Ark by the side of the road. A huge, beached ark, high at both ends, with slatted wooden sides. The Governor followed Spike's head indulgently as it panned through 180 degrees, then answered his question without it being put. 'Some kinda church,' said the Governor. 'They stuck it up not long back. Probably got a load of animals in it.' He laughed, and Betty joined in carefully.

'Do you believe in God?' asked Spike all of a sudden.

'Couldn't get to be Governor of North Carolina without,' came the good-humored reply.

'No, do you believe in *God*,' Tiggler repeated, with a directness that could easily be misread for something they didn't need.

'Honey,' said Betty quietly.

'I sure do think we're nearly there,' said the Governor's wife, straightening a box-pleat with a white-gloved hand.

In their hotel room that evening, Betty was at first inclined to be conciliatory. It must be a strain, she thought, however dandy it might be. *I* wouldn't like to get up on platforms and tell everyone for the fiftieth time what it was like and how proud it made me feel, even if it did make me feel proud and I did want to talk about it for the fiftieth time. So she mothered him a little and asked if he was feeling tired, and tried to get him to spit out any excuse as to why not once, not once *in the whole damn day,* had he mentioned her outfit, and didn't he know how uncertain she was whether primrose yellow was really her color. But this failed to work, and so Betty, who could never get to sleep unless things were out in the open, asked him if he wanted a drink and why had he gone all funny on them just before the ceremony, and if he wanted her frank opinion the soonest way to foul up the future career they'd both agreed on was for him to start asking State Governors whether or not they believed in God, for Christ's sake. Who did he think he was?

'My life has changed,' said Spike.

'Are you trying to tell me something?' Betty was normally suspicious and couldn't help noticing how many letters a famous man is liable to receive from women who didn't know him, from the Mary-Beths and all the potential Mary-Beths of the world.

'Yes,' he replied. 'You come back to where you started from. I went 240,000 miles to see the moon – and it was the earth that was really worth looking at.'

'You *do* need a drink.' She paused, half-way across the room to the frigobar, but he hadn't spoken, or moved, or gestured. 'Heck, *I* need a drink.' She sat down beside her husband with a sour mash and waited.

'When I was a kid my Pa took me to Kitty Hawk. I was twelve, thirteen. It made me into an aviator. That's all I wanted to do from that day.'

'I know, honey.' She took his hand.

'I joined the Navy. I was a good aviator. I transferred to Pax River. I volunteered for Project Mercury. I didn't get accepted at first but I kept on and they accepted me in the end. I was listed for Project Apollo. I did all the training. I landed on the moon . . . '

'I know, honey.'

' . . . and there . . . *there*,' he went on, squeezing Betty's hand as he prepared to tell her for the first time, 'God told me to find Noah's Ark.'

'Uh-huh.'

'I'd just thrown the football. I'd just thrown the football and found it and kicked it into a little crater and was wondering if I was out of range of the camera and if they'd call a foul if they spotted it, when God speaks to me. *Find Noah's Ark.*' He looked across at his wife. 'It was like, here you are a grown man and you make it to the moon and what do you want to do? Throw footballs. Time to start putting away childish things, that's what God was telling me.'

'How you sure it was God, honey?'

Spike ignored the question. 'I didn't tell anyone. I know I'm not hallucinating, I know I've heard what I've heard, but I don't tell. Maybe I'm not quite sure, maybe I want to forget it. And what happens? The very day I go back to Kitty Hawk, where it all started all those years ago, the very day I go back I see the God-damn Ark. *Don't forget what I said* – that's His message, isn't it? Loud and clear. That's what it means. *Go ahead and get your medal, but don't forget what I said.*'

Betty took a sip of her whisky. 'So what you gonna do, Spike?' Normally, when discussing his career, she said *we* rather than *you*; this time he was out on his own.

'I don't know yet. I don't know yet.'

The NASA psychiatrist that Betty consulted had a good line in nodding, as if to suggest that she'd have to tell him something far more outrageous before he'd throw down his pen and admit the fellow was minus some buttons, crazier than a bedbug. He nodded, and said how he and his colleagues had been anticipating a few *adjustment problems*, after all someone who went to the moon and looked back at the earth must be a bit like the first guy who ever stood on his head and took in the view from that direction, which might affect your *behavioral pattern*, and what with the stress of the flight and the enormous publicity attending the missions, it wasn't altogether surprising that one or two *reality shifts* might have taken place, but there was no reason to believe that their effects might be either serious or long-lasting.

'You're not answering my question.'

'What is your question?' The psychiatrist was not aware that she'd asked one.

'Is my husband – I don't know what technical term you might use, doctor – is my husband a fruitcake?'

There was a lot more nodding, this time in a horizontal rather than vertical plane, and examples of *perceptual disorientation* were given, and Spike's records were examined, on every one of which he had firmly written *Baptist*, and it seemed to Betty that the psychiatrist would have been more surprised if Spike *hadn't* heard God speak to him on the moon's surface, and when she asked him 'But was Spike hallucinating?' he merely replied, 'What do you think?' which didn't seem to Betty to advance the conversation, indeed it was almost as if *she* was the crazy one for doubting her husband. One result of the meeting was that Betty went away feeling she had betrayed her husband rather than helped him; and the other was that when, three months later, Spike put in for release from the space program there wasn't much serious opposition to his request as long as the whole thing was handled low-profile, because what was clear from the psychiatrist's report was that Spike was *minus some buttons*, crazier than a bedbug, a fifty-carat fruitcake, and that he probably believed after close personal inspection that the moon was made of green cheese. So there was a move to a desk job in general media promotions, then a Navy transfer back to trainers, but within a year of hopping around in the gray ash Spike Tiggler was back in civvies and Betty was wondering what happened when you fell off the box car of the gravy train.

It was Spike's announcement that he had booked the Moon-dust Diner in Wadesville for the first of his fund-raising get-togethers that moved Betty to wonder if the most painless thing wouldn't be to close *The Joy of Cooking* and head for an early divorce. Spike had done nothing for nearly a year except go out one day and buy a Bible. Then he'd go missing in the course of the evening, and she'd find him on the back porch, the Scripture open on his knees and his eyes turned upward to the stars. Her friends were exhaustingly sympathetic: after all it must be tough coming back from *up there* and having to readjust to the daily grind. It was clear to Betty that the fame of Touchdown Tiggler could run for quite a few years without having to put any more gas in the tank, and it was equally clear she could count on support – since fame followed by crack-up was not just American, but almost downright patriotic – but even so she felt cheated. All those years of doing what was right by Spike's career, of being shunted around the country, never quite having a proper home, waiting, hoping for the big payout . . . and then, when it comes, when those big round dollars come cascading out of the machine, what does Spike do? Instead of holding out his hat and catching them, he hits the back porch and looks at the stars. Meet my husband, he's the one with the Bible on his knees and the torn pants and the funny look in his eye. No, he didn't get himself attacked, he just jumped off the box car of the gravy train.

When Betty asked Spike what he'd like her to wear for his first public meeting at the Moondust Diner, there was some sarcasm in her voice; and when Spike replied that he'd always been fond of that primrose-yellow outfit she'd bought for when he got his medal at Kitty Hawk, she heard once again within her a voice which certainly didn't belong to the Almighty whispering the word *divorce*. But the strange thing was, he seemed to mean it, and twice, once before they departed, and again as they turned off the interstate, he commented on how fine she was looking. This was a new development she couldn't help noticing in him. Nowadays he always meant what he said, and just said what he meant, nothing more. He seemed to have left the fun, the teasing, the daredevilry up in that crater along with his football (that was a dumb stunt, come to think of it, and should have set some bells ringing earlier than it did). Spike had gotten serious; he'd gotten dull. He still said he loved her, which Betty believed, though she sometimes wondered if that was enough for a girl. But he'd lost his pizzazz. If this was putting away childish things, then childish things, according to Betty, had a lot to be said for them.

The Moondust Diner was full that April evening of 1975 when Spike Tiggler launched his first appeal for funds. Most of the town was there, plus a couple of newspapermen and a photographer. Betty feared the worst. She imagined headlines

like 'GOD SPOKE TO ME' CLAIMS GROUNDED ASTRO-
NAUT and WADESVILLE MAN MINUS SOME BUTTONS.
She sat nervously beside her husband as the local minister
welcomed him back to the community where he had grown up.
There was clapping; Spike gently took her hand and didn't
release it until he was on his feet and about to speak.

'It's nice to be back,' said Spike, and looked around the room,
giving hi-there inclinations of the head to those he recognized.
'You know, only the other day, I was sitting on my back porch
looking up at the stars and thinking about the kid I used to be,
all those years ago in Wadesville. I must have been fifteen,
sixteen or so, and I guess I was a bit of a handful, and old Jessie
Wade, God rest her, I expect many of you recall Jessie, she said
to me, "Young man, you run along screaming and shouting like
that, one of these days you'll just take off" – and I reckon old
Jessie Wade knew a thing or two because many years later that's
just what I did, though sadly she didn't live to see her prophecy
fulfilled, God rest her soul.'

Betty could not have been more surprised. He was doing a
number. He was doing a goddam number on them. He didn't
use to talk with much fondness about Wadesville; she'd
never even heard the story about old Jessie Wade before; yet here
he was, remembering it all, playing up to the folks back home.
He told them a heap of stories about his childhood, and then
some more about being an astronaut, which after all was what
they'd mostly come for, but the message behind it all was that
without these folks old Spike wouldn't have got farther than
Fayetteville, that it was *these folks* who'd really put him up there
on the moon, not those clever guys with wires coming out of
their ears at Mission Control. Just as surprising to Betty was
that he did this part of his address with all the old fun and
teasing she thought had gone out of him. And then he came to
the bit about every man's life being a process of escape and
return, escape and return like the waters in the Pasquotank
River (which was when Jeff Clayton thought it wasn't like that
on the way to the World Golf Hall of Fame at Pinehurst); and
explained how you always came back to the things and places

you'd started from. Like he'd left Wadesville years before, and now he was back; like he'd been a regular attender at the Church of the Holy Water all through his childhood, had later strayed from the path of the Lord, but had now returned to it – which was news, though hardly unexpected news, to Betty.

And so, he continued, to the serious part of the evening, to the purpose of this meeting (and Betty held her breath, thinking *nutty as a fruitcake*, how are they going to handle this bit, about God telling him to leave his football in the crater and go find the Ark instead). But again Betty had underestimated Spike. He didn't refer to lunar commands from the Almighty, not once. He invoked his faith several times, and going back to where you came from all over again, and he mentioned the difficulties that had to be surmounted in the space program; so when he finally began to explain how he'd been turning over such matters on his back porch looking up at the stars, and how it seemed to him that it was time after all these years to go looking for where we came from, and that he planned to mount an expedition to recover what could be found of Noah's Ark, which as everyone knew lay on the summit of Mount Ararat near the borders of Turkey and Iran, it all seemed to make sense, to be a logical progression. Project Ararat, indeed, could be seen as the obvious next venture for NASA; and listeners might even be free to conclude that NASA was being a little selfish, a little materialistic and narrow-minded, in concentrating solely on space flight, when there were other projects, closer to the heart and soul of the tax-payer, which might more usefully receive the benefit of their sophisticated technology.

He'd done a number, he'd done a goddam number, Betty thought as her husband sat down to a roomful of noise. He hadn't even mentioned money, he'd just asked them to honor him with their presence while he shared a few ideas with them, and if they judged he was thinking straight then he'd get off his tail and start looking for people to help him. That's my Spike, Betty found herself muttering, even though it was a rather different Spike from the one she had married.

'Mrs Tiggler, how do you view your husband's project?' she

was asked as they stood hand-in-hand before the photographer from the *Fayetteville Observer*.

'Oh, I'm behind him one hundred ten per cent,' she replied, looking up at Spike with a bridal smile. The *Observer* reported her comment, and the journalist even managed to say how striking Mrs Tiggler looked in her mustard dress with matching hat (*mustard! said Betty to Spike, I suppose he eats primroses on the side with his beef*). When they got home that night Spike seemed all charged up, like she hadn't seen him for a year or so, and there wasn't any question of him tucking off with his Bible on the back porch beneath the stars; no, he fair hustled her into the bedroom, where they hadn't done much else but sleep for quite a while, and Betty, who though unprepared for this event was not at all displeased, muttered something in their private code about the bathroom, but Spike said they wouldn't be bothering over that, and Betty quite liked him being this masterful.

'I love you,' said Spike later that night.

A few inches in the *Fayetteville Observer* begat a feature in the *Greensboro News and Record* which begat a small syndicated news item. After that there was silence, but Spike remained confident and recalled the bonfires he used to watch as a kid when it looked like nothing was happening until the whole thing burst into flame; and sure enough he was right, for suddenly he blazed across the front pages of the *Washington Post* and the *New York Times*. Then the TV people arrived, which set off another round of newsmen, followed by foreign TV and foreign newsmen, and all the time Betty and Spike worked hard (they were a team again, like at the beginning) to get Project Ararat under way. Reporters were given fact-sheets itemizing the latest contributions and endorsements, whether it was fifty dollars from a neighboring congregation, or a gift of ropes and tents from a well-known store. Soon there arose on Spike and Betty's front lawn a large wooden campaign thermometer; every Monday morning Spike, paintbrush in hand, inched up the mercury.

Not surprisingly, Spike and Betty liked to compare this critical time to the launch of a rocket: the countdown is exciting, the moment of ignition a thrill, but until you see that heavy mother of a silver tube starting to shift on her haunches and shoulder her way towards the heavens you know there is always a chance that you're in for an embarrassing and very public floperoo. Whatever Betty wanted, now she had decided to back her husband one hundred ten per cent, she didn't want that. Betty was not of a particularly religious nature, and in her private heart she didn't know what to make of Spike's experience on the moon; but she recognized possibilities when she saw them. After a year of moody Bible study and her friends being so damn sympathetic she could scream, it wasn't so bad that Spike Tiggler was back in the news again. After Project Apollo, Project Ararat – what could be more obvious than this progression, this tiny alphabetical step? And nobody, not one of the newspapers, had even suggested that Spike might be minus some buttons, crazier than a bedbug.

Spike handled it all pretty well, and never once mentioned how God had played President Kennedy in getting the whole thing rolling. This made it easier for Betty to interest people who might have been cautious if they'd sniffed anything nutsy in the scheme. Even the Governor of North Carolina was moved to forgive Spike's brusque curiosity about the authenticity of his faith and benevolently agreed to top-table a $100-a-plate fund-raising dinner in Charlotte. Betty wore primrose yellow on such occasions with a regularity which friends deemed unnecessary, not to say unfashionable; but Spike maintained that it was his lucky color. When talking to reporters Spike sometimes asked them to mention his wife's dress, which was mustard in color, as they no doubt had observed. Some newsmen, either lazy or color-blind, dutifully obliged, which made Spike chuckle when he read the papers.

He also guested on a number of religious TV shows. Betty would sometimes quiver with apprehension as yet another salesman in a three-piece suit cued in from the commercial break with the welcoming announcement that God's love was like the still center of a whirlwind, and one of his guests here today had actually been inside a whirlwind and could testify to the perfect peace within it, but how this meant that Christianity was a faith which kept you moving forward all the time, since you can't stand still in a whirlwind, which brought us to his second guest, Spike Tiggler, who had in his time traveled even faster than a whirlwind but was now looking for that still center, that perfect calm, praise the Lord. And Spike, who had gone back to his astronaut's haircut and blue suit, would keep on answering politely and never once mention – as the salesman would have loved to hear – that God had been *right there*, inside his helmet, whispering in his ear. He came across as good and simple and true, which helped the checks roll in to Project Ararat, care of Betty Tiggler, who naturally paid herself a salary.

They set up a committee: the Reverend Lance Gibson, respected or at least known through most of the state, a touch fundamentalist for some but not too left-field to scare away sensible money; Dr Jimmy Fulgood, college basketball star turned geologist and scuba-diver, who would give scientific respectability to the expedition; and Betty herself, chairperson, co-ordinator and treasurer. The Governor agreed to feature on the writing paper as Emeritus Patron; and the only glitch in the whole Ararat countdown was the failure to get the Project recognized as a charitable institution.

Some of the journalists with book-learning behind them liked to ask Spike how he could be entirely sure that the Ark was to be found on Mount Ararat. Did not the Koran say it made landfall on Mount Judi, several hundred miles away, near the Iraqi border? And did not Jewish tradition equally differ, placing the location somewhere in Northern Israel? At which point Spike would give a little touch on the charm throttle and reply that everyone was of course entitled to their opinion, and if an Israeli astronaut wanted to go looking in Israel that was fine by him, and if a Koranic astronaut did the same in Iraq, that was fine too. Skeptical reporters went away thinking that Tiggler might be simple, but he wasn't simple-minded.

Another question occasionally put was whether the Ark – assuming its theoretical location could be found – might not have rotted away over the last however many thousand years, or been eaten by termites. Once again, Spike would not be drawn, especially not into revealing how he knew it couldn't have rotted or been eaten by termites, because God's command to find the Ark clearly implied that there was something left of it. Instead, he referred the questioner to his Bible, which the questioner appeared to have come without, but which would reveal that the Ark was made of gopher-wood, which everyone agreed was extremely hard, and therefore probably resistant to both rot and termites; then Spike mentioned examples of various things miraculously preserved down the centuries — mammoths found in glaciers, the meat on them as fresh as the chuck steak from your local Giant; and he wound up by suggesting that if anything was going to be miraculously preserved down the centuries thanks to God's almighty will, then wasn't the Ark a pretty good candidate?

The Reverend Lance Gibson consulted church historians at Baptist universities to establish current thinking on the location of the Ark; while Jimmy Fulgood went into probable wind and tide patterns around the time of the Flood. When the two of them pooled their findings, they began to favor an area on the south-east side of the mountain a couple of kilometers from the summit. Sure, Spike agreed, that's where they'd begin looking, but what about his plan for starting right at the top and descending in spider-web circles so that the ground was systematically covered? Jimmy appreciated the thinking behind this idea, yet felt he couldn't go along with it from a mountaineering point of view, so Spike bowed to him on that one. Jimmy's counter-proposal was that Spike use his connections with NASA and the Navy to get a good set of aerial reconnaissance prints of the mountain, then they could blow them up and see if anything Arklike showed. Spike acknowledged this was a logical approach but wondered if God had really intended them to take short-cuts. Wasn't the whole vision of the Project as a sort of Christian pilgrimage, and didn't the ancient pilgrims always rough it? While he wasn't suggesting they take anything short of the best when it came to tents and ropes and boots and wristwatches, he did feel they should hope to feel guided by something other than modern technology once they got up there.

The Reverend Gibson's pastoral activities precluded him from making the trip to Turkey, but he would furnish spiritual back-up and constantly remind the Almighty by means of prayer that his two fellow committee-members were going about the Lord's business in a far country. Betty would stay at home and field media inquiries, which were sure to be running hot. The expeditionary party – Spike and Jimmy – was to depart in July of that year, 1977. They declined to make predictions about how long they would be away. You did not seek to outdraw the Lord, said the Reverend Gibson, unless you wanted a slug in the gut.

Various supplies had been gifted by well-wishers, church congregations and survivalist stores; and as Betty opened the parcels which continued to arrive right up to the eve of departure, she wondered at how the Project was being perceived in some quarters. A few of the offerings sure seemed less than Christian. You might have deduced from a glimpse of the Tigglers' Expedition Room that Spike and Jimmy were a couple of naked refugees being sent as hired killers to exterminate most of eastern Turkey.

They left behind a lot of old clothes, some automatic weapons, four stun grenades, a garrotte and a couple of suicide pills donated by some zealot. Their payload included lightweight camping equipment, vitamin pills, a Japanese camera with one of the new zoom lenses, credit cards, American Express travellers' checks, running shoes, a pint of bourbon, thermal socks and underwear, a large plastic bag of branflakes to keep them regular, anti-diarrhea tablets, an infra-red night-sight, water-purifying pills, freeze-dried vacuum-packed food, a lucky horseshoe, flashlights, dental tape, reserve batteries for their electric razors, a pair of scabbard knives sharp enough to cut gopher-wood or disembowel an assailant, mosquito repellent, sunburn cream and the Bible. When Jimmy secretly checked their baggage he found the folded husk of a football and a small compressed-air device for inflating it; he repacked them carefully, with an indulgent grin. When Spike secretly checked the baggage he came across a box of rubbers, which he threw away and never raised with Jimmy. The committee discussed what the expedition should take as tokens of goodwill to distribute to the peasants of eastern Turkey. Betty thought some color postcards of Spike on the moon's surface, but Spike felt this would be hitting the wrong note, seeing as they weren't on a personal ego trip but going about the Lord's business. After further reflection they took two hundred buttons commemorating the inauguration of President Jimmy Carter and his First Lady, the lovely Rosalynn, which a friend of the Reverend Gibson's had been able to let them have at way below cost, and happy to be rid of them he was.

They flew to Ankara, where they had to rent tuxedos for the fine dinner offered them by the Ambassador. Spike disguised his disappointment that most of the guests wanted to talk astronautics and seemed positively reluctant to question him about Project Ararat. Later they proved unimpressed, not to say downright miserly, when Spike in his after-dinner speech made a patriotic appeal for extra funds.

The message Betty had sent to Erzerum via Interchurch Travel about hiring a jeep or Land Rover must have not gotten through, and the expedition therefore proceeded in a large Mercedes. East to Horasan, then east-south-east for Dogubayazit. The countryside was neat, kind of pale green and pale brown at the same time. They ate fresh apricots and distributed images of the smiling Carters to small children, some of whom seemed pleased, though others continued to press for dollars or, failing that, ball-points. The military were everywhere, which caused Spike to reflect on the strategic significance of the area. It came as news to Jimmy that only a hundred or so years earlier Mount Ararat, or Agri Dagi as the locals insisted on calling it, had been the meeting-point of three great empires – Russia, Persia and Turkey – with the mountain divided among the three of them.

'Doesn't seem right, the Soviets having a piece of it,' commented Jimmy.

'Guess they weren't Soviets at the time,' said Spike. 'They were Christians like us when they were just Russians.'

'Mebbe the Lord took their slice of the mountain away from them when they became Soviets.'

'Mebbe,' replied Spike, not wholly certain of when the boundaries had shifted.

'Like, not letting his holy mountain fall into the hands of infidels.'

'I read you,' said Spike, a little irritated. 'But I guess the Turks aren't exactly Christians.'

'They're not as infidel as the Soviets.' Jimmy appeared reluctant to give up his theory at the first objection.

'Check.'

On the road north from Dogubayazit Spike shouted for Jimmy to stop the car. They got out and Spike pointed to a small stream. Gently, but unarguably, the water in it was flowing uphill.

'Praise the Lord,' said Spike Tiggler, and knelt to pray. Jimmy bent his head a few degrees, but remained on his feet. After a couple of minutes Spike went back to the Merce and filled two plastic water-bottles from the stream.

'It's the land of miracles,' he announced as they set off once more.

Jimmy Fulgood, geologist and scuba-diver, let a few miles go by, then tried to explain how it was not scientifically impossible for a stream to flow uphill. It depended on a certain weight and pressure of water higher up the mountain, and on the apparently uphill stretch being a comparatively small section of an overall descent. The phenomenon had, as far as he knew, been reported on previous occasions. Spike, who was driving, kept nodding away as cheerful as they come. 'Reckon you could explain it like that,' he commented at the end. 'Point is, who made the water to flow uphill in the first place? Who put it where He did so that we should see it as we were passing on the road to Ararat? The Good Lord, that's who. It's the land of miracles,' he repeated, nodding contentedly.

Jimmy had always found Spike an optimistic kind of guy;

here in Turkey he became frankly ebullient. Neither mosquitoes nor misfortune troubled him; his tipping showed a true Christian generosity; and he had the habit, whenever they passed a cow on the road, of winding down the window and shouting to its owner, or even just to the countryside in general, 'Drive it or milk it, fella!' At times this could get to bug you, but Jimmy was one hundred ten per cent funded by Project Ararat, so he endured such high spirits as he would have suffered bad temper.

They drove until the road ran out and the two shapes of Great and Little Ararat rose ahead of them.

'Kinda like man and wife, ain't it?' Spike remarked.

'How d'ya mean?'

'Brother and sister, Adam and Eve. The big one there and that little neat pretty one by his side. See? *Male and female created He them.*'

'Do you think the Lord had that in mind at the time?'

'The Lord has everything in mind,' said Spike Tiggler. 'All the time.' Jimmy Fulgood looked at the twin shapes ahead of them and kept to himself the reflection that Betty Tiggler was an inch or two taller than Spike.

They sorted their equipment before entrusting themselves to the two feet the Lord had provided them with. They left the bourbon in the trunk, sensing that it was wrong to consume alcoholic liquor on the Lord's mountain; neither had they any more need for the Carter buttons. They took their travellers' checks, lucky horseshoe and Bible. During the transfer of supplies, Jimmy caught Spike sneaking the deflated football into his backpack. Then they set off up the southern approaches to the mountain, the lanky ex-basketball star a few yards behind the exuberant astronaut, like a junior officer trailing a general. From time to time Jimmy's geological interests made him want to stop and examine the rock; but Spike always insisted that they push on.

They were alone on the mountain and found their solitude exalting. They saw lizards on the lower slopes, ibex and wild goats higher up. They climbed above the operational altitude of hawks and buzzards, up toward the snowline, where the only movement was the occasional dart of a small fox. In the cold nights Jimmy wrote up the expedition journal and Spike read his Bible by the stark and hissing glare of their gas-lamp.

They began on the south-eastern slope, that area of lukewarm agreement between church and science. They probed rocky gulches and looked in barren caves. Jimmy was uncertain whether they were due to find the whole Ark, preserved intact – in which case they probably couldn't miss it – or just some significant remnant: the rudder, perhaps, or some planks still caulked with bitumen.

Their first rough survey revealed nothing, which neither surprised nor disappointed them. They crossed the snowline and headed for the summit. Towards the end of their climb the sky slowly began to change color, until by the time they reached the top it appeared bright green. This place was full of miracles. Spike knelt in prayer, and Jimmy briefly joined him. Immediately below them was a gently sloping valley of snow, which ran down to a secondary peak. This could have made a natural resting-place for the Ark. But they searched it without success.

The northern side of the mountain was split by an enormous fissure. Spike pointed to where this chasm ran out, some thousands of feet below them, and said there'd once been a monastery down there. Real monks and all. Then in 1840, he said, a terrible earthquake had gotten hold of the mountain and shaken it like a dog with a rat, and the little church had fallen down, and so had the village below it, some name beginning with an A. Everyone had been killed, apparently, and even if they hadn't they would have been a bit later. See this fissure, well, four or five days after the quake a build-up of snow and water started to move down it. Nothing could stand in its way. Like the vengeance of the Lord. Wiped the monastery and the little village off the face of the earth.

Jimmy Fulgood nodded seriously to himself as he listened to the story. All this had happened, he told himself, at a time when the Soviets had owned this slice of the mountain. Of course they were Russians then, and Christians, but it proved the Lord sure did have it in for the Soviets, even before they were Soviets.

They searched for three weeks. Jimmy wondered if the Ark might be buried deep in the cornice of ice which encircled the mountain; and Spike agreed this might be possible but if so the Lord would surely indicate it in some way. The Lord would not send them upon the mountain and then conceal from them the very reason for sending them there: such was not the nature of the Lord. Jimmy bowed to Spike on this. They searched by eye, binocular and infra-red night-sight. Spike waited for a sign. Was he sure he would recognize the sign when it came? Perhaps they should search in whichever direction the wind blew them. They searched in the direction the wind blew them. They found nothing.

Each day, as the sun heated up the plain below them and the warm air rose, a halo of cloud formed itself around the mountain-top, shutting off their view of the lower slopes; and each night, as the air cooled, the cloud dispersed. At the end of three weeks they came down to collect more supplies from the trunk of the Mercedes. They drove to the nearest village, from where Spike sent Betty a card saying No News Is Good News, which struck Betty as less clear than it could have been. Then they returned to the mountain and searched for another three weeks. During this period there was a full moon, and Spike would gaze up at it every night, remembering how the present mission had begun up there in the shifting dust. One night Jimmy stood at his elbow and examined with him the creamy, pitted orb. 'Sure looks like a custard pie,' Jimmy concluded, with a nervous laugh. 'More like dirty beach sand when you get there,' Spike replied. He continued looking up, waiting for a sign. No sign came.

It was during their third spell on the mountain – agreed to be their last for the year – that Spike made his discovery. They were a few thousand feet below the summit and had just crossed a treacherous piece of scree when they came upon a pair of caves side by side. Just like the Lord stuck two fingers in the rock, they agreed. With the incorrigible optimism which Jimmy high-mindedly endured, the former astronaut jauntily disappeared into the first of the caves; there was silence, then an echoing howl. Jimmy thought of bears – even of the abominable snowman – until the continuing howl modulated, almost without breath being drawn, into a series of sporting whoops.

Not far into the cavern Jimmy found Spike Tiggler kneeling in prayer. A human skeleton was laid out before him. Jimmy sank down beside Spike. Even on his knees, the former basketball star retained a height advantage over the ex-astronaut. Spike extinguished his flashlight, and Jimmy did the same. A few minutes of purest silence passed in the cold darkness, then Spike murmured, 'We found Noah.'

Jimmy didn't reply. After a while they switched their flashlights back on and the two beams reverently explored the skeleton in front of them. It lay with its feet pointing towards the mouth of the cave, and seemed intact, as far as either of them could tell. There were a few scraps of cloth – some white, some of a grayish color – hanging between the bones.

'Praise the Lord,' said Spike Tiggler.

They pitched their tent a few yards down the mountainside and then searched the other cave. Spike was secretly hoping they might find Noah's wife, or maybe the Ark's log, but there were no more discoveries. Later, as the evening darkened, there was a hiss of compressed air inside the tent and then Spike Tiggler threw his football across the rocks of Great Ararat into the hesitant arms of Jimmy Fulgood. Time after time it thumped into Jimmy's large, ex-basketball-playing hands. His own returns were often poor, but Spike was not disconcerted. He threw and he threw that evening, until the air was cold and the two figures were lit only by the rising moon. Even so, Spike's eye was flawless; Jimmy felt the football homing in to him with the nocturnal accuracy of a bat. 'Hey, Spike,' he shouted at one point, 'not using that infra-red sight, are you?' and a chuckle came back from his barely visible partner.

After they had eaten, Spike took his flashlight and returned to Noah's tomb, as by now he had christened it. Jimmy, either from tact or superstition, remained in the tent. An hour or so later Spike reported that the position of the skeleton would have allowed the dying Noah to gaze out from the cave and see the moon – the very moon on whose surface Spike Tiggler had so recently stood. 'Praise the Lord,' he repeated as he zipped up the tent for the night.

After a while it became clear that neither of them was asleep. Jimmy coughed slightly. 'Spike,' he said, with some caution, 'It's . . . well . . . it's my perception that we have ourselves a problem.'

'We have ourselves a problem? We have ourselves a *miracle!*' Spike replied.

'Sure we have a miracle. We also have a problem.'

'Tell me how you perceive this problem, Jimmy.' The tone was amused, tolerant, almost patronizing; the tone of a quarterback who knew his arm could be relied on.

Jimmy went carefully, not being too sure himself what to believe. 'Well, let's say I'm just thinking aloud, Spike, and let's say I'm into negativity at this moment.'

'Fine.' Nothing could harm Spike's present mood. The mixture of fierce exhilaration and relief reminded him of splashdown.

'We're looking for the Ark, right? You were . . . *told* we'd find the Ark.'

'Sure. We will. We're bound to now, next time mebbe.'

'But we were looking for the Ark,' Jimmy persisted. 'We . . . you . . . were *told* to look for the Ark.'

'We were shooting for silver, we got gold.'

'Yup. I was just wondering . . . didn't Noah strike out somewhere after the Ark landed? I mean, he lived on a few centuries, didn't he, in the Bible?'

'Sure. Three hundred fifty. Sure. That village I told you about when we were on the top. Arghuri. That's where Noah had his first settlement. Planted his vines there. Had his first farm. Built his homestead up again.'

'That was *Noah*'s village?'

'Sure was. Down in the Soviet sector,' added Spike teasingly.

Things were getting less clear to Jimmy now. 'So God let Noah's settlement get destroyed in an earthquake?'

'Musta had a reason. Always does. Anyway, that's not the point. Point is, Noah settled down there. Maybe he moved on, maybe not. Anyway, what's more likely than he came back to Ararat to be buried? When he felt the weariness of Time upon him? Probably staked out that cave the moment he stepped down from the Ark. Decided that as a sign of gratitude and obedience to the Lord for preserving him he'd drag his old bones up the mountainside when he knew his hour was upon him. Like elephants in the jungle.'

'Spike, those bones in the cave – don't they . . . don't they look a little, how shall I put it, well-preserved? I mean, I'm only playing devil's advocate, you understand.'

'Relax, Jimmy, you're doing fine.'

'But they do look well-preserved?'

'Jimmy, we're talking miracles and signs here. You'd *expect* them to look well-preserved, wouldn't you? Noah was a real special guy. Anyway, how old was he when he died? Nine hundred fifty years. He was greatly blessed in the Lord's eye. Now if he had bones which were strong enough to carry him around for a thousand years, you'd hardly expect them to decay at the standard rate, would you?'

'I take your point, Spike.'

'Anything else worrying you?' He seemed to welcome Jimmy's doubts, confident he could field any ball thrown to him.

'Well, what exactly are we going to do?'

'We're going to tell the world, that's what we're going to do. And the world will rejoice. And many souls will come to the faith as a result of this discovery. And there will be a church built once more upon this mountainside, a church built over Noah's tomb.' In the shape of an Ark, perhaps. Or even in the shape of an Apollo spacecraft. That would be more appropriate, that would complete the circle.

'I'm with you about the repercussions, Spike. Let me put something to you, though. You and I are men of faith.'

'Men of science, too,' said the astronaut to the geologist.

'Check. And as men of faith we naturally wish to preserve our faith from any unnecessary slanders.'

'Sure.'

'Well, maybe before announcing the news we should, as men of *science*, check out what we as men of faith have discovered.'

'Meaning?'

'Meaning I think we should shut our big bazoos until we've run some lab tests on Noah's clothing.'

There was a silence from the other half of the tent as Spike realized for the first time that not everyone on earth would necessarily put their hands together the way they'd done for the astronauts coming back from the moon. Finally, he said, 'I think you're thinking good, Jimmy. I guess you've also got me wondering if we might have ourselves a problem with the clothes.'

'How d'you mean?'

Now it was Spike's turn to play the skeptic. 'Well, I'm only just supposing. You recall the story of Noah's nakedness? How his sons covered him up? Well, we can be sure Noah's bones are something special, but does that mean his clothes are something special too?' There was a pause, then he went on. 'I don't think we should give any free lunches to the doubting Thomases. What if Noah was laid out here in his burial robes, and after a few centuries they'd all been blown to dust and ashes. Then along comes some pilgrim – maybe some pilgrim who doesn't make it back safely through the infidel tribes – and finds the body. Like coming across Noah's nakedness all over again. So the pilgrim gives Noah *his* clothes – which would explain how he never got back through the lines to spread the news. But it means we get a serious mis-read on the carbon-dating tests.'

'You're right,' said Jimmy. A long silence ensued, as if each were half-daring the other to make the next logical step. Finally, Jimmy made it. 'I wonder what the legal position is.'

'Nnn,' replied Spike, not discouragingly.

'Who do you think Noah's bones belong to? Apart,' Jimmy added hastily, 'from the Almighty Lord.'

'It could take years to go through all the courts. You know what lawyers are like.'

'Sure,' said Jimmy, who had never been in a court-room yet. 'I don't think the Lord would expect us to go through the legal process. Like appealing to Caesar or something.'

Spike nodded, and lowered his voice, even though they were alone on the Lord's mountain. 'Those guys wouldn't need much, would they?'

'No. No. Not much, I guess.' Jimmy relinquished his brief dream of a Navy helicopter airlifting out the whole caboodle.

Without discussing it further, the ex-astronaut and the scuba-diving geologist returned to the cave with two trembling flashlights and set about deciding which parts of Noah's skeleton to smuggle out of eastern Turkey. Piety, convenience and greed were all silently present. Finally they removed a small bone belonging to the left hand plus a cervical vertebra which had fallen out of position and rolled across the right scapula. Jimmy took the section of finger and Spike the neck-bone. They agreed it would be crazy not to fly home separately.

Spike routed in through Atlanta, but the media were on to him. No, he couldn't say anything at this moment in time. Yes, Project Ararat had gotten off to a fine start. No, no problems. No, Dr Fulgood was on a separate flight, he'd had to finalize a few things in Istanbul before departure. What sort of things? Yes, there would be a press conference in due course, and yes, Spike Tiggler hoped to have some specific, perhaps some joyous news for them on that occasion. How do you feel (all dressed in primrose), Mrs Tiggler? Oh, I'm one hundred ten percent behind my husband, thrilled to have him back.

The Reverend Gibson, after hesitation and much prayer, agreed that the two portions of Noah's skeleton be subjected to scientific analysis. They sent the vertebra and the finger-end to Washington, using a trusted intermediary who claimed to have dug them up in Greece. Betty waited to see if Spike had managed to haul himself back onto the box car of the gravy train.

Washington reported that the bones sent for examination

were approximately one hundred and fifty years old, plus or minus twenty years. They volunteered the information that the vertebra was almost certainly that of a woman.

A sea-mist shifts listlessly across the black water as the seven o'clock ferry makes its way from Cape Hatteras to Ocracoke Island. The searchlight charges at the water ahead. Every night the vessel has to find its way again, as if for the first time. Marker lights, white and green and red, guide the boat on its nervous course. You come out on deck, shrugging against the cold, and look upward; but this time the mist has shut off the stars, and it's impossible to tell whether or not there is meant to be a moon. You shrug again, and return to the smoky cabin.

One hundred miles to the west, in the Moondust Diner, Spike Tiggler, holding aloft a plastic bottle of water from a stream that flows uphill, is announcing the launch of the second Project Ararat.

10

THE DREAM

I DREAMT THAT I woke up. It's the oldest dream of all, and I've just had it. I dreamt that I woke up.

I was in my own bed. That seemed a bit of a surprise, but after a moment's thought it made sense. Who else's bed should I wake up in? I looked around and I said to myself, Well, well, well. Not much of a thought, I admit. Still, do we ever find the right words for the big occasions?

There was a knock on the door and a woman came in, sideways and backwards at the same time. It should have looked awkward but it didn't; no, it was all smooth and stylish. She was carrying a tray, which was why she'd come in like that. As she turned, I saw she was wearing a uniform of sorts. A nurse? No, she looked more like a stewardess on some airline you've never heard of. 'Room service,' she said with a bit of a smile, as if she wasn't used to providing it, or I wasn't used to expecting it; or both.

'Room service?' I repeated. Where I come from something like that only happens in films. I sat up in bed, and found I didn't have any clothes on. Where'd my pyjamas gone? That was a change. It was also a change that when I sat up in bed and realized she could see me bollock-naked to the waist, if you understand me, I didn't feel at all embarrassed. That was good.

'Your clothes are in the cupboard,' she said. 'Take your time. You've got all day. And,' she added with more of a smile, 'all tomorrow as well.'

I looked down at my tray. Let me tell you about that breakfast. It was the breakfast of my life and no mistake. The grapefruit, for a start. Now, you know what a grapefruit's like: the way it spurts juice down your shirt and keeps slipping out of your hand unless you hold it down with a fork or something, the way the flesh always sticks to those opaque membranes and then suddenly comes loose with half the pith attached, the way it always tastes sour yet makes you feel bad about piling sugar on the top of it. That's what a grapefruit's like, right? Now let me tell you about *this* grapefruit. Its flesh was pink for a start, not yellow, and each segment had already been carefully freed from its clinging membrane. The fruit itself was anchored to the dish by some prong or fork through its bottom, so that I didn't need to hold it down or even touch it. I looked around for the sugar, but that was just out of habit. The taste seemed to come in two parts – a sort of awakening sharpness followed quickly by a wash of sweetness; and each of those little globules (which were about the size of tadpoles) seemed to burst separately in my mouth. That was the grapefruit of my dreams, I don't mind telling you.

Like an emperor, I pushed aside the gutted hull and lifted a silver dome from a crested plate. Of course I knew what would be underneath. Three slices of grilled streaky bacon with the gristle and rind removed, the crispy fat all glowing like a bonfire. Two eggs, fried, the yolk looking milky because the fat had been properly spooned over it in the cooking, and the outer edges of the white trailing off into filigree gold braid. A grilled tomato I can only describe in terms of what it wasn't. It wasn't a collapsing cup of stalk, pips, fibre and red water, it was something compact, sliceable, cooked equally all the way through and tasting – yes, this is the thing I remember – tasting of tomato. The sausage: again, not a tube of lukewarm horsemeat stuffed into a French letter, but dark umber and succulent . . . a . . . a sausage, that's the only word for it. All the others, the ones I'd thought I'd enjoyed in my previous life, were merely practising to be like this; they'd been auditioning – and they wouldn't get the part, either. There was a little crescent-shaped side-plate with a crescent-shaped silver lid. I raised it: yes, there were my bacon rinds, separately grilled, waiting to be nibbled.

The toast, the marmalade – well, you can imagine those, you can dream what they were like for yourselves. But I must tell you about the teapot. The tea, of course, was the real thing, tasting as if it had been picked by some rajah's personal entourage. As for the teapot . . . Once, years ago, I went to Paris on a package holiday. I wandered off from the others and walked around where the smart people live. Where they shop and eat, anyway. On a corner I passed a café. It didn't look particularly grand, and just for a minute I thought of sitting down there. But I didn't, because at one of the tables I saw a man having tea. As he poured himself a fresh cup, I spotted a little gadget which seemed to me almost a definition of luxury: attached to the teapot's spout, and dangling by three delicate silver chains, was a strainer. As the man raised the pot to its pouring angle, this strainer swung outwards to catch the leaves. I couldn't believe that serious thought had once gone into the matter of how to relieve this tea-drinking gentleman of the incredible burden of picking up a normal strainer with his free hand. I walked away from that café feeling a bit self-righteous. Now, on my tray, I had a teapot bearing the insignia of some chic Parisian café. A strainer was attached to its spout by three silver chains. Suddenly, I could see the point of it.

After breakfast, I put the tray down on my bedside table, and went to the cupboard. Here they all were, my favourite clothes. That sports jacket I still liked even after people started saying, how unusual, did you buy it secondhand, another twenty years and it'll be back in fashion. That pair of corduroy trousers my wife threw out because the seat was beyond repair; but someone had managed to repair it, and the trousers looked almost new, though not so new you weren't fond of them. My shirts held out their arms to me, and why not, as they'd never been pampered like this in their lives before – all in ranks on velvet-covered hangers. There were shoes whose deaths I'd regretted; socks now deholed again; ties I'd seen in shop windows. It wasn't a collection of clothes you'd envy, but that wasn't the point. I was reassured. I would be myself again. I would be more than myself.

By the side of the bed was a tasselled bell-pull I hadn't previously noticed. I tugged it, then felt a bit embarrassed, and climbed under the sheets again. When the nurse-stewardess came in, I slapped my stomach and said, 'You know, I could eat that all over again.'

'I'm not surprised,' she replied. 'I was half expecting you to say so.'

I didn't get up all day. I had breakfast for breakfast, breakfast for lunch, and breakfast for dinner. It seemed like a good system. I would worry about lunch tomorrow. Or rather, I wouldn't worry about lunch tomorrow. I wouldn't worry about anything tomorrow. Between my breakfast-lunch and my breakfast-dinner (I was really beginning to appreciate that strainer system – you can carry on eating a croissant with your free hand while you pour) I had a long sleep. Then I took a shower. I could have had a bath, but I seem to have spent decades in the bath, so instead I took a shower. I found a quilted dressing-gown with my initials in gilt cord on the breast pocket. It fitted well, but I thought those initials were farting higher than my arse-hole. I hadn't come here to swank around like a film star. As I was staring at these golden squiggles, they disappeared from before my eyes. I blinked and they were gone. The dressing-gown felt more comfortable with just a normal pocket.

The next day I woke up – and had another breakfast. It was as good as the previous three. Clearly the problem of breakfast had now been solved.

When Brigitta came to clear the tray, she murmured, 'Shopping?'

'Of course.' It was exactly what had been on my mind.

'Do you want to go shopping or stay shopping?'

'Go shopping,' I said, not really understanding the difference.

'Sure.'

My wife's brother once came back from ten days in Florida and said, 'When I die, I don't want to go to Heaven, I want to go shopping in America.' That second morning I began to understand what he meant.

When we got to the supermarket Brigitta asked me if I

wanted to walk or drive. I said let's drive, that sounds fun – a reply which she seemed to expect. On reflection, some parts of her job must be quite boring – I mean, we probably all react in much the same way, don't we? Anyway, we drove. The shopping-carts are motorized wire-mesh trolleys that whizz around like dodgems, except that they never crash into one another because of some electric-eye device. Just when you think you're going to have a prang, you find yourself swerving round the oncoming cart. It's fun, that, trying to crash.

The system's easily mastered. You have a plastic card which you push into a slot next to the goods you want to buy, then punch in the quantity you want. After a second or two, your card is returned. Then the stuff is automatically delivered and credited.

I had a good time in my wire cart. I remember when I used to go shopping in the old days, the previous days, I'd sometimes see small kids sitting inside a trolley as if it were a cage and being pushed round by their parents; and I'd be envious. I wasn't any more. And boy, did I buy some stuff that morning! I practically cleaned them out of those pink grapefruit. That's what it felt like, anyway. I bought breakfast, I bought lunch, I bought dinner, I bought mid-morning snacks, afternoon teas, apéritif munchies, midnight feasts. I bought fruit I couldn't name, vegetables I'd never seen before, strange new cuts of meat from familiar animals, and familiar-looking cuts from animals I'd never eaten before. In the Australian section I found crocodile tail-steak, fillet of water-buffalo, *terrine de kangarou*. I bought them all. I plundered the gourmet cabinet. Freeze-dried lobster soufflé with cherry-chip topping: how could I resist something like that?

As for the drinks counter . . . I had no idea so many different means of intoxification had been devised. I'm mainly a beer-and-spirits man myself, but I didn't want to seem prejudiced so I bought quite a few crates of wine and cocktails as well. The labels on the bottles were very helpful: they gave detailed instructions about how drunk the contents would make you, taking into consideration factors like sex, weight and body-fat.

There was one brand of transparent alcohol with a very scruffy label. It was called Stinko-Paralytiko (made in Yugoslavia) and said on it: 'This bottle will make you drunker than you've ever been before.' Well, I had to take a case of that home, didn't I?

It was a good morning's work. It might have been the best morning's work there ever was. And don't look down your nose at me, by the way. You'd have done much the same yourself. I mean, say you didn't go shopping, what would you have done instead? Met some famous people, had sex, played golf? There aren't an infinite number of possibilities – that's one of the points to remember about it all, about this place and that place. And if I went shopping first, well, that's what people like me would do. I'm not looking down my nose if you'd have met famous people first, or had sex, or played golf. Anyway, I got round to all that in due course. As I say, we're not so very different.

When we got home I was . . . not exactly tired – you don't get tired – just kind of sated. Those shopping carts were fun; I didn't think I'd ever bother to walk – in fact, come to think of it, I didn't see anyone walking at the supermarket. Then it was lunchtime, and Brigitta arrived with breakfast. Afterwards, I took a nap. I expected to dream, because I always dream if I go to sleep in the afternoon. I didn't. I wondered why not.

Brigitta woke me with tea and the biscuits I'd chosen. They were currant biscuits especially designed for people like me. Now I don't know where you stand on this one, but all my life it's been a matter of complaint that they don't put enough currants in the currant biscuits. Obviously you don't want *too many* currants in a biscuit, otherwise you'd have just a wodge of currants rather than a biscuit, but I've always believed that the proportion of ingredients could be adjusted. Upwards, in favour of the currants, naturally – say, to about fifty-fifty. And that's what these biscuits were called, come to think of it: Fifty-Fifties. I bought three thousand packets of them.

I opened the newspaper which Brigitta had thoughtfully placed on the tray and almost spilt my tea. No, I did spill my tea – only you don't worry about things like that any more. It was front-page news. Well, it would have been, wouldn't it? Leicester City had won the FA Cup. No kidding, Leicester City had bloody well won the FA Cup! You wouldn't have believed it, would you? Well, maybe *you* would, if you didn't know anything about football. But *I* know a thing or two about football, and I've supported Leicester City all my life, and *I* wouldn't have believed it, that's the point. Don't get me wrong, I'm not running my team down. They're a good team, a very good team sometimes, yet they never seem to win the big ones. Second Division champions, as many times as you like to count, oh yes, but they've never won the First Division. Runners-up, once, sure, no problem. And as for the Cup. . . it's a fact, an undeniable fact that in all the time I've supported Leicester City (and for all the time before that, too), they've never won the FA Cup. They've had a very good post-war record in reaching the Final – and just as good a one at not capturing the trophy. 1949, 1961, 1963, 1969, those are the black years, and one or two of those defeats were in my opinion particularly unlucky, indeed I'd single out . . . OK, I can see you're not that interested in football. It doesn't matter, as long as you grasp the central fact that Leicester City had never won anything but peanuts before and now they had secured the FA Cup for the first time in the club's history. The match was a real thriller, too, according to the newspaper: City won 5–4 in extra time after coming from behind on no fewer than four occasions. What a performance! What a blend of skill and sheer character! I was proud of the lads. Brigitta would get me the video tomorrow, I was sure she could. In the meantime, I took a little champagne with the breakfast I had for dinner.

The newspapers were great. In a way, it's the newspapers I remember best. Leicester City won the FA Cup, as I may have mentioned. They found a cure for cancer. My party won the General Election every single time until everyone saw its ideas were right and most of the opposition came over and joined us. Little old ladies got rich on the pools every week. Sex offenders repented and were released back into society and led blameless lives. Airline pilots learned how to save planes from mid-air collisions. Everyone got rid of nuclear weapons. The England manager chose the whole Leicester City team *en bloc* to represent England in the World Cup and they came back with the Jules Rimet trophy (memorably beating Brazil 4–1 in the Final). When you read the paper, the newsprint didn't come off on your hands, and the stories didn't come off on your mind. Children were innocent creatures once more; men and women were nice to one another; nobody's teeth had to be filled; and women's tights never laddered.

What else did I do that first week? As I said, I played golf and had sex and met famous people and didn't feel bad once. Let me start with the golf. Now, I've never been much good at the game, but I used to enjoy hacking round a municipal course where the grass is like coconut matting and no-one bothers to replace their divots because there are so many holes in the fairway you can't work out where your divot has come from anyway. Still, I'd seen most of the famous courses on television and I was curious to play – well, the golf of my dreams. And as soon as I felt the contact my driver made on that first tee and watched the ball howling off a couple of hundred yards, I knew I was in seventh heaven. My clubs seemed perfectly weighted to the touch; the fairways had a lush springiness and held the ball up for you like a waiter with a drinks tray; and my caddy (I'd never had a caddy before, but he treated me like Arnold Palmer) was full of useful advice, never pushy. The course seemed to have everything – streams and lakes and antique bridges, bits of seaside links like in Scotland, patches of flowering dogwood and azalea from Augusta, beechwood, pine, bracken and gorse. It was a difficult course, but one that gave you chances. I went round that sunny morning in 67, which was five under par, and twenty shots better than I'd ever done on the municipal course.

I was so pleased with my round that when I got back I asked Brigitta if she'd have sex with me. She said of course she'd love to, and found me very attractive, and though she'd only seen the top half she was pretty sure the rest would be in good working order too; there were a few slight problems like she was deeply in love with someone else, and her conditions of work stated that employees were fired for having sexual relations with new arrivals, and she had a slight heart condition which meant that any extra strain could be dangerous, but if I'd give her a couple of minutes she'd slip off and get into some sexy underwear right away. Well, I debated with myself for a while about the rights and wrongs of what I'd been proposing, and when she came back, all perfume and cleavage, I told her that on balance I thought we probably shouldn't go ahead. She was pretty disappointed and sat down opposite me and crossed her legs which was a pretty sight I can tell you, but I was adamant. It was only later – the next morning, in fact – that I realized *she* had been turning *me* down. I'd never been turned down in such a nice way before. They even make the bad things good here.

I had a magnum of champagne with my sturgeon and chips that night (you don't get hangovers here, either), and was slipping off to sleep with the memory of that crafty back-spin I'd achieved with my wedge at the sixteenth to hold the ball on the upper level of that two-tier green, when I felt the covers of the bed being lifted. At first I thought it was Brigitta and felt a bit bad what with her heart condition and losing her job and being in love with someone else, but when I put my arm around her and whispered 'Brigitta?' a voice whispered back, 'No, is not Brigitta' and the accent was different, all husky and foreign, and then other things made me realize it was not Brigitta, attractive lady in many ways though Brigitta was. What happened next – and by 'next' I do not imply a brief period of time – is, well, hard to describe. The best I can do is say that in the morning I had gone round in 67, which was five under par and twenty shots ahead of my previous best, and what followed that night was a comparable achievement. I am you understand reluctant to criticize my dear wife in this department; it's just that after some years, you know, and the kids, and being tired, well, you can't help dragging one another down. It's still nice, but you sort of do what's necessary, don't you? What I hadn't realized was that if a couple can drag one another down, another couple can drag one another up. Wow! I didn't know I could!

I didn't know anyone could! Each of us seemed to know instinctively what the other one wanted. I'd never really come across that before. Not, you understand, that I wish to sound as if I'm criticizing my dear wife.

I expected to wake up feeling tired, but again it was more that sense of being pleasantly full, like after the shopping. Had I dreamt what had happened? No: there were two long red hairs on my pillow to confirm the reality. Their colour also proved that my visitor had definitely not been Brigitta.

'Did you sleep well?' she asked with a bit of a cheeky smile as she brought my breakfast.

'It was altogether a good day,' I replied, perhaps a bit pompously, because I sort of guessed she knew. 'Except,' I added quickly, 'for hearing about your heart condition. I'm really sorry about that.'

'Oh, I'll muddle through,' she said. 'The engine's good for another few thousand years.'

We went shopping (I wasn't yet so lazy I wanted to stay shopping), I read the newspaper, had lunch, played golf, tried to catch up on some reading with one of those Dickens videos, had sturgeon and chips, turned out the light and not long afterwards had sex. It was a good way to spend the day, almost perfect, it seemed to me, and I'd gone round in 67 again. If only I hadn't driven into the dogwoods on the eighteenth – I think I was just too pumped up – I could have marked a 66, or even a 65, on my card.

And so life continued, as the saying goes. For months, certainly – maybe longer; after a while you stop looking at the date on the newspaper. I realized it had been the right decision not to have sex with Brigitta. We became good friends.

'What happens,' I asked her one day, 'when my wife arrives?' My dear wife, I should explain, was not with me at the time.

'I thought you might be worrying about that.'

'Oh, I'm not worrying about *that*,' I said, referring to my nightly visitor, because the whole thing was a bit like being a businessman on a foreign trip, I suppose, wasn't it? 'I meant, sort of generally.'

'There isn't any generally. It's up to you. And her.'

'Will she mind?' I asked, this time referring more definitely to my visitor.

'Will she know?'

'I think there are going to be problems,' I said, once again talking more generally.

'This is where problems are solved,' she replied.

'If you say so.' I was beginning to be convinced that it might all turn out as I hoped.

For instance, I'd always had this dream. Well, I don't mean dream exactly, I mean something I wanted a lot. A dream of being judged. No, that doesn't sound right, it sounds like I wanted to have my head chopped off by a guillotine or be whipped or something. Not like that. No, I wanted to be *judged*, do you see? It's what we all want, isn't it? I wanted, oh, some kind of summing-up, I wanted my life looked at. We don't get that, not unless we appear in court or are given the once-over by a psychiatrist, neither of which had come my way and I wasn't exactly disappointed, seeing as I wasn't a criminal or a nutter. No, I'm a normal person, and I just wanted what a lot of normal people want. I wanted my life looked at. Do you see?

I began to explain this one day to my friend Brigitta, not being sure I could put it any better than the above, but she immediately understood. She said it was a very popular request, it wouldn't be hard to fix. So a couple of days later I went along. I asked her to come with me for moral support, and she agreed.

It was just what I'd expected at first. There was a fancy old building with columns and lots of words in Latin or Greek or something carved along the top, and flunkeys in uniform, which made me glad I'd insisted on a new suit for the occasion. Inside, there was a huge staircase, one of those that divides in two and does a big circle in opposite directions and then meets itself again at the top. There was marble everywhere and freshly polished brass and great stretches of mahogany that you knew would never get woodworm.

It wasn't a huge room, but that didn't matter. More to the

point, it had the right sort of feel, formal but not too off-
putting. It was almost cosy, with bits of old velvet looking
rather tatty, except that serious things happened here. And he
was a nice old gent, the one who did me. A bit like my dad – no,
more like an uncle, I'd say. Sort of friendly eyes, looked you
straight in the face; and you could tell he stood no nonsense.
He'd read all my papers, he said. And there they were, at his
elbow, the history of my life, everything I'd done and thought
and said and felt, the whole bloody caboodle, the good bits and
the bad. It made quite a pile, as you'd imagine. I wasn't sure I
was allowed to address him but anyway I did. I said you're a
quick reader and no mistake. He said he'd had a lot of training
and we had a bit of a laugh at that. Then he took a squint at his
watch – no, he did it quite politely – and asked me if I wanted
my verdict. I found myself squaring my shoulders and putting
my hands into fists at my side with the thumbs down the trouser
seams. Then I nodded and said 'Yes, sir,' and felt a bit nervous I
don't mind telling you.

He said I was OK. No, I'm not kidding, that's exactly what
he said: 'You're OK.' I sort of waited for him to go on but he
dropped his eyes and I could see his hand moving to the top
document on another file. Then he looked up, gave a little smile
and said, 'No, really, you're OK.' I nodded again, and this time
he really was going back to his work so I turned and left. When
we got out I confessed to Brigitta I'd been a bit disappointed,
and she said most people were but I wasn't to take it as any
reflection on me, so I didn't.

It was about this time that I took to meeting famous people.
At first I was a bit shy and only asked for film stars and
sportsmen I admired. I met Steve McQueen, for instance, and
Judy Garland; John Wayne, Maureen O'Sullivan, Humphrey
Bogart, Gene Tierney (I always had this thing about Gene
Tierney) and Bing Crosby. I met Duncan Edwards and the rest
of the Man Utd players from the Munich air-crash. I met quite a
few Leicester City lads from the early days, most of whose names
would probably be unfamiliar to you.

After a while I realized I could meet anyone I liked. I met

John F. Kennedy and Charlie Chaplin, Marilyn Monroe, President Eisenhower, Pope John XXIII, Winston Churchill, Rommel, Stalin, Mao Tse-tung, Roosevelt, General de Gaulle, Lindbergh, Shakespeare, Buddy Holly, Patsy Cline, Karl Marx, John Lennon and Queen Victoria. Most of them were very nice, on the whole, sort of natural, not at all grand or condescending. They were just like real people. I asked to meet Jesus Christ but they said they weren't sure about that so I didn't push it. I met Noah, but not surprisingly there was a bit of a language problem. Some people I just wanted to look at. Hitler, for instance, now there's a man I wouldn't shake the hand of, but they arranged that I could hide behind some bushes while he just walked past, in his nasty uniform, large as life.

Guess what happened next? I started worrying. I worried about the most ridiculous things. Like my health, for instance. Isn't that crazy? Maybe it was something to do with Brigitta telling me about her heart condition, but I suddenly began to imagine things going wrong with me. Who'd have credited it? I came over all faddy and diet-conscious; I got a rowing machine and an exercise bicycle, I worked out with weights; I kept off salt and sugar, animal fats and cream cakes; I even cut down my intake of Fifty-Fifties to half a packet a day. I also had spells of worrying about my hairline, my supermarket driving (were the trolleys that safe?), my sexual performance and my bank balance. Why was I worrying about my bank balance when I didn't even have a bank? I imagined my card not working at the supermarket, I felt guilty at the amount of credit I seemed to be given. What had I done to deserve it?

Most of the time, of course, I was fine, what with the shopping, the golf, the sex and the meeting famous people. But every so often I'd think, what if I can't make it round the 18 holes? What if I can't really afford my Fifty-Fifties? Finally, I confessed these thoughts to Brigitta. She thought it time I was passed on to other hands. Brigitta's work was done, she indicated. I felt sad, and asked what I could buy her to show my gratitude. She said she had everything she needed. I tried writing a poem, because Brigitta rhymes with sweeter, but after

293

that I could only find neater and eat her, so I sort of gave up, and in any case I thought she'd probably been given poems like that before.

Margaret was to look after me next. She looked more serious than Brigitta, all smart suits and not a hair out of place – the sort of person who's a finalist in those Businesswomen of the Year competitions. I was a bit scared of her – I certainly couldn't imagine myself suggesting sex like I did to Brigitta – and I half expected her to disapprove of the way of life I'd been leading. But she didn't, of course. No, she just said that she assumed I was pretty familiar by now with the amenities, and that she would be there if I needed more than mere practical assistance.

'Tell me something,' I asked her on our first meeting. 'It's silly to be worrying about my health, isn't it?'

'Quite unnecessary.'

'And it's silly to worry about money?'

'Quite unnecessary,' she replied.

Something in her tone implied that if I cared to look, I could probably find things that were worth worrying about; I didn't pursue this. I had plenty of time ahead of me. Time was something I would never be short of.

Now, I'm probably not the quickest thinker in the world, and in my previous life I tended to just get on with the things I had to do, or wanted to do, and not brood too much about them. That's normal, isn't it? But give anyone enough time and they'll get somewhere with their thoughts and start asking a few of the bigger questions. For instance, who actually ran this place, and why had I seen so little of them? I'd assumed there might be a sort of entrance examination, or perhaps continual assessment; yet apart from that frankly rather disappointing bit of judging by the old codger who said I was OK, I hadn't been bothered. They let me bunk off every day and improve my golf. Was I allowed to take everything for granted? Did they expect something from me?

Then there was that Hitler business. You waited behind a bush and he strolled past, a stocky figure in a nasty uniform with a false smile on his face. Fair enough, I'd seen him now, and my curiosity was satisfied, but, well, I had to ask myself, what was he doing here in the first place? Did he order breakfast like everybody else? I'd already observed that he was allowed to wear his own clothes. Did this mean he could also play golf and have sex if he wanted to? How did this thing operate?

Then there was me worrying about my health and money and the supermarket driving. I wasn't worrying about them in themselves any more, I was worrying about the fact that I'd been worrying. What was all that about? Was it more than a routine adjustment problem as Brigitta had suggested?

I think it was the golf that finally made me turn to Margaret for some explanations. There was no doubt about it, over the months and years I played that lovely, lush course with its little tricks and temptations (how many times I put the ball in the water at the short eleventh!), my game improved no end. I said as much one day to Severiano, my regular caddy: 'My game has improved no end.' He agreed, and it was not until later, between dinner and sex, that I began to reflect on what I'd said. I had opened up on the course with a 67, and gradually my score was coming down. A while ago I was shooting a regular 59, and now, under cloudless skies, I was inching down to the low 50s. I could drive 350 yards without trouble, my pitching was transformed, my putts rattled into the hole as if drawn by a magnet. I could see my target score coming down through the 40s, then – a key psychological moment this – breaking the barrier of 36, that's to say two strokes a hole average, then coming down through the 20s. *My game has improved no end*, I thought, and repeated the words *no end* to myself. But that's, of course, exactly what it couldn't do: there had to be an end to my improvement. One day I would play a round of golf in 18 shots, I'd buy Severiano a couple of drinks, celebrate later with sturgeon and chips and sex – and then what? Had anyone, even here, ever played a golf course in 17 shots?

Margaret didn't answer a tasselled bell-pull like the blonde Brigitta; in fact, you had to apply by videophone for an interview.

'I'm worried about the golf,' I began.

'That's not really my speciality.'

'No. You see, when I first arrived I shot a 67. Now I'm down to the low 50s.'

'That doesn't sound like a problem.'

'And I'm going to go on getting better.'

'Congratulations.'

'And then one day I'll finally do the course in 18 shots.'

'Your ambition is admirable.' She sounded as if she was making fun of me.

'But then what do I do?'

She paused. 'Try going round every time in 18 shots?'

'It doesn't work like that.'

'Why not?'

'It just doesn't.'

'I'm sure there are many other courses . . .'

'Same problem,' I said, interrupting her, a bit rudely I suppose.

'Well, you could switch to another sport, couldn't you? Then come back to golf when you're tired of the other one?'

'But the problem's the same. I'd have done the course in 18 shots. Golf would be used up.'

'There are lots of other sports.'

'They'd get used up too.'

'What do you have for breakfast every morning?' I'm sure she knew the answer already from the way she nodded when I told her. 'You see. You have the same every morning. You don't get tired of breakfast.'

'No.'

'Well, think about golf as you do about breakfast. Perhaps you'll never get tired of going round in 18 shots.'

'Perhaps,' I said dubiously. 'It sounds to me as if you haven't ever played golf. And anyway, that's another thing.'

'What is?'

'The getting tired. You don't get tired here.'

'Is that a complaint?'

'I don't know.'

'Tiredness can be arranged.'

'Sure,' I replied. 'But I bet it'd be a sort of pleasant tiredness. Not one of those knackering tirednesses which just make you want to die.'

'Don't you think you're being perverse?' She was crisp, almost impatient. 'What did you want? What did you hope for?'

I nodded to myself, and we called it a day. My life continued. That was another phrase that made me grin a bit. My life continued, and my golf improved no end. I did all sorts of other things:

— I went on several cruises;
— I learned canoeing, mountaineering, ballooning;
— I got into all sorts of danger and escaped;
— I explored the jungle;
— I watched a court case (didn't agree with the verdict);
— I tried being a painter (not as bad as I thought!) and a surgeon;
— I fell in love, of course, lots of times;
— I pretended I was the last person on earth (and the first).

None of this meant that I stopped doing what I'd always done since I got here. I had sex with an increasing number of women, sometimes simultaneously; I ate rarer and stranger foods; I met famous people all the way to the edges of my memory. For instance, I met every footballer there ever was. I started with the famous ones, then the ones I admired but weren't particularly famous, then the average ones, then the ones whose names I remembered without remembering what they looked like or played like; finally I asked for the only ones I hadn't met, the nasty, boring, violent players that I didn't admire at all. I didn't enjoy meeting them — they were just as nasty, boring and violent off the pitch as on — but I didn't want to run out of footballers. Then I ran out of footballers. I asked to see Margaret again.

'I've met all the footballers,' I said.

'I'm afraid I don't know much about football, either.'

'And I don't have any dreams,' I added, in a tone of complaint.

'What would they be for,' she replied. 'What *would* they be for?'

I sensed that in a way she was testing me, seeing how serious I was. Did it all add up to more than a mere adjustment problem?

'I think I'm owed an explanation,' I announced – a little pompously, I have to admit.

'Ask anything you like.' She settled back in her office chair.

'Look, I want to get things straight.'

'An admirable ambition.' She talked a bit posh, like that.

I thought I'd better start at the beginning. 'Look, this is Heaven, isn't it?'

'Oh yes.'

'Well, what about Sundays?'

'I don't follow you.'

'On Sundays,' I said, 'as far as I can work out, because I don't follow the days too closely any more, I play golf, go shopping, eat dinner, have sex and don't feel bad.'

'Isn't that . . . perfect?'

'I don't want to sound ungrateful,' I said cautiously, 'but where's God?'

'God. Do you want God? Is that what you want?'

'Is it a question of what I want?'

'That's exactly what it's a question of. Do you want God?'

'I suppose I thought it wasn't that way round. I suppose I thought either there would be one or there wouldn't be one. I'd find out what the case was. I didn't think it depended on me in any way.'

'Of course it does.'

'Oh.'

'Heaven is democratic these days,' she said. Then added, 'Or at least, it is if you want it to be.'

'What do you mean, democratic?'

'We don't impose Heaven on people any more,' she said. 'We listen to their needs. If they want it, they can have it; if not, not. And then of course they get the sort of Heaven they want.'

'And what sort do they want on the whole?'

'Well, they want a continuation of life, that's what we find. But . . . better, needless to say.'

'Sex, golf, shopping, dinner, meeting famous people and not feeling bad?' I asked, a bit defensively.

'It varies. But if I were being honest, I'd say that it doesn't vary all that much.'

'Not like the old days.'

'Ah, the old days.' She smiled. 'That was before my time, of course, but yes, dreams of Heaven used to be a lot more ambitious.'

'And Hell?' I asked.

'What about it?'

'Is there Hell?'

'Oh no,' she replied. 'That was just necessary propaganda.'

'I was wondering, you see. Because I met Hitler.'

'Lots of people do. He's a sort of . . . tourist site, really. What did you make of him?'

'Oh, I didn't *meet* him,' I said firmly. 'He's a man I wouldn't shake the hand of. I watched him go by from behind the bushes.'

'Ah, yes. Quite a lot of people prefer to do it that way.'

'So I thought, if he's here, there can't be Hell.'

'A reasonable deduction.'

'Just out of interest,' I said, 'what does *he* do all day?' I imagined him going to the 1936 Berlin Olympics every afternoon, watching the Germans win everything while Jesse Owens fell over, then back for some sauerkraut, Wagner and a romp with a busty blonde of pure Aryan blood.

'I'm afraid we do respect people's confidentiality.'

'Naturally.' That was right. I wouldn't want everyone knowing what I got up to, come to think of it.

'So there isn't any Hell?'

'Well, there's something we *call* Hell. But it's more like a theme park. You know, skeletons popping out and frightening you, branches in your face, stink bombs, that sort of thing. Just to give you a good scare.'

'A good scare,' I remarked, 'as opposed to a bad scare?'

'Exactly. We find that's all people want nowadays.'

'Do you know about Heaven in the old days?'

'What, Old Heaven? Yes, we know about Old Heaven. It's in the records.'

'What happened to it?'

'Oh, it sort of closed down. People didn't want it any more. People didn't need it any more.'

'But I knew a few people who went to church, had their babies christened, didn't use rude words. What about them?'

'Oh, we get those,' she said. 'They're catered for. They pray and give thanks rather as you play golf and have sex. They seem to enjoy themselves, to have got what they wanted. We've built them some very nice churches.'

'Does God exist for them?' I asked.

'Oh, surely.'

'But not for me?'

'It doesn't seem so. Unless you want to change your requirements of Heaven. I can't deal with that myself. I could refer you.'

'I've probably got enough to think about for the moment.'

'Fine. Well, until the next time.'

I slept badly that night. My mind wasn't on the sex, even though they all did their very best. Was it indigestion? Had I bolted my sturgeon? There I was, worrying about my health again.

The next morning I shot a 67 on the golf course. My caddy Severiano reacted as if it was the best round he'd seen me play, as if he didn't know I could do 20 shots better. Afterwards, I asked for certain directions, and drove towards the only visible patch of bad weather. As I'd expected, Hell was a great disappointment: the thunderstorm in the car-park was probably the best bit. There were out-of-work actors prodding other out-of-work actors with long forks, pushing them into vats labelled 'Boiling Oil'. Phoney animals with strap-on plastic beaks pecked at foam-rubber corpses. I saw Hitler riding on the Ghost Train with his arm round a Mädchen with pigtails. There were bats and creaking coffin lids and a smell of rotting floorboards. Is that what people wanted?

'Tell me about Old Heaven,' I said to Margaret the following week.

'It was much like your accounts of it. I mean, that's the principle of Heaven, that you get what you want, what you expect. I know some people imagine it's different, that you get what you deserve, but that's never been the case. We have to disabuse them.'

'Are they annoyed?'

'Mostly not. People prefer to get what they want rather than what they deserve. Though some of them did get a little irritated that others weren't sufficiently maltreated. Part of their expectation of Heaven seemed to be that other people would go to Hell. Not very Christian.'

'And were they . . . disembodied? Was it all spirit life and so on?'

'Yes indeed. That's what they wanted. Or at any rate, in certain epochs. There has been a lot of fluctuation over the centuries about decorporealization. At the moment, for instance, there's quite an emphasis on retaining your own body and your own personality. This may just prove a phase, like any other.'

'What are you smiling for?' I asked. I was rather surprised. I thought Margaret was there just to give information, like Brigitta. Yet she obviously had her own opinions, and didn't mind telling you them.

'Only because it sometimes seems odd how tenaciously people want to stick with their own bodies. Of course, they occasionally ask for minor surgery. But it's as if, say, a different nose or a tuck in the cheek or a handful of silicone is all that stands between them and their perfect idea of themselves.'

'What happened to Old Heaven?'

'Oh, it survived for a while, after the new Heavens were built. But there was increasingly little call for it. People seemed keener on the new Heavens. It wasn't all that surprising. We take the long view here.'

301

'What happened to the Old Heaveners?'

Margaret shrugged, rather complacently, like some corporate planner whose predictions had been borne out to the tiniest decimal point. 'They died off.'

'Just like that? You mean, you closed down their Heaven and so they died off?'

'No, not at all, on the contrary. That's not how it works. Constitutionally, there would have been an Old Heaven for as long as the Old Heaveners wanted it.'

'Are there any Old Heaveners around?'

'I think there are a few left.'

'Can I meet one?'

'They don't take visits, I'm afraid. They used to. But the New Heaveners tended to behave as if they were at a freak-show, kept pointing and asking silly questions. So the Old Heaveners declined to meet them any more. They gave up speaking to anyone but other Old Heaveners. Then they began to die off. Now there aren't many left. We have them tagged, of course.'

'Are they disembodied?'

'Some of them are, some of them aren't. It depends on the sect. Of course the ones that are disembodied don't have much trouble avoiding the New Heaveners.'

Well, that made sense. In fact, it all made sense except for the main thing. 'And what do you mean, the others died off?'

'Everyone has the option to die off if they want to.'

'I never knew that.'

'No. There are bound to be a few surprises. Did you really want to be able to predict it all?'

'And how do they die? Do they kill themselves? Do you kill them?'

Margaret looked a bit shocked at the crassness of my idea. 'Goodness, no. As I said, it's democratic nowadays. If you want to die off, you do. You just have to want to for long enough and that's it, it happens. Death isn't a matter of hazard or gloomy inevitability, the way it is the first time round. We've got free will sorted out here, as you may have noticed.'

I wasn't sure I was taking all this in. I'd have to go away and

think about it. 'Tell me,' I said, 'these problems I've been
having with the golf and the worrying. Do other people react
like that?'

'Oh yes. We often get people asking for bad weather, for
instance, or for something to go wrong. They miss things going
wrong. Some of them ask for pain.'

'For pain?'

'Certainly. Well, you were complaining the other day about
not feeling so tired that – as I think you put it – you just want to
die. I thought that was an interesting phrase. People ask for
pain, it's not so extraordinary. We've had them requesting
operations, as well. I mean, not just cosmetic ones, real ones.'

'Do they get them?'

'Only if they really insist. We try to suggest that wanting an
operation is really a sign of something else. Normally they agree
with us.'

'And what percentage of people take up the option to die off?'

She looked at me levelly, her glance telling me to be calm.
'Oh, a hundred per cent, of course. Over many thousands of
years, calculated by old time, of course. But yes, everyone takes
the option, sooner or later.'

'So it's just like the first time round? You always die in the
end?'

'Yes, except don't forget the quality of life here is much
better. People die when they decide they've had enough, not
before. The second time round it's altogether more satisfying
because it's willed.' She paused, then added, 'As I say, we cater
for what people want.'

I hadn't been blaming her. I'm not that sort. I just wanted to
find out how the system worked. 'So . . . even people, religious
people, who come here to worship God throughout eternity
. . . they end up throwing in the towel after a few years,
hundred years, thousand years?'

'Certainly. As I said, there are still a few Old Heaveners
around, but their numbers are diminishing all the time.'

'And who asks for death soonest?'

'I think *ask* is the wrong word. It's something you want.

There aren't any mistakes here. If you want it enough, you die, that's always been the ruling principle.'

'So?'

'So. Well, I'm afraid – to answer your question – that the people who ask for death earliest are a bit like you. People who want an eternity of sex, beer, drugs, fast cars – that sort of thing. They can't believe their good luck at first, and then, a few hundred years later, they can't believe their bad luck. That's the sort of people they are, they realize. They're stuck with being themselves. Millennium after millennium of being themselves. They tend to die off soonest.'

'I never take drugs,' I said firmly. I was rather miffed. 'And I've only got seven cars. That's not very many around here. And I don't even drive them fast.'

'No, of course not. I was just thinking in general categories of gratification, you understand.'

'And who lasts longest?'

'Well, some of those Old Heaveners were fairly tenacious customers. Worship kept them going for ages and ages. Nowadays . . . lawyers last quite well. They love going over their old cases, and then going over everybody else's. That can take for ever. Metaphorically speaking,' she added quickly. 'And scholarly people, they tend to last as long as anyone. They like sitting around reading all the books there are. And then they love arguing about them. Some of those arguments' – she cast an eye to the heavens – 'go on for millennium after millennium. It just seems to keep them young, for some reason, arguing about books.'

'What about the people who write the books?'

'Oh, they don't last half as long as the people who argue about them. It's the same with painters and composers. They somehow know when they've done their best work, and then they sort of fade away.'

I thought I should be feeling depressed, but I wasn't. 'Shouldn't I be feeling depressed?'

'Of course not. You're here to enjoy yourself. You've got what you wanted.'

'Yes, I suppose so. Maybe I can't get used to the idea that at some point I'll want to die.'

'Give it time,' she said, brisk but friendly. 'Give it time.'

'By the way, one last question.' I could see her fiddling with her pencils, straightening them into a row. 'Who exactly are you?'

'Us? Oh, we're remarkably like you. We could be you, in fact. Perhaps we are you.'

'I'll come back again if I may,' I said.

For the next few centuries – it may have been longer, I stopped counting in old time – I worked seriously on my golf. After a while I was going round in 18 shots every time and my caddy's astonishment became routine. I gave up golf and took up tennis. Pretty soon I'd beaten all the greats from the Hall of Fame on shale, clay, grass, wood, concrete, carpet – any surface they chose. I gave up tennis. I played for Leicester City in the Cup Final and came away with a winner's medal (my third goal, a power header from twelve yards out, clinched the match). I flattened Rocky Marciano in the fourth round at Madison Square Garden (and I carried him a bit the last round or two), got the marathon record down to 28 minutes, won the world darts; my innings of 750 runs in the one-day international against Australia at Lords won't be surpassed for some time. After a while, Olympic gold medals began to feel like small change. I gave up sport.

I went shopping seriously. I ate more creatures than had ever sailed on Noah's Ark. I drank every beer in the world and then some, became a wine connoisseur and despatched the finest vintages ever harvested; they ran out too soon. I met loads of famous people. I had sex with an increasing variety of partners in an increasing variety of ways, but there are only so many partners and so many ways. Don't get me wrong, incidentally: I'm not complaining. I enjoyed every bloody minute of it. All I'm saying is, I knew what I was doing while I was doing it. I was looking for a way out.

I tried combining pleasures and started having sex with famous people (no, I won't tell you who – they asked me to respect their privacy). I even took up reading. I remembered what Margaret said and tried – oh, for a few centuries or so – arguing about books with other people who'd read the same books. But it seemed a pretty arid life, at least compared to life itself, and not one worth prolonging. I even tried joining the people who sang and prayed in church, but that wasn't really my thing. I only did it because I wanted to cover all the angles before I had what I knew would be my final talk with Margaret. She looked much as she had done several millennia earlier when we'd first met; but then, so did I.

'I've had an idea,' I said. Well, you're bound to come up with something after all that time, aren't you? 'Listen, if you get what you want in Heaven, then what about wanting to be someone who never gets tired of eternity?' I sat back, feeling a touch smug. To my surprise she nodded, almost encouragingly.

'You're welcome to have a go,' she said. 'I could get you the transfer.'

'But . . . ?' I asked, knowing that there would be a *but*.

'I'll get you the transfer,' she repeated. 'It's just a formality.'

'Tell me the *but* first.' I didn't want to sound rude. On the other hand I didn't want to spend several millennia pissing about if I could be saved the time.

'People have tried it already,' Margaret said, in a clearly sympathetic tone, as if she really didn't want to hurt me.

'And what's the problem? What's the *but*?'

'Well, there seems to be a logical difficulty. You can't become someone else without stopping being who you are. Nobody can bear that. It's what we find, anyway,' she added, half implying that I might be the first person to crack this problem. 'Someone – someone who must have been keen on sports, like you, said that it was changing from being a runner to being a perpetual motion machine. After a while you simply want to run again. Does that make sense?'

I nodded. 'And everyone who's tried it has asked for a transfer back?'

'Yes.'

'And afterwards they all took the option to die off?'

'They did. And sooner rather than later. There might still be a few of them around. I could call them in if you want to ask them about it.'

'I'll take your word for it. I thought there must be a snag in my idea.'

'Sorry.'

'No, please don't apologize.' I certainly couldn't complain about the way I'd been treated. Everyone had been level with me from the start. I took a deep breath. 'It seems to me,' I went on, 'that Heaven's a very good idea, it's a perfect idea you could say, but not for us. Not given the way we are.'

'We don't like to influence conclusions,' she said. 'However, I can certainly see your point of view.'

'So what's it all for? Why do we have Heaven? Why do we have these dreams of Heaven?' She didn't seem willing to answer, perhaps she was being professional; but I pressed her. 'Go on, give me some ideas.'

'Perhaps because you need them,' she suggested. 'Because you can't get by without the dream. It's nothing to be ashamed of. It seems quite normal to me. Though I suppose if you knew about Heaven beforehand, you might not ask for it.'

'Oh, I don't know about that.' It had all been very pleasant: the shopping, the golf, the sex, the meeting famous people, the not feeling bad, the not being dead.

'After a while, getting what you want all the time is very close to not getting what you want all the time.'

The next day, for old times' sake, I played another round of golf. I wasn't at all rusty: eighteen holes, eighteen strokes. I hadn't lost my touch. Then I had breakfast for lunch and breakfast for dinner. I watched my video of Leicester City's 5–4 victory in the Cup Final, though it wasn't the same, knowing what happened. I had a cup of hot chocolate with Brigitta, who kindly looked in to see me; later I had sex, though only with one woman. Afterwards, I sighed and rolled over, knowing that the next morning I would begin to make my decision.

I dreamt that I woke up. It's the oldest dream of all, and I've just had it.

Author's Note

Chapter 3 is based on legal procedures and actual cases described in *The Criminal Prosecution and Capital Punishment of Animals* by E. P. Evans (1906). The first part of Chapter 5 draws its facts and language from the 1818 London translation of Savigny and Corréard's *Narrative of a Voyage to Senegal*; the second part relies heavily on Lorenz Eitner's exemplary *Géricault: His Life and Work* (Orbis, 1982). The third part of Chapter 7 takes its facts from *The Voyage of the Damned* by Gordon Thomas and Max Morgan-Witts (Hodder, 1974). I am grateful to Rebecca John for much help with research; to Anita Brookner and Howard Hodgkin for vetting my art history; to Rick Chiles and Jay McInerney for inspecting my American; to Dr Jacky Davis for surgical assistance; to Alan Howard, Galen Strawson and Redmond O'Hanlon; and to Hermione Lee.

J.B.